D0711039

ONE FOR THE ROGUE

"Readers who like their Regency historicals smart, sexy, and served up with plenty of dry wit and a generous dollop of intrigue will find *One for the Rogue*, the latest sparkling addition to Collins's Studies in Scandal series, to be a rare find."
—*Booklist*

"*One for the Rogue* stands out for its fierce dedication to developing interesting, engaging, and worthwhile characters."
—*BookPage*

"The heroine, Gemma, is a geologist (yay, historical STEM heroines!) as is the hero, Cameron, and I just love watching two people with shared passions (for rocks and each other) not be able to resist falling in love!"   —*Book Riot*

"A fine conclusion to a Regency series dedicated to celebrating the intellectual and artistic achievements of women."
—*Kirkus Reviews*

Also by Manda Collins

The Rogue Goes On

TWO NOVELS IN ONE

Wallflower Most Wanted

&

One for the Rogue

MANDA COLLINS

St. Martin's Paperbacks

This is a work of fiction. All of the characters, organizations, and events portrayed in this book are either products of the author's imagination or are used fictitiously.

Published in the United States by St. Martin's Paperbacks, an imprint of St. Martin's Publishing Group

For information, address St. Martin's Publishing Group, 120 Broadway, New York, NY 10271.

www.stmartins.com

ISBN: 978-1-250-84812-3

Our books may be purchased in bulk for promotional, educational, or business use. Please contact your local bookseller or the Macmillan Corporate and Premium Sales Department at 1-800-221-7945, ext. 5442, or by email at MacmillanSpecialMarkets@macmillan.com.

Printed in the United States of America

St. Martin's Paperbacks edition / August 2022

10 9 8 7 6 5 4 3 2 1

Wallflower Most Wanted

For Janga, whose support in those early days of drabbles and Bon Bon fanfic is a big part of why I'm published. Our mutual love for a certain author's work sparked a friendship that's withstood kerfuffles, drama, and real life struggles and I look forward to decades more.

Chapter 1

Consumed by the need to capture the scene in front of her before the light changed, Miss Sophia Hastings didn't notice the newcomers until it was too late.

She'd struck out early that morning—an unusual occurrence for her—carrying her own equipment to her favorite spot at the edge of the Beauchamp House property, atop the chalk cliff overlooking the sea.

The desire to capture the morning light dancing over the waves had been building in her for days. It was always thus with her artistic motivations. Every painting she'd ever completed had begun as the kernel of an idea: a hint of color, a flicker of light, a touch of shadow. And slowly, over time—while she worked at other tasks—the idea would grow from thought to need. And she would give in to the impulse that made her try—however fruitlessly—to capture what she saw on canvas. Sometimes what she saw was a scene she'd crafted with models and costumes and props. But other times, like today, the scene was one that nature had provided for her. And that meant bringing her tools to the spot that nature herself dictated would give the best view.

Having removed her slippers so that she could feel the solid earth beneath her stockinged feet, she dashed her brush across the canvas, blending grays and blues and a hint of white in an energetic frenzy. Her arm arced in wide sweeps, mimicking the movement of the waves below and the wind that whipped around her. She'd been working for almost an hour, and was in that otherworld where her awareness of her own surroundings was dimmed by the vision before her, when several things happened at once.

A deep male voice sounded from somewhere in the trees behind her.

Footsteps crunched on the pebbled beach below.

And she lost her balance in the middle of a particularly energetic brush stroke, tumbling over the edge of the cliff.

The fall itself seemed to happen in an achingly slow unfurling of time, though in actuality it took only seconds for her to drop the ten or so feet from the precipice to the rocky beach. And somehow she managed to twist in such a way as to land on her feet and not her head.

Unfortunately, one of those feet landed on a rather sizeable stone that twisted her ankle.

She'd no sooner hit the ground than a large male form knelt beside her on the beach.

"My God. Are you hurt?"

Sophia blinked, and looked up into the alarmed face of Lord Benedick Lisle, vicar of Little Seaford. With a visage that was almost too fittingly angelic, his clear blue eyes and unruly brown curls had set every female heart in the vicinity into a flutter since his arrival some months earlier. And as an artist, with an eye for beautiful forms, Sophia couldn't help but notice that the vicar was almost perfectly made. That he possessed an innate decency and sense of humor was perhaps gilding the lily.

Now, however, his usual good humor was replaced with real concern.

"Of course you're hurt." He didn't seem to need a reply,

which was good because she'd lost her breath from the fall. "No one can fall that far and remain unscathed."

He waited a moment, just taking her hand in his, watching her with a mixture of concern and wonder. Shoving away her response to his gaze, she began assessing herself for damage. Her arms and upper body seemed fine. But her right ankle was throbbing and when she gave it an experimental flex, it made her cry out in pain.

"It's my ankle," she said through gritted teeth. It was mortifying to be in this situation. Not only because the vicar—who was undoubtedly the most handsome man in the county—was seeing her in such a vulnerable state, but also because he'd likely think this was some sort of ruse to get him to notice her. Not that he was vain—quite the opposite—but the unmarried young ladies of Little Seaford had all but turned vicar hunting into a sport. Why should he think she'd be any different?

But Lord Benedick didn't seem to be overly concerned about his hide, for he gave a grim nod. "I'm just going to feel for broken bones, Miss Hastings," he assured her solemnly. "Let me know if something pains you."

Moving back so that he could get to her foot—which was bare but for her stockings—he very carefully slipped his large hand beneath her heel and lifted it. Sophia bit her lip to keep from voicing her pain at the movement, and when he probed the joint with steady fingers she nearly levitated.

For a moment, all she felt was white hot pain.

"Easy," he soothed, lowering the offending extremity gently to the ground. "There's no sign of a break. At least not that I could feel. I think you'd better get Dr.—"

He broke off at the sharp bark of a shout from the clifftop above them.

Sophia's eyes flew to his as she recalled the man's voice she'd heard right before she fell.

She opened her mouth to tell him when Benedick raised a finger to his lips. Realizing that it might be best if they weren't discovered, she nodded.

"Damn you," the man cried. "I knew I should have seen to this business myself. You're far too soft to deal with our problem. Can you be relied upon to eliminate our little stumbling block if necessary?"

The other man's voice was too low for them to hear, but it seemed to be placating, because the first man's next words were calmer. Something about their location allowed his utterance to float down to the beach below with amazing clarity. "See that you do," he said in the tone of a man who has little patience with excuses. "If this scheme doesn't work out, I will hold you responsible. And I am not kind to those who disappoint me. You've been loyal enough so far. I hope you won't allow yourself to be weakened by your loyalty to people who don't care about you. I am the one who truly understands you. Only I can help you rise above your circumstances and achieve the success you deserve."

There was something familiar about the man's voice. But Sophia was still too shaken from her fall to concentrate on it.

Once again, they heard the low mumbling of the second man. Then, the sound of footsteps shushing over the dead leaves of the little wooded copse indicated that the two men were leaving.

Sophia and Lord Benedick were silent for a few minutes more, just to be sure the men were gone. The sound of the sea, battering into the shore again and again, punctuated their breathing while they waited. The sun, which had been wan when Sophia first came out that morning, had gone behind a cloud, and Sophia shivered a little.

"Who was that?" she asked glancing up at the cliff, almost afraid the two men would climb over. "Even only hearing one side of their conversation I know it was not about their plans for the village fete."

"I'm not sure," Lord Benedick said, following her gaze upward. "Perhaps it's best if we forget we heard that. It was clearly not intended for public consumption. And the louder man did not sound like the sort of person who would take kindly to having interference in his business."

Sophia turned to him in surprise. "I should have expected that attitude from other men, Lord Benedick, but I should think as a man of God your first responsibility is to help people. And clearly someone is in grave danger. We just heard one man tell another that he must be prepared to eliminate someone."

"I am aware of what we heard, Miss Hastings," he said stiffly, "but you are in no condition to look into the matter. We must see to getting you back to Beauchamp House. Whatever we overheard can wait for that at least, can it not?"

As if the conversation were over, he rose easily to his booted feet and put his fists on his hips. He rather looked like an avenging angel, now, Sophia thought sourly. An avenging angel who was urging caution.

She knew very well when she was being fobbed off. Still, she was determined. Her own sense of justice insisted. "Very well, Lord Benedick. It can wait. But do not think to dissuade me from learning more about those men. If someone is truly in danger we must do something to protect them."

At her vehemence, something in his gaze softened. "Very well, Miss Hastings. I will commit to learning more. But for now we must get you to the house."

She nodded, and was about to ask him for a hand up when he bent and gathered her into his arms, lifting her as if she weighed no more than a feather.

The jolt to her injured ankle, however, soon replaced any

shyness at being lifted bodily from the ground. Her head swam a little as the chalk cliffs spun by her as she was propelled upward. Closing her eyes against the disorientation, she concentrated on getting past the painful moment. When it had abated some, she took a deep breath and became aware of the warmth of the hard male chest against her side, as well as the bergamot mixed with pure male scent of him.

"I'm sorry," he said, and she realized she must have made a noise at the pain. "I'll do my best not to jostle you as we go up the sea stairs, but it will be impossible to avoid some bumping. It is the nature of stairs, I'm afraid."

She looked up into his eyes, which were once more creased with concern. She needed to be careful or she'd find herself enjoying this sort of tender care a bit too much. "Thank you, my lord," she said with a firmness that was as much for her as it was for him. "I will try to keep my cries of pain to a minimum."

Sophia was only half-joking.

"Good girl," he said with a nod. "Let's get you home."

Lord Benedick Lisle, vicar of Little Seaford, had been on his morning walk along the seashore when Miss Hastings had quite literally fallen from the heavens. Or at the very least from the clifftop.

One minute he'd been studying the crumbling stone sea wall that marked the boundary of the Beauchamp House property, and the next a female body was hurtling down from above.

He'd been too far away to do anything but watch in shock as he tried to make sense of what he was seeing. Then, he broke into a run. When he reached her side, he realized it was Miss Sophia Hastings, one of the four Beauchamp House heiresses.

She was an exceptionally lovely young woman—he might

be a vicar, but he was still a man, and he doubted the Archbishop of Canterbury himself would be able to resist the pull of Miss Hastings' ample charms—but it was her spirit that made her truly beautiful. Whereas other young women with her looks might have gone to London and taken the *ton* by storm, or searched for a wealthy husband, Sophia was a painter of some skill and she was determined to make her mark. Which meant she spent a great deal of time in her studio, or painting outdoors. And when she wasn't working, she was surrounded by a cadre of young men from the village. She hadn't, so far as Ben could see, given any of them an indication that she was interested in more than flirtation, but she somehow managed to handle them without allowing them to get too competitive over her.

Ben had considered entering the fray himself, but with his own duties in the parish he hardly had the time for friendship, much less anything more serious. And, if he were being honest, as a vicar, he needed a certain sort of wife. He had watched his brothers Archer and Freddie fall in love and marry, and he certainly wanted the sort of partnerships they enjoyed with their wives. But he also had to be pragmatic when it came to choosing a bride. A vicar's wife would need to be content with sharing him with the parish. A vicar was never off duty. If someone were ill, or suffering, he had to be ready to leave at a moment's notice. And his wife would need to be someone who shared his dedication to caring for the people of his parish. Who wouldn't worry about getting her gown a bit dirty when she visited the homes of people who worked the land. Who could converse with all sorts of people, be they noble or commoner. He wasn't sure that Miss Hastings possessed those qualities.

Of course, that was putting the cart before the horse. But he was a sensible man, and he was perhaps a bit too prone to overthink things. And if truth be told, he was unlikely to find Miss Hastings in a quiet moment to assess whether they could even be friends. She was always chatting with someone or working on one of her paintings.

If he'd wished for a few minutes of uninterrupted conversation with the lady, however, he hadn't wished for it to be while she was in excruciating pain.

He tried to be as gentle as possible while he climbed the sea stairs, but it was impossible to be as smooth as a well-sprung carriage, and by the time they reached the gardens behind Beauchamp House, he was panting from exertion and Miss Hastings' face was white with pain.

As they neared the fountain, he heard a shout from the house and Lady Serena Fanning, who served as chaperone to the heiresses, came hurrying out followed by the Duchess of Maitland—Lady Serena's sister-in-law and one of the four heiresses.

"What's happened?" Lady Serena asked as she reached them. Her strawberry blond hair was coiled tightly around her head in a rather severe style, but Ben knew she was fond of her charges. "Sophia, my dear, are you hurt?"

"I hurt my ankle," Sophia said through clenched teeth.

"But how?" Daphne, Duchess of Maitland, asked, her brow furrowed. "I thought you were painting this morning."

"Perhaps we can discuss this inside?" Ben asked. Sophia wasn't heavy per se, but he wasn't exactly Gentleman Jackson either and he didn't want to drop her.

"Come," Serena said and he followed her through the gardens toward the terrace where two French doors opened into a drawing room.

It was a comfortably appointed room with warm rose walls and a pair of overstuffed sofas before a low fire.

"Here is fine," Sophia said indicating one of the sofas. Ben lowered her as carefully as he could onto the cushion and inhaled the lemon scent of her hair just before he pulled away from her.

Stepping back, he found himself clasping his hands behind his back to stop the impulse to reach for her again.

"Perhaps you can ask Greaves to send for the doctor, Daphne dear," said Serena, who was obviously in caretaking mode, putting a pillow behind Sophia's back, and bringing her a light blanket.

"Stop fussing, Serena," the patient protested. "I'm perfectly fine."

"You are not fine," her chaperone corrected her. "But I will leave you be for a moment. I'll see if someone can find your sister. There's no telling where she's got to looking for her rocks."

Without waiting for a reply, Serena turned to Ben. "If you'll wait here a moment, I'll go get some ice for Sophia's ankle and ask cook to send some refreshments."

And then she was gone.

The urgency of the need to get Sophia up to the house had erased any awkwardness between them during the long walk, but now there was a tension between them. Not liking to loom over her, Ben lowered his tall frame onto the sofa across from her.

"You're in good hands, I think," he said, breaking the silence. "Lady Serena seems quite competent."

Sophia ignored his small talk and got right to the heart of the matter. "Thank you for rescuing me, my lord. I don't know what I'd have done if you hadn't happened along." Her blue eyes were bright with sincerity. "Not to mention what would have happened if those men on the bluff had discovered me."

At the reminder of the conversation they'd overheard, Ben's gut tightened. He didn't like to imagine that scenario. "I want you to promise me that you'll concentrate on healing and not try to investigate the matter on your own. I'll handle it."

She tilted her head. "You'll investigate it? I thought you said it was best to leave it alone?"

"As you said, someone is in danger." He wasn't sure what exactly he would do, but he knew he had to keep her away from the matter. There had been menace in the man's voice. And he sounded like the sort who would not take kindly to prying eyes in his business. "I'll ask a few questions."

Her pretty lips pursed in frustration. "It's not fair that I'm injured. I would like to know what they're up to."

He was entirely unsurprised that she was already chafing at the constraints of her injury. And it had only just happened. For her sake he hoped it would heal quickly.

"What if I promise to tell you what I learn?" he offered her. He didn't add that this way she could remain out of the matter, which would ensure her safety. He had a sneaking suspicion that she wouldn't give a fig for her own safety if it meant protecting someone else's.

Like a queen accepting a favor from a serf, she gave a regal nod. "I suppose that will have to do," she said with a moue of distaste. "Though I do wish I could go with you. Who do you intend to question first?"

He was saved from response by the arrival of the butler Greaves carrying a laden tea tray. "Miss Hastings," he older man said gravely, "May I say how unhappy I am to hear of your injury?" He gave a deep bow.

"Thank you, Mr. Greaves," Sophia said with a sweet smile for the butler. "It is an annoyance, but these things happen in the pursuit of one's craft."

Ben rather thought most artists avoided tumbling over seaside cliffs, but kept his own counsel on the matter.

He watched in amusement as the butler, who clearly had a soft spot for Sophia, handed her a cup of tea and a plate of biscuits. "Lady Serena told me to serve you, Miss. She is fetching your sister from upstairs."

"Thank you, Greaves," Sophia said, sipping her tea. "You may go. Lord Benedick will keep me company while we wait for Gemma and Serena."

Ben wasn't positive, but he thought he saw a flicker of disappointment cross the man's face before he gave a brisk bow and left the room, closing the door behind him.

"He's a sweet man," Sophia said, "but overly solicitous at times."

"He certainly holds you in some affection," Ben remarked. He might as well have been invisible for all that the butler noticed him.

Sophia gave a slight shrug, but didn't comment on the matter. Instead she changed the subject. "I wonder if you might do me a favor, my lord."

He nodded. "Of course. Whatever I can do to make you comfortable."

"It's just that my canvas and easel and paints are all still on the bluff," she said sheepishly.

Of course. She hadn't exactly carried them down to the beach as she fell.

Ben stood. "I'll go retrieve them for you." She obviously cared about her materials and wanted them to be in good hands.

"I could ask a footman," she added in a low voice, "but I thought maybe you could look in the little wooded area and see if our arguing men left any traces of themselves behind."

Ah. Not a bad idea, actually. "I'll be off then. I've got about an hour until I'm to meet with the altar guild."

"Oh." She looked a little guilty. "I don't wish to take you away from your work. I'll send a footman."

But Ben was already eager to get to the copse to look around for himself. "I have the time, Miss Hastings," he said, crouching beside the sofa where she reclined with her ankle elevated. He took her hand and squeezed it. "I will bring your things back, though I may not have time to come in and report to you. But I'll send a note round if I find anything."

Her dark lashes lowered as she looked down at their joined hands. When she looked up and met his gaze, her smile was one of relief. "Thank you for keeping me apprised. I know you'd rather I stay out of this business, but I can't help but feel responsible for whomever it was they were discussing."

"You can only do what's in your power," he said, trying to reassure her. "But I share your concern. They were rather rough customers."

Stroking his thumb over the back of her hand, he reluctantly let her go and stood.

"Wish me luck," he said with a crooked smile.

"Just don't tumble over the edge," she said wryly. "I won't be there to rescue you."

Chapter 2

As it happened, Dr. Holmes was unable to come that afternoon because he was attending to another patient in the next county.

Lady Serena was concerned, but Sophia was convinced that it was only a sprain, and once she'd been helped to her bedchamber by two sturdy footmen, she allowed her maid to tuck her into bed with ice for her ankle and agreed to rest.

"I know you must be disappointed about missing Mr. Morgan's ball this evening," Ivy said, from where she perched on Sophia's bedside. "Of all of us, you're the lady most likely to be found dancing the night away."

She, Daphne and Gemma had come to check on her after luncheon. Only the sisters, Sophia and Gemma, had known one another before their arrival at Beauchamp House. But since then, the four ladies had built strong friendships. They each had expertise in separate disciplines, but they all appreciated the difficulties of being a female in the arts and academe, so offered one another support not only as friends, but also as fellow pioneers. And when both Ivy and Daphne had found themselves in danger thanks to tasks given them by their benefactor, Lady Celeste Beauchamp, they'd grown even closer.

Sophia frowned at her offending ankle. "I'd forgotten about the Morgan Ball," she said.

She'd been looking forward to the entertainment at the industrialist's newly refurbished country estate, which he'd bought for what was rumored to be a ridiculously large sum from a deeply indebted nobleman. It would be the neighborhood's first chance to see what was purported to be one of the most expensive renovations in Sussex history. According to local gossip, Morgan had chosen the south coast for his country home because he claimed to have a fondness for history and the location was near to Hastings—where William the Conqueror had claimed victory.

No one quite knew what to make of the self-made man who had made appearances in Little Seaford and the surrounding towns occasionally over the past year or so. By all accounts he was brash and a bit rough, but Sophia wasn't really concerned with his manners. She would really like to discuss his textile mills in the north, the conditions of which she'd learned about thanks to a letter from her Aunt Dahlia in Manchester.

If my sources are right, Peter Morgan is in Sussex for no other reason than to buy himself a seat in the Commons without having to face a local population who has suffered from his dangerous factories. He stood by and did nothing while the women and children working in his factories fell ill from cotton lung, and what's more, were torn limb from limb by his wicked machinery. And now he would flee from Manchester, where his perfidy is known far and wide. He seeks to whitewash his reputation in the waters of the sea.

It can hardly be a coincidence that a little bird informs me one of the local members in that same vicinity has recently decided to give up his seat in the Commons. You must do all you can, my dear, to keep this awful man from what will be nothing less than theft. It is bad enough that the

*working men who give their lives and labor to make En-
gland great are kept from the vote, but to also ensure that
government positions are handed out to the very industrialists who crush those same workers is monstrous.*

*Be vigilant, dear Sophia! And pray urge that stubborn
sister of yours to do so as well. I know I taught you both better than to sit by while the weak are bullied by the strong!*

Sophia had, of course, promised her aunt to learn all she
could about the man, and if she had to miss his first entertainment, she'd lose her chance. Not to mention she was as
curious as anyone else to see the spectacle of the newly em-
bellished interiors of Morgan's house. Aunt Dahlia would
likely be disappointed in her, but she was human after all,
and liked to be dazzled as much as the next person.

She mentioned none of this to Gemma, however, who, as
Aunt Dahlia had said, was stubborn and if truth be known,
was far less interested in the workings of the political system than in her own pursuit of knowledge.

"You may have forgotten the ball," Gemma said tartly,
"but I cannot imagine that your usual little coterie of admirers has. They will be cast into despair when they arrive to
find you are not there. A shame, really, since it is one of my
chief pleasures in life to watch them persist in the face of
your polite indifference."

Tugging at one of Sophia's locks, she added with a saucy
grin, "I can't imagine why they are so taken with you.
You've always got paint in your hair."

Sophia made a face. "At least I don't have dust from dirty
old stones under my fingernails," she retorted. "And besides,
my gentleman callers can hear about my accident from me.
I'm going to the ball."

All three of her companions gasped.

"You can't!" Gemma said, her mouth agape.

"Sophia," Ivy said with a sigh. "I don't see how, unless

you wish to bring Thomas and Walter in the carriage with us so that they might carry you around on a litter like the king in his younger days."

"You won't be able to dance," Daphne said, looking puzzled. "What would be the point?"

"Oh ye of little faith," Sophia said with a wave of her hand. "I will simply use the walking stick we found in the attic during our initial explorations of the house. I'm sure with the sturdy arm of some strong gentleman, and the walking stick, I'll be able to hobble along quite nicely."

"I never met a more stubborn person in my life," Gemma said with a shake of her head. "You're worse than Aunt Dahlia."

"It's because of Aunt Dahlia I must go," Sophia protested. Then, she explained what her aunt had told her about Mr. Peter Morgan and his possible political aspirations. "So, you see, I need to find out what he's about. And what better place to do that than his first large entertainment in the neighborhood. How a man entertains says a lot about him."

"Why didn't Aunt ask me to look into Morgan?" Gemma asked with a frown. "I care about women and children."

How to explain that one's sister had a bit of a one-track mind? To one's sister?

Daphne, who was not known for either her tact or propensity for biting her tongue, saved her the trouble. "Gemma, you'd never be able to concentrate long enough. You'd start daydreaming about one of your fossils and would lose track of the conversation."

Gemma looked offended and looked to Ivy then Sophia for support. "Am I really that bad?" she demanded when they only gave pained shrugs in response to her questioning look. "I'm not that bad."

"Dearest, you were so lost in thought about some issue

with your research," Sophia said not unkindly, "that you tried to put on a hat *while you were already wearing a hat*."

"That was one time!" Gemma protested. "And it was a very thorny issue."

"It's nothing to be ashamed of," Ivy assured her with a kind smile. "You're very dedicated to your work. It's quite admirable. But even you must admit that you aren't precisely interested in anything quite as much as fossils and the possibility that giant lizards once roamed about the countryside."

Gemma shook her head, her light brown hair a little frizzy as it escaped its pins. "I don't mean to do it. It's just that I'll start thinking about something and then everything disappears."

"It's the same for me and maths," Daphne said with a nod of agreement.

"We all do it," Sophia assured her. "I fell from the chalk cliff because I was so absorbed in my work, for heaven's sake."

That diverted everyone.

"I thought you tripped walking on the shore," Gemma said with a frown. "You didn't tell me you fell from the cliff. Sophia, you might have been killed."

She gave her sister an impulsive hug. "Thank goodness you weren't hurt worse."

"How did you come to fall?" Daphne asked. "If you stay far enough from the edge, it's safe enough."

Quickly Sophia explained how she'd been startled by a man's voice behind her, and how Lord Benedick had come upon her.

"Who was it you heard?" Ivy asked. "That's Beauchamp House land. If there are trespassers we should let Kerr and Maitland know." The Marquess of Kerr and the Duke of Maitland were nephews of the bluestockings' benefactor, and more importantly, the husbands of Ivy and Daphne.

Sophia frowned. It hadn't occurred to her that the men they'd overheard were trespassing. But it was also possible that one or both of them had some association with Beauchamp House. The idea gave her a chill.

Mistaking her shiver for a more general fear, Ivy tried to reassure her. "Since both Daphne and I were accosted here, Kerr is quite firm about ensuring the safety of the house. He and Mr. Greaves have made sure that all the footmen are trustworthy, and there are new locks on all the doors. Even if someone were to wander onto Beauchamp House land, there's no way he could get into the house without someone knowing."

Sophia nodded. She had to tell Lord Benedick about her new insight into the quarreling men. He hadn't sent round a note, which she assumed meant he hadn't found anything in the copse. But she could speak to him tonight at the ball.

To Ivy she said, "I trust Kerr. Whoever the man was, I don't think he meant me any harm. He was speaking with someone else and they were far too involved in their own conversation to notice anything else."

"I'm just glad that Lord Benedick happened to be walking on the beach when you fell." Ivy's eyes behind her spectacles were wide with concern. "You might have been stranded there for hours."

"I wish I'd been there to see him carrying you from the shore up the sea stairs," Gemma said with a wink. "It must have been quite romantic."

"I was far too busy trying not to cry out every time my ankle was jolted," Sophia said wryly. Though she had noticed just how very muscular the vicar was on their journey. And she'd been tempted to snuggle her face into his neck more than once. But she wouldn't admit that now.

"Then how on Earth will you manage to go to the ball?" Ivy asked. "You're being stubborn to the point of lunacy, Sophia."

"I will manage," Sophia assured them with a calm she didn't feel. She was still determined to go. Though she wasn't quite as sanguine about her ability to withstand hours on her feet as she let on. But Aunt Dahlia needed her. And she'd made a promise.

"Now, you should all go and let me rest so I can look my best."

When Daphne and Ivy had gone, Gemma came and sat beside her sister on the bed.

"You weren't too distracted to notice the vicar's strong arms," she said with a sly look. "I've seen the way you look at him. He's the only unmarried man in the village who doesn't dance to your tune. And you like that."

"He's a handsome man," Sophia said blithely. "I'd hardly be human if I failed to notice. And between us, he's quite strong."

"You do like him," Gemma said with a grin.

"Of course I like him." Sophia refused to be baited. Whatever attraction she might feel for the vicar was not nearly as important as finding the identities of the men they'd overheard. And there was the matter of Peter Morgan and his political ambitions. She had plenty to keep her occupied without adding a *tendre* to the list.

"Now, please go find some old rocks to examine so that I may rest."

Gemma gave her a disappointed look, but took herself off.

Ben had been unable to find anything in his search of the little wooded area where their mysterious arguers had been hidden. He had quite easily found Miss Hasting's easel, canvas and supplies. The painting was still a little wet, and promised to be intriguing when it was finished. The way she'd captured the light and colors of the sunrise on the sea was impressive. He'd never been particularly artistic himself, but seeing work like this made him wish he had that sort of talent.

He reflected on the matter that evening as he drove his gig to the country estate of Mr. Peter Morgan, where the industrialist was set to hold his first public entertainment in the neighborhood. It hadn't occurred to him to ask Miss Hastings if she'd planned on attending, but given the state of her injury, he had little doubt that she'd have to send her regrets. Which was a shame. He'd enjoyed her company, and had hoped to reassure her that she shouldn't worry overmuch about what they'd overhead. But that could wait until later.

The line of carriages in the gently curving drive of Morgan House was impressive. Clearly the rest of the residents of Little Seaford were just as curious to see the inside of the mansion as he was. Having handed over the reins, he was greeted by a few parishioners as he made his way to the receiving line.

"Good evening, Vicar," said Mr. Josiah Almond, a member of the local gentry, whose estate was just on the other side of Beauchamp House. He was a widower of middle years, whose children were grown, and a regular churchgoer. He was also a bit of a gossip. In a lower voice, he said with a wink, "I see you've come to see what this Morgan fellow is about just as the rest of us have. I don't mind telling you I hope his refreshments live up to the promise of his taste in building materials."

Almond gestured to the marble beneath their feet. And if Ben's memory served from when his mother had been refurbishing the Pemberton ducal residence, the gilt molding and fabric-lined walls of the Morgan entry hall were quite expensive.

"I have a feeling you won't be disappointed, Almond," Ben assured the older man. If his assessment was correct,

Morgan was intent upon impressing his neighbors. Everything about his home seemed to promote the idea that Peter Morgan was a rich, successful businessman. Was it a bit over the top? For Ben's tastes, yes. But then, he'd grown up in a ducal household that was built for similar purposes, and had long ago come to see the finery for what it was, a show of power. He had no need for such flummery. But the powerful did. And it would be hypocritical to take his father's show of wealth as a given while criticizing Morgan for doing the same thing.

Further discussion was stalled when they reached the place where Morgan, his wife and sons stood greeting their guests. Morgan himself was a large man, whose large belly was as much a show of wealth as any bit of gold in his home. His wife, on the other hand, was rail thin. She was pretty enough, with guinea gold hair that was still unmarred with gray. While Morgan greeted Mr. Almond, Ben took Mrs. Morgan's hand.

"Thank you so much for the invitation, ma'am," he told her sincerely. "I am always grateful for the chance to get out in the evening."

Mrs. Morgan smiled at him. "You are quite welcome, my lord. I'm sure our little home isn't what you're used to, but I hope you will be comfortable."

The description of what must be thirty rooms at the least, as a "little home" might have had Ben spraying his beverage, if he'd been unlucky enough to be drinking at that moment. As it was, he had to tamp down his natural response for the easygoing expression he'd perfected over the years of being the recipient of odd confidences from his flock. "I'm quite sure I will be most comfortable, Mrs. Morgan. But let us discuss the most important thing. I hope you'll reserve a set for me?"

The bit of flirtation did the trick and she blushed. "You

rogue," she said without heat as she batted him on the arm with her fan. "You know I'm past the age for dancing, but if I were not, you may be assured I would not be able to turn down the most handsome man in the village. Aside from my Peter, of course."

"What's this?" said the man himself as he turned from Mr. Almond, who was moving along the line to the younger Morgans. "I hope you're not trying to lure my wife away, Vicar."

There was no menace in the man's tone, but Ben could hear a slight thread of pique, as if he didn't take the matter seriously but couldn't help but be a little annoyed. Whether because Ben was younger, or higher born, he couldn't say.

"Of course not, Mr. Morgan," said Ben smoothly. "Only inquiring if your dear wife was dancing this evening. But alas, she has informed me that she is not."

"She would make all the young ladies green with envy if she did," Morgan said putting a proprietary arm around his wife. "I don't blame you a bit for asking."

Then, obviously considering that matter behind them, he changed the subject. "What do you think of Morgan Manor, eh? I don't mind telling you I'm quite proud of it. Designed the place m'self, did you know that? From the ceilings to the floors. No expense spared, I can tell you. I wanted it to be a jewel on the coast, and so it is."

Ben blinked at the boast. "It's quite a sight to see," he said truthfully. "And I can tell that you put a lot of thought into every detail."

Morgan beamed. "I knew you'd understand. I'll bet it rivals your father's place in the country, eh? Of course it does. His place must be a hundred years old at least. And has none of the modern conveniences we've got here."

The Duke of Pemberton had actually had modern plumbing installed several years ago, but Ben wasn't about to get into a competition with Morgan over whose home was better. "It is indeed over a hundred years old," he confirmed. "And nowhere near as modern as this. You are to be congratulated."

Before Morgan could use the pause to add more comparisons to his father, Ben continued, "I was just telling Mrs. Morgan how thankful I was for the invitation. I'm looking forward to this evening's entertainment. Thank you, sir."

The industrialist looked a bit frustrated at being unable to continue his explanation of how he had bested the Duke of Pemberton, but the person behind Ben diverted his attention then, and with an over-hearty handshake, he sent the vicar on his way.

After exchanging greetings with the Morgan sons, who were typical young men, with shirt points and hair that were higher than advisable, Ben stepped into the ballroom, which was already teeming with guests.

To his surprise, however, his eye was captured by a familiar head of auburn-tinged dark hair amongst the chaperones and wallflowers.

He couldn't see the lady's face, as she was at the moment surrounded by a circle of young men, but it was most certainly Miss Sophia Hastings, holding court. No doubt having taken to the side of the ballroom thanks to her ankle injury, but here at the Morgan ball nonetheless.

"Evening, Vicar," said a male voice from beside him. He looked up and the Duke of Maitland handed Ben a cup of watery-looking punch. So much for Mr. Almond's hopes for lavish food and drink, he thought wryly. "It tastes better than it looks."

Since Ben had performed the duke's marriage ceremony not long after his arrival in Little Seaford, he and the other man had become friendly.

"Why aren't you dancing with your bride?" Ben asked, taking the cup and sipping. It did indeed taste better than it looked. Perhaps Mr. Almond wasn't to be disappointed after all.

"She's over there lecturing the schoolmaster, Mr. Pinter, about something having to do with maths," Maitland said with a shrug. "I don't pretend to understand half of what she says about all that business. But it makes her happy, and that's enough for me."

Ben had known as soon as he met the couple that they were fond of one another, despite the circumstances that had led to their hasty marriage. And though they seemed on the surface to be a mismatch, given that the duchess was one of the most gifted mathematicians in the nation, and the duke . . . was not, they made it work. And Maitland had even agreed to live the rest of the year in Little Seaford, away from his own properties, so that his wife might fulfill the requirements of her inheritance at Beauchamp House. Of course, the duke was also the nephew of the former owner of the home, Lady Celeste Beauchamp, so he already felt at home in Little Seaford. But Ben didn't know many men who would adjust their lives in such a way simply to please their wives. And considering that Maitland's cousin, the Marquess of Kerr, had done the same thing, it was clear that the men in that family doted on their wives.

Ben looked across the room to where the blond duchess did indeed seem to be explaining something to Pinter, using her hands to sketch figures in the air. "Pinter looks a bit non-plussed," he said to the duke.

"Probably because she knows more about the subject than he'll ever forget," Maitland said with a shrug. "But he'll be all right. He likes her. And is far better at accepting a woman as his superior in an academic subject than most men in his position would be. He's a good fellow, Pinter."

The two men were quiet for a moment as the musicians began warming up, and the buzz of conversation around them picked up. It was unusual for Ben to remain unmolested by the female population for so long, but he supposed it was because they were slightly afraid of the duchess, and he was currently standing next to her husband.

"Heard you rescued Miss Hastings from the shore this morning," Maitland said, turning to give Ben a curious look. "I didn't know you were in the business of rescuing damsels in distress. Though I suppose being a vicar and all, it's part of the job."

He felt his ears redden at the other man's teasing tone. "I'm sure if anyone else had come upon Miss Hastings, he too would have done what he could to help her."

"But how many men would have carried her a quarter of a mile—up treacherous sea stairs no less—to help her?" Maitland asked. "I'm quite fond of the chit, but I don't even think I'd have tried it."

"I couldn't leave her there," Ben argued. He didn't add that they'd just overheard a man threatening murder, so leaving Sophia on the shore would have been dangerous in more ways than one. "And it wasn't as difficult as all that."

His aching biceps told him differently, but he wasn't going to admit to it here and now. The less emphasis he put on the physical exertion it had taken to get Sophia from the shore to the house, the better. He didn't want the duke or anyone else at Beauchamp House thinking he'd helped her out of some sort of *tendre*. As lovely as Miss Hastings was, she was not the sort of lady he should be associating with. He would need to, when the time came, marry someone who would make a good vicar's wife. Nothing he'd seen of Miss Hastings had indicated that she was so disposed.

"You do know there's a secret passageway from the shore that leads into the house, don't you?" Maitland asked with a raised brow. "I should have thought Sophia would have told you. It has stairs as well, but it's a damned sight shorter than all the way up the outer stairs, across the lawn and through the garden."

Ben blinked, not sure what he was hearing. "Are you telling me Miss Hastings might have saved my back by telling me of a shorter route? Why didn't she tell me?" He thought back to the long trek from the beach to the house. He had a sudden inclination to give Miss Hastings a lecture—complete with gesticulations rivaling those of the Duchess of Maitland.

"I daresay she was too overset by pain to remember it," Maitland said thoughtfully. "She's not the sort to keep something like that to herself on purpose. She's a good 'un, is Sophia."

Good 'un or not, Ben thought with a frown, he was going to have a word with her about it. If for no other reason than to assure himself that he'd not been hoodwinked into helping her. The ladies of the village had tried all sorts of machinations to get close to him. He had difficulty believing someone like Sophia, who obviously had her own ambitions, would do such a thing, but who was he to claim knowledge of the female brain?

He was about to excuse himself to go speak to her, when Peter Morgan stepped onto a small dais at the front of the room, which he hadn't noticed before. It wasn't unusual for a host to say a few words at the opening of a ball. But something about this felt different.

With a gesture to the musicians, indicating they should be silent, their host began to speak.

From her seat at the side of the ballroom, Sophia wished for the hundredth time that she'd listened to her sister and stayed home. Her ankle was throbbing, and the circle of young men around her, rather than distracting her from her pain, were only annoying her with their competition to see who was willing to do more for her. She could only drink so many cups of punch, and she flatly refused to let them carry her about the room like a pasha. It had been lowering enough to hobble into the room with her walking stick.

She'd had visions of holding court from her perch with the matrons and wallflowers, but hadn't actually thought through the grueling process of getting from the carriage to said perch.

Fortunately, the sound of the musicians warming up signaled that her suitors would have to go soon and dance with those young ladies who hadn't fallen from the cliffside that morning. Her injury could be counted a benefit in that instance at least.

"Your attention, ladies and gentlemen," came the sound of their host from the front of the ballroom. And fortunately, Sophia's young gentlemen had the sense to move so that she could see where Peter Morgan had taken a position at the dais situated near the musicians.

Sophia wondered, a little thrill of electricity running down her spine, if as her Aunt Dahlia had predicted, Peter Morgan was going to announce his intention to run for the vacant seat in the Commons.

"Thank you all for coming tonight," said Morgan with a broad smile, which he made sure to beam over everyone in attendance. At least the ones in the ballroom at the moment. "It is with great pride that my wife Millie and I welcome you into our new home away from home. Our little jewel on the coast. As most of you know, I've made my home for most of my life in Manchester, but since our arrival in Little Seaford, we've been most cordially welcomed by you and the rest of the villagers. I've met with Mr. Givens, the mayor, and have listened to his concerns. And I've made it my business to become involved in local activities, like the upcoming art exhibition, the board of which I am now a member. I mean to make it clear to you, the residents of Little Seaford, that I will put as much effort and energy into the wellbeing of our village, as I have done with my businesses."

There was a smattering of applause from the room at large, but from one side of the room, where the two Morgan sons and their friends had gathered, came a raucous cheering. Obviously, the man had brought his own audience, which could be counted on to cheer in the right spots.

Sophia glanced around the room, and noticed that with the exception of the cheering lads, the rest of the guests looked puzzled. And in some cases, troubled.

When the cheering had died down—at the behest of Morgan, who gave a gesture in his sons' direction—he continued. "It is my great pleasure to announce that I intend to run for the vacant seat in this district for the House of Commons. And I hope all of you will give me your support!"

Once again, the cheering group erupted into huzzahs. And there was a bit more applause from the main room. It was more polite, however, than genuinely enthusiastic.

Since she'd been forewarned by her aunt, Sophia wasn't surprised, but she was puzzled at Morgan's decision to make the announcement at what was ostensibly an entertainment for the upper echelon of Little Seaford society. If he had wished for a large cheering crowd, surely a more public celebration would have been far more conducive to that.

"Now, without further ado, I shall allow you to get on with what you've come for," Morgan said, beaming out over the room. "Let there be dancing."

He gestured to the musicians, and they began playing, and Morgan, looking as pleased as if he'd just delivered a New Year's infant, led his rail-thin wife, Millicent, out onto the dance floor in the first dance.

"I suppose that is what Aunt Dahlia was speaking of," said Gemma from where she'd come to stand beside Sophia's chair.

"Indeed," Sophia said. "Only I didn't expect him to make the announcement tonight."

"I'm not sure anyone did," Gemma said with a nod to the guests, who were slowly making their way onto the dance floor. But there were several small groups of gentlemen who seemed to be in deep conversation. "It seems to have set some of the local tongues wagging, that's certain."

One thing their host had mentioned, however, had caught Sophia's attention and it was far more personal for her than her aunt's request to keep an eye on Morgan. "What do you suppose he intends, getting himself a seat on the art exhibition board?" she asked her sister. "What can he possibly know about art?"

But Gemma gave her a speaking look. "What does anyone in this village know about art, excepting you and the Primbles with their group of artists at Primrose Green? Isn't the owner of the livery stable on the board?"

"Yes, but Mr. Essex has a very keen eye," Sophia argued. The man had chosen very complimentary colors for the exterior of his establishment, after all. "And besides, I know that all of the board members—Mr. Morgan excepted—have the best interests of the village at heart. And they will judge impartially. We don't know what sort of motives Mr. Morgan has for affiliating himself with the art board."

"One would imagine he simply wishes to ingratiate himself with the local populace," Gemma said. "Though it is difficult to know what any man will do. They are fickle creatures to be sure."

Sophia supposed her sister was close to the truth. Still, since she intended to enter the exhibition this year, she was concerned that the entry of Morgan onto the board of directors would affect her chances of having her pieces shown. "You're likely right. He will simply sit on the board and let the others take charge. It is no doubt his intention to use the meetings to solicit support from the other business owners in the group."

"Are you afraid that he will try to keep you out of the show?" Gemma asked, her eyes narrowing. "Sophia, your work can be a bit controversial, but no one in Little Seaford is the least bit interested in censoring you. This is hardly the wilds of Yorkshire. Most of the gentry hereabouts spend their springs in London and summers on the road between here and Brighton. They are quite sophisticated."

But Sophia wasn't sure that Morgan had the purest of motives. Her aunt had seemed to think he was going to run his campaign with a view toward capitalizing on the populism that had grown stronger in the years since the Peterloo massacre, where fifteen people had been killed when cavalrymen stormed into a crowd demanding parliamentary reform in St. Peter's Fields, Manchester. For many years now, a growing contingent of the population had been protesting the inequities of the voting system, the cutting—by industrialists like Morgan—of wages when the market shifted, and the Corn Laws, which imposed a tariff on foreign grain, and meant the people were forced to buy more expensive British grain. It was quite canny actually, Sophia thought, for Morgan to choose to run for his seat in Sussex, where he was relatively unknown, as opposed to in Manchester, where his reputation as a factory owner would hardly do him any good.

"He could make quite a name for himself as a reformer if he were to come out against the scandalous paintings of an upstart young lady who would do better to stay at home embroidering," Sophia told her sister. "It's what I'd do if I were in his position."

"Well, I think you're being far too suspicious," Gemma said with a shake of her head. "You're seeing plots where none are there."

Before Sophia could respond, she spotted a couple of her usual cadre of admirers headed their way.

"Don't go," she hissed to Gemma, as her sister gave her a pat on the arm, then hurried away to where Daphne was speaking to the local schoolmaster.

But it was too late.

"Ah, Mr. Walsh, Mr. Ellis," she said with more enthusiasm than she felt. "What a delight to see you again."

Chapter 3

A few minutes later, she was wishing desperately that Gemma would return.

Or Daphne.

Or anyone who could get her away from the utterly tedious pair of young men who were currently monopolizing her attention.

"If you don't mind my saying so, Miss Hastings," said the Honorable Mr. Toby Walsh, handing Sophia a glass of punch, "you aren't at all what I expected when the mater told me about the bluestockings up at Beauchamp House back when you first arrived."

"Nor me," said his friend Walter Ellis, making use of the quizzing glass that looked ridiculous in the hand of such a young man. "I never knew it was possible for pretty chits to be smart." Perhaps realizing his words were not exactly flattering, he colored a little and added, "That is to say, I'd never . . ."

Needing to get out of the ballroom before she said something she'd regret to her two remaining hangers-on, she stopped Ellis with a hand on his arm. "I wonder if I could trouble the two of you for a favor?" she asked, showing none of the irritation she felt with the two young men on her smooth visage. "I see the Vining sisters there by the potted lemon tree looking a bit down pin. They're quite shy, you know, and I know they would simply fly into the boughs with happiness if two handsome young fellows like yourselves would ask them for the next set."

When Mr. Ellis looked as if he would object, Sophia added with a speaking look, "I believe their marriage portions are quite generous, and I cannot imagine your Mama would object to your at least making an effort in that direction."

Since the young man's mother had complained to Sophia earlier that she despaired of young Walter ever showing an interest in a suitable young lady, she knew that was an understatement. And Walter, perhaps realizing the truth in what she said, exchanged a look with his friend. "Perhaps one dance won't hurt, eh Walsh?"

Calculation in his eyes, Walsh turned from his friend back to Sophia. "One dance. But you must promise to give me a personal viewing of your paintings in the exhibition next week."

Not wanting to be outdone, Ellis echoed, "And me. For you must know I am interested in your painting above all things."

Since Sophia doubted young Mr. Ellis had ever contemplated art or its creation in all his one and twenty years, she wasn't convinced. Even so, if she were going to get out of this ballroom and off her aching ankle, she had to concede. "I'll give you both a tour of my studio, but you must hurry before the Vining girls abscond."

With promises to seek her out later, the two men hurried over to where the well-dowered Vining sisters stood whispering to one another.

Freed from the last of her coterie, Sophia breathed a sigh of relief and rose carefully from her chair to make her escape. Like her fellow heiresses, she'd been chosen to inherit Beauchamp House because of her renowned intellect and skill. In her case, it was her talent as a painter and her knowledge of art in general. Her work had been shown all over England, and she'd gained a reputation for art that both pushed the boundaries of what ladies were expected to depict on the canvas and called attention to those issues that might better, in some opinions, be hidden from view. Now, however, she wasn't thinking about her work, or anything but getting out of the ballroom before she was besieged again by young men looking for flirtation and a bit of scandal.

"I don't suppose you'd like a steady arm to help you get to wherever you're going," said a male voice from behind her.

A frisson of awareness ran through her as she recognized the voice of Lord Benedick, whom she'd spent far too much time thinking about since he'd rescued her from the shore.

Of course he'd be here at the most talked about social event to happen in Little Seaford in months. As the local vicar, he was practically required to attend. And as one of the town's most eligible bachelors, his absence would likely have caused a revolt amongst the village's unwed—and even some married—female population.

Sophia herself was not immune to the clergyman's charms. Certainly not after he'd carried her against that broad chest as if she weighed no more than a feather. And she'd had more than one improper dream about the man since his arrival. And yet, she knew all too well that a woman like her had no business with a man like him. Not only was he, as a duke's son, far above her reach socially, but he was also a man of God. And she and God weren't precisely on good terms.

Still, a supporting arm, when her ankle was aching from having all the blood rush to it for the past hour, was something she couldn't pass up. "I must confess, my lord, that I would accept the arm of the devil himself at this moment if he were kind enough to offer it."

Taller than her by at least a head, Benedick stepped closer and with courteous expediency, slipped an arm around her back and let her rest against his solid form for a moment. It was no more intimate than the waltz that had already been performed once that evening, but it was closer than Sophia had ever been to him and she could feel the warmth of his body through the barrier of their clothing.

Even so, the throbbing of her ankle overrode any feelings of euphoria or attraction she felt at the contact.

Unable to stop herself, she gave a sharp intake of breath when she accidentally put weight on it.

"Easy there," he said, his blue eyes shadowed with concern, "I think perhaps you might better sit down."

But she shook her head. "I have to get out of this room before I'm trapped again."

He didn't bother to ask who would do the trapping, only said, "Where to?"

"Somewhere less crowded," she said through clenched teeth, her painful ankle threating to make her cry out.

It had really been beyond foolish for her to attend tonight's festivities.

"Your wish is my command, my lady."

Giving up control of their destination to her companion, Sophia concentrated instead on maintaining her composure.

Fortunately, they were near a door leading into a side corridor, so they were able to slip away without being waylaid. And before she knew it, Sophia found herself seated on a long settee with her offending ankle propped on a fluffy cushion.

"We must stop meeting like this," Benedick said as he took a seat in a low-slung chair near her. "One could almost accuse us of taking a tour of the couches of lower Sussex."

"I imagine the Pavilion at Brighton has much better settees

than this," Sophia said, with a look of mock disdain for the piece of furniture upon which she currently lounged. She should be mortified at being forced to accept help from the vicar again, but instead she felt a sort giddy excitement at seeing him again.

Quite a dangerous thing, really, if she allowed herself to dwell on it.

Which she most certainly would not.

Benedick didn't seem to mind. "I can assure you, Miss Hastings, that the Pavilion also has far less gilt." He accompanied the remark with a comical wide-eyed glance around the room, which did indeed look as if it had been decorated by King Midas himself.

After they shared a laugh, he leaned forward, his elbows on his knees. "I had thought you would forgo tonight's entertainment given your injury this morning. Has no one ever told you to take better care of yourself?"

It was certainly what her sister and friends had said to her before they set out this evening, but Sophia was hardly going to admit that in the face of a gentle scold from the man who'd come to her rescue twice in the same day now. "What is the fun in staying home while everyone else is out dancing?" she said with a toss of her head. "Besides, I came at the request of a dear relation who needed me to be here for our host's announcement tonight."

His brows rose. "Someone who knew that Morgan would announce his political campaign?"

Deciding, given their shared experience that morning, that he was a safe person to share her aunt's information with, Sophia nodded. "My aunt works with a group in Manchester where Morgan's factories are located. She heard from her contacts there that he'd decided to run for the seat here, far from where his business dealings might sour the local people on him. She asked me to do what I could to stop him. Which meant attending the ball tonight."

"But surely she'd have understood if she knew you'd injured yourself," he said not unkindly. "One must admit to human frailty from time to time, Miss Hastings."

"Of course she would have done," Sophia said with a frown. "But some things are more important than personal difficulties. And besides, I wanted to hear what he had to say for myself. There will be plenty of time to rest tomorrow."

"One cannot help but admire your determination," he said. His blue eyes were warm with what looked like appreciation, though Sophia suspected that was just her imagination. "What did you think of Morgan's speech, then?"

Thankful to be off the subject of herself, Sophia leapt at the conversation thread. "It was remarkably short," she said. "I suppose I'd expected something more elaborate, but he must be saving that for when he talks to the villagers. He will certainly need the support of those in attendance tonight, but it will be the more skeptical farmers who own their own smaller plots of land he'll need to convince."

"Then I should think an assembly ball would have been more suited to his political needs," Benedick said. "But that would not have allowed him to show off his magnificent palace."

"Precisely," Sophia said with approval. "He must reassure everyone of his wealth and power, so that they will put their lot in with him. Aunt Dahlia mentioned in one of her letters that his speeches in Manchester before he made the decision to come south were very focused on shifting the balance of power back to the people. Unfortunately his treatment of those same people in his factories—particularly the women and children who work in them—made it impossible for him to gain any sort of support in the north. Nearly everyone had a friend, or a neighbor or a relation who had suffered thanks to cuts in wages, or injuries on the job, or worse."

"You don't suppose the conversation we heard this morning might have had some bearing on the announcement tonight?" Benedick asked, his face darkening.

It hadn't occurred to Sophia, but thinking back to what the men had said, she nodded. "It's possible. Political intrigue is certainly one interpretation to put on the matter." In fact, the more she reflected on the one man's vehemence about "eliminating a stumbling block" the more this explanation made sense. She was already composing a letter to her aunt in her mind, when Benedick's next words penetrated her fog of concentration.

". . . so, you must agree with me now that this is not something a young lady should be involving herself in," he said in a placating tone. "The men we heard were quite serious. I hope you will allow me to look into the matter. I have friends who work with the Home Office who may be able to . . ."

"Certainly not," Sophia interrupted him. "I do appreciate your concern for me, Lord Benedick, but I'm hardly a frail young thing to be wrapped in cotton wool. If you intend on doing any sort of investigation into the conversation we overheard, I must insist upon being a part of it."

"With all due respect, Miss Hastings," said the vicar, looking as if he'd like to tug on his hair in frustration, "you are injured, and you must know that men are far more likely to divulge secrets to other men than they are to a beautiful young woman whom they are trying to impress."

She tucked away the fact that he'd just called her beautiful to be examined at another time. "Are men so weak that they cannot manage to speak sense in the presence of a lady?" she demanded. "If that is the case then I believe we should immediately cease spouting the fiction that women are the weaker sex. For I am quite certain any woman of sense can say what's on her mind no matter how many men are looking on."

"I was merely making a general observation, Miss Hastings," said the vicar, his color rising a little at the retort. "In my experience, men, especially powerful men such as our host, have a tendency to put their best face forward in the presence of ladies. It is human nature. And you cannot deny that such things happen when ladies are in the presence of men they wish to impress too."

Thinking back to the antics of Mr. Walsh and Mr. Ellis earlier, Sophia relented. "I suppose there is some truth in what you say. But I do wish there was some way to remove the silliness of vanity from such important matters. Can we not simply talk sense without constantly being concerned about how we appear to the opposite sex?"

At that Benedick relaxed a little and grinned. "My dear Miss Hastings, what you are asking is the impossible."

His smile was infectious and in spite of her determination to "talk sense" Sophia found herself smiling back.

He continued, then, his blue eyes meeting hers in amusement. "I should certainly think you've become accustomed to having men make cakes of themselves in an effort to win your approbation."

"No more than you have, Vicar," she said with a raised brow. "Unless I've imagined the bevy of unmarried ladies who linger after church every Sunday in hopes of gaining a kind word from you."

"Touché," he said softly. "So, we are agreed that both gentlemen and ladies are prone to making fools of themselves when it comes to impressing one another. Where does that leave us?"

"It leaves us with the fact that I insist upon being a part of whatever you intend to do to find out what those two men were talking about this morning," she said calmly. "And while I admit that I might need to give myself a few days to recover from my injury, I will not allow you to pat me on the head and send me on my oblivious way."

The vicar shook his head at her vehemence, and leaned back in his chair, stretching his long legs out before him. "Miss Hastings, has anyone ever told you you're stubborn?"

"I believe you implied it not five minutes ago, my lord," Sophia responded with a sweet smile.

Chapter 4

He'd only meant to see Miss Hastings comfortably seated, but Ben found himself taking the chair across from her as soon as she'd got comfortable on the settee.

It had been impossible not to be aware of her all evening as the crowd of men—ranging from young men just home from university to wealthy friends of their hosts, men of a certain age on the lookout for a pretty paramour—ebbed and flowed as she flirted and dismissed them. He'd discussed Mrs. Brown's rheumatism while Sophia accepted punch from a young man with high shirt points. He'd assured Mr. Stevens, the local butcher, that he'd greatly enjoyed the side of beef the man had gifted him while she laughed at some quip from the Northmans' steward. Then, when finally the last man had gone, he'd made his way to her side for the first time that evening.

Only to find her mouth tight with pain as she tried to stand on the ankle that had made it impossible for her to dance.

He could have told her it would be a bad idea to attend a ball on the injury she'd sustained that morning, but he was now more sure than ever that Miss Sophia Hastings made up her own mind about things.

Now, he was forced to admit the fact again, since she'd just effectively backed him into a corner over allowing her to help him look into the contretemps they'd overheard that morning.

"I suppose you've left me with no choice but to work with you," he admitted with a rueful shake of his head. "You drive a hard bargain, Miss Hastings."

"I learned from my Aunt, my lord," she said with a grin. "Aunt Dahlia is quite good at getting what she wants from a negotiation. And so am I."

Clearly.

Just then, the clock at the end of the gallery began to chime.

Had they really been here alone for so long? Ben should have felt panicked at the notion, but instead he felt only a protective urge for Miss Hastings' reputation. "I'll just go find your sister, now, shall I? You've stayed long enough to make an exit without comment."

He watched as she stared down at her slippered foot for a moment. When she looked up at him, it was with a slight frown of frustration. "Yes, all right. I disliked making the others leave before they were ready, but it's been a few hours now."

It was on the tip of his tongue to remind her that her sister, with whom he'd danced earlier, had been ready to leave hours ago, but he stopped himself. Instead, he stood, and glanced down at her. "Is there something I can do for you before I go look for one of your party?"

But as he'd expected, she shook her head. "Go. The sooner we can call for the carriage, the sooner we can leave." For a moment he saw just how much of an effort it had been to keep up the pretense that she was not in pain.

He laid a hand on her shoulder. Nothing more than a show of support. Then headed in the direction from which they'd come.

And almost collided with Miss Gemma Hastings as he reached the door leading into the ballroom.

"Lord Benedick," said the brunette, who while she shared some resemblance to her sister, wasn't nearly as breathtaking as Sophia. At least, not in Ben's opinion. "Have you see Sophia? The last I saw her she was surrounded by her usual coterie, but she disappeared while I was dancing and though she insisted that her ankle was merely strained, I know it must be hurting like mad."

Though Sophia hadn't asked him to, once he'd sent Gemma to where she could find her sister, Ben went in search of either the Marquess of Kerr or the Duke of Maitland. He found Kerr and his wife, unfashionably conversing with one another, at the edge of the dance floor.

"I knew she was fibbing," said Ivy, Marchioness of Kerr with a shake of her head. "Of course we'll see she gets home safely. Thank you so much for looking after her, Lord Benedick. I doubt any of those cloth heads who pester her every time she sets foot out of the house would have done so."

Since his assessment of those men was similar, Ben didn't argue. Instead he said, "Why don't I see that she gets to the driveway safely, while you see that the carriage is readied. If you're not quite ready to leave yet, I can see her home. I know her sister is with her so it would be perfectly proper."

But the marchioness, who was looking rather pale, demurred. And Kerr agreed. "I was ready to get Ivy home an hour ago, so this simply gives us a good excuse. But I do appreciate you getting Sophia to the carriage. Maitland and Daphne came in their own rig so there's no need to worry about them."

Relieved that plans for getting Sophia away from there were in hand, Ben turned to go back to the gallery when he was waylaid by his host.

"Lord Benedick," said the nascent politician. "I hope you'll give your father, the duke, my best."

Since to Ben's knowledge, his father, the Duke of Pemberton, had never met Morgan, it was an odd request, but

hardly the first of its kind. People were always trying to ingratiate themselves with his father. And Ben was just a means to
an end.

"I will, Mr. Morgan," he assured the man. "And I thank
you very much for this evening's entertainment. I've been told
balls are rare in this neighborhood, and from what I've seen
of the dancing tonight, everyone is very much enjoying it."

Morgan preened. "I invited a number of people from
town as well, you know. Thought I'd bring a bit of town polish to the rustics, don't ye know?"

Since the neighborhood boasted any number of members
of the *ton,* Ben thought that was rather stretching it a bit, but
he didn't correct the man.

"Well, I thank you, but now I'm afraid I must be on my
way. I've a sermon to write and . . ."

When the industrialist stayed him with a hand, Ben fought
the urge to remove it. "I hope you'll tell me something, my
lord," Morgan said in a low, confiding voice. "What do you
make of the ladies up at Beauchamp House?"

At the mention of Beauchamp House, Ben stilled.

"What of them?" he asked silkily. He might not live in
the pockets of the Beauchamp House ladies, but he'd performed the marriage of the Duke and Duchess of Maitland
and he counted them as friends. And there was the matter
of Sophia, whom he found far more attractive than was pru-
dent. Something about Morgan's tone told him that the man
had nothing positive to say about them.

"Well, I mean to say," said Morgan with a shrug. "It's not
right, is it? Ladies wasting their time with pursuits that are
better suited to men? I'm not one for book learning at the
best of times, but I see it's something that must be done. But
it don't seem natural for ladies to do such things. My Millie certainly would never think to read poems in English,

much less in that heathen Greek. And I've heard from some friends in London that the painter, Miss Hastings, I think, well, she paints things that aren't fit things for ladies to be dwelling on."

It wasn't the first time Ben had heard such sentiments about the inhabitants of Beauchamp House. Indeed, he most often heard the complaints from other ladies in the neighborhood who didn't know what to make of the unconventional lady scholars, who were also better than average—and Sophia's case, much more than average—looking. But he wasn't in the mood for such piffle and he was within an inch of telling his host so, when Morgan continued his speech.

"I understand that Miss Hastings will have a couple of her works in the art exhibition next week," the man said his eyes narrow with judgment. "I was hoping you'd lend your voice to mine as well as a few other concerned citizens who'd like to make sure that whatever she brings is fit to be seen by our wives and daughters."

It was something that was better discussed in private, not in the middle of a crowded ballroom where anyone might overhear them. And Ben was already late getting Sophia down to meet the waiting carriage. But as there was no way on earth he'd ever agree with this man's narrow minded attempt to censor Sophia's work—work he'd seen and admired in the months since making her acquaintance—he simply said what he was thinking. "No, Mr. Morgan. I will not lend my voice to this effort. I believe Miss Hastings is a talented artist—one of the best I've ever seen—and I look forward to seeing her work in the exhibition."

With a short bow, he continued, "Now, if you'll excuse me, I must be off. Thank you again for a pleasant evening."

He felt the other man's gaze on his back, but he didn't much care at the moment. His desire to get Sophia out of this house had only increased with Morgan's words. Not glancing behind him, he made his way back to the gallery.

To Sophia's mortification, her slow progress from the gallery to the ground floor made it necessary for Benedick to lift her up into his arms and carry her most of the way down to the carriage. So, for the second time in twelve hours, she found herself being bodily carried by the vicar.

It was the stuff that village gossips dreamed of.

And it would make her an object of scorn for every unmarried young lady in the county.

"It's only a bit farther," she protested, when Benedick stopped and made the suggestion. She wasn't sure why, but she knew that while allowing him to carry her would indeed spare her ankle, it would prove uncomfortable in a more personal way. "You see," she said, biting back a gasp of pain as she limped along past her sister and the vicar down the stairs, "I can do it."

"And you'll damage your ankle," Gemma chided, "perhaps irreparably. What if it's broken, Sophia? Do you wish to become an invalid?"

Since the offending joint had swollen more in the time since they'd arrived that evening, Sophia feared her sister might be correct.

"Come, Miss Hastings," Benedick said with a kind smile. "I won't bite. And you must admit that at the rate we're traveling now it will be next week before we get downstairs."

"Oh I do wish you would dispense with Miss Hastings and call me Sophia," she said crossly. "It seems nonsensical given the frequency with which you're compelled to carry me about like a sack of potatoes."

She felt as well as heard his laughter. "I suppose that's acceptable," he said, "Sophia." He said her name a few seconds after, as if savoring the taste of it on his tongue. "And you must call me Ben."

"Very well, Ben," she said, with a brisk nod, almost hurrying over the syllable, as if to prove to him that she wasn't feeling a little thrill at the small bit of impropriety.

Then, before she could continue, the vicar had lifted her into his arms with an ease that was surprising to her despite the evidence of his strength when he'd carried her from the shore. He was much stronger than his lean build had led her to believe. Especially when one considered that she was not the sort of fashionable waif favored in the fashion plates these days. Despite her pain, she couldn't help but feel the hard muscles of his arms and chest where she cradled against him. And her relief at having her weight off the ankle almost had her sagging against him. Still she managed to keep some modicum of decorum.

They were almost to the second landing when they were met by their hostess, who gasped when she saw them. "My dear Miss Hastings, whatever has happened?"

"Only a sprained ankle, Mrs. Morgan," Sophia assured her, wishing the woman away. Though he'd not shown any signs of flagging, she didn't wish to test Lord Benedick's—Ben's, she mentally corrected herself—strength farther than necessary.

"Oh dear, I am sorry to see you in such pain, Miss Hastings," said Mrs. Morgan, a lovely, if not terribly intelligent woman, whose sweet nature seemed at odds with her brash husband. "I've suffered from sprains myself and they do get worse before they get better."

Then her face turning serious, she asked, "Have you passed my husband on your way down? I thought he was having a little chat with Mr. Penn in the library, but no one seems to have seen them."

Mr. Barnaby Penn was a local art dealer whose shop

was the sponsor of the upcoming Little Seaford Exhibition. Could it have been Penn she and Ben had overheard in the gallery? It was impossible to get a good look at the vicar's face in her current position, but she felt him stiffen at their hostess's words.

"I'm afraid we haven't seen him, Mrs. Morgan." Sophia could feel his deep voice reverberate through his chest. "Now, I'm afraid I must get Miss Hastings to her carriage."

At the reminder of his burden, the matron flushed. "Of course, of course. I hope you'll feel better soon, Miss Hastings."

There was no opportunity for conversation about what their hostess had revealed since Gemma was with them, and it was minutes later when he was lifting her into the spacious Kerr carriage that Ben told Sophia in a low voice, "I'll call on you tomorrow and we'll talk."

She felt the tickle of his breath against her ear, and breathed in the clean hint of bayberry and warm male as he pulled away and gave her a nod. "I hope you'll be feeling more the thing tomorrow, Miss Hastings," he said in a more normal tone that might be overhead by the others. "Do take care of yourself."

Alone in the carriage, she listened as he exchanged a few pleasantries with the marquess and Ivy. While they were still speaking, Gemma was handed in by a footman. Settling into the seat across from Sophia's she said wryly, "I'll wager that was more adventure than you were expecting from this evening."

Now that she was out of view of Ben and the rest of the ball-goers, Sophia felt a mantle of exhaustion fall over her. "You have no idea," she told her sister, leaning her head back against the plush squabs of the carriage. "It was foolish of me to go to the ball. I'll admit it now. But only to you."

"Stubborn to the end, I see," her sister said with a snort. "But don't try to change the subject. You know very well I was talking about your rescue at the hand of the most hand-some vicar in three counties."

"Since I know very well you've not met all the vicars in three counties, I will have to respectfully disagree." Sophia raised a brow but didn't raise her head. "I will admit he's good looking though. But there's no need to weave some romantic tale about it. He was simply being a gentleman."

"A gentleman who saw to your every comfort and looked as if he wished to ride home with us to see you safely tucked up in bed." She knew without looking her sister was wearing her I-know-I'm-right expression.

At that moment, Lord Kerr handed Ivy into the compart-ment, and Sophia was saved from replying to her sister's ab-surdity. It took a minute for them to get situated, what with Sophia's foot propped on the cushion where Ivy would have gone. They ended up riding the short distance with the mar-chioness seated rather improperly on the marquess's lap.

Sophia might have hoped this would mean they'd not wish to converse, but in that she was sorely mistaken.

"I believe you've got a champion in our vicar, Sophia," said Ivy with a grin once Kerr had given the coachman the signal and the carriage began to move. "He seemed quite at-tentive, did he not, Kerr?"

"Far be it from me to cast any man's behavior in a certain light," the marquess said with a hint of amusement in his voice. "But I do agree that Lord Benedick seemed to be more concerned for our Sophie's injury that he might have done with, say old Mrs. Mason."

"You're all, as Maitland would say," Sophia said from where she'd settled into her corner of the coach, "dicked in the nob."

"We'll see," Gemma said sweetly.

Not wanting to hear more, Sophia closed her eyes and feigned sleep the rest of the way home.

Chapter 5

Ben only had a couple of servants at the vicarage, which was a tidy red brick house with a pretty walled garden at the back and, as he'd learned not long after his arrival, a secret passageway leading from the cellars into a series of smugglers tunnels that opened out onto the beach just below Beauchamp House. His predecessor had been severely injured thanks to a miscreant's misuse of the passageway, and Ben had been happy enough to see that door sealed to prevent mischief.

Since he didn't keep a carriage of his own, he'd accepted a ride home from the Morgans in the coach of the local magistrate, Squire Northman, and his wife. It had been a brief drive, but he was grateful to step down and bid them goodbye thanks to Mrs. Northman's incessant chatter. He was also fairly suspicious that she'd felt his thigh for one moment when the conveyance hit a rock, but perhaps he was simply imagining it. It had been a strange evening. And there was no denying his senses were on high alert thanks to the moments spent cradling the luscious Miss Hastings against him.

The lantern at the door to the vicarage was flickering merrily when he shut the gate behind him. Though he'd instructed his manservant Jeffries not to wait up, that fellow was still conscious of the harm done to his previous master on his watch, and kept his own conscience on such matters that related to caring for the new vicar. And sure enough, the door opened wide when he stepped up to it.

"My lord," Jeffries said bowing. "I hope you had a pleasant evening."

Ben peeled off his gloves and handed the man his coat and hat. "It was well attended, and though I suspect Morgan wished for a crush it was hardly that."

"My lord, I must inform you that while you were gone you received a visitor."

Ben stopped just as he reached the stairs leading to his rooms. "Who—"

Before Jeffries could respond, an all too familiar voice spoke up. "I hope you'll excuse the late hour, Ben, but it couldn't be helped."

Arrested, he turned to see his younger brother, Lord Frederick Lisle, lounging against the door jamb of the front parlor.

With a cry of surprise, Ben pulled the other man into a hug, which quickly devolved into their childhood habit of wrestling for the upper hand.

"Hah," the vicar taunted when he'd managed to get his elbow around Freddie's neck, "I still have it!" He knocked his knuckles on his brother's head before turning him loose.

When he'd been set free, his younger brother shook his head, straightening his cuffs and cravat. "One would have thought that your years in the church would have taught you a sense of decorum."

"Oh, I have plenty of decorum in the right company," Ben said with a grin. "But you're my little brother. I had to greet you properly."

Dismissing Jeffries for the evening, he led Freddie upstairs to his study, and once they were settled in front of the fire with glasses of brandy, he waited for an explanation. While it wasn't unheard of for one of the Lisle brothers to visit another unexpectedly, Freddie had only recently celebrated the birth of his second child and it wasn't like him to leave his wife, Leonora, on her own at such a time.

They chatted a little about news from their parents, and their brother Archer, whose wife was expecting. "And I suppose you've heard that Cam is giving a paper at the royal society this week. One of his bits about bones or fossils or whatnot." Freddie, nor indeed any of the other Lisles, had never been able to understand where Cameron, the second to last of the brothers, had got his love of all things ancient. It wasn't as if the family were Philistines. They appreciated history and knowledge, but Cameron needed to touch everything he learned about. And spent his days digging into the earth in search of artifacts from the past.

"I'm glad for him," Ben said, taking a sip of his drink, "but better him than me."

"Amen to that," Freddie agreed. "I'm quite sure I'd nod off before the first presenter finished a paragraph."

"What of Rhys?"

Their eldest brother, Rhys, Viscount Lisle, heir to their father, the Duke of Pemberton, had, the last time Ben had spoken to him, been considering an extended stay on the continent. Since their father was in his prime, and needed little assistance in the running of the various Pemberton estates, he was a bit restless with life in the country. And London was far too full of matchmaking mamas for his comfort.

"On an extended stay at the hunting box in Scotland," Freddie said with a frown. "I had given him any number of contacts in Paris when he was making plans, but at the last minute he changed his mind. If you ask me, there's some trouble with a woman, though you know how tight-lipped he is about such things."

Rhys had never been one to discuss his affairs with his younger brothers. Perhaps since their father had instilled his position as the eldest, and therefore the role model, from the time he was small. Ben remembered quite well how in awe of his brother he'd been when they were children. It was as if he could do no wrong. No high spirits. No misbehavior. He was the perfect child. And as they'd grown, he's continued to be the one who pleased most everyone. There were lapses, of course—he was human. But Ben had often thought it must be very difficult to show so little weakness all the time.

Freddie's theory that a woman might be involved was not without merit. The few times they'd seen their eldest brother act out, it had been over some affair of the heart. Or some other, less romantic organ.

"I'd say we'll find out soon enough," Ben said wryly, "but it's Rhys. He might blurt it out in his cups at Christmas, or we'll never know."

"True." Freddie raised his glass. "To the brothers Lisle. Wherever they may be."

They drank deep, and sat in companionable silence for a moment.

Then, no longer able to hold back his curiosity, Ben said, "Speaking of locales, I don't suppose you wish to tell me that brings you here with no advance warning so soon after little Libby's birth?"

At the mention of his new daughter, Freddie's face softened, and Ben was reminded once again of how much his brother had changed since his marriage to Leonora. Once the most eligible bachelor on two continents, Freddie had settled into life as a husband and father as if he'd been born to it. And in a way, if their father was anything to go by, he had been.

"You know I wouldn't have left them without good reason, Ben," he said, his expression turning serious. "It's important, and I thought worth a quick trip down here to speak to you in person."

Setting his glass aside, Ben leaned forward, his elbows on his knees. A listening posture.

"You remember Mainwaring does a bit of work for the Home Office from time to time?"

"I do," Ben replied. The Earl of Mainwaring was one of Freddie's oldest school friends and was well known to all the Lisles.

"Well, his man in the Home Office has some concerns about some dealings in this area, and Mainwaring immediately thought of you when he heard of the locale."

It wasn't exactly routine for a minister with the Church of England to become involved with the affairs of the Home Office, but nor was it entirely out of the ordinary, Ben knew. He'd never been asked to do so before, however, and was a little surprised that the earl had thought of him so readily. It wasn't as if they were as close as he and Freddie.

As if hearing his questions, Freddie explained, "I'd just given him a rundown of family news and mentioned that you'd accepted a position in Little Seaford. So, it must have been in his mind when the fellow from the government spoke to him."

There was something else, however, that made the hairs on the back of Ben's neck stand on end. That conversation he and Sophia had overheard was still fresh on *his* mind. And it was far too coincidental to imagine that there was more than one conspiracy at work in their little village.

With a quick nod, he indicated that his brother should continue.

"According to Mainwaring, your tiny Sussex village has over the past year or so been flooding the homes of the newly rich and shall we say, artistically unfamiliar, with forgeries of valuable and coveted paintings."

Immediately, Ben thought of Sophia, though it pained him to do so.

How long had it been since her arrival at Beauchamp House?

Almost nine months exactly.

"What makes them think that the culprit is in Little Seaford?" he asked, careful not to reveal what he was thinking.

"They've traced the origins of the forgeries to one of the two galleries in the village," Freddie said, his mouth twisted in amusement. "Who would have thought a tiny village like this would have more than one gallery? I'd say it barely has enough inhabitants to sustain one."

"There's an artist's colony at Primrose Green," Ben said distractedly as he tried to recall if Sophia had ever sold her paintings through the local galleries. He wasn't as familiar as he might have been with her work because most of his time since arriving in the village had been spent getting to know his parishioners and ministering to the poorer families of the area. He'd attended a few social gatherings at Beauchamp House and the other gentry residencies, but he was hardly so well acquainted with Sophia that he knew the details of her business transactions.

To his frustration, Freddie noticed his shift in attention. "You've thought of someone," he said with a sharp gaze.

Ben cursed himself for a fool and despite his instinct to protect Sophia, he decided to trust his brother.

"There is a local artist." He leaned forward with his elbows on his knees, looking down so that Freddie couldn't read his expression. "She's been here for about the same amount of time as you've indicated. But I have no notion of whether she sells her work through either of the local galleries. I don't know enough about her art to assess whether or not she'd be able to create the sort of copies you're talking about."

He looked up and saw that Freddie's expression had turned sympathetic. "That's the way of things, is it?"

Unable to remain still, Ben stood abruptly and began to pace. "Don't make assumptions," he said, rubbing the back of his neck. "I barely know the lady. But I have found her to be a pleasant enough companion and I suspect she is quite talented since she's one of the four Beauchamp House heiresses."

This had Freddie cocking his head. "Is she indeed? Of course we'd heard about Lady Celeste's unusual bequest, since Leonora runs in intellectual circles—the sort that welcome ladies, I mean. But I don't think I knew there was an artist amongst them."

"A classicist, a mathematician, an artist and a naturalist," Ben said. "But surely she would have no reason to do paint forgeries now that she's safely in Beauchamp House." He didn't add that he wasn't convinced that she had the sort of questionable morals necessary to pass her own work off as someone else's.

"Isn't there some sort of contest amongst them?" Freddie asked. "Whoever remains longest gets to keep the house?"

"Yes," Ben said, waving his hand in dismissal. "But I think they've agreed at this point to simply share the house amongst themselves. Two of the ladies have married peers, and have no need of the house as a domicile, and the other two, Miss Hastings the artist, and her sister Miss Gemma, the naturalist, would be content to share, I think. As far as I can tell, she has no need for funds."

"It is difficult to know what goes on beneath the surface

with some people, Ben," Freddie said gently. "For all you know the lady has gambling debts or dressmakers bills or some other sort of financial troubles."

But Ben couldn't see it. Then, something occurred to him. In context of what Freddie had said about the forgeries, he ran back through the conversation he and Sophia had overheard at Morgan's.

"Would people who trade in forged art be the sort to eliminate a conspirator who no longer pulled his weight in the scheme?"

Freddie's gaze sharpened. "Absolutely."

Quickly, Ben related the details of what he and Sophia had overheard.

When he was finished his brother gave a low whistle—something their mother would have skinned him for if she'd been there to hear it. "I'd say you stumbled onto the very men Mainwaring is looking for," he said with a slight shake of his head. "What are the odds?"

But Ben was lost in his relief that Sophia was no longer a suspect. His gut had told him she couldn't possibly be the person Mainwaring hunted, but it was calming to know that was true.

"And you have no idea who these two were you overheard?" Freddie asked. "There was no hint of an accent? Or perhaps a phrase someone you know uses?"

"No, neither Sophia nor I could decipher who they were. Their voices were simply too low."

"Sophia, is it?"

Dash it. Ben knew better than to speak to Freddie when he was fatigued. His brother was a master at reading his weaknesses.

"Miss Hastings," he corrected himself. "I misspoke."

"Did you, indeed?" Freddie didn't seem convinced. "So,

it was the Beauchamp House artist you were secreted with when you overheard our schemers? That is fascinating. Tell me more about this lady, whom you know so little about."

"Freddie?"

"Yes, Ben."

"Shut up."

Chapter 6

Sophia spent a restless night, both because of her ankle and plagued by memories of the conversation she and Ben had overheard. Though ice from the icehouse helped with the swelling, the next morning it was still paining her enough that she welcomed Serena's suggestion of sending for the doctor again.

"At the very least he can feel if anything is broken," Serena said, her blue eyes dark with sympathy. "And perhaps give you something for the pain."

Having managed only to move from her bedchamber into the adjoining sitting room, Sophia sighed. "You know I detest being ill," she said, "but it is time to call Dr. Holmes. I thought perhaps when he was unavailable yesterday that I should be well enough, but it's time for him to look at it."

"Good girl," Serena said with a nod of approval. "I'll go send for him at once."

The chaperone left her alone, and Sophia slumped back against the settee.

If she didn't have such a fear of becoming like her mother, who took to her bed at the slightest hint of illness, she'd have agreed more readily to calling in the doctor. But though she loved both her parents, she had no wish to emulate either of them. Her father, the younger son of a Yorkshire baronet, made a prosperous living for himself as a solicitor in York, and had married as much for social standing as for affection. The former Miss Laetitia Gorham, now Mrs. Hastings, was a beautiful but rather spoiled beauty, whose wealthy parents had indulged her every whim. And her husband had continued doing so, allowing her to take to her bed with smelling salts at the least provocation. That Sophia and Gemma had gained any sort of standing in their chosen fields of study was entirely due, Sophia was convinced, to their Aunt Dahlia, the eccentric younger sister of Mr. Hastings, who lived with them.

It was from Dahlia that Sophia first learned to hold a paintbrush, and Dahlia who taught both Sophia and her sister that though they'd been born female, they were entitled to use the intellect they'd been gifted with to better themselves and the world. If it hadn't been for their aunt, Sophia strongly suspected she and Gemma might have developed into the same sort of empty-headed young ladies she'd seen on the ballroom floor last evening.

Theirs had been an unconventional upbringing, to be sure, but it had led them to be chosen by Lady Celeste Beauchamp to be her heiresses, and for that she had to be grateful.

She did wish, at this moment, however, that she'd been a bit less enthusiastic with her painting yesterday. Though, she reflected crossly, if it hadn't been for the mysterious men on the bluff she'd not have gone flying over the edge.

Sophia wasn't left long to brood, however.

Only moments after Serena's departure, Ivy, Daphne and Gemma crowed into her cozy sitting room, followed by a maid carrying a tea tray.

"We thought you might need a bit of cheering up," Ivy said from where she'd settled onto an overstuffed chair beside the tea table. "And tea always makes things better."

"But you said we were going to quiz her about her *tête-à-*

tête with Lord Benedick." Daphne's nose crinkled in confusion as she perched on the arm of the sofa where Gemma sat. "I do so hate it when I'm disappointed like that. Maitland has some very interesting theories about how they passed the time and I wished to prove him wrong."

Gemma and Ivy groaned at their friend's words, but Sophia simply sighed and rubbed the spot between her eyebrows, which was suddenly feeling tight.

"Daphne," Gemma chided, her wide mouth quirked with frustration, "that was the part we weren't going to talk to Sophia about, remember?"

"No, no," Sophia said with a "pray-continue" gesture, "by all means, make your inquiries. Though I'm afraid the details of my time with the vicar last night will be sorely disappointing to you."

"Well, you cannot blame us for being curious," Ivy said, handing her a cup of steaming tea. "Lord Benedick is deliciously handsome and his manner last night when he tucked you into the carriage was quite solicitous."

A memory of that moment when he'd been close enough to kiss flashed into Sophia's mind, but she ignored it. "He is a kind man, who took it upon himself to help me. It's hardly surprising given his vocation. I daresay he'd have done the same if it had been Gemma or Serena who needed his assistance."

"I've never seen him look at Serena the way he looked at you," her sister said dryly. "Though if you wish to pass it off as mere Christian kindness, then I suppose that's your right."

But Daphne looked disappointed. "Do you mean to tell me that nothing happened when you and the vicar were alone in the gallery?"

Thinking back to the conversation she and Ben had overheard, Sophia thought that Daphne's assessment wasn't entirely incorrect, but kept her own counsel on the latter.

Instead she said, "Nothing like what you lot were hoping for. I must say I thought marriage would have both of you focused on your own affairs, but it would seem that it's turned you into hopeless romantics. Not every conversation is a prelude to a kiss, you know."

"They cannot help themselves," her sister said reaching for an almond tea cake. "It's like an illness they can't help but wish on everyone else."

Setting the silver teapot back down on the tray, Ivy then dropped a lump of sugar in her own tea and stirred it. "Just you wait, Gemma," she said with a knowing smile. "It will happen to you and when it does I will be the first to congratulate you."

"Then I hope you will live to see that day," Gemma replied. It would take more than teasing to convince her sister that love was something she should consider, Sophia knew. Another personality trait that could be laid at their parents' door. "Though I cannot think it will happen in either your lifetime or mine."

"Never say never, my dear Gemma," was Ivy's only response as she sipped her tea. "There was a time when I thought no man could possibly be secure enough in himself to want a wife who could match him in wits and sense. But then I met Quill."

To Sophia's surprise, it was Daphne who played the peacemaker. "We only want you both to be happy, Gemma," she said with a sweet smile. It was times like this that made friendship with the unconventional mathematician worthwhile. "I certainly never thought a man like Maitland of all people could bring me such joy. But here we are."

Seeing the mulish set to her sister's jaw, Sophia intervened before she could say something cutting. "And do not think we don't appreciate it." She gave her sister a speaking look and Gemma had the good grace to look sheepish. "Of course we do. Especially since we've seen your transformations for ourselves. But you must know we have to make our own ways. And sadly, there are no more of Lady Celeste's nephews coming to stay, so it might take a while."

Ivy colored a little. "I'm sorry, ladies. I just want your happiness, as Daphne says."

The marchioness could be a bit autocratic at times—not because of her title, but because she was used to knowing exactly what she wanted—but she meant well, and Sophia loved her, bossiness and all. Sophia's ankle gave a throb of pain then, and she winced, adjusting the cloth covered ice on it.

"Oh, dear," Ivy said, noticing Sophia's discomfort and setting down her cup and saucer. "We shouldn't have descended on you like this. You're obviously in pain."

A brisk knock at the door sounded before Sophia could respond.

"Only look who's come to look in on you, Sophia," said Lady Serena brightly, as she preceded Ben into the room.

The vicar looked a bit nonplussed to see all four of the Beauchamp Bluestockings assembled, but soon regained his aplomb.

He was dressed for the country, in a pair of fawn breeches that showed his muscular legs to perfection, and a cutaway coat that did nothing to hide the broadness of his shoulders. But it was the way his gaze zeroed in on her once he stepped into the room that made Sophia's breath catch.

"Good morning, ladies," he said, bowing. "I had hoped to see you up and walking, Miss Hastings, but I'm sorry to see that is not the case."

To Sophia's surprise, he proffered a small posy of pink roses and nasturtium to her. "I had my housekeeper choose these. I'm afraid I'm hopeless at such niceties. In town one only needs the services of good florist, you see."

Their hands brushed as she took the bouquet, and to

cover her blush, she buried her nose in the blooms. "They're lovely, my lord. Thank you so much."

Ivy and Gemma exchanged a look, and soon they rose and none too gently pulled Daphne along to join them. "I've just recalled that we were planning to organize the library section on animal husbandry this morning," Ivy explained as she and Gemma dragged a protesting Daphne from the room.

"I'll send up the doctor when he arrives, Sophia," said Serena before she too decamped.

Left alone, with a half empty tea tray between them, Sophia and Ben stared at one another in disbelief.

Then burst out laughing.

"Oh, I am sorry," Miss Hastings, said as she wiped tears of mirth from her face. "I don't know what has got into them. It's as if they've never interacted with human beings before."

He was glad to see she'd kept her humor intact despite her injury and last night's disturbance. On his walk over to Beauchamp House, Ben had debated whether to share what he'd learned from Freddie last night with her. There was no need to drag her into the matter, especially if, as the conversation they'd overheard had indicated, the men involved were ruthless.

Now, settled across from her in a tastefully appointed sitting room, he welcomed the moment of levity. Faced with the sight of her draped ankle, propped on a tasseled pillow, and the obvious shadows beneath her blue eyes, he was reluctant to add to her worries. Though he knew he must do so before the visit was over.

"There's no harm done," he said, leaning back a little in a surprisingly comfortable armchair. "And they are clearly fond of you."

The easy manner between the ladies of Beauchamp House had been something that struck him when he first met them. It was not unlike the sort of bonds formed at school. And with the various upsets and disturbances they'd faced together over the past year—including attempts on two of the ladies' lives—those ties were more than skin deep. These friends genuinely cared about each other.

"Yes," she said with a rueful shake of her head. "I just wish they didn't all turn into Mrs. Bennet from *Pride and Prejudice* when a gentleman calls."

At the mention of Miss Austen's novel, he grinned. "So long as they don't cast me in the role of Mr. Collins. I am a vicar, but I hope that is where the resemblance ends."

This surprised a laugh from her. "I hardly think Mr. Collins would be the recipient of longing gazes from nearly every female in three counties," she said tartly.

"Do not go on about that again," he chided, referring to their discussion the night before. "I'm of no more interest to the ladies of the village than the next man."

"If you say so," Miss Hastings replied, not convinced. "Though I suspect there is a surfeit of baked goods in the vicarage kitchens that would contradict you.

"Well, I do say so, Wallflower," Ben returned. "There is nothing unusual about the ladies of a village trying to feed their bachelor vicar. It's a time-honored tradition."

Her response to the endearment—warmth in her cheeks and a nervous nibble of her lower lip—sent a jolt of awareness through him. He might not be moved by the blandishments of the other women in the village, but putting this particular lady to the blush was dangerous to his own peace of mind.

"The tea is still warm," she said with false brightness. "Shall I pour you a cup?"

Taking the proffered distraction with gratitude, he agreed and watched as she drew the teapot toward her and began fussing with the silver.

"Have you learned anything more about the mysterious men we heard last night?" she asked, as she handed him a cup and saucer.

Something of his dilemma must have shown on his face, because Sophia gave a little gasp as she looked up. "You have. Who were they? Do you know who it is they mean to harm?"

If he revealed to her what Freddie had told him, it might just endanger her further. But the intelligent gleam in her eyes told him that keeping the information to himself would likely do nothing to dissuade her from searching for more news on her own. Which might be even more dangerous.

"I received a visit from my brother Freddie, that is, Lord Frederick Lisle, last evening after the ball," he began. Keeping his explanation as vague as possible, with no mention of the Home Office, or the possibility of a network of criminals involved in the business, told her that it was suspected a forger was working in this part of the country. "He thought he'd better warn me since the miscreant might be one of my parishioners."

"That seems an odd bit of information for a gentleman about town to acquire," Sophia said, a line appearing between her tawny brows.

"He has friends in the government," Ben said with a slight shrug. Nothing he said was false. He simply didn't go into the complex details or dangerous implications of the matter with her. She was injured, after all, and as a lady could hardly set out to capture the ruffians on her own. He would tell her the whole truth if the need arose. Now was not the best time, however. To Ben's relief, she seemed to accept his explanation at face value. "I suppose Little Seaford is as good a place as any for an art forger to work," Sophia said thoughtfully. "It takes only painting supplies and a store of sufficiently aged canvas."

"And there's no shortage of artists here," Ben added wryly.

"The proximity of the artist's colony at Primrose Green certainly makes it a safe place to hide in plain sight."

Sophia looked thoughtful. "The man yesterday said that they wished to wait until their man had shown his work in the exhibition before ridding themselves of him. Perhaps I can ask the Primbles for a list of everyone who has submitted work for it."

Mr. and Mrs. August Primble were the owners of Primrose Green, a local manor house that had been in August Primble's family for generations. When he inherited and married, he and his wife made the unconventional decision to open the house and grounds to artists in need of lodging and support. Thus was born the artist's colony at Primrose Green. The setting so close to the sea gave the inhabitants ample fodder for their work, and the Primbles got to pretend they were as talented as the artists who lived with them. They were not, but Ben had found them to be sensible people despite their eccentricities.

They were also the organizers of the annual Exhibition to which Mr. Morgan had referred. It was open to anyone in the county who wished to exhibit their work, but the largest number of works by far came from Primrose Green.

"There might be a hundred names on that list." Ben couldn't keep the frustration from his voice.

But Sophia didn't seem worried. "I'd say closer to thirty at most. There are only twenty or so places at Primrose Green and there aren't that many of us in the county at large."

"They were definitely discussing a man, which narrows it a bit too."

Though success in the world of art was often bestowed upon males, it was also the case that any young lady with a rudimentary knowledge of watercolors was encouraged to enter the exhibition. Which meant the list of men entered might be even shorter, he was relieved to realize.

"How on earth did your brother manage to arrive on the very night we heard them planning a murder?" Sophia asked, shifting a little in her seat. Her position, reclining along the length of the sofa, made it necessary for her to twist her torso to face him.

"We surmised it must have been coincidence," he said, moving to perch on the arm of the sofa so she needn't contort herself to face him. At her expression of surprise, he shrugged. "You're already in pain from one injury," he explained. "I don't wish to cause a crick in your neck as well."

"Thank you," she said, with a grateful smile. "Now, what is our next move?"

"Your next move is to rest your ankle and do as Dr. Holmes says," he said firmly. At her look of outrage he raised a staying hand. "My brother is here for the next few days and we will look into the matter. I promise to keep you informed of any developments. But if you are to be present for the exhibition, and to show your own work, then you need time to heal."

Sophia scowled. "I detest that you are right," she said crossly.

"It does happen sometimes." He stood, and moved to take her bare hand in his gloved one. "I'll bring Freddie to meet you tomorrow. You'll like him. He's the charming brother."

Not waiting to hear her reply, he left, closing the door to the sitting room firmly behind him.

Chapter 7

To Sophia's great relief, Dr. Holmes pronounced that her ankle was not broken, only sprained, and after wrapping it tightly with strips of cotton, he advised her to give it rest, and prescribed a mild sedative for when the pain prevented her from sleeping.

If she had been worried that she would spend the next few days in isolation, however, she was disabused of that notion by the steady stream of callers that began not long after the physician had bid her good day.

"I was unable to rest a moment longer until I inquired after your injury, Miss Hastings," said Mr. Toby Walsh, his intricately patterned waistcoat causing Sophia's eyes to cross slightly. With a flourish, he proffered an overlarge bouquet of crimson roses. Sophia accepted them with a smile of thanks, but couldn't help but glance at the smaller nosegay the vicar had brought her, which was now in a vase of water on the marble mantelpiece. There was no denying that the red roses were lovely, but they seemed overblown and loud in comparison to the pink and white flowers.

Handing the bouquet to her waiting maid, Sophia smiled with more warmth than she felt. "You are too kind, Mr. Walsh, but as you can see, I am no more injured now than I was last evening. I pray you will set your mind at ease."

A knock at the door heralded the arrival of another visitor.

"Ah, Walsh. I might have known you'd be here." Mr. Walter Ellis shot a narrow-eyed glare at his friend before stepping forward to bow to Sophia. "Miss Hastings, how relieved I am to see that you've suffered no ill effects from overtaxing your . . . ah . . . limb at the ball."

Instead of flowers, he proffered a small stack of books. Sophia was surprised to see that it was the three volume set of Frances Burney's *Evelina*.

"M'sister is quite fond of this one, and I recall how dull it was to be laid up when I broke my leg," the young man said sheepishly.

Touched by his thoughtfulness, Sophia gave him a genuine smile. She already had her own dog-eared copy of the novel, but his gesture made her rethink her earlier assessment of the young man's character. Perhaps Mr. Ellis wasn't quite as silly as his friend.

As if to add further proof to this realization, Mr. Walsh spoke up, clearly jealous of the attention his friend's gift had garnered him. "I daresay the library at Beauchamp House has plenty of novels in it, Ellis, old fellow. It was stocked by a lady, after all. Personally, I don't care for them. Far too much nonsense in them."

If he'd wanted to elevate himself, however, this was entirely the wrong thing to say. But before Sophia could give him a richly deserved set down, it was delivered by Gemma, who had been quietly watching their interactions from her chair near the window.

"I daresay you're one of those gentlemen who hides his novel reading from his friends under the supposition that it is unmanly," she said with a sad shake of her head. "But I've found that men of intellect and sense enjoy a bit of fictional escape every now and again. Perhaps you should ask Lord Kerr or the Duke of Maitland which authors they prefer. Unless, of course, you consider them unmanly in some way?"

Sophia hid a smile at the myriad of emotions flitting over young Mr. Walsh's face. He seemed unable to decide whether to take offense, or to thank her for her suggestion. Perhaps recognizing that they were outgunned, Mr. Ellis clapped his friend on the back. "Let us leave Miss Hastings to her rest, Walsh. I have a feeling we've outstayed our welcome."

Reluctantly, Mr. Walsh agreed and soon was accompanying the other man from the room, leaving Sophia alone with her sister.

"You were a bit hard on poor Walsh, weren't you?" Though Sophia knew her sister had never been one to suffer fools gladly, but nor was she one for delivering a strong rebuff to an unarmed opponent.

"Perhaps I was." Gemma smoothed the skirt of her deep green gown, as if needing something to do with her hands. "But I've had a surfeit of gentlemen pretending to some sort of divine gift of intellect that gives them the right to pass judgment on whatever we ladies choose to occupy our time with."

Blinking, Sophia tried to recall when she'd seen her sister so annoyed. It wasn't as if she was meek or mild. But in general Gemma was an even tempered and steady sort of lady, who wished to pursue her own studies in natural history and ignored most other distractions.

"Strong words," she said aloud. "Has someone in particular said something to push you over the edge?"

Suddenly restless, Gemma rose and moved to examine Sophia's bouquet on the mantle. "I have received a rejection today from the editor of the *Annals of Natural History*. For my article outlining the three fossils I've unearthed since we came to Beauchamp House. They are significant finds, I believe, and could do much toward explaining some of the history of this part of England. But he claimed that because I am a lady, and unaffiliated with any particular institution or legitimate scholar, my work cannot be verified or given the aegis of his publication."

Sophia was all too familiar with the bias against scholarship conducted by the so-called fairer sex within most of the scholarly world. But it did at times seem that the greatest misogyny lay with the sciences. "Who is this horrid fellow and what must he look like? I will sketch a caricature of him for you to use on your archery target." It was a process the sisters had practiced since girlhood—Sophia providing the exaggerated image of whomever had crossed them, and Gemma filling said image with arrow holes. Childish, perhaps, but infinitely satisfying.

Turning, Gemma faced her sister, her pretty countenance wreathed with irony. "I'm not quite sure what he looks like but he is no doubt thin as a rail with a giant wart on his nose."

Laughing despite her sister's upset, Sophia made a mental note to sketch the miscreant as a gift for her sister as soon as possible.

Still, it was clear that her sister's ire was not going to be diminished by a few calming words and a cathartic drawing.

"You might write this fellow a reply," she said reasonably. "Outlining all the reasons you think he is wrong, and perhaps suggesting that he learns to curb his prejudices when it comes to choosing articles for his publication."

"That's a brilliant idea," Gemma said, brightening.

"I'm not finished," said Sophia raising a hand. "Write the letter, seal it and write his direction on it. Then, burn it."

"Burn it? Why?"

"Because you don't wish to burn bridges. What if you need this fellow at some point in the future? Burn the irate letter then write another, more reasonable one. Post that one and see what his reply is."

Even the calmer letter would win Gemma no favors, Sophia knew, but one of the reasons Lady Celeste had chosen her sister to come live at Beauchamp House was her determination in the face of adversity from the scientific establishment: which meant male scholars. And Sophia herself had fought against similar unfairness from the Royal Academy, which was reluctant to show the paintings of ladies who didn't confine themselves to landscapes or portraits.

She was proud of her sister, and despite her concern over her possibly raising the ire of this editor, she knew that confronting him about his dismissal was necessary.

At least she hoped they would not.

"I know it's difficult to be turned down." Sophia watched as Gemma returned to her chair and began to drum her fingers on the arm. Placing a gentle hand over her sister's, stopping the motion, she continued, "You mustn't let such things get the better of you, my dear. You and I both know how intelligent and talented you are. The rejection of a single man and a single journal will not change that."

Gemma turned rueful eyes to her. "I know you are right," she sighed. "But I was so looking forward to seeing my findings in print. And I thought—perhaps foolishly—that this editor would turn out to be a fair-minded man . . ."

Gemma nodded and Sophia couldn't help but give her arm a comforting squeeze.

"Let's talk about something more pleasant," Gemma said with a determined effort at cheer. "Lord Benedick is certainly paying a lot of calls on you these days."

Sophia felt her ears redden. "That's hardly the case. He was merely checking in on me this morning. And the visit with Lord Frederick will be to introduce him to the household at large." That Lord Frederick's visit was also planned to give her more information about the possible art forger run amok in Little Seaford was something she couldn't reveal just yet.

But she was confident that despite her fascination with Ben's person, his increased attentions sprang not from affection on his part, but from a desire to get to the bottom of the conversation they'd overheard.

"Whatever you say," Gemma said, not looking convinced. "But, I think I know what a gentleman with an interest looks like at this point—having seen both Lord Kerr and the Duke losing their hearts to Ivy and Daphne."

"Don't be absurd," Sophia chided. "We are friends. And he simply wished to check in on me."

"Hmph. I'm not sure I believe you, but I will let you have your little self-deceit." Rising, she gave her sister a brief hug. "Shall I see if Gladys will bring up a luncheon tray for you?"

Sophia's stomach gave an emphatic growl. "I suppose that's a yes," she said with a raised brow.

After his visit to Beauchamp House, Ben stopped in at a local farmer's house to look in on that man's mother, who was ill.

Giving comfort to the sick and looking after his parishioners was an aspect of his work that he found especially fulfilling. He'd always been interested in people. And though one might think that growing up in a ducal household would have turned him into a different sort of man altogether, his father had instilled a sense of responsibility and stewardship in all his sons. It had been Ben who accompanied their mother on visits to the tenant farms when he was a boy. He'd watched and learned as she held the hands of the sick, asked after the health of families, and counseled when asked for advice.

Neither of his parents were typical for their rank, something he'd quickly learned once he went to school and began socializing with others of their class. And he was grateful for it. Their teaching had made it possible for him to perform his duties as a man of the church with ease. At least, the caring for his flock part. Church politics was something altogether different, and an aspect of his calling he avoided at all costs.

Having offered what comfort he could to both the sick old woman, who was unlikely to survive the pleurisy in her lungs, and her son and his wife, Ben was in a contemplative mood when he returned to the vicarage. It was difficult these days to see families suffering from the loss of their elders without putting his own parents in their place. Though both the Duke and Duchess of Pemberton were in excellent health, there was no denying they were getting older and the time would come in the not too distant future when he'd have to say goodbye to them.

But he was snapped out of his brown study by the troubled look on his manservant's face when he stepped inside. Taking off his hat and coat, he handed them to Jeffries, who took them as he spoke.

"My lord," the older man said, his bushy gray brows drawn together in concern, "You have a visitor. I put him in the front parlor, but I believe your brother happened upon him before I could introduce them."

Ben bit back a sigh. While a competent butler, and a dab hand with a cravat, Jeffries had a tendency to become overset at the oddest times. When important figures from the village paid calls, for example. He was well able to handle lords and ladies, but let the mayor call at the vicarage and Jeffries became skittish as a cat.

"I feel sure my brother will not embarrass the household, Jeffries," he said wryly as he pulled off his gloves. "Who's called?"

Recovering himself, the butler looked slightly abashed and said, "It's Mr. Peter Morgan, my lord. I told him you were away for the morning, but he insisted on waiting. He seemed quite agitated."

There was a slight censure in his tone, but Ben ignored it. Jeffries might be intimidated by the industrialist's bluster, but he wasn't.

His response to the butler was a noncommittal sound.

Curious to see what Freddie was up to, he followed the sound of conversation. And when he opened the door, it was to find his brother lounging with one booted foot on his knee in Ben's favorite chair near the fire. In contrast to Freddie's relaxed pose, Morgan was standing before the fireplace, his back ramrod straight, a scowl on his blunt features. Neither man's demeanor changed when Ben entered the room.

"Mr. Morgan," Ben said, shutting the door behind him and stepping forward to shake the man's hand. "I am sorry to have kept you waiting. I hope my brother and my staff have made you comfortable."

The set of Morgan's jaw said that the opposite was true, but someone had instilled basic good manners into him, and he gave a short nod. "Yes, your brother has been welcoming." And that, apparently was all the time he wished to spend on pleasantries. "I wish to speak to you about a very important matter, Lord Benedick and I need to do so in private."

Ben exchanged a look with his brother, who gave a slight shrug and rose. "I'll just take myself off to the library, then. It was quite interesting to speak with you, Morgan. Quite interesting."

And giving a slight bow to the man, he slipped out of the room, shutting the door behind him.

With Freddie's departure, Morgan seemed to relax very slightly. Ben made a mental note to quiz his brother about what must have been a very odd conversation. Freddie could talk the hind legs off a goat, but he had a feeling that Morgan wasn't the sort to fall into easy conversation with a man he'd

dismiss as a useless fribble based on his apparent lack of gravity. Of course, there was more to Freddie than met the eye, but
Morgan wouldn't know that. And likely wouldn't care.

"Can I call for some refreshment, Mr. Morgan?" Ben asked
once they were alone. "Tea, or perhaps something stronger? I
believe I've got a bottle of brandy in the sideboard."

But Morgan shook his head. "What you can do for me,
Reverend Lord Benedick, is to use your influence to ensure
that the upcoming art exhibition in our village is safe from
the polluting influence of a Miss Sophia Hastings' work."

Chapter 8

Ben rocked back on his heels at the other man's mention of Sophia.

"I'm not sure what you mean, sir," he said with a mildness he didn't feel.

"I have been assured by someone very close to her that Miss Sophia Hastings plans to place three highly improper paintings in the exhibition," Morgan said with a scowl. "One, in fact, depicting a common whore, and another showing a child on the brink of death. I do not know the subject matter of the third one, but I have no doubt it will be equally repellent."

The vicar could see that Morgan was not the sort to listen with any seriousness to an explanation of art and the role it played in pushing for social change. Or, for that matter, to discuss the fact that some of the most explicit and disturbing paintings he'd ever seen were religious in nature. This was a man who merely needed to hear a few words of describing the painting's content to determine its unwholesomeness.

That the artist in question was Sophia Hastings, whose very presence in a household of lady scholars was questioned by some in the village, was not lost on him either.

Still, as the minister to the whole of Little Seaford, he had to do what he could to see things from every point of view—even those that made him itch to abandon his clerical collar and challenge the holder of said opinion to a fist fight.

"I'm not sure what you wish me to do about the paintings to which you refer, Morgan."

"You must use your office as the spiritual leader of this village to keep that woman from exposing not only my wife but all the gentle ladies of the district to such filth. The innocence of our wives and daughters must be protected at all costs." Stifling his instinct to plant the other man a facer, Ben pretended puzzlement. "I'm not sure I see what the problem with Miss Hasting's work is. Is the fallen woman depicted in the nude?"

Morgan scowled. "Not that I've heard," he conceded, "but it needs only the implication that the woman in the painting makes her living on her back. I want no daughter of mine looking at such a person. Even on canvas."

"But surely you've read about Mary Magdalene in the gospel, Mr. Morgan. If our Savior can bring a woman who once plied that trade into his flock, then I don't see the harm of showing another such lost soul in art. Knowing Miss Hastings, I have little doubt that the painting will be quite tasteful, and will likely carry a moral message. She might be a bit unconventional, as are all the ladies at Beauchamp House, but she is hardly a purveyor of indecency."

"Jesus also consorted with lepers, my lord," said Morgan tightly, "but that doesn't mean I wish my family to do so. It is my job as their protector to keep such ugly facts of life out of their purview. And as a leader in the village of Little Seaford, I extend that protection to all the innocent ladies and children of the town.

"As for Miss Hastings, my lord," he continued, "I find it difficult to believe a woman who looks like she does is unfamiliar with the sort of scenes she shows in her art. Her father is barely a gentleman, I think. She would do well to preserve what reputation she has instead of flaunting the proprieties as she does. I cannot think either she or her sister will escape their time in that very unconventional household without ruining themselves."

Vowing silently to ask Kerr or Maitland for a bout of fisticuffs as soon as he extricated himself from this interview, Ben clenched his jaw against a string of profanity.

Still, he wasn't required by his vows to allow men like Morgan to speak ill of ladies, no matter how unconventional their circumstances might be.

"I should be more careful about what I said about the very dear friend of both the Duchess of Maitland and the Marchioness of Kerr, sir. You may have your opinions about the suitability of the Misses Hastings, but I can assure you that they are not without friends. And I believe any attempt on your part to slander them with such musings in public would be met with a very sharp rebuke from both the houses of Maitland and Kerr. Not to mention, that I myself count the Hastings sisters as friends, and have never seen a hint of the character flaws you suggest."

As he warmed to his subject, he felt his temper rise. Who was this uncouth lout to cast aspersions on Sophia's reputation solely because she'd been gifted by God with a beautiful face and a curvy figure? Was Morgan's own wife—whose looks, to be honest, paled in comparison—to be considered virtuous because she was plain? Good character wasn't determined by one's physical beauty or lack thereof.

"I also cannot see how you are able to determine the morality or immorality of Miss Sophia's paintings without having laid eyes upon them yourself." He could see that Morgan wished to respond but wouldn't let him get in a word. Not yet. "I understand you may not be all that familiar with art, sir. However—"

There Morgan cut him off. "I am actually quite familiar

with art, Lord Benedick," he said with a sniff. "I have the pleasure of acting as the patron of a very talented young man whose work is what art should be—uplifting, moral, beautiful and entirely appropriate in mixed company. Mr. Thomas Ryder is everything that Miss Sophia Hastings is not. And I intend to see to it that his work is given a place of prominence in the exhibition."

Ah, Ben thought. So Morgan was worried that Sophia's paintings would eclipse those of his protégé's. It was quite possible that the man was indeed as worried about protecting the fragile sensibilities of Little Seaford's ladies as well, but it was far more likely that he was trying to eliminate competition from Sophia. That he had suggested the Hastings sisters were no better than they should be in order to elevate his favorite was despicable, however.

"And who is this Thomas Ryder you've taken under your wing?" he asked aloud, unable to keep a hint of skepticism from his tone. "A local fellow?"

The exhibition was intended to be a showcase for the artwork of local painters and the grand prize—an exhibition in a very influential London Gallery, which had been secured by the head of the artist's colony at Primrose Green—had the potential to bring the winner to national prominence.

"He is a young man I have brought with me from Yorkshire," Morgan said grudgingly, as if he knew exactly what Ben was thinking about the exhibition's intent. "But as he resides with my family now, he is a local. And since Miss Hastings is only a latecomer to Beauchamp House, I cannot think that you would consider the matter of length of residence to be a problem."

He had a point, Ben acknowledged, with a nod of his head. Still, there was something havey-cavey about this business. Deciding he'd had enough of Morgan's bluster, Ben gave him a friendly but cool smile. "As you may have guessed,

I cannot support you in this matter. I would encourage you to wait until Miss Hastings' work is unveiled before casting aspersions on it, but I can see that advice would fall on deaf ears. I see nothing about the subject matter in general that would endanger the souls of my congregation, and in fact, I can only think that seeing how the less fortunate among us live would do a bit of good."

He offered his hand in a gesture of goodwill, but was not surprised when Morgan ignored it and stomped to the door. Wrenching it open, his large frame filling the doorway, he turned to glare at Ben. "You'll regret this, vicar," he said with a scowl. "I am an influential man in these parts. And I have friends in the church. When the Archbishop of Canterbury hears about this, you will find yourself in a much less convivial post."

Since the archbishop was his mother's first cousin, Ben had no worries on that score. Whatever influence Morgan thought he had, it was far less than that the Lisles wielded. He might dislike the politics of his position, but that didn't mean Ben was unwilling to use them when necessary.

Especially when it was in support of his innocent friends who were being targeted by a bully.

"I hope I'll see you Sunday, Mr. Morgan," he said to the man's retreating back, unable to stop himself.

When the front door closed behind him, Ben heard Freddie come downstairs and into the parlor.

"What. An. Ass." His brother said in his wry way.

Though Ben didn't disagree, he wasn't quite so comfortable dismissing the man altogether. He'd clearly got it into his head to ruin Sophia's reputation. And that was something Ben wasn't going to stand for. Not because he was attracted to her, he told himself, but because what Morgan was doing was both unfair and wrong.

"I very much wish that Peter Morgan was one of the

men you overheard at his ball," Freddie said emphatically. "It would be quite satisfying to see him in manacles being hauled off to jail."

Ben didn't disagree. It was perhaps unchristian of him to wish the other man ill, but he was human. And his sense of justice demanded that Morgan see some sort of ramifications for his unfairness toward Sophia.

"I just can't be sure," he said aloud. But silently, he agreed. It would be eminently enjoyable to see Morgan get his comeuppance. Not Christian, perhaps, but every man had his trials.

Even vicars.

By the afternoon, thanks to Dr. Holmes' tight wrapping of the joint, Sophia's ankle was feeling improved enough to make her chafe at the restrictions of her injury. The physician's manipulation of the joint had shown it to be only sprained, not broken, and he'd assured her that it would be much more the thing in a week or so. For the pain, he'd suggested laudanum, but Sophia disliked how it made her feel, so as an alternative he recommended willow bark tea. And with the assurance that he'd look in on her again in a few days, he left her to take a much needed nap.

When she woke several hours later, she felt better, and the swelling in her ankle had abated considerably.

She tried to keep herself occupied with a book, but soon the dullness of the sickroom got the better of her.

A short time later—having endured the indignity of being carried bodily up to the third floor by a footman—Sophia found herself settled comfortably on the settee in her attic studio.

Upon her arrival at Beauchamp House, after paying a visit to the magnificent library with its gilt trimmed shelves and intricately patterned recessed ceiling, her next priority had been to see the studio space Lady Celeste had spoken of in her letter. Taking up what might have originally been intended as a nursery, the open room ran the width of the house and its wall of windows overlooked the manicured gardens, the rolling green beyond, and finally the cliffs and sea beyond that.

Sophia had yet to enter the room without a sharp intake of breath at the sight. In the daytime, the view of the countryside leading to the sea could be bright with sun and blue skies, or more often, gray with roiling clouds and hints of rains to come. At night, especially when the moon was visible, the view was just as compelling.

But it was the natural light that streamed through those windows into the chamber that made it special. As any artist would surely agree, light was a chief consideration for anyone who put brush to canvas. And whoever had designed this room—no doubt Lady Celeste—had known that better than most.

Without the wall of windows, the shape of the chamber would have put Sophia in mind of a barn. Especially with the peaked roof. But the skylights in that roof, coupled with the plethora of windows, not to mention the smell of turpentine and oil, marked it as exactly what it was. A magnificently appointed artist's studio.

And it was all hers.

At least for the next six months.

She and the other heiresses hadn't discussed what would happen if all four of them managed to remain in Beauchamp House for the full year stipulated in Lady Celeste's will, and therefore inherited equal shares in the house. Ivy and Daphne had remained in spite of their marriages to titled men who had multiple houses of their own. But both Kerr and Maitland had been nephews of Lady Celeste, so therefore had sentimental attachment to the house itself. There was little chance at this point that Beauchamp House would become the sole property of any of them.

The studio, however, Sophia secretly thought of as her own.

With its multiple easels and ingeniously devised rolling walls that could be hung with works in progress and used to form smaller rooms within the large one, the studio was more perfect that she could have ever imagined for herself. And stocked as it was with canvas and supplies and everything she could possibly need, it was as close to heaven as she would get on this earth.

Now, however, thanks to her ankle, she was unable to put the room to its proper use. At least not for painting. She had instructed the footman to move one of the rolling walls— hung with her three paintings for the exhibition—to a spot where she could sit back and examine them as a critic might.

The first, which she'd titled "Fallen" was of a scene outside the entrance to a theatre. In the foreground, black carriages disgorged their wealthy occupants who paused in mid-laugh, mid-step, amid the chatter of the *haute ton* seeing and being seen, entirely at home in their world—its confines as real as the carriage interior they'd just stepped out of, if invisible. Lamps hung on either side of the wide doorway, paling in comparison to the almost blinding light of the entryway. And just to the right of the steps leading into the theatre, in a small recess between the stair rail and the iron gate of the next building, lay the crumpled figure of a woman. Her shiny gown, its bodice too low for propriety, was rucked up a little to show her calf. And thrown out to her side, her hand was open, relaxed. In the palm rested a shining gold guinea. Sophia had purposely left the woman's face in the shadows, because women like that are so often unseen by the type of people who are blithely walking past. It was perhaps a bit too literal a symbol, but she thought it worked. At least she hoped it did.

Her stomach clenched at the idea of unveiling it for the residents of Little Seaford to judge. In the time since she'd come to the seaside village, she'd come to, if not love the residents, at the very least respect them. They might not be quite comfortable welcoming her or the other bluestockings into their bosom, but neither did they hold the heiresses in contempt, in part because despite her eccentricities, Lady Celeste had been a favorite among them.

This painting, Sophia knew without consulting them, would not be something they immediately understood or appreciated. It was, she feared, a bit ahead of its time. And would cause a bit of a stir among her neighbors. But it was the other percentage of Little Seaford's inhabitants—the artists at Primrose Green, the local gentry, and the educated, somewhat cosmopolitan few—she hoped to speak to. That contingency might not like the painting, but they'd appreciate its technique, and might even agree with its message. Hopefully, it was these visitors to the exhibition who would also serve as judges.

The thought of the exhibition reminded her of the overhead conversation and once again she felt a pressing need to find out whose life was in danger. And to warn him. Even if the man was a forger, he didn't deserve to die for it.

She cursed her injured ankle again and rested her head against the back of the settee with a sigh.

Which is when she heard the knock on the door of the studio.

"I hope you don't mind the disturbance, dearest," Gemma said as she stepped into the room, followed by Ben and a man who could only be his brother Freddie. The two men weren't enough alike to be twins—Ben's hair was slightly darker, and curlier, and his build was a bit less lean—but they had that general similarity that couldn't be pinpointed but marked them as having emerged from the same set of parents. "Lord Benedick and his brother, Lord Frederick Lisle. They said it was a bit urgent."

Sophia was surprised to receive a second call from the vicar in the same day, naturally, but her sister's mention of necessity gave her pause.

"What is it, my lord?" she asked, attempting to sit up straighter. "Has something happened?"

Sophia didn't miss the hesitation before Ben said, "Well, not precisely . . . that is to say . . ."

"It's no worry," she assured him with a smile. "My sister told me some of what you overheard at the ball last evening. But I'm off to work for a bit now. I'll leave you to it." To Sophia she said pointedly, "Do not overtire your injury. You may have bullied the footmen to carry you up here, but they can just as easily be instructed to take you back to your bedchamber." And with that admonition, she left them. Leaving the door of the attic rooms ajar for propriety's sake.

"You told your sister about what we overheard?" Ben asked with a slight frown.

"I was in pain and needed some distraction," Sophia told him baldly. "And Gemma is trustworthy. She won't tell anyone. Not unless I tell her she may."

"Don't be a stickler, Ben," said Lord Frederick, stepping around his brother to take Sophia's hand in his and kiss it. "I'm the handsome one, Miss Sophia," he said with a wicked grin. "I regret, however, that I'm taken, so you should dampen any pretensions you have toward my very handsome person."

"If Leonora heard you say that she'd have your guts for garters," Ben said wryly. "And stop flirting. It's quite true that you are taken and you should stop raising expectations."

"If I may be so bold as to speak," Sophia cut in, "I am in no danger of succumbing to your charms, Lord Frederick, powerful as they are. Though I do thank you for exerting yourself on my behalf."

With an unrepentant grin, Freddie bowed again. "She's got spirit," he said to his brother. "I like that." To Sophia he said, "I do apologize, my dear. Old habits die hard, I'm afraid, and I find it impossible not to flirt, especially when it offers such a rare opportunity to tweak my brother's nose."

Sophia shook her head a little, dazzled despite herself. Then, having collected herself, she said, with what she hoped was credible sobriety, "Perhaps you should both bring a chair over and explain what it is that has you here in such haste. Especially when I thought we'd agreed to see each other tomorrow, Lord Benedick."

Exchanging a look she could not read, the brothers retrieved chintz-covered wingback chairs from where they sat on either side of a trestle table, and moved them to sit facing Sophia's settee.

"Well?" she prompted when they'd settled. "What is it?"

Ben's mouth tightened. "Someone has taken it into his head to challenge your entries in the exhibition. He claims they're obscene. And he asked me, as the vicar of the parish, to support him in it."

Chapter 9

"I suppose it's Mr. Morgan who finds my work so objectionable?" Sophia asked, her blue eyes narrowed with annoyance.

Ben had only been mildly surprised to learn that she'd abandoned her sitting room for the art studio. It was impossible to imagine her sitting quietly while she waited for her ankle to heal.

The room itself was impressive. Large enough to allow for paintings of all sizes, and with a view that could inspire even the most novice of artists to capture it. Lady Celeste Beauchamp had been an accomplished woman, with talents ranging from classics to mathematics. But this room made it clear that she had as much love for art and painting as she did for the others. This was a shrine to color and light and had been carefully crafted as the perfect space for creation.

Now, settled across from where Sophia reclined on the settee, he was relieved to see that she appeared better rested than she had that morning. Though the news of Morgan had put a crease between her tawny brows.

"It is, indeed, Morgan who has come forward asking that your paintings not be shown in the Exhibition," he responded. "He hasn't even seen them, but apparently the description of their content was enough to convince him that they are inappropriate for a public event that will include mixed company."

"He must have seen the title and description that I turned in to the exhibition committee," Sophia said, her rosy lips pursed with anger. "Because no one has seen them but the members of this household and the servants. And after the difficulty we had with disloyal footmen in the past, Kerr and Maitland have made quite sure that our men now are corruption proof."

"Who might have shown him your submission forms?" Freddie asked, serious now that they were discussing Morgan. "Is there someone on the committee who is particularly friendly with him? Or who might have alerted him to the content of your work?"

Ben watched as she thought about the question. Her rose colored gown showed her creamy complexion to advantage, and he couldn't help but appreciate the way the bodice—which was all that was respectable—framed her bosom. When he looked up, Freddie caught his eye and gave him a wink. Caught out, he gave himself a mental shake and turned his attention back to Sophia's face.

"There are any number of people on the committee who might have alerted him," she said grimly. "He's done a good job of ingratiating himself with many of the village leaders. Times have been difficult for the farming families since the bad harvests a couple of years ago. And that in turn has affected business in the village shops. Morgan has been quite good at using that discontent to his advantage, playing the benevolent industrialist, making contributions to local groups that were in need of funds. Offering jobs at his estate. People are grateful to him. And willing to overlook some of his more questionable pronouncements."

"Such as crying foul over artwork that just happens to call into question the morality of his own wealth?" Ben asked.

"Precisely," Sophia said with a nod. "I knew, of course, that the factory worker painting would draw his ire. His own textile mill in Yorkshire is responsible for any number of child workers being killed in the machinery, or dying more slowly from cotton lung. He feels guilty, and I want him to."

"May we see them?" Ben asked, suddenly needing to see the works that Morgan found so obscene.

"Of course." Sophie gestured to the area behind them.

Turning, Ben saw for the first time that what he'd thought was a partition, was actually a rolling wall of sorts. And it was hung with three paintings. He'd been so focused on Sophia when they entered the room he'd been blind to the details of what hung on the walls.

He and Freddie rose so that they could look fully at the works.

And he was nearly overwhelmed by them.

If you didn't look closely, it would be possible to miss the crumpled prostitute in the first painting. The light and animation of the theatre entrance was so engrossing. And yet, it gave pathos to the fallen, forgotten woman whose death was of no concern to the rich and powerful who passed only a few feet away. It was dark, and engrossing, and perhaps one of the most provocative works of art he'd ever seen.

Beneath it was a different tableau—it had the same effusive use of light as the other had—that depicted a child lying lifeless on a bed, his mother weeping at the bedside. In a small vase on a bedside table was a cotton blossom. Impossible to get in England, of course, but it was symbolic here. A nod to the cotton mill that had taken the boy's life. On the floor lay an advertisement for child workers at just such a mill. It was nameless, but Ben could well imagine Morgan seeing his own factory in the image.

"You have real talent, my dear," said Freddie at last, turning to face Sophia. "I admit to having a certain degree of skepticism when I heard you were a painter. There are so many who fancy themselves artists simply because they're able to pick up a brush and daub on a few spots of color. But these are . . ." he seemed, to Ben's amusement, at a loss for words. Freddie Lisle was very rarely unable to find something to say.

"They're powerful," Ben said moving to take Sophia's hand. He found himself needing to convey his appreciation with touch. Which was odd, but the artwork had engendered strong emotions in him. Despair for the people depicted, anger at those who had put them in such straits, and oddly, thanks to the skill and beauty of the art itself, hope. "I, too, I must admit, was not expecting such dramatic work from you."

At Sophia's frown, he raised a staying hand. "Not because I thought your paintings would be boring. It's just that your personality is so . . ."

He searched for a word—well aware that he was in the same position his brother had been in. And to his disappointment, Sophia made no move to supply one.

"You're so effervescent," he finally settled on. "You're funny and frank and you have such a practical demeanor. I suppose I didn't imagine you would have such bold and challenging things to say in your art."

Sophia gave his hand a squeeze. "I think that's the most insightful thing anyone has ever said to me about my work."

Reluctantly he let her go and moved back to sit in his chair facing her. If Freddie weren't there, he'd have been sorely tempted to pull her into his lap and hold her. Which was utter madness. But it seemed that madness was becoming his default emotion in her company.

"I am rather prosaic about most things," she continued, staring down at her hands. "It comes of having impractical parents, I think. Gemma and I had to fend for ourselves when it came to the practicalities. But that doesn't mean I am without feeling." She looked up and met Ben's eyes. He could see that she was sincere and a bit defensive. "I feel things very strongly. But it's not always convenient to dwell on emotions when you're concerned about making sure cook will have dinner ready, or the laundry maid won't ruin your best gown. Beauchamp House had allowed me the luxury, for the first time in my life, of letting my emotions flow onto the canvas. I can say without exaggeration that this is my best work. And it was done here, in this very room."

Ben wanted to question her further about her life with her parents. Where had they been while she was seeing to the running of the household? As far as he knew they were both still living. So, why had she been burdened with such chores? But he could see it wasn't the time for that discussion. Instead, reluctantly, he turned the subject back to Morgan.

"How can we ensure that Morgan doesn't get his way?" he asked. "These paintings deserve to be seen. They deserve to hang in the exhibition along with the other locals' art. You are just as much a resident of this village as they are. And I would venture to guess that no one else's work will be as powerful or carry as necessary a moral message."

"We'll need to speak to the committee," Sophia said with a martial glint in her eye. "And I know just where we should begin."

"Not to dampen the fight to get your paintings seen, Miss Hastings," Freddie said, "but there is also the matter of the forgery ring, and its implications for the nation's safety, operating out of Little Seaford. I believe my brother told you we think the conversation you overheard at the Morgan Ball could be related?"

Ben bit back a curse as he saw Sophia's expression turn from excitement to annoyance. "We discussed the possibility of a forger, of course, but not a forgery ring. And certainly nothing about it affecting England's security. I hope this isn't another of your attempts to protect me, Vicar, for I will tell you here and now, that I will be quite put out with you if that is the case."

For a man who'd been seconded by the Home Office, Ben thought darkly, his brother had an extraordinary skill for spilling secrets.

"I can assure you, Miss Hastings," he said aloud, "I intended to tell you about the full extent of the plot and its interest to the Home Office just as soon as I was able. I only learned of it myself last evening when my brother showed up unannounced on my doorstep."

All of which was the truth. However, he chose not to tell her that he'd planned to keep the news from her until she was recovered from her injury, and therefore less likely to risk her health through overexertion. If it was a sin, it was by omission. And surely keeping her from harm would be looked upon as a virtue by anyone other than the lady he was attempting to protect.

He had the distinct feeling that Sophia was not convinced, and yet, she didn't argue. With a raised brow, she turned to his brother and said, "I suppose I'd best hear the whole tale, then."

But Ben didn't want her to know about something that might put her in danger. "Perhaps when you're more recovered, Miss Hastings," he said with a speaking look at his brother.

"Lord Benedick, you begin to annoy me," she said with a tilt of her head, her blue eyes lit with a spark of pique. "My brain has not been injured. Only my ankle, which the last I checked, is incapable of reason. I should hate to think you are one of those tiresome males who believes us to be the weaker sex, who cannot endure more than two thoughts in our heads at a time."

The accusation stung. Especially since he'd only just finished telling her in plain terms what Morgan thought of her paintings. "Miss Hastings," he said, feeing an unaccustomed wash of anger, "I thought we understood one another better than that. Of course I don't see you—or any woman—as unintelligent merely because of your sex. I merely wished to ensure that you do not come into danger by knowing more than you should about matters that are known to only a handful of people. My brother and myself included."

Sophia opened her mouth to respond, but Freddie spoke up, holding up a staying hand to stop them both from speaking. "If I may interrupt, Miss Hastings, being married, myself, to a headstrong, intelligent lady, I do understand your annoyance with my brother. But having known him for many more years than you have, I can attest to the fact that he is the least likely man of my acquaintance to dismiss a lady's mind as inferior. He is, however, quite concerned with the safety of everyone who falls within the scope of what he sees as his responsibility."

He wasn't wrong, Ben reflected, but it was damned uncomfortable to be summed up so easily.

"I can assure you that he knew nothing about the government's interest in the forgery ring until I told him not long after my arrival last evening," Freddie continued. "I cannot say whether he intended to tell you before my clumsy revelation, but my guess is that he would have told you eventually. Just hadn't decided when to do so."

Ben met Sophia's eyes, which had softened at his brother's words.

Looking a bit sheepish, she said, "I suppose I should apologize, Lord Benedick. Perhaps I am more snappish than usual thanks to a lack of sleep."

"Think nothing of it, my dear," he told her with a smile. Then, unable to let the moment pass without owning up to his own wrongdoing, he admitted, "I might have been waiting to tell you about the Home Office later, as Freddie said.

But not because I think you to be inferior. Simply because I thought Morgan's threats against your paintings were enough to bring to you while you were under the weather."

Sophia sighed. "I suppose that's not entirely a bad idea. As much as it pains me to admit it."

Quickly, Freddie gave her a summary of what the Home Office knew about the criminal activity they suspected was centered in Little Seaford.

"I had no notion," she said when he was finished. "And you really work for the Home Office?"

Ben gave a soft cough at his brother's momentary pique at the skeptical tone in her voice. Then, his good nature overcoming his wounded pride, Freddie gave an elegant shrug. "They are, at the moment, short of investigators. And my friend who works with them recalled that Ben had been living here, so thought he might be drafted into service."

"Which I am, of course happy to do," Ben said with a shrug. "I am in a position to know most of the families in the area."

He gave Sophia a mischievous look, "And perhaps a friendship with one of Little Seaford's foremost artists can help me understand more about painting and the art world."

She shook her head. "I might have known you'd find a way to charm your way back into my good graces."

"My dear Miss Hastings," Freddie said, raising his quizzing glass, "he is a Lisle. Of course he is charming."

She didn't comment, but said, "I do believe I know just the people we need to ask about both Mr. Morgan's objections and who might be involved in any sort of art forgery in the area."

"Don't keep us in suspense." Ben thought perhaps Sophia was enjoying the prospect of a fight. Not the need for it, certainly, but she wasn't someone who backed down from a challenge. And she now had several.

"Of course you already know them, Lord Benedick." Sophia said with a grin. "But I believe your brother will enjoy making the acquaintance of the Primbles."

They were just the sort of people Freddie would find fascinating.

"Freddie, old son," he said, clapping his brother on the shoulder. "I believe you're in for a rare treat. And Miss Hastings is perfectly correct. The Primbles, whose home is an artist's colony of sorts, will be able to ensure Morgan doesn't get his way, as well as give us some idea of who among the local artists might be involved in the forgery ring."

Freddie's brows rose with interest. "Then lead the way to these fonts of artistic wisdom."

Before Ben could remind him of Sophia's infirmity, she spoke up.

"Tomorrow," Sophia promised with a gesture to her ankle. "I'm afraid today I'm still not up to a carriage ride. And if the two of you try to go visit our resident eccentric artists without me I will never forgive you."

Ben knew from her tone that she was serious. "I wouldn't dream of it, Miss Hastings. Though I've met the Primbles in my capacity as vicar, we will need your artistic credentials to lead the way. I don't know a Rembrandt from a Rubens."

"We would never be so ungentlemanly as to leave you behind, Miss Hastings," Freddie said with a hand over his heart. "No matter how much my brother urges me to do otherwise, I will not allow him to abandon you."

To Ben's amusement, Sophia only pursed her lips a little at Freddie's foolishness before turning to speak to him. "I trust you, Lord Benedick," she said. And it was hard not to read more than was likely intended by the words.

"I shall see you tomorrow, gentlemen," she continued with a firm nod. "You may pick me up at ten in the morning. And

I promise not to make you wait overlong for me to find just the right hat."

"You didn't tell me she was considerate as well as a lovely, brother," Freddie said in a stage whisper.

Ben took his brother's elbow to his ribs with good humor, though he didn't miss that Sophia's color rose at the bit of flattery.

He'd have liked to have a few moments alone with her to assure himself that she was indeed improving, but there were lines of fatigue around her eyes that told him she was in more pain that she professed.

"Get some rest," he said aloud, though his tone was gentler than his words. "We'll see you tomorrow and determine whether you are ready for a jostling drive then."

Before she could argue, he and Freddie bowed and took their leave.

Later that evening, Sophia was reading in bed when, to her surprise, Lady Serena came to her.

"You seem to be feeling better," she said with a gesture to Sophia's injured ankle as she took a seat in the chair beside the bed. "I take it Dr. Holmes' treatment has helped?"

Setting her book aside, the first volume of *Pride and Prejudice,* which she'd sought out after her discussion of it with Ben that morning, Sophia nodded. "And rest," she admitted sheepishly. "I am ready to admit that my decision to attend the ball last evening was not my finest decision."

Serena's blue eyes, so very like her brother the duke's, lit with mischief. "Oh how I could use that information to my advantage. An admission of wrongdoing from one of the Hastings sisters!" She clasped her hand to her chest in mock astonishment.

"I am hardly the only lady in this household with a reluctance to admit fault," Sophia said with a sniff. "And besides, I seem to recall you were not so eager to call for the physician when you had a cough last month."

To her credit, Serena lifted her hands in surrender. "You are right. I am just as bad as any of you heiresses."

Once their shared laughter had diminished, however, she got to the point of her visit. "Dearest, while you are here at Beauchamp House, I am not only your friend, but also your chaperone. And as such, am here to serve as your guardian in the absence of your parents."

Having some notion of where this conversation was headed, Sophia shifted uncomfortably. Though she and Gemma had never been outright disobedient to their parents back in Manchester, nor had they been particularly slavish to their wishes. For one thing, doing precisely what their mother wished them to do would have meant spending days on end in a darkened room with a cloth soaked in lavender water on their brows. For another, Aunt Dahlia, who had a far more outspoken persona than either her brother or sister-in-law, had taken her nieces under her wing almost as soon as she came to live in the Hastings household.

Sophia could hardly wave away the older lady's concerns by telling her that she needn't worry since Mr. and Mrs. Hastings were indifferent parents at best and neglectful at worst. She could only imagine poor Serena's response to that sort of confession.

In truth, her parents weren't that bad. Mama and Papa simply delegated the day-to-day care of their daughters to Mr. Hastings' sister Dahlia, who'd come to live with them. Mr. Hastings was far too busy with his work as a solicitor, and Mrs. Hastings was so often taken ill that she couldn't accompany her daughters on social or educational outings.

Still, Sophia understood what Serena was getting around

to. And the subject wasn't one she was particularly eager to discuss.

Before she could respond, however, Serena pressed on. "It cannot be a surprise to you that I should come to you about this early on. Especially given the . . . precipitate manner in which both Ivy and Daphne managed to find themselves wed. That my own cousin and brother were the gentlemen who compromised them is not precisely something I am proud of. In fact, I daresay if there were a governing body of chaperonage, I should have already found myself summarily dismissed long ago."

Despite herself, Sophia giggled. At Serena's scowl, she held up a protesting hand. "You must admit, Serena, that it's amusing. And I hardly think anyone who cares about such things places the blame at your feet. Special licenses are quite common among the peerage, are they not? And besides that, both Ivy and Daphne are known to be unconventional. It can hardly be a surprise to either the village of Little Seaford on the *beau monde* that their marriages were secured in hasty fashion."

But Serena was not to mollified. "You might find it amusing, my dear, but it is deadly serious to me. I am responsible for the four of you. And I've done a terrible job of watching over Ivy and Daphne. I do not mean to make the same mistakes with you and Gemma."

Sophia didn't pretend not to know from which gentleman in particular Serena was supposed to protect her. "You are leaping to conclusions about the vicar and me that are far too premature. I enjoy Lord Benedick's company, it's true. But I am hardly the sort to make a suitable vicar's wife. I'm not even sure I believe in all the teachings of the Church of England. And aside from that I'd be provoked into jealousy every time one of his flock batted an eyelash at him."

That she did harbor an attraction for him despite her sensible objections to any sort of match between them was something Sophia would simply need to control. Once their shared investigation into the forgery ring was over, she would simply go back to her painting and leave him to be snapped up by some wholesome lady more suited to becoming a clergyman's helpmeet.

Serena, however, didn't appear to believe Sophia's protestations. "You might claim otherwise, but I've seen you together. He's smitten with you, or at the very least, taken. It would only take the slightest bit of encouragement on your part to have him eating out of your hand."

"You make me sound like some sort of biblical temptress, Serena," she said with a frown. "I've hardly got the sort of stunning beauty that makes men of God abandon their principles and sin with abandon."

To her surprise, Serena shook her head. "You really don't know, do you?"

"Know what?" Sophia asked, plucking nervously at the bedclothes. She was growing uncomfortable with all of this talk of attraction and temptation.

Wordlessly, Lady Serena took her hand. "My dear girl, you are beautiful. I know any number of ladies in London who would sell their teeth to have a figure like yours. Not to mention your passion for your work only adds to your charm. Together, these traits are almost irresistible. I'm not surprised Lord Benedick finds you fascinating. My only shock is that we don't have more than a few local gentlemen paying calls on you weekly."

Sophia felt her face heat. "You needn't exaggerate, Serena. I know I'm far too short and . . . round . . . to be fashionable. And you and I both know that the gentlemen who call here are not just for me. I have a good mind that Mr. Tewksbury comes only to see you, in fact."

At that, Serena's cheeks turned red. "I will admit Tewksbury might not be here for you, but the rest are. Gemma never makes an appearance and Daphne and Ivy are married. And while your figure might not be in fashion at the moment, you are most definitely the sort that most gentlemen prefer."

It wasn't hard to guess that in this case, Serena was very likely speaking of her belated husband and his preferences. She was tall and willowy—like Lady Celeste, she'd once told them. And though she was quite pretty, she would never be called buxom. Though the heiresses didn't know the entire story, it was known among them that Lord Fanning had not been good to her and that Serena still bore some of the emotional scars of his ill treatment of her.

She gave her chaperone's hand a squeeze where she still held it. "I thank you, Lady Serena," she said with a soft smile. "I still don't quite believe you, but I'm grateful for the compliment. And while I beg leave to disagree with you that any gentleman would find himself overcome with lustful thoughts over my person, I will endeavor to rein in my charm when in the company of our handsome local vicar."

Serena sighed. "I don't mean for you to hide your light under a bushel. And by all means if you wish to allow Lord Benedick to court you, I will not object. Just please try for a bit more discretion than Ivy and Daphne managed. That's all."

That made Sophia laugh. "Since it will not be at all necessary, I have no qualms about making that promise. I will even make you a small wager. If, by chance, I am forced to marry by special license, I shall gift you with whichever of my paintings you wish. Even one of those I've promised elsewhere."

Serena's eyes narrowed. "And what shall I do for you if I lose?"

"You will accompany Ivy, Daphne, Gemma and me to London on a shopping trip," Sophia said without blinking.

"I should like to see you devote a bit of time to yourself for a change. You spend so much of your daily life tending to Jem and looking after us. You deserve a bit of fun."

Serena's young son, Jem, was a favorite with the heiresses and his older cousins, but Sophia knew well enough what a handful he could be. And though the widow would deny it, she gave far more to others than she received.

For the barest moment, Serena's eyes lit with excitement at the prospect of a holiday. Then, as if reality had intruded upon her like a wet blanket, she grew serious again. "It's a nice thought, but really I have far too much to do here, and Jem . . ."

"Jem will be perfectly content to remain here with his favorite uncle and cousin." Sophia countered. "And I know the others would like the opportunity to do something for you after all your kindnesses to us."

"Gemma won't like it," Serena said stubbornly. "Nor will Daphne. They both detest shopping."

"Well, we will find some other activity to entertain them while we're in London," Sophia said with a shrug, hiding her triumph at the note of concession in Serena's voice despite her argument. "So, I will simply have to keep myself from marrying by special license in the next month or so. I don't believe I've ever won a wager so handily."

With a shake of her head, Serena rose. "Don't count your winnings yet, old thing," she said in a tolerable impression of her brother, the Duke of Maitland. In her normal voice, she added, "I don't know what it is about this house, but it is clearly endowed with some sort of magnetic properties that lead sensible young ladies into mischief. And I intend to protect both you and your sister from following Ivy and Daphne down that selfsame path."

When she was gone, Sophia chuckled merrily to herself.

"Magnetic properties, indeed." She wished her ankle weren't throbbing or she'd have searched out the others to tell them.

Picking up her book again, she began to read. But in the back of her mind, she was already planning which shops she'd take Serena to on their trip to London.

Chapter 10

To Sophia's relief she slept the night through, and the next morning she was able to put weight on her ankle without the blinding pain of the day before. There was still some discomfort, however, but she was able to have breakfast with the rest of the household without needing to be transported there by one of the footmen.

She did allow Greaves, who was replenishing the tea and coffee service at table, to bring her a plate of toast and eggs. It was customary for residents of the house to serve themselves at breakfast, but she was a favorite with the butler, and he made sure she was settled.

"Thank you, Mr. Greaves," she told him with a smile. "You're too good to me."

The older man, so proper most of the time, gave one of his rare smiles. "Of course, Miss Hastings."

Then he hurried from the room.

"If I hadn't seen it, I wouldn't have believed it," Lord Kerr said with a grin from his place beside Ivy. "You've wrapped poor Greaves 'round your finger. I can't be sure but I think he was blushing."

"Hush, Quill," Ivy chided. "Sophia is just being herself.

She cannot help it if the majority of the male population succumbs to her pretty face."

"You're hardly an antidote," Sophia told her friend with a laugh. "In fact, I'd say as a whole we're not a bad looking group."

"Intermarriage within the aristocracy leads to exaggerated features on most of the offspring in the *ton*," Daphne said as she spread marmalade on her toast. "Statistically, Kerr, Maitland, Serena and myself should be frightful looking. Fortunately, we've all managed to turn out rather attractively. It's a wonder, really."

"I, for one, am relieved to have escaped the overlarge ears and weak chin of my fellow aristocrats," said her husband, the Duke of Maitland, raising his teacup with a flourish. "Else Daphne might never have set her cap at me.

"I did no such thing," his wife responded without rancor. "I simply noted that you were a handsome man and acted accordingly."

"Yes," Gemma intervened before Daphne could expound on the subject, "and we all know the outcome."

"We do, indeed," Ivy agreed with a grin. "Now, speaking of good-looking aristocrats, I couldn't help but notice that our vicar paid not one but two calls on our Sophia yesterday. I know he takes his duties as minister seriously, but that seems a bit overly conscientious to me. What say, you, Sophia? Has our vicar fallen prey to your winsome ways?"

This sort of teasing was *de riguer* for their group, so Sophia didn't take offense at her friend's words. Though she had hoped that no one would notice Ben's second appearance at Beauchamp House yesterday.

Even so, she had to tell them about Morgan's threat to have her paintings taken out of the exhibition at some point.

Quickly she told them the reasons for Ben and Lord

Frederick's visit, including the presence in the village of an art forger.

When she'd finished, her friends were gratifyingly angered on her behalf.

"I wish we'd declined the invitation to that man's ball," Ivy said fiercely. "He has rubbed me the wrong way since he first arrived in Little Seaford, and now I am convinced he's the worst sort of hypocrite. His kind always has a fancy woman in town while he condemns the rest of the world for their perfidy."

"What can we do?" Daphne asked, cutting to the heart of the matter. "Shall the duke and I pay a call on him and let him know he's crossed a line? I have no fears about playing the outraged duchess for a good cause. Just say the word."

"Alternatively," Kerr said thoughtfully, "Maitland and I could go alone. Talk to him man to man. His type enjoys bullying women, but rarely stands up to other men. Indeed, it would be quite pleasant, I think, to put the man in his place. He's swept into the village as if he owned it and seems to think everyone else should accept his leadership. Last I heard, the village has a competent mayor in Mr. Givens."

But the idea of any of them approaching Morgan and possibly riling him further made Sophia nervous.

Morgan, like most men of his station, found it galling enough that he'd worked—or rather, his factory workers had—for his every penny when aristocrats simply inherited their wealth through the good fortune of birth. Maitland and Kerr were not as snobbish as some others of their class, but they did possess that certain bred-in-the-bone sense of authority that Sophia sensed would anger Morgan. He was both jealous of them and resentful.

"I do appreciate your championship," she told the cousins. "Indeed, I am grateful for all of you. So much. But I believe this is a matter that requires an appeal to a higher authority."

Gemma blinked. "Lord Benedick is going to pray for you?"

Sophia laughed. "I imagine he will, as vicar, but I was talking about someone else. A higher artistic authority. The chairman of the Little Seaford Art Exhibition, Mr. Primble."

"Oh, excellent," Maitland said with a grin. "For all of his eccentricities, Primble isn't a man to stand for interference in his art business. I once saw him deliver a withering set down to Mrs. Northman, the Squire's wife, when she attempted to give one of the artists in the Primrose Green colony some suggestions for how he should frame his painting. I don't think a Beau Brummell at the height of his influence could have been more cutting."

"I hope it won't come to that," Sophia said with a slight shudder. Mr. Primble could indeed be sharp, and that might be just as counterproductive with Morgan as being approached by Maitland and Kerr would be. "Instead, I believe Lord Benedick and I will be able to persuade Mr. Primble to simply ignore Morgan's request. He is, after all, the chairman of the exhibition committee. And he has an appreciation for art that challenges."

Just then Mr. Greaves returned with the news that Ben and his brother Lord Frederick Lisle had called. "I have put them in the drawing room, Miss Hastings. I took the liberty of sending your maid for your hat and cloak."

Ignoring the grins of the rest of the table, Sophia thanked him, and when the butler was gone, stood with the help of her walking stick. "Now, if I've amused you enough this morning, I'll just be off to pay a call at Primrose Green."

"Good luck," said Ivy as Sophia made her way to the door. "And be sure to bring Lord Benedick and his brother for luncheon. I have a feeling this visit will leave you needing sustenance."

Chapter 11

The following morning, Ben and Freddie waited in the drawing room for Sophia or word that she was not well enough to accompany them to call on the Primbles.

Ben had suspected she was a bit overconfident about the degree to which her twisted ankle would have healed by this morning, but he hadn't been able to say no when she all but begged them not to leave her behind. And he hadn't been lying when he said that he and Freddie would need her artistic expertise to communicate with any sort of sense at the artists' house. If she was unable to accompany them, they'd simply have to put the visit off until she was recovered enough.

While the brothers waited, they wandered the well-appointed chamber, examining the various objects d'art and paintings Lady Celeste had used to adorn the room. The walls were hung with blue fabric and the inset ceiling was decorated with plaster reliefs in an ivy pattern. But it was the smaller items that lined the mantle and the recesses in the walls that caught the eye.

The shepherdess figurines of the ordinary drawing room were far too tame for late Lady Celeste.

The mantle, for instance, was lined with several figures that seemed in the style of the Elgin Marbles. Upon closer inspection, however, Ben realized that they were all different depictions of the god Priapus—at least that's what he assumed given the outsized proportions of the genitalia of the statues in comparison to the rest of their bodies.

On the other side of the room, Freddie must have encountered something similarly shocking because his usually unflappable brother gave a short laugh, which turned into a coughing fit when Sophia entered the room.

"Oh dear, Lord Frederick," she said with a frown, "I'll just call for some water for you."

She was almost to the bell pull when Freddie recovered himself. "Not at all, Miss Hastings. I'm well, I assure you."

And to Ben's relief, Sophia was also looking much improved.

Though she still limped a bit, her eyes had lost the shadows beneath them, and her cheeks glowed with renewed energy.

"Good morning, Miss Hastings," he said to her, offering a bow. "I hope your appearance means you will be able to accompany us to visit the Primbles."

Sophia glanced at the mantle behind him, and seemed to hide a smile before responding. "Yes, you're quite correct. My injury is almost healed. And thanks to Lady Celeste's walking stick, I shall be able to come along with you. Shall we be off?"

Offering her his arm, Ben escorted her from the room, feeling his brother's amused gaze on his back as they walked. He was always pleased to see his siblings, but he'd be damned glad when Freddie went back home. It was difficult enough to maintain his calm demeanor in the face of Miss Hastings' beauty, but he felt like a damned schoolboy under the watchful eye of his younger brother.

When they reached the entryway, where Greaves was

ready with Sophia's pelisse and hat, Freddie took his own hat and bowed to Sophia. "I'll be riding Ben's gelding to Primrose Green. He's got my curricle for the two of you, in deference to your injury."

With a wink in Ben's direction, he exited and hurried down the front portico of the house.

Sophia and Ben followed at a more sedate pace, and when they reached the curricle, he lifted her by the waist into the vehicle. It took no more than a few seconds, but the brush of her warm body against his coupled with her sweet rose scent had him a little light headed.

By the time he'd climbed up beside her and taken the reins from the groom, he'd regained his composure.

They were silent as he steered the light carriage over the gravel drive and toward the road leading to Primrose Green, which was on the other side of the village from Beauchamp House.

"Your brother seems nice," Sophia said, which almost made him laugh. Polite chitchat was not what he expected from Miss Sophia Hastings.

Even so, he responded easily. "He's a good man. Pesky as younger brothers often are, but since he's married and become a father, he's much more himself, I think. Freddie was always a bit wild. Certainly the most prone to get into scrapes of the Lisle brothers. But Leonora has had a calming influence on him."

"Marriage has that effect on some men," Sophia said with a nod. "Though his wife is Leonora Craven Lisle, is she not? Certainly not the sort of staid society wife one would think of as a steady hand."

Freddie's wife, Leonora, was a celebrated poet and had been rather famous in her own right long before she married Freddie. "I thought the same thing before I met her," Ben said with a shake of his head. "But it turned out that far from being the sort of flighty, head-in-the-clouds poet one might expect, Leonora is rather comfortingly sane."

He turned to glance at Sophia, where she sat beside him with one hand holding her hat in place thanks to a burst of wind. "She's not unlike you, to be honest. She has that same sort of practicality mixed with idealism. I think you'd like each other if you were ever to meet."

From the corner of his eye he could see that she'd colored a little. "Thank you. It's a high compliment to be compared to someone of her stature."

"I only tell the truth," he said with false seriousness. "I'm a vicar, you know. It's in the vicar handbook."

"The Ten Commandments, you mean?" she asked with a raised brow.

"That would be one of them, yes," he conceded with a sniff.

"Far be it from me to question you about church business, vicar." Her tone was solemn, but there was a twinkle in her eye.

"See that you do not, Miss Hastings," he returned. "See that you do not."

After a brief, companionable silence, he said what he'd been thinking since she first walked out with the cane. "You seem to be feeling better."

"Yes, thank goodness," she agreed, the relief evident in her voice. "I was afraid it would be worse today and keep me from accompanying you. And I really do think you'll need me to translate for you with Mr. Primble."

"Come now," Ben said. "I've met the man, and we had no trouble understanding one another."

"It's not that communication is the issue," she said with a shrug. "It's more that I will need to plead my case with him. Artist to artist."

"But I thought Primble wasn't much of an artist himself."

"Oh, he's not," Sophia assured him. "He's dreadful. But he fancies himself one, and that is all that's needed for him to take up my cause. An attack against one of us is an attack against all in his eyes. It's one of the reasons he turned Primrose Green into a colony. He wanted somewhere that artists could be together, in the spirit of community. Us against the world."

"It sounds rather intoxicating," Ben said, seeing when he glanced at her that she looked a bit like a champion. "Why aren't you at Primrose Green?"

Sophia gave a snort of laughter next to him. "Because while I appreciate the ideals that the Primbles promote, I do not trust them to protect my reputation. And, scandalous as Beauchamp House can be to some, Primrose Green is far more dangerous. There's a reason there's only one lady artist in that house and she's over fifty. The male artists who reside there are, not to put too fine a point on it, rogues every one of them."

Ben had known that the Primbles' household, filled as it was with various unrelated artists, was odd, but the trouble Sophia mentioned hadn't occurred to him. Suddenly he was quite glad she hadn't chosen to join the artist's colony.

"Sounds like you made the right decision, Wallflower," he said with quiet vehemence. He made a mental note to make sure she stayed in his view while they were at the colony.

"Oh, not that ridiculous nickname," she said with an impatient noise. "I'm the least wallflowerish person you've ever met, I'd wager."

"I wouldn't say that," he responded, not looking her way, but feeling her gaze on him. "I suspect you fancy yourself a sociable, chatty sort. And you are, to a point. But there's also a bit that you hold in reserve, Miss Hastings. As with the emotions you show only in your art, I think there's another side of your personality. A shyer side. That you tamp down when you're in company."

"You've thought a great deal about this, haven't you?" she asked wryly, though when he turned to look at her, there was hectic color in her cheeks. He must have hit a nerve. "Well, perhaps I am more complex than I let on to social acquaintances. But I don't think you're as cheerful and sunny as you pretend to be when you're playing the role of vicar."

Her shrewd analysis took him off-guard a bit. He was, as a general rule, an easy-going man, but there were times when even he didn't feel as chipper and pleasant as his position required of him. But he'd learned long ago that not unlike Descartes, with his admonishment to kneel down and pray in order to become a believer, it took only a concerted effort to project good humor for it to eventually convert itself into the real thing.

"I'm no more a simple character than you are, Miss Hastings," he agreed. "I may even have hidden depth. But that's for you to learn at a later time. For it would appear we're on the drive leading to Primrose Green."

He watched as Sophia turned and noted that they were indeed on the straight drive leading up to the red brick manor house that was covered in ivy.

"So we are," she said with a brisk nod. "I think I see your brother just ahead of us."

And sure enough, Freddie, riding Ben's gelding Gabriel, was almost at the end of the drive.

"So you do, Sophia," he said. It was a little heady how good her name felt on his tongue. And with that thought he tamped down his attraction for his companion and focused on the meeting ahead of them.

Sophia soon found herself, along with the Lisle brothers, following the Primbles' rather slovenly butler down a narrow hallway toward a pair of French doors.

As they walked, Sophia with one hand on her walking stick and the other resting on Ben's arm, she couldn't help but notice that every available inch of wall was covered with paintings. It hadn't occurred to her that the artistic output of a household with multiple artists in it would of necessity need space in which to hang their works. Did the colony have so little luck selling their pieces, she wondered?

She'd only ever been in the drawing room of Primrose Green on social occasions. And then it had only been a couple of times. The general aesthetic of the Primbles seemed to be "more is better." Not unlike this hallway with its abundance of paintings, from landscapes to portraits to classical scenes, the drawing room was a showcase of other sorts of *bric a brac*. From figurines, to tapestries, to mirrors.

"It's a veritable museum's worth of not very good art," Freddie said in a low voice that only Sophia and Ben could hear.

Before they could reply, they reached the doors, which opened directly onto a wide sweep of green lawn. Sophia had forgotten that Primrose Green boasted one of Capability Brown's gardens. Rather than remaking it in the current style, the Primbles had maintained the artificial lake, faux antique Greek urns and follies along the lake's edge and the tangles of trees and shrubbery beyond. On the expanse of green just near the house, were the Primbles and several of their residents, set up with easels and palettes as they tried to capture the landscape around them on canvas.

In the distance, Sophia could also see a man busy at another easel while several people in what looked to be Greek attire posed against the columns of the largest of the follies.

The butler announced their arrival, and after some initial pleasantries, the Primbles were ushering them back inside to a library that was, thankfully, filled only with books.

"My dear Miss Hastings," said Evelyn Primble once she'd seen Sophia's ankle properly elevated on a leather sofa, "you must take better care. It is the height of foolishness for an artist as talented as you to risk permanent bodily harm. You need your physical strength to do your work justice."

The lady of the house was, by appearances, exactly what one would imagine when attempting to conjure the dictionary definition of a lady artist. Attired in a brightly colored patterned tunic, with a belt cinching the waist and a rather unwieldy turban covering her hair, Mrs. Primble gestured broadly with her hands when she spoke, and was, in general, the sort of woman who took up a great deal of metaphorical space in a room.

Her husband, by contrast, looked like a prosperous businessman, a banker perhaps, or a lawyer. His clothes, while following the customary country uniform of breeches and frock coat, were drab in comparison to his wife's. But he was a pleasant enough fellow, if a bit dull in the shadow of his butterfly of a wife.

Mrs. Primble now turned to Ben with a scowl. "What on earth do you mean, Vicar, escorting this young lady out and about with such an injury? I thought you had more sense than this. She is a treasure, and we need her in top form for the exhibition."

"Now, mother," Mr. Primble chided "Miss Hastings is perfectly able to make her own decisions. It's not the vicar's fault . . ."

Exchanging an amused look with Ben, Sophia interrupted before the Primbles could continue their treatise on her well-being. "Actually, Mrs. Primble, the exhibition is precisely why we've come. That, and—" she gestured to Freddie who'd been watching the whole exchange with the enthusiasm of a small boy at Astley's Amphitheatre for the first time, "—something a bit more complicated that Lord Frederick has brought to our attention."

The husband and wife paused in their chatter and also exchanged a speaking look. Though Sophia had no notion of what it could mean.

"Then this calls for something stronger than the tea I've sent for," Mrs. Primble said. "I know it's not even time for luncheon yet, but I get the sense that this is serious business."

"I'll wait for the tea, thank you, Primble," said Ben to their host, who had produced a bottle of brandy from the sideboard.

"I will too," Sophia said with an apologetic smile. "I could do with a strong cup."

"Suit yourselves," Mrs. Primble said with a shrug as she handed a glass to Freddie. "Now, what's this business you've brought to us?"

Quickly, Ben outlined Peter Morgan's objections to Sophia's paintings being displayed as part of the exhibition. As he spoke, Mrs. Primble in particular became more and more incensed. By the time he'd finished with Morgan's threat to have him removed from the parish, both Primbles were nearly trembling with outrage.

"How *dare* that here-and-thererian, who has only himself arrived in this county within the last year or so, imply that Miss Hastings is not resident enough to show her paintings!" Mrs. Primble hissed. "That trumped-up figure of an artist he had under his wing is no more a painter than I am a blacksmith! His work is derivative at best, and near-forgery at worst."

"Miss Hastings," Primble assured her with a determined look, "you may rest assured that so long as Mrs. Primble and myself retain our positions on the exhibition committee, your work will have a place in our show. Not only is it thought-provoking and unlike anything else to be exhibited, but the fact that Lady Celeste Beauchamp herself chose you from the dozens of other female artists of a similar caliber gives you a stamp of approval that outshines any quibble that Peter Morgan might have. The man's a Philistine, and doesn't know good art from a machine in one of his blasted factories."

"While your support is reassuring," Sophia told them sincerely, "I cannot help but fear that he will find a way to turn the other committee members against me. The amount of largess he's pumped into local coffers speaks quite loudly. Especially during a time of diminished prosperity."

But Mrs. Primble seemed to have no worries. "You let us handle the matter, Miss Hastings. He might have money to flash about, but we are not without influence in the village. I will see to it that your art is displayed in a place of prominence, where it can do its work of stirring emotions."

Despite her reservations, Sophia felt a sense of relief at the Primbles' promises. They did hold a great deal of sway with the townsfolk, who held the artist's colony to be an eccentric attraction that made their village more interesting to tourists, whose custom had become important while the crops were failing.

"Now," Mrs. Primble said, as if they'd put the matter to rest, "what was this other business you wished to see us about?"

Rather than outline the entirety of what the Home Office believed about the forgery ring, Freddie told them only that a forger was suspected to be in the area and that the authorities were searching for him.

It would have been easy to assume that because of their eccentricity, the Primbles were foolish. But the shrewd look that came into Mrs. Primble's eyes as Freddie spoke told Sophia that she, at least, was up to every rig.

"And you think we might know who this forger is because

we have an abundance of artists in our own household." It was a statement, not a question. And Sophia was pleased that Freddie didn't try to fob her off with a half truth.

"It is not unreasonable to think that the house in the area that shelters the most painters might be the first place to search for our culprit," he said with a nod. "I don't wish for you to betray a trust, of course. But as artists yourselves, you know that works that falsely purport to be the valuable creations of the world's finest craftsmen devalues everything in the market. You cannot wish your own works, or those of your residents, to lose value because of this charlatan."

Primble moved to slip a hand around his wife's waist, as if to give her support while she took in the news.

"There is someone, Lord Frederick," he said, his jaw tight with emotion. "Someone who once was a resident here, but has since gone on to enjoy the auspices of another patron. His work, while technically strong, never had enough originality to set it apart from that of anyone else's. There was no spark. No *je ne sais quoi*. When he was approached by Peter Morgan with an offer of patronage, he leapt at the chance. And he has, since moving into Morgan's household, found some degree of success. Though I wouldn't say his work is any better than it was before. It does help to have the backing of a man with a great many friends who have the funds but not the taste to furnish their mansions with art."

"You're speaking of Thomas Ryder, then?" Ben asked, his eyes sharp with interest. "I didn't realize he'd once been a resident at Primrose Green."

"Not for terribly long," Mrs. Primble assured him. "He didn't get along with the others, for one thing. A house like this, where many temperaments must live in harmony, isn't the best place for someone who is unwilling to cooperate with his peers. He often chose the best models and locations for his works without any concern for anyone else who might have previously made arrangements to use them. He had a rather mercenary approach to art itself, seeing it as a means to an end, rather than something to be created from one's soul. He didn't fit in here, and to be honest, when he left to go to Morgan's we were all relieved."

Chapter 12

Sophia had never met Ryder, though she'd been aware that Morgan had taken a painter under his wing. He'd been there the night of the ball, though he'd given her a wide berth because of her injury. He had danced every set and seemed interested only in those young ladies who had the boon of a large dowry to illuminate their charms. It sounded as if he painted with the same venial intent as he sought a wife.

"And you think he's good enough to reproduce the works of the Old Masters?" Freddie asked, rising from his chair, restless now they'd learned of a suspect.

"Absolutely," said Primble with a nod. "He might not be very creative when it comes to choosing his own subjects, but his brushwork is outstanding. And he often made it a point to teach himself the techniques of great artists in an attempt to improve his own work. He's one of those poor creatures whose paintings are flawless, but unfortunately don't depict anything particularly new or interesting."

Sophia was gaining a new respect for the Primbles' knowledge of art and painting. Like most people, she'd assumed that they surrounded themselves with artists because they lacked talent themselves. But the ability to differentiate between mediocre and excellent work was a talent in and of itself. Perhaps there was a reason for the hallway of not very good paintings. Something besides simply displaying the works of their students in a place of prominence.

Having elicited the information they'd come for, Ben also rose, and moved to stand beside Sophia's settee, holding her walking stick for her.

"I cannot thank you enough for your help, Mr. Primble." He shook the man's hand. Then, turning to their hostess, he bowed over her hand. "Mrs. Primble, you have saved us a great deal of trouble with your candor."

"I'll add my thanks, as well," Sophia said as she rose from the settee on her own power, but with Ben quickly offering a supporting arm. Really, she was much improved and didn't need quite this much assistance. But she couldn't help but admit it was no hardship to feel his strong arm beneath her fingertips.

"You are welcome, my dears." Mrs. Primble beamed at them. "I detest it when a man attempts to silence a lady. Especially when he uses ridiculous charges of impropriety and obscenity to do it. I would venture to guess that a great deal of what men like that consider obscene are simply things that bother their conscience. If he gives you another bit of trouble you must come to me, Miss Hastings."

"What will happen to Ryder?" asked Primble once they'd reached the entryway of the house. "If it is him, I mean? It's entirely possible that there's someone else in the area with a gift for copying. It's not an unusual way for artists to learn. And the odds of him being the only one in the area to use it are slim."

"I don't know at this time," Freddie responded. "But I must ask you to keep this conversation to yourselves. We do not wish Mr. Ryder or Morgan to learn that he's a suspect now. If we are to catch him, we need him to remain unaware of our interest."

"Of course," Mrs. Primble assured him as he kissed her hand. "We will be silent as the grave. But you must let us know what happens, Miss Hastings. I expect a full report once the business is over."

Since Sophia had no notion of when that would be, she made the promise easily. If she was, for some reason, gone from Beauchamp House by the time the business with the forger was resolved, then Mrs. Primble would simply have to understand.

Once they were outside, and Freddie's horse and the curricle had been brought around, the brothers made arrangements to meet back of the vicarage once Ben had returned Sophia to Beauchamp House.

"Miss Hastings," said Freddie with a crooked grin. "I leave for London this afternoon, so I shan't see you again this visit. But I wish to say how pleased I am to have made your acquaintance. I feel sure we'll see one another again, but in the meantime I hope you'll take care of yourself."

He bowed low over her hand and kissed it.

There was no denying that Lord Frederick Lisle was a charmer. And that he was as handsome a man as she'd ever seen. But Sophia found she much preferred the understated wit and easy-going nature of Ben. Even so, she was pleased to have met the sauciest Lisle brother.

"You take care yourself, my lord," she said with a grin. "And please tell your wife she has several admirers in the village of Little Seaford."

He nodded, and once he was in the saddle, gave a tip of his hat and was off.

Ben grasped Sophia by the waist and lifted her into the curricle. Had she imagined the spark when their eyes met? She resisted the urge to press her hand to her chest. By the time Ben was up on the seat beside her, she'd managed to regain her composure.

Once they were settled, he gave the horses a signal to move and they were off.

"You'll miss him when he's gone, I think," Sophia said into the sound of the horses' hooves on the gravel lined drive.

"Of course," Ben said with a shrug. "He's family. He might drive me mad at times, but he's my brother."

"I know too well how that feels," Sophia laughed. "It's a good thing Gemma and I spend so much time devoted to our own pursuits. For if we had to spend our days in one another's pockets, I very much fear one of us would end up with severe bodily harm."

They spent the rest of the drive back to Beauchamp House in a discussion of the various merits and drawbacks of siblings.

When they reached the circular drive before the tidy manor house, Sophia was surprised to see an unfamiliar gig being led to the stables.

"A visitor?" Ben asked as he noticed her frown.

"It would seem so," she replied, trying to recall if anyone had mentioned expecting callers today.

He made quick work of lifting her from the curricle, and insisted on escorting her into the house, though Sophia was quite certain she could make it on her own.

"I took Mrs. Primble's admonishment quite seriously," he told her with a grin. "It's not every day I'm raked over the coals for risking a young lady's health. Not many people will dare question a vicar's behavior. Unless he behaves very, very badly."

At the twinkle in his eye, Sophia found herself imagining just the sort of situation in which Ben might do so. Perhaps Freddie wasn't the only charming Lisle brother, she reflected.

Just then, as she handed her hat and gloves to a waiting

Greaves, she heard raised voices from the front parlor just off the entry hall.

"Who's visiting, Greaves?" she asked the butler, who looked none too pleased at the din in the next room.

"A gentleman came to see Miss Gemma," he said with a moue of distaste. "Only he didn't ask for Miss Gemma Hastings, but G.E. Hastings."

Not waiting for further explanation, Sophia moved toward the parlor, followed closely by Ben. Greaves gave a sharp knock on the door before opening it on a tableau of a man and woman in combative stance.

Her sister, her arms akimbo, was scowling as if she'd like to toss the gentleman out on his ear.

While the gentleman, in travel-worn garments, and sporting a head of familiar-looking light brown curls, looked equally put out.

Behind her, she heard Ben give a groan. "Cam, what the devil are you doing here?"

Ben wasn't sure who he'd expected to find exchanging heated words with Gemma Hastings, but it certainly wasn't his brother Cameron.

But, rather than admit that, yes, it was unusual for him to be in Beauchamp House, let alone Little Seaford in general, Cam did what he always did and turned the question around. "I might ask you the same thing, Ben. Are you acquainted with this . . . this . . ." he gestured to Gemma with a rare bout of speechlessness then found the word he was looking for, ". . . harpy?"

Beside him, Ben felt Sophia stiffen, while Gemma made a noise that was something between a snort and a howl. "You, sirrah, are a boor and a scoundrel and I will thank you to take yourself out of this house at once!"

"How do you know this man?" Sophia asked both Gemma and Ben.

When it appeared that Gemma wasn't ready to speak, Ben did so. "This rapscallion, who has clearly lost every bit of the social graces drilled into us at our mother's knee, is my brother, Lord Cameron Lisle."

Having calmed down a bit, Cameron had the good grace to look sheepish at Ben's reminder of social niceties. Bowing prettily, he said to Sophia with a grin that was not unlike Freddie's, "At your service, ma'am."

"This is Miss Sophia Hastings," Ben said tersely. "Miss Gemma Hastings' sister."

Cameron's light blue eyes glanced from one sister to the other, then back again. Finally able to see the resemblance.

"Ah," he said, infusing the syllable with a great deal of feeling.

Pulling away from Ben, Sophia limped over to her sister, brandishing her walking stick with a bit more force than he thought entirely necessary. Still, heeding the warning, Cameron stepped away from the sisters to stand near the window where he could see the room at large. He'd once told Ben it was a trick he'd picked up in his travels, to ensure that he could never be taken by surprise. Clearly he was more unnerved by the Hastings sisters than he was letting on.

"What made you think it was acceptable for you to upbraid my sister in her own home, my lord?" Displeasure dripped from her every word. Ben had never seen Sophia in protective mode, but he had a feeling that, if necessary, she'd toss his brother bodily from the room.

It was quite exhilarating.

He was prepared to back up her question with one of his own if Cam proved recalcitrant, but to his secret amusement, his brother's ears reddened under Sophia's gimlet gaze and he looked as if his cravat had suddenly tightened itself.

"I . . . ah . . . it was badly done of me, Miss Hastings," he said, flags of red in his cheeks. "I'm afraid I lost my temper and . . ."

He was interrupted by a lusty sigh from Gemma, who was also looking sheepish. "It wasn't entirely his fault, Sophia. When I found out who he was I couldn't contain my indignation and I'm afraid I let my temper get the best of me."

Sophia's reddish brows lowered. "Well, I wish you would inform us just who Lord Cameron is besides Lord Benedick's brother, for I must confess, I find myself quite at a loss."

Then, as if she could no longer stand to be on her feet, she moved to collapse into an overstuffed chair near the fireplace. When neither Gemma nor Cam spoke up, she said, "Well?"

Ben went to stand beside Sophia's chair and watched as his brother and Gemma exchanged a series of looks that clearly were full of import. But it was in a language he had no idea how to translate. Finally, Gemma walked over to the chair beside Sophia's and sat.

"You recall I told you about the article I submitted to the *Annals of Natural History*, the one that was rejected?" Gemma addressed her sister without looking at either of the men in the room.

"Oh," Sophia said, almost without thinking. Then, understanding dawned and she said again, with a wide-eyed look toward her sister, "Oooooh!"

Next she turned her narrowed eyes on Cam, and unless Ben was very much mistaken, his brother had made an enemy of both Hastings sisters at this point. If looks could kill, Cam would, at the very least, be mortally wounded.

"So, this is the narrow minded cloth-head who refused to publish your findings?" she asked Gemma, aghast.

"I say," Cameron objected. Though whether it was to being called narrow minded or a cloth-head, Ben couldn't tell. "I gave it the same sort of evaluation as I give every submission. It was interesting, but not particularly ground-breaking."

"Oh, I'm sure you gave it the same sort of evaluation as you give every article *written by a female* that crosses your desk," Gemma said hotly, crossing her arms over her chest. "I wouldn't be surprised if you read only the first three paragraphs before tossing it aside."

Before they could embark on another round of arguments over the paper, Ben broke in with the question that had been plaguing him. "We know now what set you at loggerheads, but why are you here, Cameron? In this house. Arguing with Gemma in person? Could this not have simply been settled by mail?"

At that, Gemma turned bright red.

Sophia turned to stare at her sister. "Gemma, what did you do?"

"You recall you told me I should write a letter to the editor who rejected me?" Gemma asked, looking as if she would rather be anywhere but in this room.

"Two letters," Sophia said. "Yes. One saying how you really felt, and the other more calm and thoughtful."

Gemma nodded and Ben saw dawning horror on Sophia's face. "You sent him the angry one?!"

"I got them mixed up!" Gemma said heatedly. "This is what comes of listening to your advice about writing two letters! Any other sane person would write one angry letter, tear it up and then think about something else."

"I was trying to help you make a case for yourself," Sophia said, hectic color in her cheeks. "When ladies are attempting to enter fields that are traditionally male, it sometimes takes a bit of persuasion to convince the male establishment to accept them."

"If my findings weren't enough to make him accept me," Gemma said tightly, "then maybe it's not a field I want to be a part of."

Not liking the sight of the two sisters, usually so supportive of one another, at odds, Ben asked tentatively, "Surely this letter can't have been all that upsetting, Cameron. You've been to the ends of the earth, for heaven's sake. You've been insulted by people all over the world."

His brother raised a brow. "You make me sound like the most delightful fellow, Ben. But, to correct you, yes this letter was all that upsetting. Miss Hastings called into question everything from my virility to my intelligence to my ability to sit a horse. I came here because she signed it with her initials only so I thought she was a man. I came to challenge this G.E. Hastings."

Ben's eyes widened. "What?"

Sophia turned to her sister. "I thought you said he knew you were a lady when he rejected your paper."

Gemma shrugged. "I send out papers under both my real name and with only my initials. I assumed this one was under my real name because it was a rejection."

"Gemma." The censure in Sophia's voice couldn't have been more shame-inducing if she's been a fifty-year-old governess. "You called this poor man all manner of names without cause."

"I'm not an imbecile." Gemma said the words grudgingly. Then, to Cameron, she said, "It was badly done of me. I should have checked to see if you knew I was a lady or not. I realize now that my letter didn't really state my reasons that the paper should be published, but was rather a series of insults and epithets loosely strung together."

"How did he even receive it?" Sophia asked. "You only told me about the letter yesterday. It hasn't had enough time to reach Oxford. Or Cambridge. Or wherever it is Lord Cameron resides."

At that Cameron looked a bit rueful. "I've actually been in Lyme these past few months. That was the direction I gave on my letter to G.E. Hastings."

"Mrs. Tompkins said she'd have her son deliver it since he had plans to go to Lyme this morning," Gemma agreed stiffly.

Ben turned to his brother in astonishment. "You've been living just down the coast for months and never once came to see me?"

"I'm here now," Cameron said with a shrug. "Besides, you know how village life gets under my skin. I know hardly anyone in Lyme aside from the people I employ to help me search for fossils. If I came here you'd have me introduced to the entire village within a few days and I'd have no peace."

Despite his annoyance at his brother's avoidance of him, Ben couldn't help but admit that he had a good point. It was a vicar's job, in part, to know his parish. And he would very likely have had Cameron meeting and greeting the whole of the village if given the chance. He also had to admit that he would have done so in part to take some of the pressure off himself from the local matchmaking mamas.

"Fine," he said with a shake of his head.

"So, you came here to confront G.E. Hastings?" Sophia asked, a glint of amusement in her eyes now. It was, after one got past the initial alarm of the scene they'd walked in on, an amusing scenario.

"Yes," said Cameron with a grin. "And not only was G.E. a lady, but she's got a sharper tongue than a Billings-gate fishwife."

"Gemma." Sophia's sigh this time was exasperated.

"I was angry, Soph," her sister responded. "You know how I get when I'm angry."

Seeing that the worst of the storm had passed, Ben turned to Sophia. "Perhaps some tea?"

With a sigh that was half exhaustion half amusement, she gestured to the bell pull. "By all means."

Chapter 13

The Lisle brothers did not stay for luncheon, given that Lord Cameron and Gemma were still at odds, their tacit agreement to stop shouting notwithstanding.

Unfortunately for Sophia, this meant that much of the discussion amongst the Beauchamp heiresses—Kerr and Maitland having left that morning for London to take care of business matters—was of the sudden abundance of Lisles in their small part of the county. Not that she was an authority on the subject. It was just that her friends seemed to see her as some sort of window into the minds of the Lisles.

"I suppose it's not that unusual for the vicar's brothers to visit him," Ivy said as she picked up her soup spoon. "It's just the appearance of two of them separately at around the same time. Don't you agree, Sophia? What does Benedick say?"

"I am hardly the man's confidante," Sophia said with frown. "We are working together on the matter of a possible forger, and he was kind enough to take my side against Mr. Morgan, but it's not as if we have spent hours together discussing our feelings."

"You must have talked about something on the drive to and from Primrose Green this morning," Daphne said, tilting her blond head in that questioning way she had. Normally Sophia found it endearing, but today it had the opposite effect.

"You seemed quite friendly when you burst in on Lord Cameron and me," Gemma offered with a shrug.

She wasn't sure why, but Sophia felt cornered, and she didn't care for it at all.

"I wasn't expecting the Spanish Inquisition," she said tartly. "Would you like to go get the thumbscrews, Daphne? I'll wait."

Ivy bit back a laugh. "My goodness, it would appear that someone is sensitive over the subject of our handsome vicar."

"I am nothing of the sort," Sophia said crossly. "I simply do not enjoy being interrogated by my friends. And my sister. We didn't quiz you when you were suddenly going off with Lord Kerr on various errands alone."

"But that implies that your errands with the vicar are of a similar nature," Daphne said triumphantly. At Sophia's scowl, she added with a shrug, "It's logic. You cannot argue with logic, Sophia."

"Can we not just enjoy our meal without discussing the vicar, or his brothers, or your sudden baseless speculations about the nature of my friendship with him?" It was odd even to Sophia that she was so overset by their teasing. She only knew that whatever it was she had with Ben was new enough to be fragile and might not stand up to the harsh light of day. And aside from that, she had other things to worry about. Ensuring that the most important work of her life was part of the exhibition. Perhaps then she would think about whatever it was she and the vicar had been tiptoeing around.

Besides. She'd seen enough infatuations of a few days' duration to know that it was far too soon to think about Ben in those terms. For all she knew, he'd meet the love of his life when he was paying calls in the village and not give her a second thought.

To her surprise, since her sister was often her most ardent teaser, it was Gemma who came to her rescue. "I suppose we've nettled you enough. Though I hope you will remember this when it comes time for you to scold me about my behavior with Lord Cameron."

"My maid told me she heard the shouting from the laundry," Daphne said with an admiring glance at Gemma. "I must admit I enjoyed hearing that you gave the male editor of a scholarly journal a set down. I've known several in my time who deserved worse."

"Do not encourage her," Sophia said, giving her sister a speaking look. "It might have been cathartic, but it really is not the thing to shout at a gentleman you don't even know. Though I do know your nerves were overset, Gemma, you must know you crossed a line. As did Lord Cameron. It was badly done on both your parts."

"So much for not scolding me," Gemma said under her breath. Aloud she said, "I am sorry for losing my temper. It was not becoming. And I am grateful you arrived when you did."

"And I'm sorry you were so upset," Sophia said, grasping her sister by the hand. "I must confess, I find it difficult to believe that Lord Cameron's manners are so lacking given . . ."

"I thought we weren't going to speak of the Lisle brothers any longer," Daphne cut in. "I really wish someone would ensure that we keep this conversation on track. I don't know if I'm coming or going."

Sophia felt a pang of conscience. Daphne was right. She was being hypocritical.

"Good point, Daphne," she said with a nod. "I broke my own rule."

They were silent for a moment as they concentrated on the delicious fish pie cook had presented for luncheon.

"Where is Serena today?" Sophia asked, noting for the first time that their chaperone—and sister to the Duke of Maitland—was absent from the table. "She would have reined us in before we came to such a pass."

"Jeremy has a cold, poor dear, and Serena is sitting with him while he's feeling poorly," Ivy said with a sympathetic frown. "She's taking a tray in the nursery."

Though the boy was old enough to have been sent away to school, Serena was determined to keep her son at home and away from the often brutal realities of Eton for as long as she could. Sophia couldn't blame her. Especially given the bad behavior the boy had already witnessed from his now deceased father.

"I'm sorry to hear it," Sophia said aloud. "Is there anything we can do?"

"She says not." Ivy shrugged. "I already asked. And Dr. Holmes had a look in on him yesterday when he was here to see you. He says it's nothing to worry about."

Both Lady Serena and Jeremy had become dear to the heiresses in their time at Beauchamp House, and the ladies discussed possible trinkets available in town they might purchase for the child. Nothing too dear, but well suited to divert an ailing child from his misery.

Once they'd settled on a plan, the conversation turned to the exhibition.

"You didn't tell us what the Primbles said about your paintings, Sophia," Gemma said. "Are they going to back you against Morgan?"

"Yes," Sophia said, pleased with that portion of the visit

to the Primbles. She filled them in on what the couple had said regarding her place in the exhibition, and their assessment of Ryder as the possible forger.

"Is he the unpleasant fellow who none-too-subtly attempted to determine the amount of each potential dance partner's dowry before he would sign their dance cards?" Gemma asked with a look of disgust. "He is not terrible to look at, but I confess I cannot understand why any of the young ladies present consented to stand up with him."

"He has the unqualified support of his patron." Ivy's mouth pursed in distaste. "Ryder himself might not have wealth or talent, but he has the support of Morgan. And Morgan is not without some degree of influence. Both in Little Seaford, and in some circles in a certain part of London. He may not be a pillar of polite society, but he holds some sway in the middle class. And like it or not, many genteel families with land have a need for the infusion of funds that a connection to Morgan might give them."

If it had been Morgan she and Ben overheard at the ball, perhaps the politician's support of Ryder wasn't as strong as they thought. Without any means of identifying the voices they'd heard, however, it was entirely possible it was someone else who threatened murder. Given her own animus toward Morgan, it would be so much more satisfying to learn he was a criminal. But the truth of the matter was she had no idea. Not with any degree of certainty.

"Did any of you get the feeling that anyone else was particularly interested in Ryder at the ball?" she asked her friends. "Not ladies, but perhaps men who seemed to be taking him under their wing. In a manner similar to the way Morgan did?"

"He seemed to be very friendly with the mayor, Mr. Ivens, and of course Mr. Framingham, but he owns one of the galleries in town, so that's not unusual," Gemma said. "Why do you ask?"

At the mention of Framingham, Sophia's heart began to beat faster. As owner of one of the two galleries in town, Framingham was in a prime position to sell forged paintings. He had the connections in town that would allow him to know exactly what sort of works the newly wealthy middle class were seeking to furnish their homes with. And he knew which artists were least likely to draw suspicion from the authorities. It was much less risky to attempt to sell a forged version of a work by lesser-known Renaissance artists, than, say Tintoretto. And Framingham would know that.

Surely it wouldn't be out of the ordinary if she were to pay a visit to Framingham's gallery while they were in town purchasing things for little Jeremy.

"So," she said, trying to sound casual, "are we all agreed that a trip to the village is in order this afternoon? I should also like to look at the selection of ribbon at White's. My chip bonnet is sadly in need of refurbishing and I'd like a little project to take my mind of this business with Morgan."

To her relief, no one seemed to guess the secondary reason for her enthusiasm for the shopping excursion. And, not too much later, all four ladies were settled in the open carriage, on their way into Little Seaford.

Jeffries was waiting at the door when Ben arrived back at the vicarage from Beauchamp House, accompanied by Cam.

That another of the vicar's brothers had arrived for a visit seemed not to faze him. But the note that had come while Ben was out seemed to be burning the hand that held it.

"This came for you, my lord," he said with a speaking look as he handed it over. "It was tucked into the door jamb. I found it just after you left this morning."

It wasn't unusual for Ben, as the local clergyman, to receive anonymous notes, deliveries of produce as tithe, and even once a cage of chickens. But something about this note must be troubling his butler.

"What's amiss, Jeffries?" he asked, ignoring the smirk on Cam's face. His brother's wandering allowed him to get through life without the responsibility of personal servants. He claimed it was the best way to live, though Ben had his doubts.

"It's just that this arrived without me knowing it, my lord," the butler said in a low, harassed voice. "I always know when someone is delivering something. Even the chickens."

Since the chickens had been rather loud it wasn't exactly a glowing example of the man's all-knowing nature.

"Well, it does happen sometimes," Ben reassured him. "Even the sharpest eye can miss a detail from time to time."

That didn't seem to appease the man, but he took himself off to the kitchens to perhaps vent his frustration on the cook.

"I suppose I'll take myself off, then," Cam said with a wry grin. "When you begin dealing with domestic issues, it's time for me to go back to my vagabond life."

"You just got here," Ben said, not really surprised, but not willing to let his brother off the hook either. "At least Freddie stayed a couple of days when he breezed through."

"I came to confront the man I thought had insulted me," Cam said with a shrug. "Now that I've discovered he's a lady, I have no more need to be here."

"You can't cozen me, brother. I saw the way you looked at her when she wasn't looking at you." Ben had been amused to see his usually diffident brother fall under the spell of Gemma's spirit. She was lovely—though he was partial to her sister's softer beauty, of course—and Cam had definitely been intrigued.

"And that is exactly why I need to leave," Cam said

ruefully. "I might be attracted, but a smart man removes himself from danger before it becomes a real risk. You'd do well to do the same if you know what's good for you."

"Perhaps I'm not so fearful of getting caught," Ben said with a shrug. In fact, he was rather certain he'd found the woman he wanted to spend the rest of his life with.

It took a moment for the realization to sink in.

He blinked.

He wanted to get caught. He wanted to marry her.

Miss Sophia Hastings.

Ben felt the uncanny sensation of rightness that came from knowing his own mind.

He'd only experienced it one other time in his life: when he decided to follow his heart and join the church.

Despite the fact that he was grinning like an idiot, however, his brother was, as per usual, oblivious.

"To each his own," Cam said with a shake of his head. "I'm going to go back to my happy bachelor life and leave you to your little artist. Don't want any of that nonsense rubbing off on me. It's bad enough Archer and Freddie have fallen."

One day, Ben thought wryly as he cuffed his brother on the shoulder. One day Cam would succumb to love's siren song.

However he might try to avoid it.

"The next time you come for a visit, please endeavor not to overset my lady or her sister," he said aloud. Though despite the chiding remark, he was sad to see him go. He missed his brothers, living as he did, away from them.

But Cam didn't seem to mind the scold. "I'll do my best, though you know I've got a particular knack for setting up ladies' backs."

And with an answering clap on his elder brother's shoulder, he took himself off.

When he was gone, Ben took the anonymous note to his

study, poured himself a brandy, and broke the seal on the missive.

I HAVE INFORMATION ABOUT THE PAINTINGS. COME TO
FRAMINGHAM GALLERY TODAY AT 3PM
A FRIEND

He'd donned his hat and coat again and was on his way into the village before the brandy settled again inside the cut crystal glass.

Chapter 14

The drive into the village wasn't a long one, but Sophia took the time while Daphne and Ivy were in their own conversation to speak with her sister.

Touching Gemma on the arm, she asked in a low voice, "Are you sure you're well after your contretemps with Lord Cameron this afternoon? He did seem to be remorseful later, but he was quite harsh to begin with."

Gemma, who had been scanning the horizon, likely hoping for a glimpse of the sea, turned to her with a laugh. "Of course, my dear." She gave her a half hug. "It takes more than a dressing down from that sort of man to dim my enthusiasm."

She lifted a dark brow and countered, "I should ask you if you're sanguine that he'll quite likely be your brother-in-law. It's a shame such a self-important prig should be related to a man as delightful as Lord Benedick."

Sophia felt her face burn. "I shouldn't be so quick to assume any sort of permanent match between the vicar and me, Gemma," she said hastily. "We are friends, that is all. If something more should come of our association . . ."

But Gemma was no more ready to believe Sophia's denials than Sophia was prepared to believe Gemma had emerged from that afternoon's argument unscathed. "It's as plain as punch that he's smitten. Why on earth would he have brought both his brothers to visit you in the space of week if he felt otherwise?"

"That was because of the business with the forger," Sophia said with a shake of her head. "At least, that's why he brought Lord Frederick. And we are his closest neighbors so it's hardly a surprise that he would call with his houseguests."

Her stomach flipped at the notion whatever it was between them could lead to something permanent. Of course she was hardly unaware of the logical conclusion of mutual attraction, but then, too, she knew that most meetings of the mind lasted only a few days before one or the other party lost interest and moved on.

"You may pretend to yourself that it's nothing more than good manners that has the vicar paying calls so often," Gemma said with a shake of her head. "But that doesn't explain the way his eyes follow you whenever you're in a room together."

"Since when are you so observant?" Sophia asked pettishly. She wasn't accustomed to Gemma being the one to point out home truths to her and not the other way round.

"You might think me a daydreamer, sister," Gemma chided, "But that doesn't mean I'm entirely without the ability to notice what's right under my nose."

Then, as if unable to keep from admitting the truth, she added, "And Daphne and Ivy are convinced you'll make a match of it. Once they pointed it out, I saw for myself the truth of it."

Sophia gave a frustrated sigh. There were many things she appreciated about living amongst the most intelligent ladies she'd ever known, but having that intellect turned upon her own life was not one of them.

"Oh, do not take on so," Gemma said, patting her on the

hand. "We all quite like him. And it never hurts to have a man of God on one's side in a fight."

That only made Sophia's heart twist. "Gemma," she said in a hushed tone. "What do I know about being a vicar's wife? I'm not even particularly devout. And I certainly know nothing about keeping house or running a village fete, or whatever it is a clergyman's helpmeet is expected to do."

At that confession, her sister's brow furrowed in sympathy. "I'm probably the wrong person to ask, dearest, given that I too know little about the sorts of things other ladies are taught from the time they're small. I cannot regret our unconventional education, but I would not have objected to at least a bit of household management from Mama in addition to the lessons Aunt Dahlia gave us."

At the mention of Dahlia, Sophia's head snapped up. "That reminds me that I've a letter for her in my reticule. I do wish the mail coach ran faster. I should like to know what she thinks about Mr. Morgan's possible involvement in the forgery scheme. She might know whether he has any connections to the art world in Manchester."

Though her mention of Dahlia was indeed sparked by her sister's words, it was also true that Sophia had taken advantage of the opportunity to change the subject. She did have concerns about her suitability as a wife should the attraction with Ben turn to something more serious, but she didn't want to dwell on the matter. Especially when so many other important matters were on her mind.

Gemma seemed to accept the diversion and they chatted about their aunt for a few moments until the carriage came to a stop in the village.

She waited for Ivy and Daphne to go inside before she lay a hand on her sister's arm. "I've just remembered I need to stop in at Framingham's to see if he knows where in the exhibition hall my paintings will go. I'll only be a minute."

Gemma rolled her eyes. "I should have known," she said with sigh. "Why didn't you just say you wanted to question Framingham?"

"Keep your voice down," Sophia hissed. "I don't want everyone in the street to know my plans."

"And what are those plans?" Gemma asked in a lowered voice. "You are not a Bow Street Runner, Sophia. And recall what sort of danger Ivy and Daphne found themselves in when they began meddling in dangerous matters. They were almost killed."

Sophia gaped at her sister. "They only began asking questions because Lady Celeste asked them to. She may not have known about this particular business, but she would certainly be against it if she had. Any artist with integrity would be."

Looking as if she knew that argument was futile, Gemma threw up her hands. "I give up. You're going to do what you think best anyway. You always have. Just promise me that you'll be careful." Her gaze softened. "You're my only sister and I cannot afford to find another one."

"I promise," Sophia said with an answering smile. Her sister might be the only person in the world who could set her back up in mere seconds, but she was also her dearest friend. "Now, go inside and make my excuses. I'll only be a few minutes."

In the intervening hour before he was expected at Framingham's shop, Ben paid a call at the home of a local widow, Mrs. Debenham. A sweet-tempered lady of middle years, she'd been left to raise three daughters on her own when her husband died only a year or so ago of influenza.

Though she'd seemed to be coming out of her shell a bit now that her official mourning period was over, he'd noticed her waiting to speak to him after services this past Sunday. But when he'd finally managed to extricate himself from a particularly loquacious elderly parishioner, Mrs. Debenham had been gone.

He'd always been adept at reading people. Even as a child he'd been able to anticipate what his brothers or parents would say or do, sometimes before they themselves seemed to know it. It was a skill that had served him well in his calling. Persuasion and guidance were almost as important in the vicarage as preaching.

So, he'd known something was amiss with Mrs. Debenham, and for the moment, set aside his anticipation of the meeting at Framingham's to focus on his duty as a vicar.

The door was opened by Miss Temple, the widow's spinster sister who had come to live with her after Mr. Debenham's untimely death.

To Ben's concern, her expression when she recognized him was one of relief. "Oh, Vicar, I'm so glad you're here. I told Helen she needed to speak to someone in authority about this."

Before he could ask just what "this" could be, he was ushered into the tidy front parlor of the Debenham house, where he saw Mrs. Debenham seated on a long sofa, a handkerchief crumpled in her hand. She'd obviously been weeping.

On seeing Ben, however, she sat up straighter. Wiping at her face, and sliding a hand over her hair, she said in a thick voice, "Lord Benedick, what a mess you must think me."

She made to rise, but Ben urged her to remain seated. Rather than take a chair, he crouched on his haunches in front of her, and took her hand. "My dear Mrs. Debenham," he said in a calm tone, "whatever can I do to help?"

"Oh, but I—," she protested, shaking her head. "That is to say, I shouldn't—"

"Helen," Miss Temple said in a bracing tone, "Tell him. Someone needs to know what that man did."

At the mention of a man, Ben's heart sank. He knew all too well what indignities could be visited upon the persons of those ladies without male relatives in the house. Especially by those opportunistic men who saw such women as easy prey.

Mrs. Debenham's brown eyes filled with tears at her sister's words. "Oh dear me. I am sorry, Lord Benedick," she said in a broken voice. "It's really not such a calamity as my sister makes out."

Though Miss Temple made a frustrated sound behind them, Ben said nothing, waiting for the widow to speak in her own time.

Once she'd gained her composure, she took in a deep breath and said, "I suppose if you're here, I do need to speak of this with someone. And you've always been kind to me, Lord Benedick. Especially after my husband died."

"Tell him," Miss Temple said, though this time, Ben noticed a pleading tone in her voice. Whatever had happened, it had truly overset the widow's sister.

"It's a little thing, really," Mrs. Debenham said, her pale complexion reddening a little. "It's just that when I was leaving the stationer's last week I ran into Mr. Morgan and his friend, the artist, Mr. Ryder."

At the mention of Ryder, Ben's focus sharpened.

Aloud he said, "What happened, Mrs. Debenham?" Knowing both Morgan and Ryder were involved, he had no expectation that the matter was a "little thing" as she'd characterized it.

"I had just stepped out into the street, when Mr. Morgan and Mr. Ryder approached. And since we'd been introduced, I greeted them, then made as if to continue on. But Mr. Morgan, well, he stopped me."

Ben's jaw clenched but he said nothing. At the very least, the fact that the encounter took place on a public thoroughfare told him the physical assault he'd feared was unlikely.

"He had spoken to me in the past," she said in a tight voice. "You know how some gentlemen are with widows?"

She didn't wish to say aloud what he'd told her, that much was obvious, but Ben knew well enough the attitude she spoke of.

"He urged Mr. Ryder to continue on without him," she said. "And I guessed he'd attempt to persuade me again. And I was correct. Only this time, he was much more . . . forceful."

"What did he say, Mrs. Debenham?" Ben asked, keeping his voice even with some difficulty.

"He asked me again, and I declined, of course. But then he said that if I continued to refuse him, he would spread it about that I'd consented, and I'd be ruined." Her mouth was tight with anger. "He wanted to frighten me into doing as he wished, Lord Benedick. And he knows how important my reputation is. Especially when I've three young daughters to see well matched in the next few years."

The anger that washed over him was familiar. It was the same kind he dealt with whenever he witnessed the kind of brute cruelty humankind could visit upon one another. More than ever, he wanted to find some connection between Morgan and the forgers so that the industrialist would pay not only for those crimes, but the ones like this against Mrs. Debenham. The poor woman had already been through enough difficulty to last a lifetime. That Morgan had seen fit to heap more upon her with his lewd suggestions and threats was really the outside of enough.

"Your sister was right to urge you to tell me, Mrs. Debenham," he said in a comforting tone. "I hope you will never fear informing me of any difficulties you may have. All the sin in this instance is Morgan's, not yours. And though I know it might be embarrassing to confess such an encounter, such bullying needs to be brought into the light if it is to be combatted."

"Oh, but I hope you won't speak to anyone about it, Vicar," she said with an expression of alarm. "If word should get out . . ."

"Of course I shall tell no one," he assured her, rising to his feet. "But I do beg your permission to have a word with Mr. Morgan on the matter."

Mrs. Debenham swallowed, but nodded as her sister sat down beside her and took her hand. "I would appreciate that, Lord Benedick. Though I do wish it wasn't necessary."

"As do I, my dear," he said with a reassuring nod. "But I find much of the time men like this need only a few choice words to put them in their place. And as frustrating as it may be, they often listen to objections from other men with far more attention than those from ladies."

"He's a brute," Miss Temple said with a scowl. "Trying to pass himself off as a gentleman when he has no more manners than a pig in the pen."

Ben agreed with her, but could hardly say so given his role in the conversation. Instead he only nodded. "He needs to know that such threats are unacceptable."

If necessary, he'd use his father's status as a duke to enforce his rebuke. Ben had few qualms about leveraging the privilege he'd been born with to effect good in the world. He had little enough use for it in his everyday life. Let his accident of birth persuade Morgan to behave himself.

Assured that Mrs. Debenham had been calmed, and confident that her sister would take good care of her, he left the little house and stepped out into the bright light of the main street of Little Seaford.

Sophia waited until the door had closed behind Gemma before crossing to the other side of the street to Framingham's Gallery. Its window had several prints by well-known artists, and a few original paintings by lesser-known ones. But the sign on the door proclaimed the shop to be a purveyor of fine art.

When she stepped through the door, the first thing she noted was that there seemed to be no one in the main gallery. The counter where one would expect Mr. Framingham to position himself was empty.

She rang the bell on the counter, then began to wander the room.

For a gallery in a small coastal village, it boasted some pieces by several rather well-known artists. But she was not surprised to see some work from the residents of Primrose Green in the mix, some of it quite good—like a landscape by Mr. George Rollins, and a still life by Mrs. Primble herself— and some of it rather mediocre—like an oil on canvas of what appeared to be a depiction of the death of Achilles by Morgan's protégé, Thomas Ryder.

As she often did, Sophia became immersed in the art around her, taking in each brush stroke, examining the scale, perspective, and composition of each work. So engrossed was she that as she stood before Ryder's painting, she was unaware that someone was standing behind her until he spoke.

"What are you doing here?"

Unable to stop herself, Sophia let out a little squeak of surprise at the intrusion and spun around at once to face her accuser.

To her surprise it was not Mr. Framingham, but Thomas Ryder—his dark brow lowered with menace—who stood behind her. His entire mien was one of aggression and for a moment, Sophia feared for her physical safety. He was not a small man, despite his occupation, and though she was no slight thing, he could easily knock her unconscious and carry her away with no one the wiser. At the thought, her heart, already racing, beat faster.

"You are not welcome here," he continued, pointing an

accusing finger. "Not after all the trouble you've been causing me. Asking questions at Primrose Green. Sticking your nose where it doesn't belong. Framingham is a friend of mine and I know he would agree."

He wasn't a particularly large man, but there was no mistaking the menace in his tone.

Gaining control of her growing sense of alarm, Sophia imposed a calm she did not feel over herself before she spoke. "Hello, Mr. Ryder," she said, offering her hand. "I don't believe we've been introduced. Though it would appear that you already know who I am."

"Indeed I do, Miss Hastings," Ryder said with a scowl, ignoring her proffered hand. "You're the busybody who doesn't know how to mind her own business."

As he spoke, he stepped closer, forcing Sophia to crowd back against the wall to get away from him. She was grateful she had her walking stick with her, but she was unsure of whether she'd be able to wield it with enough force to do more than stun him. Still, she couldn't let him get away with his threats.

"Forgery is the business of every artist who cares about the integrity of their work. Surely you can see why I would wish to investigate the possibility of such a thing happening here in my own village. You should be interested too, Mr. Ryder," Sophia said calmly. Though her stomach was clenched with anxiety, she maintained a façade of calm.

"I don't know what that's got to do with me," he asked crossly. " And you've got some nerve to call yourself an artist. From what I've heard, you're no more than a provocateur with a paintbrush and a desire to stir up trouble. What I paint is what people wish to buy, to display in their homes, to look at every day and appreciate. What you paint is obscene and no decent person would wish to look at it in an exhibition much less put it in a place of prominence in their home. People like you disgust me."

"You mean artists with original ideas who attempt to provoke thought in their viewers?"

Sophia knew as soon as she said the words that it was unwise to needle the man, and the flare of genuine rage in his eyes made her cringe backward, though there was nowhere for her to go. She watched in horrified slow motion as his clenched fist rose as if he would strike her. She lifted her walking stick and was about to raise it to block the blow, when she saw someone tackle the artist from behind.

Surprised, she lowered her stick and watched as Ben, his face a mask of barely leashed anger, tussled with Ryder, finally managing to pin the other man's hands behind his back.

"Even a boy in the schoolroom, Ryder, knows that a gentleman does not raise his hand against a lady," Ben said through his teeth as he easily held the scowling artist. "I believe you owe Miss Hastings an apology." Ryder gave them both a mulish glare. "Fine," he said. "My apologies, Miss Hastings."

She waited for him to go on, but it appeared that those were the only words of amends he was prepared to make. Even so, Ben let the other man go.

"You should both learn to mind your own business," Ryder said flatly. "This is something that could prove dangerous to both of you. And if you know what's good for you, Miss Hastings, you'll choose not to show your work in the exhibition. Morgan is a powerful man and what he says in the town goes. You'd do well to remember that."

Ben had moved to her side and they watched as Ryder strode away and out the front door of the gallery.

Once he was gone, Sophia felt herself begin to tremble, and with a low curse, Ben pulled her against him and wrapped his arms around her. She buried her face in his shoulder and let him hold her. Taking strength from his nearness and sheer physical presence. They were blocked from view through the window and from the other part of the shop by a large floor-to-ceiling piece that was propped against a pillar.

"I could have killed him with my bare hands when I saw him looming over you," he said into her hair, holding her tightly against him. "I don't think I've ever been that fiercely angry in my entire life."

"Thank goodness you happened by." She had been prepared to use her walking stick against Ryder, but it would have required her to put her full weight on both ankles. And there was no guarantee the injured one would hold up to such stress without the assistance of her cane. "He was prepared to strike me. I could see it in his face. His stance."

Rather than respond, Ben made a low noise that was almost a growl. And without a word he bent his head to hers and took her mouth with a kiss as much a claiming as a caress.

Ben had been telling the truth when he told Sophia he'd never felt such rage.

Coming on the heels of Mrs. Debenham's revelation about the way Morgan had treated her—and knowing that Morgan was the artist's patron—the sight of Sophia in range of Ryder's raised fist had filled him with a primitive desire to hurt the other man. Not to simply stop him from harming Sophia. But to lift him bodily and beat him with his bare fists.

It was a new, and somewhat disturbing bit of self-discovery, and if Sophia hadn't been there to witness the whole thing, he might not have been able to control himself. He wanted to believe his conscience would have been enough to pull him back from the edge, but the truth was that seeing Sophia in peril had flipped some sort of switch within him. And whether it was instinct or some other force, it had been as strong as any he'd ever felt.

And just as instinctive was the need to pull her into his arms. To give comfort, true, but also to prove to them both that this connection between them, new as it may be, was real, and though she might not know it yet, she was his.

At first his kiss was firm, a sort of claiming, and Sophia kissed him back with just as much emotion. But soon the softness of her lips against his and the feel of her curves pressed against him made him gentle the caress. He stroked his tongue over the seam of her lips, asking for entry and when she opened beneath him like a flower, he took the invitation. Her mouth was hot and wet and he bit back a groan when her tongue met his. This was what he'd needed, he realized. Holding her, feeling her life force pressed against him, proving to him in the most physical way that she was safe and alive and his.

They stood together for several long moments, lost in each other. So, it was a surprise when a shout sounded from somewhere beyond them.

"Oh God! No!"

Ben and Sophia pulled away from one another and turned as one toward the direction from which the outburst had come. Sophie started forward, heading further into the shop, and to the source of the noise.

But Ben put a staying hand on her. "You'd better let me go first. We don't know what's going on back there. And with the threats Ryder made and the talk of illegality, it might be dangerous."

Sophia looked as if she wanted to argue, her blue eyes narrow with impatience. But she must have seen the practicality of his words, for she allowed him to step in front of her and lead the way toward the door then into the storage area in the rear of the gallery.

The door itself was ajar, and Ben indicated with a finger to his lips that Sophia should remain quiet while he stepped inside.

She gave a nod and he pressed the door open fully and saw that the storage area was actually being used for that purpose. Stacked against the walls were paintings of all sizes and types; some were framed, some were not, and some appeared to be unfinished. There were also easels, and various other stands for displaying works of art, mostly paintings, but there were some that seemed better suited for sculpture and pottery. It was not particularly tidy, but there seemed to be nothing out of the ordinary for such a storage room.

With one exception.

Just beyond the table inside the door, where it was obvious someone had been working on a framing project, the pieces of an ornate gilded frame lay beside a canvas face down on the surface. And just beyond that, stood Ryder, his head down, staring at the scene on the floor before him.

There was no question in Ben's mind that Framingham—for it was he whose battered body lay bleeding on the floor of his own shop—was dead. No one could lose the amount of blood pooled on the floor beneath him and live.

"Ryder," Ben said, stepping forward, "what happened?"

The other man, who so lately had looked at both Ben and Sophia with undisguised dislike, now seemed relieved to see them. "I don't know. He was like this when I came back here."

Then he seemed to realize that they might not have the most flattering interpretation of his presence there. He raised his hands in a gesture of innocence. "You saw me only minutes ago. He's obviously been bleeding for an hour or more. I didn't do this."

As much as he'd have liked to see the man punished for

what he'd done to Sophia, Ben was forced to admit that Ryder was correct. The timing made the possibility highly unlikely.

"We know," he said with a nod. Then, he made his way over to the body of Framingham, and wordlessly knelt beside him. He said a silent prayer that the man's death had been swift and that he'd not felt too much pain, and placing his hand on the dead man's forehead, he said the words that would entrust his soul into the hands of his Creator. "Through the merits of Jesus Christ thine only son our Lord. Amen."

Ryder and Sophia, who had stepped forward to stand beside him, stood watching as Ben closed the dead man's eyes and rose to his feet. "We'll need to alert the authorities," he said to Ryder, who nodded, his face pale as he looked everywhere but at the corpse between them.

"I'll go," he said, obviously eager to get out of the close room.

He was gone before either Ben or Sophia could respond.

Stepping around the body, Ben put an arm around Sophia and gently led her back toward the door and back into the gallery proper. "You shouldn't have come in here," he said. "You didn't need to see that."

But Sophia, though she let him lead her away, wasn't so ready to agree. "Why should you have to see it while I'm sheltered?" she asked, slipping her arm through his. "It must be just as upsetting for you as it is for me."

He couldn't help but smile at her oh-so-rational response. "It's not that it doesn't upset me," he reasoned, "it's that you don't need that scene in your mind. I've seen death. It's one of the most difficult parts of my calling, but a necessary one. And an inevitable part of life."

"But this," he continued, turning to face her, feeling more exhausted than he'd ever been. "This is not inevitable. It's the worst part of what one human being can do to another. And I should have protected you from it."

When she slipped her arms around him it was to offer comfort. And selfishly he took it. He'd seen death before, but what had been done to Framingham was a level of savagery that left him shaken.

"Sophia?" called a female voice from the front of the room. "Are you still here?"

Reluctantly, he pulled away from her and they walked back toward the door, where they found not only Gemma but Ivy and Daphne hovering just inside the entrance.

"Ah," Ivy said with a twinkle in her eyes. "Good afternoon, Vicar. I might have guessed it was you who waylaid Miss Hastings."

But something about both his and Sophia's expressions must have alerted her to the fact that something was very wrong.

"Oh no," she said, her own face turning from teasing to serious. "What's happened?"

"Are you well?" Gemma asked, stepping forward, gazing at her sister as if she could divine the source of Sophia's angst through sheer will. "Did something happen? Did someone harm you?"

Ben would have responded, but Sophia pulled away from him and gave her sister a little hug. "I'm fine," she said, before turning to address the others who were watching with varying degrees of concern. "There's been a . . . that is to say, Mr. Framingham is . . ."

"Framingham has been murdered," Ben cut in, thinking it best to tell the truth of the matter. "We don't know who did it, but it seems that he must have been dead when Sophia first entered the shop. Ryder has gone to alert the authorities. The magistrate, I suppose." It was too late for the doctor to do much good.

"Dear God," Ivy put a hand to her chest. "Another?"

It had only been a few weeks after Ben's arrival in the area that a man had been found murdered in the library at Beauchamp House. These ladies were not entirely unfamiliar with violent death, much as he wished Sophia had been spared this particular encounter.

"Statistically," Daphne said, sounding at once authoritative and worried, "it seems highly unusual that three people so far removed from the criminal underworld should be murdered within the same general area."

"Indeed," Sophia said with a nod to her friend. Ben saw that she gave the other woman a squeeze on the arm. "It is unusual, I think. Right now, though, I think we should probably leave so that when the doctor and the magistrate get here we won't be underfoot."

"Squire Northman will wish to speak to you," Gemma reminded her. They were well acquainted with Northman from his investigation of the previous deaths they'd been connected to.

"Then he can do so at a later time," Ben said firmly. "Let me see you to your carriage. At least I hope you came by carriage." He gave a speaking look in the direction of Sophia's injured ankle. She was leaning heavily on the walking stick at this point and it was no doubt paining her.

"Yes, we brought the carriage," she said wearily. "And I've never been so grateful for it."

The others preceded them from the shop, and Ben took the moment of privacy to squeeze her hand. "I'll come speak to you as soon as I learn anything. Though I may be tied up with Framingham's family for a while this evening. No doubt this will be a surprise to his wife and children. And I need to ensure that they've got sufficient support."

She turned and touched his cheek with her gloved hand. It was no more than that, but he felt it like a more intimate caress. "Take care of yourself," she said softly. "And watch Ryder. He was stunned by the sight of Framingham, but he's not entirely uninvolved, I think."

"Yes, ma'am," he said with a grin. Then, when they'd reached the place where the landau was waiting, he lifted her by the waist and tucked her into the empty seat beside Gemma.

"Keep an eye on her for me, ladies," he said with a tip of his hat.

Sophia looked surprised, but not particularly displeased by his admonition.

And as he watched the coachman flicked the horses with the whip and they drove away.

Chapter 15

After dinner that night, still rattled from the murder of Mr. Framingham and not wanting to be alone, Sophia asked the other ladies to join her for tea in her studio. She wasn't sure why, but she felt as if art itself were under attack. Especially after Thomas Ryder's harsh words about her work, and seeing poor Framingham dead among the paintings and canvases of his workroom. Someone—maybe Ryder, and definitely others—was cheapening the heart and soul of what made art valuable by creating fakes. And though she was certainly in no way comparable to the great artists whose work had been forged, it chilled her to think of a fellow artist carefully stealing every brushstroke, every carefully plotted decision about composition simply to make a profit.

"I don't think I've been up here since you finished your pieces for the exhibition," Ivy said as she and Daphne followed Sophia and Gemma into the studio.

The natural light from the windows and skylights was absent now that the sun had gone down, and the room was somehow cozier in the glow of lamplight. Even so, it was bright enough for Ivy to spot the fallen woman painting from the doorway and she and Daphne made a beeline for it.

"Oh, Sophia," the marchioness said with wonder and sadness in her voice, "it's magnificent."

Sophia never knew how to accept compliments about her work. She liked it, obviously, but there was also a sort of awkwardness that came from confronting the fact that another person—sometimes a stranger, though in this case a friend—was looking at something that had come directly from her soul. It was rather like having one's diary read aloud in a crowded room.

Before she could respond, Ivy continued. "It's heart-wrenching. The contrast between the gaiety of the theatregoers and the utter sadness of the dead woman just steps away. Have you seen something like this? How did you decide to paint it?"

They moved to settle around the low table in the corner where the servants had laid the tea service and a plate of cakes. Sophia's maid had wrapped her ankle in the way the doctor had showed her and because it had swollen again in the wake of the day's activity, she had it propped on an ottoman.

"It was a small article in the *Times*," she answered once they each had a cup and saucer in hand. "Just a paragraph, really, about a woman found dead near the Royal Opera House. No details. Other than to say that she had died of exposure. Something about the juxtaposition of the dead woman and the site of so many of polite society's evening entertainments struck me as particularly shattering. And my imagination did the rest."

"Have you ever been to the Royal Opera House?" Daphne asked, brow furrowed. "I went once during my first season. This is a remarkably accurate depiction." She sounded as if she suspected Sophia of some sort of witchcraft. "Though, there was no dead woman, fallen or otherwise, in that area. At least not that I saw."

Sophia hid a smile. Daphne could be a bit literal at times.

"Our Aunt Dahlia took us to London many times over the years," Gemma said. "Including the Royal Opera House."

"During the day it was galleries and museums and parks," Sophia said with a smile of remembrance, "but in the evenings she took us to the opera, and plays, and fed our minds with great performances."

"She sounds as if she would have got along well with Lady Celeste," Ivy said with a grin. "I wonder if they ever met."

It was something Sophia had thought about before. Her aunt and Celeste had been of an age, and could have attended some of the same entertainments in London when they were young. And they certainly seemed to have similar leanings toward intellectualism and the arts. Still, she had no way of knowing. There had been no mention of her in Celeste's diaries which they'd had to read in order to find out who had killed her.

"I shall write to her and ask," she said aloud, " And until I hear back, I propose we behave as if they did."

She raised her teacup in a toast. "To Dahlia and Celeste— the two ladies who made me what I am today!"

"And the same for me," Gemma said, raising her own cup. Then, Ivy and Daphne followed suit and they drank to the mentors.

"Speaking of Celeste," Ivy said when they'd finished, "I wonder what she would have made of this forgery business. I know what she would have said regarding Morgan and his ridiculous attempts to stop you from showing your work, Sophia. But as a painter herself, she must have had opinions about forgery and schemes like the one Lord Frederick alerted his brother to. I know there have been instances in the world of historical artifacts when people have attempted to pass off fakes as original fragments of Sappho, for instance. It makes me ill."

It was something Sophia had thought about, especially given that this particular scheme was taking place in the very village where Celeste had lived. The Home Office had only timed the forgeries coming out of Little Seaford to a year ago—several months before the heiresses had arrived at Beauchamp House, and only weeks before Celeste's death. Though it was possible their benefactor had known something was going on, it was far more likely she was too sick to know or care.

"I feel sure she would have had objections," Sophia agreed. "But I'm not sure the timing is right. Though I suppose it is possible the scheme began before the authorities realized it was going on. It seems to have run too smoothly to be a new endeavor."

"And from what you and Benedick overheard," Gemma reminded her, "they don't seem to be loyal to whichever artist they use to create the forgeries. It's possible there was someone before this latest one."

Which reminded Sophia of something. "But what happened to Mr. Framingham doesn't make sense given what we heard. It was clear from the conversation that they would be eliminating an *artist*. Not an art dealer. Why was Framingham killed and not Ryder—if he is the one who is painting the forgeries?"

In the chaos of the afternoon's events, the conversation about the artist had slipped her mind. But now it was like a sore tooth she couldn't stop poking at.

"I know we're talking about the artist, but I just realized about Framingham," she continued. "Of course we don't know that he was involved in the scheme at all. It's purely conjecture on our part. But it seems too coincidental that a forgery scheme and the murder of an art dealer would happen in the same village."

"Perhaps Framingham objected to the plan to eliminate the artist?" Daphne, who had been unusually quiet, seemed to be thinking seriously about the matter. "If, as you say, Ryder was there to see him, that means they had some sort of relationship. Perhaps he didn't wish to see Ryder killed or exiled or dealt whatever punishment the men you overheard meant to inflict."

For someone who didn't generally wish to deal in hypotheticals, it was a logical enough explanation for why Framingham might have been killed.

"I believe you might be correct, Daphne," Sophia said with a nod. "And it would explain why Ryder was so overset about the murder. Obviously anyone would be chilled to find a body, but his reaction seemed outsized if the two men were merely acquaintances. Still, we don't know for sure that Ryder is the artist in question. He's unpleasant, to be sure, but he could simply be what he seems: Morgan's protégé. Whatever the case, he and Framingham were connected in some way we don't yet know about, I'm sure of it."

They were silent for a moment as they contemplated the complicated puzzle.

"I still cannot help but think Celeste must have known something," Gemma said, finally. "She had her eye on everything that was happening in this area. She had friends all over the county. The art community among them."

"Unless she left some sort of trail," Sophia said with a shake of her head, "as she did with the quests she left for Ivy and Daphne, I don't see how we'll ever know."

"You're sure there was no mention of it in your letter from her?" Ivy asked. Her own request from Celeste to search for the person who killed her had come via a letter she'd left to be given to her on her arrival at Beauchamp House.

"Or perhaps in the papers you received on your inheritance?"

Daphne prodded. Celeste had given Daphne the clues she needed to find a long lost treasure in the letter she received with the news of her being chosen as an heiress.

"No," Sophia assured them. "Nothing like that. Believe me, as soon as I realized how your missives from her contained clues to the mysteries she wished you to solve, I scoured my own letters like mad. Both Gemma and I did. But we found nothing."

"And she gave no letters to Serena to give to you either." Daphne's words were a statement, not a question.

But Ivy was not ready to give up. "With Daphne's puzzle," she said thoughtfully, "she used ciphers hidden within the text of the letter to speak to her. What if she did something similar with you, Sophia?"

"I'm not sure I know what you mean." Sophia was beginning to get a headache. Surely if Celeste had meant to leave her some quest she'd have been straightforward with it as she had done with Ivy and Daphne. She had a feeling they were looking for clues where none existed.

"What if she left your clues in the form of a painting? Or paintings?"

The final clue to help Daphne in her search for a long lost Scottish treasure had been hidden in plain sight in a painting. So, the idea wasn't entirely without merit. "Then where is the painting? There are several stored in one of the cabinets in the corner, but they weren't in any place of prominence when we arrived. I assumed they were simply works that Celeste had chosen not to display in the house. Some lesser known but still valuable pieces by continental artists."

Ivy tilted her head. "Don't large houses usually store things like that in the attics? I know when we were at Kerr House, the housekeeper told me that they rotate pieces on display based on family preference, and in some cases the season. But they're all stored in the attics."

Sophia hadn't actually thought about the paintings in the cabinet since she'd found them on her arrival. Since she shared ownership of the house, she hadn't felt comfortable removing the works of art already on display throughout the rooms, and there was enough storage space already in the studio that she didn't need that particular cabinet.

"It wouldn't hurt to take a look," she said with a shrug. Then, feeling sheepish, she asked, "Could one of you bring them over here? I dislike admitting it, but I cannot contemplate walking even as far as it takes to get to the cabinet."

Gemma gave her a look while Daphne and Ivy went to retrieve the paintings. "I knew you were overdoing it today." Sophia knew her sister's disapproving look all too well.

Then, in a lower voice so the others wouldn't hear her, Gemma continued, "No one will think less of you if you give yourself time to heal, Sophia. You are not Mama. And no one will ever mistake you for her."

At the mention of their mother, who had wielded her imaginary illnesses and time in the sickbed with the precision of a sharpened sword, Sophia felt breathless for a moment. Had she been doing that? Pressing on because she couldn't stand the idea of being assumed to be an exaggerator? It was possible, she acknowledged. Grateful to her sister for pointing it out, she squeezed her hand. "You may be right. I do have a tendency to abhor the sick room because of her. I promise to rest my ankle tomorrow."

Then Ivy and Daphne arrived carrying armloads of canvases which they propped against the ottoman at Sophia's feet.

"This is all of them," Ivy said, slightly breathless from her exertion. "I thought there would be more."

"No," Sophia said, feeling a bit foolish for not realizing

the possible significance of the cabinet before now. "I should have known they were special since there weren't that many of them. But I was so thrilled that this studio was to be mine I barely gave them a glance before I shut the cabinet and went about my business."

She picked up the first one in the stack, using both hands because of its size and the heaviness of its gilt frame.

It was clearly a Rubens. It bore all the hallmarks of the Flemish artist's work. A female nude, whose soft, lush body was the central focus of the painting, was seated at a fountain, hunched over to hide her nakedness. But it was her fearful expression as she cringed from the two men crowding into her that told the tale. She knew well how this woman felt—it was the same terror she'd felt that afternoon when Ryder threatened her.

This was, Sophia realized, a painting of the story from the book of Daniel about Susannah, an innocent wife who is spied upon while bathing by two nefarious men who then threaten to falsely say she's been meeting her lover if she doesn't agree to let them have their way with her. She refuses, the men accuse her publicly of having a lover and she is sentenced to death. At the last moment, the young man Daniel appears and demands the men be questioned, and when their stories don't add up, Susannah is declared innocent and freed and the men who slandered her are put to death.

It was a story that always angered Sophia when she thought of just how precarious a woman's virtue could be when men took it into their minds to bring them down. True, Susannah was proved innocent, but she shouldn't have needed to be.

More important than the story depicted in the painting at the moment, however, Sophia realized was the significance of the painting itself.

She knew it was Rubens. It had to be. But it was also, if she recalled correctly, famously missing. There were several versions of *Susannah and the Elders* that were said to have come from either Rubens or his studio. But this particular version was only known because of an engraving of it by another man. The painting itself had been presumed missing for hundreds of years. It certainly wasn't known by the art world to be hidden in a cupboard in Lady Celeste Beauchamp's studio cabinet.

"What is it, Sophia?" Gemma asked, her eyes worried. Clearly Sophia had been quiet for too long.

Instead of answering her, Sophia flipped quickly through the other works leaning against the ottoman.

What she saw made her heart race. She wasn't sure what it meant, but she knew what she saw with her own eyes.

"These are all forgeries," she said, a sense of unreality washing over her. "They are all forgeries of paintings that are known to be missing or lost."

Chapter 16

Ben was bone tired when he left the Framingham house, where he'd spent the better part of the afternoon consoling the grieving wife and children of the murdered man.

It was never easy to console a family who had lost a loved one unexpectedly, but this was different from his experience thus far as a minister. He'd never before had to explain to a wife that her husband had died not by an accident or illness, but by another man's hand. He would never forget as long as he lived the sound of Lucy Framingham's shriek when he informed her that her husband was dead. And then, again when she learned it was murder. He'd been a bit more circumspect with the children, who were too young to understand much beyond the fact that their father had gone to heaven. But their sadness and puzzlement had been, in its way, as affecting as their mother's reaction.

Fortunately, Mrs. Framingham's sister and her husband lived in Little Seaford, and were able to come take control of things in the aftermath of the master of the house's death, and he was able to leave secure in the knowledge that he'd done what he could for them.

And always in the back of his mind as he interacted with the dead man's family was the note he'd received that morning when he and Cam had returned to the vicarage from Beauchamp House.

It was dark as he took the reins of his horse from the stable boy he'd paid to hold him, and almost without intending it, he found himself steering Gabriel toward Beauchamp House. Even if it was just for a moment, he needed to see Sophia before he would be able to sleep tonight. And after witnessing the agony the Framingham family was enduring, he needed to assure himself that she was safe and secure and away from whatever ugliness was lurking in Little Seaford.

Despite the late hour, a groom was at the ready to take Gabriel's reins. Ben was composing his explanation to Greaves for the late call, but was surprised when the butler opened the door before he even reached the landing.

"Lord Benedick," the butler said, bowing. "Is something amiss? Has something happened?"

Belatedly, Ben realized that the household hadn't exactly been a stranger to death and destruction over the last year.

"I apologize for alarming you, Mr. Greaves," he said with genuine regret. "As far as I know, the duke and Lord Kerr are in good health. I am here to see Miss Hastings, I'm afraid."

But the butler's expression did not brighten. "Something has happened to her parents. I'll have both Miss Hastings and Miss Gemma come downstairs and see you in the drawing room."

Dash it, he was making a mull of this. "No, no, nothing like that, Greaves."

Ben rubbed a hand over his face as the butler stared at him.

"I simply wished to assure myself that Miss Hastings is well. That's all. I realize it's unusual, and possibly inappropriate, but you must have heard about what happened in the village today . . ."

He let his voice trial off, hoping the man would see his exhaustion and take pity on him.

To his relief, Greaves' eyes shone with understanding. And something else Ben wasn't able to interpret. "Of course, my lord. Of course. The ladies are in Miss Hastings' art studio at present and I'm sure they will be happy to see you."

At the news Sophia was surrounded by her sister and friends, he almost demurred and left. The prospect of greeting a room full of inquisitive ladies was more than he was ready to face. But nor was he prepared to leave without at the very least laying eyes on Sophia.

So it was that he found himself following the aging butler upstairs to the attic art studio. After Greaves knocked briskly, he stepped inside and announced Ben, and Ben was relieved to see that only Sophia was there. She was on the settee where she'd been when he and Freddie visited her before. Only this time instead of her own paintings she had a stack of unfamiliar ones arrayed on the floor and ottoman next to her.

"Ben," she said, her voice revealing her surprise and a husky note that indicated she might have been napping. "I know you said you'd come speak to me, but I thought you'd been too involved with the magistrate or Mrs. Framingham."

With the silence and discretion that were the hallmarks of a good servant, Greaves slipped out of the room, shutting the door behind him.

Unable to stop himself, Ben gathered her into his arms, and somehow ended up with Sophia in his lap, his face buried in her neck

"I hope this is all right," he said, leaning his cheek against her bosom. "I just . . . I needed you."

But Sophia didn't protest. She simply held him. And stroked her hand over his back. Offering the comfort he so desperately needed.

"Was it very bad?" she asked softly. "You don't have to tell me. I know it was."

He lifted his head and leaned back against the settee. "I've ministered to the grieving before. Many times. It's never easy, but nor is it entirely without some sort of optimism. Even if it's just that their loved one is no longer suffering. Or will be with God. But I've never had to tell a woman her husband has been murdered."

"I'm so sorry," Sophia said, now leaning her head on his chest. "You're a good man. To do this job that not everyone would be able to do."

He laughed at that. He couldn't help it. "It was the church or the army. And I have no stomach for war. I may have chosen the church because I had some idea that I liked helping people. But it's a bit different in practice than it was in my imagination. I did go with my mother to visit the tenants on my father's estate. But for the most part, they welcomed us. That's not always the case with the vicar. Nor is it as easy as bringing a basket of food and going on my way."

"But that's why it's so admirable," Sophia said, lifting up so that she could look him in the eye. "You know how difficult it is. How thankless it can be. And you do it anyway. You look after the members of your parish—both those who attend services and those who don't—and you do it without seeking thanks or accolades. You do it because it's your job. But also because it's the right thing to do."

He saw the admiration in her eyes, and shook his head. "Don't make a saint of me, Sophia. I'm a man. Nothing more. I do the job I've been called to do. But I am not without flaws. Without sin."

At that she gave a saucy smile, and he was suddenly reminded of the impropriety of their pose. And how good it felt to have her soft curves pressed up against him.

"I never said you were a saint, vicar," she said softly. "In fact, I'm rather hoping you aren't. Because I would like it very much if you kissed me again."

"Would you, indeed?" His gaze went to her lips, pink and full and inviting. He'd have to be a bloody saint to ignore that invitation.

"I would," she said, and before he could make the decision himself, she leaned in and kissed him, just a meeting of mouths. But enough to give him a taste of what was to come. Pulling back just a fraction, she said against his lips, "But I'm happy to do it for you."

His exhaustion, which had so lately hung upon him like a pall, disappeared at the taste of her mouth on his. Curious, and eager to see what she'd do, he let her explore. Savored every nibble of her teeth on his lower lip, then when her tongue dipped into the seam of his lips and prodded for entrance, felt the caress echoed in his groin. Unable to hold back, he opened to her questing mouth and took the lead, lifting his hand to hold her head to his, taking the kiss from an exploration to something more carnal. They molded themselves together, as if any breath of air between their bodies was the difference between life and death. And Ben felt his hunger for her rising, as he cupped her generous breast in his hand, and felt her gasp at the caress.

He would have liked nothing more than to take her here, now, and give them both the release they so desperately needed. He was certain it would be good, and he was sure now—whether Sophia knew it or not—that she was the woman he wanted for his wife. But something about the moment, perhaps that little gasp when he stroked his thumb over the peak of her breast, brought him back to reality. And unfortunately, reality meant that they had to stop.

Reluctantly, with a strength he had doubted he had within himself, he pulled his head back and said her name.

"Sophia." Deprived of his mouth, she'd simply moved on to his neck. "Sophia, stop."

He felt the moment she heard the note of firmness in his voice. She stilled, and pulled back a little to look at him.

"We have to stop," he said, breathing hard even as the words left him. "We must stop now or I won't be able to."

Ben watched as her eyes went from drowsy with passion to a level of alertness that was admirable given the situation.

Wordlessly, she climbed off of him, and sat a few inches away from him. She spent a few seconds smoothing the skirts of her deep blue gown, though they hadn't really gotten to the point where it was an issue.

"I'm sorry," he said, his voice sounding rough to his own ears.

"If you apologize for despoiling me or some other such nonsense, Lord Benedick Lisle," she said in a tone of warning, "I don't know what I'll do. But you won't like it."

He laughed a little at her fierceness, and the hint of frustration in her voice that echoed his own. "I wouldn't dream of it, my dear." He lifted her hand and kissed the center of her palm. "I am sorry we had to stop, but I am not sorry for what just happened."

She was silent for a moment, before she turned to look at him. As if to gauge the truth of his words. What she saw must have satisfied her because she gave a nod of agreement. "Good. Because I'm not sorry for what happened either."

"Then we are in agreement," he said with a smile.

Not quite ready to leave yet, but needing something to spark a change in subject, his eye fell on the paintings that had been strewn around her when he came in. "What are all these?" he asked, indicating with a jerk of his head he meant the artwork. "That doesn't look like one of yours."

At his words, Sophia let out a gasp. "Oh! I almost forgot. Ben, I think these are some of the forgeries. We found them in the cabinet here in the studio. I believe Lady Celeste was purchasing them to keep them off the market."

For the second time that evening, his fatigue evaporated. "Tell me everything."

Chapter 17

"I'm happy to come with you, my dear," Ivy told Sophia the next morning as they finished up breakfast.

Greaves had just informed the assembled ladies of the house that Squire Northman, the magistrate for this county, had arrived to question Sophia about the murder of Mr. Framingham.

Not long after she told Ben about the cache of forged paintings they'd found in the studio, he'd taken his leave with the promise to come back this morning. He hadn't yet arrived, however.

Even so, Sophia was prepared to answer the man's questions as thoroughly as she could. The memory of the dead man was still fresh in her mind, and she'd even awoken twice in the night in a cold sweat thanks to it.

"I believe I can manage," she told Ivy with a smile. "Though I appreciate the offer. I know both you and Daphne have had your own moments with the Squire."

"I was a suspect at one point," Daphne pointed out, as she buttered her toast. "Northman is not the most pleasant of men, but he is persuadable when the truth is there to lay out before him. I believe he is a bit frightened of Maitland, though. It's a shame he isn't here to go into the interview with you. He was most useful during mine."

Sophia rather thought Maitland had been so fierce with Northman because he was in love with Daphne, but she didn't point that out to her friend.

Instead, she rose, with the aid of her walking stick. "I'm sure it will be routine. I barely knew the man and from all appearances he was already dead while I was in the gallery. So, there's nothing to be concerned about."

She wasn't sure if she was reassuring her friends or herself.

Just as she neared the door of the breakfast room, Gemma came barreling up. "I overslept," she said, slightly breathless and looking as if she'd dressed hastily. It was unusual for the always punctual Gemma to be late for anything. "I haven't missed breakfast, have I?"

"You haven't," Sophia said, hiding her smile at her sister's unusual state. "But I'm off to meet with the magistrate. I'll see you later in the morning."

At the mention of Northman, Gemma's eyes snapped to attention. "Do you wish me to go with you?"

Sophia gave a lusty sigh. "Why is it that everyone thinks I need a keeper with me so that I might answer a few questions from the magistrate? I'm hardly infirm or lacking intellect."

"Of course you aren't, dearest," said Gemma putting a hand on her arm. "But you were overset last night. And the Squire has a tendency to be a bit unscrupulous when he asks his questions. You're the most, well, tender of us. I simply don't wish him to cause you discomfort."

Did they really see her that way? Sophia wondered. It was true perhaps that of the four heiresses she was the most soft-hearted. But she wasn't one to weep at the drop of a hat, or to become tearful at the least provocation. She saw herself as rather practical and unemotional. It was rather jarring to think that her sister and friends saw her any differently.

She was saved from further speculation on the matter by the arrival of Greaves followed by Ben, who despite the late hour of his departure the evening before looked well rested and handsome in his form-fitting trousers and pristine cravat.

"Lord Benedick has arrived, Miss Hastings," said Greaves rather needlessly, given that Sophia could see the man with her own eyes.

"Yes, thank you, Greaves," she told the butler nevertheless. One thing she could count on, at the very least, was Greaves' scrupulous attention to protocol.

"I believe Squire Northman is here to question you?" Ben asked, only a fleeting intensity in his gaze indicating that he remembered as vividly as Sophia did their encounter in the studio the evening before. But the next instance he was all politeness and manners. "May I sit in with you? It will perhaps be easier for him to question us both at the same time. And I can offer you some support."

Sophia purposely ignored the look of smugness on her sister's face, then let Ben take her arm.

In a low voice as they made their way to the drawing room, he asked, "Are you well this morning? Yesterday was quite exhausting and I know your ankle was paining you last night."

Sophia made a noise of impatience. "I wish everyone would stop treating me as if I am made of cotton floss. I am perfectly capable of enduring a trying day. And while my injury still aches a bit, it is nothing I cannot handle."

Her voice rose as she spoke, and to her embarrassment she realized she'd nearly been shouting by the end.

If she was afraid he'd be offended, however, she was mistaken.

Ben laughed and pulled her arm closer to him. "I can see I'll need to have more respect for your strong will, Sophia. I forgot for a moment that you were unlike any other lady of my acquaintance. Forgive me?"

The apology was said so sweetly she couldn't reject it without seeming churlish. "Yes, I forgive you," she said crossly. "And I suppose I'm sorry for ripping up at you. It's just that everyone seems to think I'm some simpering artist who wears her every emotion on her sleeve."

"I don't think that," he said sincerely. "And I daresay your sister and your friends don't think that either. They're just concerned for you after yesterday's ordeal. And they wish to help you. It's what we do for the people we love."

She supposed he was right. Then, realizing what he'd said, she asked, with a sideways look, "Am I unlike the other ladies of your acquaintance?"

"Most certainly," he said without hesitation. Then, in a lower voice, he added, "I don't wish to kiss them until they make the little greedy noises you made last night."

At the reminder of her response to him the night before, and his to her, Sophia felt her entire body suffuse with heat.

Then, as luck would have it, they were at the door to the drawing room.

He gave her a knowing grin, the wretch, before opening the door and ushering her inside.

Squire Northman, a gruff, no-nonsense leader of the local gentry, at whose home Sophia and the other heiresses had dined on a number of occasions, was today in his magistrate guise. That is to say, he was his usual self only more intimidating. He'd been accompanied by his secretary, who, Sophia knew from past experience, took notes during these interviews.

"It's about time, Miss Hastings," he said without preamble as Sophia, followed by Ben, entered the room. "I've been cooling my heels for a quarter of an hour or more. I know you ladies take your time dressing, but this is serious business."

'Good morning to you, too, Mr. Northman," Sophia

said without referring to his complaint. "I hope you won't mind, but I've a twisted ankle and will need to sit for this interview."

It was both a way of putting him in the position of behaving like a gentleman rather than a lawman, and also a way for her to get off her ankle, which had begun to throb.

Looking somewhat chastened, the older man nodded. "I didn't mean to be so harsh. M'wife tells me I'm rag-mannered at times. Please sit, Miss Hastings."

As she took a seat in the large wingback chair near the window overlooking the garden, the magistrate turned to Ben, who had been silent thus far.

"Vicar," Northman said with a slight bow. "I'm pleased to see you're here as well. I can question you both about this business and maybe get to the bottom of things."

To Sophia he said as he began to pace before the fire, "I don't mind telling you, Miss Hastings, that I believe there must be something in the water at Beauchamp House, for now it's three of you involved in this sort of thing. I don't hold with ladies getting mixed up in murder. It would be a sight better if the four of you would keep yourselves to yourselves and stay at home with your needlework."

There was so much to object to in the statement, Sophia wasn't even sure where to begin. She was saved from doing so by Ben, who'd come to stand beside her chair, his hand warm on her shoulder.

"Perhaps you should get to the questions about Framingham rather than giving commentary on the behavior of the Beauchamp House heiresses, Squire," he said with a raised brow. "We all wish to see whoever killed the man caught and punished, do we not?"

Looking frustrated, but resigned, the magistrate gave a

slight shrug, then turned to his secretary, who'd been silent throughout the proceedings so far. "Be sure to write all of this down. This is important business."

Not waiting for a response, he turned back to Sophia. "I believe the vicar told me last night, Miss Hastings, that you were in the gallery for some time before you heard the shouts of Mr. Ryder from the storage room?"

Sophia gave him the details of her visit to the gallery— minus the kissing once Ben appeared on the scene—and concluded with finding Ryder standing over the body of Framingham. When she was finished, the magistrate looked, if anything, more grave.

"And you heard nothing before Ryder came upon you alone? No shouts, no crashing around?" Northman asked, his bushy brows lowered with intensity.

She'd gone over the scene again and again in her mind last night, but she could recall no unusual noises or sounds coming from any part of the gallery. "Nothing, Mr. Northman. And if Mr. Ryder had been stabbing Mr. Framingham before he accosted me, then wouldn't he have been bloody?"

The magistrate looked taken aback that she'd mention something so graphic, but reluctantly nodded. "It's unlikely that the person who killed Framingham could have done so and not become . . . messy in the process."

"Do you remember if Ryder came through the front door as you did, Miss Hastings?" Ben asked, turning to look at her. "Is it possible he came from the direction of the storage room and the rear entrance of the gallery?"

Northman looked as if he would object to Ben usurping his duties as questioner, but seemed to think the question was a good one, because he indicated with a wave of his hand that she should answer.

"I can't be sure," Sophia answered truthfully. She'd spent at least an hour last night before finally falling asleep trying to remember the exact details leading up to the discovery of Framingham's body. "I don't recall hearing the front door, but I was also in a bit of a . . . a daze, I suppose you'd call it. I get that way sometimes when I'm engrossed in a painting. I'm still there, my physical presence is still there, but my mind is . . . elsewhere."

Northman gave a grunt, as if this was the sort of nonsense he'd expect from a lady artist.

But Ben gave her shoulder a squeeze. "It's that way with me and reading sometimes. My tutor used to say that he could have shot a pistol in the room and I'd not hear it."

"So you can't know for sure if Ryder was in the back, having words with Framingham before he came upon you, or if he breezed in from the street none the wiser?" Northman demanded. "I can't say as I'm surprised, since it seems to me that the fellow is a bit slippery."

Since Sophia's opinion of the other artist was not much better, she didn't argue. Though she did wonder if they should inform the magistrate about the forgeries. "Perhaps you know already since you're in contact with the authorities, Squire—" she began, only to be interrupted by Ben.

"—but Ryder is a protégé of Mr. Peter Morgan and both men had dealings with Framingham in relation to the upcoming art exhibition in the village," the vicar finished, his hand on her shoulder squeezing to indicate she should go along. "You should perhaps speak with Mr. Morgan."

It was difficult not to gape at Ben as he spoke, but Sophia managed it.

Just.

Chapter 18

He wasn't sure why, but some instinct warned Ben that telling Northman about the forgery scheme would be risky.

It wasn't simply that they'd possibly discovered a connection between Sophia's benefactor and the fake art—though that was something they'd not been able to examine closely enough yet. Nor was it the fact that they were investigating the forgery scheme under the nose of Northman himself.

But both of these together added up to a compelling reason, so far as he could determine, to keep the information regarding the forgeries to themselves for the time being. He'd once heard his brother's friend the Earl of Mainwaring say that a good investigator had to trust his instincts. Well, if that was the case, then this was Ben trusting his.

Added to that was the fact that he'd paid a call on Morgan that morning to offer the man a strong, albeit somewhat restrained, warning against further intimidation where Mrs. Debenham was concerned. At first the man had attempted to excuse his behavior.

"You're a man of the world, vicar," Morgan had said with a joviality that made Ben wish fervently he didn't have a duty to eschew physical violence. "Mrs. Debenham is a sweet little thing. You can hardly blame me for being taken with her."

"As a matter of fact, Morgan," he'd said through clenched teeth, "I can blame you. Especially when in the face of the lady's refusal you threatened to ruin her reputation."

If he expected Morgan to respond with anger, he was soon disabused of the notion. "Of course I didn't threaten her. Is that what she said?"

Ben could hardly call the man a liar to his face without there being consequences. And as much as he'd like to put a bullet in him, vicars weren't precisely encouraged to go about dueling. No matter how justified the cause might be. Instead, he said calmly, "She did indeed say that. And I am inclined to believe her. Though, if you deny it, I have no choice but to accept that."

Morgan's eyes narrowed at that, but he didn't say anything in response.

"Of course," Ben continued, "if it were true, then I might be inclined to have a word with my father about the matter. He has a great deal of influence in the government, you understand. And if he were to take an interest in a local political race, like the one here, for example, well, his word in the right ear could make or break a candidacy."

At that the industrialist scowled, and he muttered an imprecation.

"I see I've made myself clear," Ben said with a tilt of his head. "I look forward to hearing from Mrs. Debenham that you've sent her a letter of apology. As well as a donation to the local widows and orphans fund in the name of her late husband."

"Now see here, vicar," Morgan spat out. "You can't make me . . ."

"Do you really wish to face the ire of the Duke of Pemberton, Mr. Morgan?" Ben asked blandly. "I can assure you, my father is many things, but a friend of those who intimidate helpless women, he is not."

The other man's lips tightened, and his eyes blazed with temper.

"Fine," he said tightly. "Now, if you've no more to say, I have work to do."

It had been a satisfying meeting for Ben, but here and now with Sophia and Northman, he was all too aware of the magistrate's friendship with the industrialist. Perhaps Northman had no idea that his friend was a boor and a bully.

But Ben thought that was unlikely. Men like Morgan were the sort who assumed everyone else thought the same way they did.

Aloud, he repeated his assertion that the magistrate should speak with Morgan.

"I know he's a friend of yours, Squire," he said, aware of Sophia's curiosity as if it were a palpable thing. "Morgan may be able to give you more information about both Ryder and Framingham. Perhaps the murder has something to do with the upcoming art exhibition."

He realized his mistake the moment the words left his mouth. And to his frustration, the opening he'd given Northman didn't pass the man unnoticed.

"I believe you are expected to have some paintings in this exhibition, Miss Hastings," the magistrate said, turning his gimlet eye on Sophia.

"Yes," she agreed, remaining poised. But then, he knew she always was when speaking about her art. Sophia was nothing if not knowledgeable about her craft. "I have a few paintings that I plan to show."

"And you had a disagreement with Morgan over the suitability of these paintings, did you not?"

Northman was remarkably well informed about the inner workings of the local art world, Ben thought. But he supposed it was possible that Morgan had confided in him.

"We've never spoken about the matter," Sophia corrected

him. "Mr. Morgan has not seen fit to discuss it directly with me. But more to the point, though I am aware of Mr. Morgan's objections, I have heard nothing about Mr. Framingham agreeing with him. Nor have I spoken with the poor man, if it comes to that. So, I'm not sure what my work has to do with what happened yesterday."

"Morgan tells me that he spoke with you, as well, about the matter, Lord Benedick," said Northman. "Is it possible you went to speak with Framingham since he was on the committee organizing the exhibition? To persuade him that Morgan was wrong about your lady friend's paintings?"

"Miss Hastings is a friend, Northman," Ben said tightly. "And I will thank you to be respectful to her. As to whether I spoke with Framingham about the exhibition, I did not. Nor, I believe, did Miss Hastings. As she has already told you."

He'd had just about enough of the man's questions and insinuations. And if he and Sophia were to find any answers regarding the murder or the forgeries, they needed the magistrate to leave.

"If you have no more questions," he said, drawing upon every ounce of hauteur growing up the son of a duke had instilled in him, "I believe Miss Hastings needs to rest now. She is, as you can see, injured, and the events of yesterday were quite distressing for her."

Northman's eyes narrowed for the fraction of a second as if he were trying to see past Ben's outward manner and into his mind. But it was clearly not possible, so he relaxed a little and nodded. "I may need to come back and speak to you again, Miss Hastings."

With an indication to his secretary that they'd finished their business, the magistrate and his minion left the room, closing the door behind them.

When enough time had passed for them to be out of earshot, Sophia turned to Ben with an irritated look. "Why did you stop me from telling him about the forgery? He might be able to help us!"

"And he might just as easily have told us to mind our own business and leave it all to the authorities," he returned, aware even as they spoke about such a serious topic that they were currently alone in the room. Try as he might, it was damned hard to control his baser instincts when he was in her company. Not particularly impressive for a man of the cloth, he knew, but he was, after all, just a man. He might have chosen the church, but that didn't mean he'd lost all feeling below the waist. Certainly not in Sophia's company.

Her huff of frustration brought him back to the matter at hand.

"He could have told us that, yes, but you were asked to look into the matter by the Earl of Mainwaring," she argued. "Does that not make you a colleague of sorts to the magistrate?"

Ben rubbed his neck. "It's not that simple. Mainwaring asked me to look into the matter. It's not as if I've been authorized by the Home Office, or anything like that."

"Well," she said tartly, "if he didn't wish you to investigate the matter properly then he shouldn't have asked in the first place. Though it's entirely possible Framingham was killed for some reason having nothing to do with the forgeries, I cannot help but think otherwise. So, the scheme Mainwaring asked you to look into has become vastly more complicated."

"Of course it has," he answered with a shrug. He prowled across the room to lean his shoulder against the marble mantelpiece. "But that doesn't mean we cannot still unravel it."

"I admire your optimism," she said with a wry look. "So, what do you propose we do next?"

He thought for a moment before he wandered back over to the chair across from hers and lowered his tall frame into it. "I think we need to look at what we know so far."

"All right," she agreed. "First, thanks to your friend Mainwaring, we know that someone has been selling forged paintings through the village of Little Seaford, to the newly rich, to furnish their homes."

"We also know that Peter Morgan," Ben said, leaning back in his chair, "who has lived in the area for about the same timespan as the paintings have been appearing on the market, has many friends among those who might wish to purchase such paintings."

"And at the cliffs, we heard two men, one of whom might have been Morgan," Sophia said, ticking off a third finger, "arranging to get rid of the artist who has been supplying the forgeries."

"An artist we believe to be Ryder."

He watched as Sophia leaned her chin on her hand. "If Ryder is indeed the artist," she began, "then why is it that Framingham is dead?"

"You mean why Framingham and not Ryder?" he asked, curious.

"Yes," she said, lifting her ankle as if it was in pain.

"Here," Ben said gruffly, took her foot gently in his hands, removed her slipper and rested her heel on his thigh. "You should stay off the foot altogether today."

"Not you, too," she said with a scowl. "Acquit me of knowing how to take care of myself, please."

"Of course I know that," he said with a frown. "But you try a bit too hard to be the strongest person in the room. Compared to the other ladies in this house, you might seem like the soft one, but I suspect that's just your beauty giving a false impression, Wallflower. You're beautiful, it's true, but stubborn. And you can flirt and chat and make small talk, but that doesn't mean you're weak or fragile."

She was quiet for a second, arrested by his words. "You purport to know a great deal about me, my lord."

"I make it my business to know . . . people." He'd almost

slipped and said *you*, which would not have been appropriate yet. There was still much they needed to resolve before
he could think about speaking to her as frankly as he wished
to. But soon.

Sophia's gaze rested on him for a moment. As if she
were trying to figure him out. Then, as if realizing it was an
impossible task, she shook her head a little.

"I believe we were discussing why it is odd that Framingham would turn up dead instead of Ryder," she said,
bringing them back to the topic at hand. "Could it be that
Framingham was one of the men we overheard?"

That was a possibility. "And Morgan—or whoever it was
that we overheard, double crossed him?"

It was entirely possible that there had been a falling out
amongst the conspirators.

"Perhaps Framingham no longer wished to sell the forged
paintings?" Sophia suggested. "Or wanted a larger cut of the
profits?"

Either option was possible. It was also possible that they
were overlooking a more straightforward option. "What if
Ryder found out that Morgan and Framingham were plotting to get rid of him?"

Sophia's eyes grew wide. "But I thought we'd decided he
couldn't have been the killer because his clothes were free
of blood?"

"There's nothing to say he didn't hire someone else to kill
the fellow, then went to the gallery to check his handiwork,"
Ben said with a shrug. "And spent a bit of time threatening
you to give himself an out."

His jaw clenched at the memory of Ryder standing over
her yesterday. It wouldn't disappoint him in the least if they
discovered the other man was a murderer and saw him hang
for it. He knew the Gospel said to turn the other cheek, but

when it came to Sophia he found himself feeling decidedly Old Testament.

"Perhaps we shouldn't spend too much time on the why," Sophia said after a bit of thought. "We can't know the why until we know the who. That will tell us the why."

It was a good point, he had to admit. "Very well. We suspect both Ryder and Morgan. And there are likely others we don't know about."

"There are also the paintings Celeste collected," Sophia reminded him. "I didn't have time to search more thoroughly for any notes or explanations she might have left about them, but knowing how she documented things for Ivy and Daphne, I cannot imagine she left that cache of paintings for me without some kind of clue as to why they were there."

"Then it would seem we have a task before us, Wallflower," he said. And without waiting for her consent, he lifted her into his arms.

"What are you doing?" she squeaked. "I'm perfectly able to walk, Ben. Put me down."

"You are injured and if you won't be so sensible as to stay off your ankle, then I will have to ensure you do so myself." He began walking toward the door of the drawing room.

"Where are you taking me?" she asked, her arms clasped tightly around his neck.

"To your studio," he said as he kicked the door shut behind them. "To search for Celeste's letter to you."

They had reached the second floor landing when Daphne came striding down the hallway toward them.

Sophia felt her cheeks heat as she prepared for the duchess—an unconventional one, but a duchess nonetheless—to comment on the scene of Ben with Sophia in his arms. But to her surprise, when Daphne stopped in her tracks at the sight of them, she laughed.

"Well, isn't this a bit of a scandal," she said with a shake of her head. "Sophia, I hope you know what you're doing."

"We are going to search for a letter from Lady Celeste in my studio," Sophia said with as much dignity as she could muster in her present position. "You are welcome to join us. And Ivy and Gemma as well."

But Daphne didn't seem fooled. "Ivy and Gemma are immersed in the library," she said with a keen look. "I was headed downstairs to post this letter to Maitland. Though I might need to add a few lines, now."

"I hope you'll give the duke my best," Ben said mildly as he shifted a little on his feet. "Is he expected to return soon?"

"In a few days," Daphne said, turning her attention to Ben. "I hope he won't need to give you a stern talking to, Lord Benedick."

Sophia had never wished more for the floor to open beneath her and swallow her up. But that would not help given that Ben would be devoured with her.

"I cannot imagine that he will," he responded with a shrug. "My intentions are entirely honorable, I assure you, Duchess."

At that Sophia turned, needing to see his expression. He looked right back at her, his gaze as steady as a rock.

He was serious, she realized, her heartbeat increasing.

"I am glad to hear it," Daphne said with a nod. "I guessed as much, but it never hurts to get confirmation. I'll just leave you to it, then."

And to Sophia's surprise, she continued her trek downstairs, and left them to continue theirs upstairs.

"What did you mean by that?" she demanded once they were out of earshot. She wished desperately that he would set her on her feet so that she could question him properly.

It was difficult to interrogate someone while he was holding you in his arms.

"Just what I said," he returned mildly as they reached the door to her studio. With more ease than seemed fair, he managed to open the door and carry her inside without any trouble.

She waited until he'd placed her gently on the settee she'd spent so much time on these past few days to continue her questions. As if he expected no less, Ben took the chair across from her and leaned forward with his elbows on his knees. Ready for her to go on.

"But, we don't really know one another," she said with a frown. "And my family isn't nearly as aristocratic as yours. Papa is the son of a not very prosperous baronet. And he himself is a solicitor. Not smart at all."

The look he gave her was one of disappointment. "Have I ever indicated to you that I care about any of that?"

"Well, you will care very much when you see how small my marriage portion is," she said with a raised brow. "I know younger sons have to make their own way in the world. And I cannot imagine I'm the sort of wife who will make your position in the clergy comfortable. Surely the archbishop frowns on vicars' wives who call attention to themselves by painting scandalous pictures."

She didn't dare look at him to see if he agreed with her. Part of her was convinced that the idea of their marrying was mad and would lead to scandalous ruin. The other part desperately wanted him to tell her she was being a fool and that he'd marry her no matter what. She wasn't sure which of these parts she wanted to trust at the moment.

"It might surprise you to realize that I am not impoverished and in need of a rich bride to keep me in the style to which I've become accustomed," he said wryly. "Do you suppose I went into the church because my father tossed me out on my ear without a cent to my name? I went into the church because I wished to be of help to people. The politics, the edicts of the archbishop, these hold little interest for me."

That gave her pause. She wasn't sure what she'd thought regarding his financial situation, but she had assumed he needed a bride with a sizeable dowry.

Before she could reply, he continued, "I have made investments with my monthly allowance from the ducal estate which have grown into a respectable fortune. And, though I dislike admitting it lest you think me of the same ilk as Morgan, I own, along with my brothers Freddie and Cam, a cotton mill in Manchester."

Sophia blinked. "I . . . you . . . what?" He could not have shocked her more if he'd just informed her that he turned into a wolf when the moon was full.

"When Freddie came back from France, he had some funds he wanted to invest. He did the research and Cam and I were both looking for something to do with our savings."

"But, how can you do that?" she demanded. She tried to recall that this was Ben, who was so kind to his parishioners, who had comforted the family of the murdered Framingham. Who had kissed her as if she were the most precious gift in the world. But she had questions. How could she not? "How can you put little children to work? And subject them to unhealthy conditions that will ruin their lungs? Eventually kill them?"

"Of course we do not employ children," he said, his mouth tight with displeasure at the idea. "And we offer honest work for a living wage. I do not pretend that ours is morally superior to any other factory in the north, but we have taken steps to ensure that the conditions are as safe as we can make them, and that the children of our workers—most of them women—are offered an education."

Slightly abashed, she said, "I've heard other men, like

Morgan, say that it is impossible to run a factory without child labor. How did you manage it?"

"Men who say that are lying to themselves to justify their practices," he said harshly. "It is certainly possible to do it. But it is not without its detractors. And not from where you'd think it. Regularly our managers are accosted by children and their parents demanding that we employ them. Because they need the wages. I've done what I could to ensure that there is someone on staff at the factory to assist those people in whatever way we can. But going against the grain is not without risk."

He meant that in more than one sense, she knew. Marriage between them would not be without risks. Or without its detractors, she knew. She could only imagine what the reaction of the archbishop would be to hearing about *Fallen*. Ben would be demoted or worse.

"I should have known you'd find a way to run a factory in a manner that helped the most people," she said a little sadly. Because there was no way she could ruin this gentle man's professional life by tying his lot to hers.

"I had hoped you knew me better by now," he said carefully. "But," and he smiled crookedly at this, "I tend to forget we've only truly known each other for a few days. For all that we've been acquaintances since I arrived, I don't think I began to actually see or know the real Sophia until I saw your paintings."

If he'd schemed for a hundred years to find a way to reach her heart, he couldn't have found a surer way than through her painting. It was the most direct representation of the hopes and dreams and sorrows and pain she felt in her very soul. And that he could see her now—and she knew it wasn't just easy flattery—was as close to being understood as she'd ever felt.

"I hadn't intended to do this yet," he said, his gaze intent now, as if trying to read her thoughts, "but surely you must know my intentions are honorable. I wouldn't have kissed you without being prepared to pay for them with my hand in marriage. I've never met anyone like you, sweet Sophia. And perhaps I could marry some empty-headed society lady with a large dowry and more hair than wit, but we both know I'd be miserable with that sort of wife. I want you. With all your zeal for reform and need to call attention to the less fortunate in your work. The archbishop might not like it, but to be frank, I don't give a damn."

As he spoke, her heart, already faster than normal, began to pound. Her hands grew damp. And her stomach flipped with nerves.

"Sophia." Ben was on one knee now, and she felt her eyes begin to fill as he took her hand. "Marry me. Make me the happiest of men."

And to her everlasting shame and embarrassment, she fainted.

Chapter 19

Good heavens.

Ben quickly gathered Sophia into his arms and attempted to rouse her from her faint.

He hadn't spent a great deal of time imagining the way his future beloved would respond to his marriage proposal, but he dashed well had not considered that she might fall into a swoon over it!

"Sophia?"

Fortunately for them both, she opened her eyes almost immediately. He watched in mixed concern and amusement as the emotions flitted over her face. First confusion. Then, a smile as she saw him leaning over her—a good sign, surely? Then her eyes widened and a look of horror washed over her.

"Oh no." She shook her head and tried to sit up. Wanting to do whatever it took to make her comfortable, he assisted her to sit up on the settee beside him.

"I cannot believe I did that," she groaned. "I do not faint, Ben. Never. Not even when Tommy Travers spilled punch down the front of my favorite gown at the assembly ball."

She covered her face with both hands. "I am mortified."

"Well, I think the burden of shame lies with me," he said wryly. "I am, after all, the man who managed to make you faint dead away at the notion of marriage to me. If my brothers ever get wind of this, I will never rest easy again."

At that she dropped her hands, and threw her arms around him. "No," she said squeezing him hard. "You mustn't blame yourself or your words. It was a perfectly lovely proposal. I was simply overcome, I think."

She pulled away from him so that he could see the sincerity in her eyes. "You did nothing wrong. I've just had so much excitement these past few days and I haven't really been sleeping well, and I suppose I didn't eat much at breakfast and it all caught up with me."

"Perhaps we should ring for some sandwiches and tea," he said with a practicality he wasn't especially feeling. There was still the matter of his unanswered proposal hanging between them. Though he'd be a churl to bring it up again when she was obviously famished and overset.

"A good idea," Sophia said with a smile. "You always know what to do to make me feel better, Ben."

And to his surprise, she leaned in and kissed him. Then snuggled against his shoulder as if they'd not just enacted a scene from a Restoration farce.

"Do I take that to mean you've accepted my proposal?" he asked, half fear, half hope.

She pulled away from him again and gave him an exasperated look. "You don't honestly believe I fainted from shock and disgust, do you?"

Well when she put it like that . . .

Feeling sheepish, he shrugged. "One doesn't like to presume . . ."

Her laugh was clear and bright and just what he'd needed to hear.

"Of course I accept your proposal, you fool." She shook her head, loosening a few silky strands of brown tresses from her chignon to lightly trace the skin of her neck. "I'm not sure your optimism over the reaction our betrothal will elicit from the church hierarchy is founded, but if you're willing to take a chance on me, then I will take a chance on you."

For the first time in a quarter hour at least, Ben felt himself relax. And with a slight whoop, he pulled her to him and kissed her again. Properly this time, with every ounce of joy and hope and passion he felt when he was with this remarkable woman.

When she came up for air, her cheeks were delightfully pink and her hair was even more disheveled.

Though he would have liked to continue on in that manner, her stomach gave an annoyed growl. "I suppose I'd better send for those sandwiches," he said with a grin.

Just as he pulled the bell, a knock sounded on the door and Gemma called from the doorway, "Sophia, Lord Benedick, I'm afraid there's a bit of a disturbance downstairs and I fear it's something that only you can deal with."

"Come in, Gemma," Sophia called to her sister with a hint of amusement. "We've news."

Cautiously, as if she expected to find them in, at the very least, a passionate kiss, Gemma stepped into the room enough to see that they were both fully clothed with several feet between them.

"Oh," she said, her smile rueful. "I wasn't sure. . . . that is to say . . ."

"What is going on downstairs?" Sophia asked, clearly wanting to ensure there was no trouble before she made any sort of announcement.

At the reminder, Gemma's smile turned into a frown. "The Bishop of Chichester is downstairs with your father, Lord Benedick. And neither looks particularly happy."

"What?" Ben was not entirely surprised by the arrival of the bishop. He'd expected Morgan's next move in the attempt to discredit Sophia would be to have the bishop rein him in. But he was genuinely shocked to learn his father was here. "Why are they here and not at the vicarage?"

"They said they called there first and learned from your man that you were here." Gemma seemed as nonplussed as he felt. "I've left them downstairs with Daphne and Ivy. I think perhaps it's best to limit their time with Daphne before someone takes offense."

That was an understatement.

Sophia, who had taken all of this in without a word, set about smoothing her hair and righting her gown. Though it wasn't in any sort of disarray that he could see. Using her walking stick, she stood and offered him her arm. "Shall we go downstairs and see what these gentlemen want?"

He'd known he'd have to inform both the church and his parents about the betrothal at some point, but he hadn't supposed it would be quite this soon.

Still, he took her arm. "You're able to get downstairs like that?" he asked. Her eyes showed the memory of how she'd gotten upstairs earlier.

"Yes," she said with prim dignity. "I believe I can make it."

"Then I suppose we should go see what all the fuss is about."

Sophia rather felt as if she were stepping on stage when she and Ben stepped into the drawing room, where Greaves had placed the Duke of Pemberton and the Bishop of Chichester. As she limped in, both men turned to give her polite, but rather searching looks.

To her amusement, the bishop was still holding one of the phallic figurines from the mantle. Which he hastily put back as he stepped forward to greet them.

"Lord Benedick," the church leader said with a regal inclination of his head. "What a surprise it was to find your father was calling upon you here, rather than at the vicarage, as well." He was a tall, reed-thin man with what Sophia imagined was a permanent look of impatience on his long face. "Are you so frequently from home that your parishioners have begun seeking you out here as well? That's hardly proper."

A flash of exasperation crossed the duke's face as he ignored the clergyman and addressed his son. "You're looking well, Benedick. I hope you'll introduce us to your friend?"

At the reminder Ben gave her a look of apology. She imagined he'd been just as nonplussed by the bishop's introduction as she had.

"Miss Sophia Hastings, I'd like you to meet my father, the Duke of Pemberton," he said with a gesture toward the man whom she would have picked from a room full of other peers as his father. Like Ben, and indeed Freddie and Cam as well, the duke was tall with a strong if not particularly bulky build. His dark brown hair was a shade darker than his son's, and he had brown eyes, which must mean that his sons had inherited their blue eyes from their mother. "Papa, this is Miss Sophia Hastings. Her father is the son of Sir Giles Hastings of York. And she is assisting me with a particular matter that the Earl of Mainwaring has asked me to look into. It has to do with art and as Miss Hastings is herself a celebrated oil painter, she has been a valuable resource."

He made no mention of their, admittedly nascent, betrothal, but Sophia felt a pang of disappointment at the omission. Though she supposed that had more to do with the other man who stood waiting for an introduction.

"I'm very pleased to meet you, Miss Hastings," the duke said, bowing over her hand. "Like Gussie, here, I too was surprised to find my son here rather than at the vicarage, but I understand now. How could he possibly stay away when such beauty was here at Beauchamp House?"

It was clear where the Lisle boys had got their charming

manners from, Sophia thought with a blush. "You are kind to say so, your grace," she said with a smile.

Then she turned to face the bishop, who was not nearly as pleased with her as the duke seemed to be.

"Your grace," Ben said, his presence at her side giving Sophia a boost of courage as she faced the annoyed ecclesiastical, "Miss Sophia Hastings. Miss Hastings, this is his grace the Bishop of Chichester."

"I had rather hoped to have a word with you alone, Benedick," the clergyman said with a sniff. "Would that be possible?"

"Don't be so stiff-rumped, Gussie," the duke said with a frown. "If Benedick says they're investigating something for the Home Office, then that's what they're doing. Whatever issue you have with him can't be more confidential than that."

If anything the bishop's nose and mouth grew more pinched. "Perhaps, Pemberton, you should mind your own business. And as it happens, since Miss Hastings is the reason for my visit to this Sussex backwater, I believe it would defeat the purpose to counsel your son about her while she's in the room."

"We're both standing right here," Ben reminded them with a little wave. "And as it happens, I have a guess as to what brought you here, Bishop."

"First," the duke said, with a look at Sophia's white-knuckled grip on her walking stick, "I believe we should sit down and discuss this like civilized people."

He offered his arm to Sophia. "Miss Hastings, may I?"

She exchanged a look with Ben, who seemed to shrug with his eyes—something she'd never known possible—and decided it was safe to take the duke's offered arm. Soon she was tucked up in her favorite overstuffed chair near the window with an ottoman at her feet to elevate her ankle.

Once the men were seated in chairs around her, with Ben

taking the seat beside hers so they presented a united front, the duke, who seemed to be the unquestionable leader of this meeting, indicated with his hand that his son should continue.

"My guess, your grace," he said to the bishop, "is that you've had a complaint from a member of my parish about Miss Hastings. Perhaps a complaint that I've been spending too much time with her? Or that I recognize her at all given the content of her artwork? Does that sound familiar?"

"That may have been the gist of what I was told," the bishop said with a grudging nod. "And that you've been using your position as vicar to intrude upon matters that do not concern you. I might add that the person who made this complaint is a respected member of the community."

Sophia had little trouble guessing he meant Peter Morgan. And it surprised her not a whit that the bishop thought him respected.

"My son has already explained this, Gussie," said Pemberton, his leg crossed over his knee, perfectly at ease in what must be a difficult meeting for his son. Clearly he was not intimidated by the bishop. That much was obvious by the way he referred to him by what must have been a childhood nickname. "He and Miss Hastings are working together on a matter at the behest of Mainwaring. Whom you and I well know works for the Home Office. If he is able to fulfill his duties as a vicar, then I don't see what the problem is."

"I'm quite able to defend myself, sir," Ben said to his father, who lifted his hands to indicate his son had the floor. "Though, your grace, I do not believe there is anything to defend here. As my father said, Miss Hastings and I are working together on something for Mainwaring. It involves art forgery and more than that I cannot say. But I can assure you that I have not neglected my duties, and having seen Miss Hastings' paintings, I can assure you that they are far from what Morgan claims them to be."

It was all perfectly true, but Sophia couldn't help but feel a bit of frustration at his decision to omit the news of their betrothal. Wouldn't that reassure the vicar about the time they spent together? While she did appreciate that the investigation for the Home Office was perhaps a stronger argument for their closeness, the betrothal would remove the appearance of impropriety at least. Or so she thought.

If anything, the bishop seemed to grow more annoyed. "What business has the Home Office to co-opt my clergymen to perform their nasty little tasks? I've a mind to pay a call on the Home Secretary himself to complain."

None of the others responded to that, which Sophia assumed was a rhetorical question. And if it wasn't, there was no response they could give that would assuage his pique.

"Morgan has done a great deal for this village, Benedick," he continued in a scowl. "In fact, I believe his donations have made the living at Little Seaford one that is no longer the kind of pittance once seen here. You risk him reducing the amount of his tithe by going against him. And of him withdrawing some of his funding for your pet projects like caring for the village poor. Are you prepared to do that?"

Sophia watched as Ben's jaw tightened. She could see that he was holding his temper on a tight leash, indeed.

"Are you suggesting that I cease investigating a matter at my country's behest in order to appease a man who would use donations to the church as a means of getting what he wants?" his words were clipped and cold.

"I warned you about the politics of the church when you came to us, my boy," said the bishop with a shrug. "It is part of the job, no matter how much you dislike it. Of course you must render unto Caesar when necessary, but do not forget what duty you owe to the church and your parish."

He gave a pointed look at Sophia, who felt her back stiffen. "I notice you glossed over Morgan's other accusations regarding Miss Hastings." He did not elaborate, but it was clear from the way his eye roved over her what his meaning was. "Perhaps I should remind you as well that there are certain moral standards to which we expect you to adhere."

At that both Ben and duke stood. "Now see here, Gussie. If you're going to accuse my son of—"

"Don't be tiresome, Pemberton. I'm not accusing him of anything. But there is the appearance of impropriety. And that, I think, is enough to cast doubt on the nature of his relationship with Miss Hastings." The bishop had stood as well. "It might all be perfectly innocent, but it is what his parishioners think that matters. Once he has lost their confidence . . ."

"I doubt very much I've lost anyone's confidence who knows me," Ben said, his anger radiating off him. "And I will not have you cast aspersions of Miss Hastings' good name without so much as a bye-your-leave. It might change your opinion to know that I have only today asked her to be my wife and she has accepted. So, I will ask that you moderate your manner of speaking about her or I will be forced to complain to the archbishop."

At his announcement, Sophia struggled to her feet. "Benedick, you needn't have told him about this now."

She'd wanted him to announce their betrothal before, but now it felt like a play in a chess game. And she could see from the bishop's high color and pursed lips that it hadn't calmed his anger.

"I beg to differ, young lady," the bishop said coldly. "Now is the perfect time, because it tells me that the rumors are true. It is of course, your choice whom you take as a wife, Lord Benedick. But if you choose this route, your career will not be an easy one. You have not shown yourself to be a political man when it comes to rising in the church, but know if you do this that your chances of rising will forever be dimmed."

"Because Miss Hastings and I have been seen in one another's company too frequently?" Ben asked with incredulity.

"Because Miss Hastings paints what more than one of your parishioners has complained to me is obscene. Dead prostitutes? Dying children?" The bishop made a noise of disgust. "It is unfit for a man to paint such scenes. Much less a lady." He said the last word with a degree of skepticism that indicated he doubted her claim to the title.

Sophia clenched her fists in an effort to keep from striking the man. He was, of course, entitled to make judgments based on the content of her art, but to use them as a bludgeon against Ben was inexcusable. His career thus far with the church had been, so far as she knew, blameless. Was he to be censured solely based on the friendship of a few months' duration? She knew of church elders who had carried on affairs of decades duration who had escaped punishment. That Ben would find himself in such a situation because of her was enough to make her want to howl at the unfairness of it.

Like powerful men before him, the bishop also liked to have the last word, apparently, because once he'd said his peace, he swept from the room.

Leaving a pregnant silence behind him.

Chapter 20

"Gussie always was an egotistical fool," said the duke into the silence that fell in the wake of the bishop's departure. Then, turning to Sophia, he offered her his hand. "My dear Miss Hastings, I am very pleased to hear of your betrothal to my son. His mother and I had given up hope that he'd ever choose a bride."

Ben tried to shake off the pall of the bishop's words on him. His anger over the man's criticism of Sophia was foremost in his mind, especially when she herself had been forced to listen to his nonsense. He knew well enough that the church wished its clergymen would marry bland, selfless women who would make good helpmeets and be seen and not heard. But he'd long known that wasn't the kind of match *he* wanted. And certainly after meeting Sophia and seeing her determination to right societal wrongs with her work—something that spoke to his own sympathy for those who by accident of birth were stuck in the lower class—he'd known that she was what he wanted.

That his father, after only a few moments with her, was welcoming her to the family said more than any of the bishop's dismissive speeches.

"Thank you, your grace," Sophia said, though Ben could hear the note of falseness in her voice. "I wonder if you wouldn't mind giving me a few moments alone with your son? We have much to discuss, I think."

Though he was focused on Sophia, Ben couldn't mistake the look of warning his father sent him. He was all too aware of the danger, there, however.

"Certainly, my dear," the duke said with a smile. "I'm in need of a rest after all of Gussie's bombast. I do hope we'll see one another again before I travel on to visit Cam down the coast."

He kissed her on the cheek before bidding Ben a quick goodbye, and then he too was gone.

Leaving Ben and an obviously overset Sophia alone.

He knew something was seriously wrong when he moved to take Sophia's hand and she pulled away.

"Come now," he said in a cajoling tone. "You aren't taking what the bishop said to heart, are you? My father obviously approves, and his opinion is far more important to me than the bishop's is."

She turned from where she'd been facing out the window and he saw that her face was white. "Yes, I do take it to heart when the man who holds the future of your career in the church in his hands claims that a match with me will ruin you. While I am, of course, pleased to have your father's blessing, I cannot help but be troubled by the bishop's censure."

Ah. She was worried for him. "I told you before that I am not dependent upon the church's funding. And unlike the Roman church there isn't really a way for him to defrock me. The worst he can do is scold. Which he has done." He moved closer, reaching out to touch her arm. He was relieved when she didn't pull away.

He ran his hand down her arm until he'd taken her hand in his. "I'm sorry that I waited until that precise moment to reveal our betrothal, however. It made it look as if I was inventing it on the spot in order to escape his chastisement."

"I doubt it would have made a difference," she said, moving closer to let him hold her against him. "He had already made up his mind about me before he came to Little Seaford. Morgan must have placed a great deal of money in the hands of the right people to get the bishop himself to come to deliver a set down in person."

Relieved that she wasn't angry at him so much as the situation, he took a moment to enjoy the feel of her against him. To smell the fresh lemony fragrance of her hair, and the warmth of her skin.

"I have no doubt that Morgan is quite skilled at the business of paying off those he thinks will be of use to him at some point," he said, stroking a comforting hand over her back. "He is a businessman with a businessman's conviction that money will buy whatever he wants—including the silencing of a critic."

At his words, she stiffened and pulled away. "You don't suppose he contacted the bishop because of what happened with Framingham?"

Ben frowned. "What do you mean?"

"Just that someone must have been worried to silence Framingham permanently," she said with a pointed look. "What if Morgan knew that he'd contacted you before he died? If it was indeed Framingham."

He considered it. He'd wanted—because of the man's behavior with Sophia—the culprit to be Ryder, but it was entirely possible that the murderer was someone else. Someone with more at stake than an itinerant artist did.

Someone who stood to lose an empire if his scheme was uncovered.

"We need to find that note from Lady Celeste," he said with a sense of urgency. If Morgan had either killed Framingham or had him killed, then his next target might be the people who were trying to bring him down. He wasn't worried for his own safety. But if it had been Morgan who sent the bishop information about Sophia, then he just might see Sophia as a threat as well as Ben.

And he would let Peter Morgan harm Sophia over his dead body.

Taking Sophia's hand, he led her upstairs to search for the clue that would lead them to the truth.

In the studio again, Sophia made immediately for the ornate Jacobean cabinet in the corner, where she'd first discovered a collection of documents and diaries relating to Lady Celeste's art dealings. She had given her works as gifts and kept a journal with the title of each painting and the name of the person she'd gifted it to.

As if by agreement, she took a seat and Ben handed her stack after stack of loose pages and other ephemera from the late artist's collection.

"I don't understand why her art papers are so disorganized when the rest of her papers were so very tidy," Sophia said as she opened a letter that seemed to be from an art dealer in Brighton. "Though given the breadth of her interest, I suppose she couldn't do it all."

Ben turned from pulling out a bound journal from the cabinet. "You don't suppose someone has already searched this collection? And that's why it's in such disarray."

The possibility hadn't occurred to her and Sophia thought it over for a moment. Could someone have sneaked into the studio and rifled through Lady Celeste's papers without her knowing about it? It was true there were a couple of months between the lady's death and the arrival of the heiresses. Serena had been here, of course, but she wouldn't have done such a thing.

Then, a thought occurred to her. Someone else in the house might have decided to conceal a letter for her from

Lady Celeste. Someone who might think he was protecting her from danger.

"I think I might know who has the letter Lady Celeste left for me," she said with a sigh. If she was right, he would be mortified at being caught out. But there was no time for that now. A man was dead and they needed every bit of information they could gather.

"Who?" Ben asked, his brows drawn.

"Ring the bell pull and we'll find out if I'm right." Sophia said rubbing the spot between her eyes that was beginning to throb.

She hoped she was correct. If she wasn't, then she wasn't sure where they'd be able to search next.

Chapter 21

Greaves himself arrived in answer to the bell, and Ben was struck by the realization that the butler seemed to have a soft spot for Sophia.

It wasn't all that unusual for a butler to respond to a bell from a member of the family, but it did seem that Greaves was, more often than not, the one who came running when Sophia called.

"Miss Hastings," the older man said, offering her a slight bow. Then, turning to offer another to Ben. "How may I be of assistance?"

He seemed to take the presence of Ben in the room as unexceptional, though as an upper servant, Greaves was skilled at keeping his opinions to himself.

"Mr. Greaves," Sophia said from her perch on a high-backed chair near the cabinet they'd been searching, "is there something you'd like to tell me? Perhaps something relating to a note Lady Celeste left with express instructions for me?"

Ben watched fascinated as the man's upright posture sagged a little. Folding his arms over his chest, he leaned back against the cabinet to watch the interaction between Sophia and the major-domo.

"Miss Hastings," Greaves began with a tight-lipped frown,

"you must understand it was for your own protection. I cannot imagine Lady Celeste would have wished you to put yourself in the sort of danger both Miss Ivy—that is, the Marchioness of Kerr—and the Duchess of Maitland found themselves in when they followed my late mistress's directives. I know it was not my place, but I . . . that is to say, my affection . . ."

Before he could say more, Sophia stopped him, raising a hand. "Mr. Greaves, how could you?" she asked, looking both disappointed and touched. "You know it's not your place to make decisions like that. Not only has your decision to hold back Lady Celeste's letter or note, or whatever it was, put me in more danger, but it may very well have got Mr. Framingham killed."

At that, the butler flinched. "Of course I never intended to do anything that would harm anyone, Miss Hastings. I was only trying to keep you safe."

"I know that," she said with a sigh. "And I know you have a soft spot for me. But you must always know that more information is better in these situations than less. If I don't know all the facts then how am I to make a rational decision about how to approach this situation? Lady Celeste's letter might contain information that would keep both me and Lord Benedick safe from harm rather than endangering us."

Looking abashed, Greaves nodded. "I only thought to do what would keep you out of danger, Miss Hastings. I knew at the time I was breaking every tenet of my profession. But after what happened to the others, I couldn't stomach the idea of such a thing happening to you." He looked up, his eyes bright with emotion. "I will submit my letter of resignation to Lady Serena in the morning. I only hope you'll give me time to gather my things and search for a new position."

Sophia, Ben could see, was moved by the butler's confession. It was obvious that she held him in just as much affection as he held her. "I don't think that's necessary," she said briskly. "You were acting out of concern—rather like a father—and as my own father is not here, I cannot help but think that he would heartily approve of your actions. I must warn you, however, that you must, in future, resist the impulse to hide things from the ladies of this house. You are perhaps of a generation that sees ladies as less capable of handling danger or difficulties. But I cannot stress enough that such a notion is wrong-headed."

Greaves closed his eyes for the barest second, letting relief show in the set of his shoulders. Then, before Ben's eyes he pulled himself together and stood up straight and proud. "You are far more generous than I deserve, Miss Hastings," he said stiffly. "I will not make this mistake again. My apologies for allowing my emotions to cloud what I knew to be my duty as a servant."

"And now," Sophia said firmly, "you must bring me the letter or note, or whatever it was, that Lady Celeste left for me. It is imperative that Lord Benedick and I are able to find out just who it is we are looking for. And who killed Mr. Framingham."

With a nod, Greaves bowed again and excused himself to go get the note.

When he was gone, Ben turned to Sophia, who was looking a bit rueful. "I suppose it was obvious the man thinks of you as his special charge," he said gently. "But how did you know he'd taken the letter?"

Shaking her head, Sophia said, "I wasn't positive. But it suddenly occurred to me that there was one person in the house who would wish more than anyone else to keep me from harm's way. And when I recalled his response to my ankle, I realized that it could be no one else."

"He'd have been sacked in any other household in England," Ben pointed out. He tried to imagine what he'd have done if he learned Jennings was hiding things from him. But the situation was different, he supposed. He was a grown man, and though Sophia was a strong, capable woman, society hadn't yet come to the realization that ladies were able to make their own decisions. Greaves was a product of his upbringing and despite serving as butler to Lady Celeste—who was most certainly not a conventional lady—he must have made the mistake of seeing Sophia as one. Not to mention that his affection for her had made him fearful on her behalf. As Ben well knew—thinking back to his reacting to seeing Ryder's arm raised to her—fear of seeing Sophia harmed could inspire all sorts of rash behavior.

"But this is not any other household in England," Sophia said firmly. "And for all that he's made our task of finding who's behind the forgery and Framingham's murder more difficult, I cannot be angry with him. He's a dear man and has taken excellent care of us all. I believe much of the time there's a tendency to see servants as cold and emotionless. Interchangeable. And I know well enough that there's nothing farther from the truth."

Ben moved to stroke her arm. "You are extraordinary."

As he watched, a blush crept up from her neck and into her cheeks. "I'm nothing special," she responded with a slight smile.

He was calculating whether he had enough time to kiss her before the butler came back when the man himself returned.

Presenting a sealed letter to Sophia, Greaves bowed. "Again, I apologize, Miss Hastings. It won't happen again. You have my word."

Taking the proffered missive, Sophia nodded. "I know it won't, Mr. Greaves. Thank you for doing the right thing."

With another bow, the butler began to walk back to the door. He was almost there when Sophia called after him. "Mr. Greaves?"

He turned, "Yes, Miss Hastings?"

"Thank you for looking out for me." She gave him a smile guaranteed to melt the sternest heart. "I don't believe my own father could have done a better job of it."

Ben wasn't certain, but he thought the old man blushed before he gave a brisk nod and slipped from the room.

Once Greaves was gone and the door closed behind him, Sophia slipped her thumb beneath the wax seal bearing the imprint of Lady Celeste's ring.

She was frustrated by Greaves' actions, of course. But she couldn't help but feel that his impulses had come from a desire to protect her. She didn't approve of his decision to keep the letter from her, but she couldn't condemn the man or order him dismissed because he'd acted out of affection and loyalty. It simply wasn't something she could do and remain content with herself.

Ben watched her closely as she unfolded the parchment and began to read aloud.

> *My dear Sophia,*
> *I cannot tell you how pleased I am that an artist of your talent and vision has agreed to come to Beauchamp House. You are likely unaware of it, but I attended the exhibition of your work in York two summers ago, and that is what convinced me that I could choose no other painter to join the group of ladies to whom I intended to leave my home. (That your sister is a celebrated naturalist in her own right, and therefore was perfect to round out my quartet of scholars, was a happy coincidence.) Welcome to your new home. I hope that you will find my studio—where I have spent many happy hours engrossed in my own, far less impressive, work—is congenial to your artistic eye and that you will produce more of your wonderful work here.*
> *As with your fellow scholars, I have a task which I*

believe you in particular are best suited for. In no way am I insisting that you undertake this investigation, but I do believe that if you choose not to, the very artistic world which you cherish so much will suffer. The decision, however, is yours.

Now, the facts. For some time now I've been aware that one of the galleries in the village has been selling forgeries of some very valuable paintings to buyers who are either unaware that the paintings are fake, or don't particularly care. I stumbled upon the matter when I visited Mr. Framingham's gallery one afternoon and came upon the man himself wrapping a painting that looked familiar, while a Mr. Richard Nettles, as he was introduced to me, waited. I had come to pick up one of my own pieces which I'd asked Framingham to frame for me. It was only a quick glimpse, but I was certain I'd either seen the work Framingham was wrapping before—or I'd seen it described. It was Italian, that much I knew. And after consulting one of my collections of art books in the library, I realized that the painting was by Tintoretto. The Temptation of Eve, which dated to 1578. But I knew one other detail about the painting that my books didn't. This particular work had been part of a collection of some thirty valuable works of art that were purchased from a French Nobleman who was desperate to buy passage for his family out of France as the revolution raged around them. The purchaser was none other than my father, the fifth Duke of Beauchamp, who was in France on business at the time. You will find enclosed with this note a list of those paintings, which were lost in a shipwreck while crossing the English Channel. My father, was, of course, unharmed as he'd returned to England a month before. He was quite upset over the loss, however, and would often lament it when in his cups.

The realization that this Mr. Nettles had purchased

what was surely a forgery was troubling to me, and I approached a friend with ties to the Home Office with the information. That avenue, however, was not productive. So, I endeavored to learn more from Framingham. After a few pointed questions, wherein I hinted that I would like to buy a painting similar to that of Mr. Nettles, I learned the man had been recommended to Framingham by a newcomer to the area, Mr. Peter Morgan. I'd met the man before and found him to be just the sort of bombastic fellow I abhorred, who had no real love for art, but instead saw it as a means of elevating his own stature. I also learned that several more of Morgan's friends had also purchased paintings at his behest. The identity of these paintings confirmed my suspicions. Someone had a list of the paintings that were lost in the Channel and was painting them to order for the unsuspecting amongst Morgan's set, who doubtless didn't know Michelangelo from Vermeer, much less were able to tell a forgery from the real thing.

I sent my man of business to each of the homes where the forged paintings were now on display, and one by one, he purchased six of them. These six you will find here in the studio cupboard where I put them for safe-keeping. I did not tell the authorities about the scheme because there was one particular detail that my man learned upon his visits to these middle class homes which made that impossible.

Framingham had told all of the buyers that the paintings in question had come from the collection of an unconventional member of the aristocracy: one Lady Celeste Beauchamp.

That someone has been forging works that my father lost at sea is one thing. That they would attribute the previous ownership of said paintings to his daughter was outrageous. Not only did it make my father look like an *insurance cheat, but it also made me out to be complicit in the matter. I could no more report that to the authorities than I could turn myself in to them. Besides, I'd already gone to them with the news and they'd chosen to either ignore me, or conduct their own investigation without informing me of the details.*

On top of this, my illness has made it difficult, if not impossible, for me to handle the details and day-to-day investigation into this matter. Which is why, my dear Sophia, I leave it in your capable hands. As a fellow artist, I know you will find the notion of these valuable works of art being reproduced as bold as you please, without concern for the harm it does to the wider world, as abhorrent as I do. And as one of my four heirs, I hope you will see the insult to my good name as an insult that must be answered. I am unable to do so, but I hope that with some assistance, you will.

Feel free to ask my nephews and Serena for assistance should you need it. And please, be careful. I fear that whoever is behind this will not like being exposed for the charlatan he is. I have my suspicions that Morgan may have something to do with it, but right now it is only a suspicion. I hope that you will find some bit of truth that will prove it one way or another. And if it turns out he is innocent, well, I suppose even one wolf cannot be responsible for all the lost sheep in the world.

Be well, my dear girl, and be safe.

Yours in love for the arts,
Lady Celeste Beauchamp

Chapter 22

From behind the letter which she'd been reading, Sophia produced another sheet which was a list of the paintings Lady Celeste had mentioned. At the top of the page was a heading, which read "Items Lost in the sinking of the *Mary Frances*, May 17, 1788, while crossing the channel from Calais to Bristol." Beneath it was a list of some thirty paintings, the titles and artists of which made Sophia's breath catch. These were works that if they hadn't been lost would be worth hundreds of thousands of pounds. At the bottom of the page was the scrawled signature of the fifth Duke of Maitland, who must have written the list, since it was in a different hand.

"Lady Celeste certainly didn't do things by halves," Ben said as he took the list from Sophia and scanned it. "When she left tasks for you all, she made certain they weren't easy ones. I have an imagine of her in my head as a goddess on Mount Olympus crafting labors for Hercules."

He had a point, Sophia had to admit, as she moved to take out the paintings she and the other heiresses had placed back into the cabinet after looking at them earlier in the week. "I can't believe she stumbled onto a scheme like this simply by chance," she said, staring down at a work that rather skillfully recreated a painting by Vermeer called *Girl with a Fan*. It skillfully, faithfully mimicked the famous Dutch painter's use of light and the portrayal of one of several female models he used again and again. How close it was to the original, Sophia couldn't know until she compared it to a print in one of the collections in the library, but she had a feeling it was close. "If she hadn't recalled the list of paintings her father had lost, she would never have put it together that the work she saw being wrapped by Framingham was a forgery at all."

"What I want to know," Ben said thoughtfully, as he held the list, "is who knew about the lost paintings? Was it widely known that the schooner went down with a fortune's worth of artwork on it, or did the family manage to keep it quiet? I know it was likely a coup for the duke to purchase such a collection, but the loss of it would have stung. I can imagine he'd do what he could to keep news of the sinking—or more particularly what went down on it—a secret."

"That's something we'll need to ask Serena, and perhaps Kerr and Maitland when they return from London, about," Sophia said. "They may have heard family stories. Though I believe the duke himself died before they were born."

"If it was kept a secret, then how did Ryder get hold of it?" Ben asked, as usual his jaw tightening at the man's very name. "He had to know which paintings he was meant to re-create. And I think we're no longer in any doubt that he is the one who has been painting them, are we?"

Sophia shook her head. It was possible someone else had been the artist in question, but she'd seen his work during their visit to Primrose Green. And the brushwork, the mixing of colors, it was all very similar to the works she was looking at now. "I think it is him, yes," she said. "And I would very much like to ask him whether he has any conception of the harm his forgeries have done. Not just in Little Seaford, but also in the art world as a whole."

At that, however, Ben shook his head. "Absolutely not," he said with a finality that put her back up. "I will speak to the man if it's necessary. But you are to go nowhere near him."

"You are being unreasonable," Sophia pointed out with a scowl. "I can speak to him about the paintings themselves. Artist to artist. And perhaps I can convince him to tell us who else is behind the scheme. Especially when he learns that Morgan was planning to get rid of him."

"And I'm not comfortable with you being in the same room with the fellow," Ben countered. "He raised his hand to you, Sophia, or have you forgotten? I can't speak for my actions if he does such a thing again."

She was at once touched by his concern, and annoyed at his high-handedness. Must all the men in her life insist upon protecting her from herself?

Standing, she moved to slip her arms around his neck, and though he was still annoyed, she felt him relax a little at her nearness. "I cannot imagine he would be so foolish as to do something like that again, Ben. He's a forger, not a fool. And if you're with me, he'll have even more incentive to behave."

"Don't think I don't realize what you're doing," he said, even as he slid his hands over her bottom and pulled her closer. "I know when I'm being coaxed, Miss Hastings."

She leaned in and kissed him, just letting her mouth brush across his. "I was Sophia before. Why the formality?"

"I am trying to be a gentleman, Sophia," he said on a sigh as she nibbled over his chin. "And you're making it dashed difficult."

She knew exactly how difficult his struggle was—she felt the evidence of his body's attempt to overcome his mind pressing against her stomach.

"I don't need a gentleman just now, Ben," she whispered

against his ear. "I need a man. That's all. Not a vicar. Not a lord. Not a gentleman. Just a man."

Ben felt a shudder run through him as Sophia nipped his earlobe.

She was going to be the death of him.

But there was one particular part of him that came to life whenever she was near, and it was making a very good argument for the opposite.

"I can't just throw you over my shoulder and have my way with you like a barbarian," he said through clenched teeth. "You deserve to be wooed. To be taken in a bed, with proper attention to detail."

His hands stroked over her back as he spoke, however, encouraging her as she kissed a path down his neck.

When she stopped, he almost wept. "Ben," she said in a firm tone. "I know what I want. And I do not care about hearts or flowers. I don't need a proper bed. I only need you. And as shocking as this might be to your delicate sensibilities, I want you."

As she spoke, she met his eyes and he found himself awed again by her ability to cut to the heart of the matter. To get past his reservations and respect for the conventions and to speak the truth of what lay between them. "You're sure?" he asked, his voice husky with desire. "Because I'm willing to wait."

Her mouth quirked into a half smile before she kissed him hard on the mouth. "I know you are and I love you for it. But I am not."

Some recess of his brain where his primitive desires lay took over then, and he lifted her into his arms and carried her over to the settee, which was bathed in afternoon light. Gently settling her onto the sofa, he all but sprinted to the door and turned the lock.

When he returned, he found her sprawled over the deep red

velvet of the cushions, her cheeks pink with desire and looking like a sumptuous banquet meant only for him. Never letting his eyes leave her, he shrugged out of his coat and waistcoat and tossed them aside. Then came his cravat, which was a bit more difficult given the slight trembling of his fingers. It went into pile with his coats. His boots took a bit more time, but he removed them with what he considered admirable speed. Turning, he saw that she was gazing appreciatively at him.

"Don't forget to remove your shirt," she said in a sultry tone. "I want to see you."

It was the work of a moment to pull the fine lawn over his head and another minute more before he could gather her against him and reverse their positions on the settee, with him on the bottom, and her sprawled over his chest.

When their mouths met, it was surprisingly gentle. He felt as if he'd been waiting for this moment from their first meeting. Though he hadn't known it at the time. He'd only known then that she was the most beautiful thing he'd ever seen and he wanted her. That thought, like so many that went against his values as a gentleman and a clergyman, had been suppressed. But here, now, he was as fully himself as he could recall feeling in years. With Sophia, Ben was, as she'd said she wanted, just a man. A man who wanted more than anything in the world to make love to the woman in his arms.

He took his time with her, savoring every soft stroke of her tongue, and answering with parries of his own. Their bodies pressed together, his naked chest against her clothed one, while he explored the rest of her with his hands. While she sighed into his mouth, his hand wandered over the generous curve of her hip, and down over her thigh to gather the loose fabric of her gown and slide it up, inch by inch, until her stockinged leg was exposed and he touched the naked flesh just above her garter.

She gave a gasp against his mouth, then gave a slight tilt

of her hips, encouraging him to move his hand up further. At the same time, he used his other hand to pull down the bodice of her gown, exposing the bosom he'd been dreaming of for weeks. Even from the way she was positioned, in the shadows, he could see that her breasts were every bit as beautiful as he'd imagined. Unable to hold back, he bent his head to take one rosy tip gently between his teeth before laving it with his tongue. Sophia gave a gasp of pleasure and writhed a little against him.

Needing to feel her beneath him, he flipped their positions until she was on her back and he was kneeling over her, where he could worship one breast with his mouth while he stroked and caressed the other with his hand. Beneath him, Sophia gave a little cry as he suckled her and he felt her hips buck against him, which was sweet anguish to his cock nestled as it was between her thighs. Taking his hand from her breast, he slipped it beneath her gown and stroked up, up until he reached the heart of her, where the gathering wetness revealed the depth of her desire. He stroked a finger over her clitoris while at the same time giving a decadent suck at her nipple and Sophia almost bucked off the sofa.

"Ben," she gasped, unable to stop her body's response to the caress. "Oh."

He did it again, this time stroking a finger over her opening, then plunging one inside. Then another. Judging by Sophia's little cries of bliss, she was coming undone. And one more stroke had her crying out again and bucking against him in earnest again and again before she finally lay still and panting.

Quickly, efficiently he got her out of her gown, and stockings and undergarments, and when she was lying naked before him, Ben felt his chest constrict at the sight. He had never, in all his life, seen a more beautiful sight.

The eyes she lifted to him were drowsy with pleasure, but

she raised her arms to him and he shucked off his breeches and went to her. Finally, at last, skin against skin.

"It might hurt a bit," he warned her, not wanting the realities of their joining to be a surprise to her. As she'd pointed out to Greaves, she deserved to make her own decisions based on the facts. "But I will do all I can to ensure it doesn't last."

"I'm not worried," she said with a smile. "I want you. I want this. Judging by what you just did with your hands, I cannot imagine you're bad at it."

He sent up a prayer of thanks to his years before taking holy orders, where he'd learned quite a bit about bringing as much pleasure as he received. Sex, he'd always considered, was a gift from God. That he was able to share that gift with the woman he loved, was a blessing.

"I'll do my best," he said solemnly, kissing her before he reached between them and pulled her knee up over his hip. Fitting himself against her, he pressed forward thinking of any distraction he could to ignore the hot, wet clasp of her body around his.

Sophia was quiet, as if holding her breath, but he felt her hands clasp his shoulders as he stroked into her. And when he finally, blissfully, seated within her she gave a slow exhale. "No pain," she said softly as they both adjusted to the feel of their joined bodies.

Then, unable to control himself any longer, Ben began to move.

Chapter 23

Sophia wasn't sure what she'd expected the act of love to be like. She'd, of course, learned long ago from naughty books found in her parents' library, and a hidden book of etchings she'd found in the library here at Beauchamp House, what the act entailed. But none of that had captured what it would be like with Ben. With his careful attention to the way she responded to his touch, and the intense look of satisfaction in his eyes as he wrung every last gasp from her while he stroked her with his hands. It was more than anyone could capture on the page, and she was strangely giddy from the emotions it stirred in her.

Now, in what should have been an embarrassingly awkward pose with him braced over her on one arm, she was instead filled with a sense of deepest elation and joy. But as he pulled out of her, and ever so slowly pressed back inside, she felt something else building within her. And her body began to move of its own volition, following him as he pulled away. This was something far more than simple release. As she looked into his eyes, hazy with passion, she felt the bond between them strengthen and wrap them in a cocoon where only they two existed.

His kiss as he plunged into her was needy, desperate.

And she answered him caress for caress, stroke for stroke. They moved together in a dance she knew was not unique to them, but it felt as if it was. As if they were the only two people in the world.

And then she couldn't think at all, as his every stroke ignited another small spark within her and she was lost in an explosion of desire, where every touch sent her higher into the flames.

Then, as if knowing she needed it more than anything, Ben slipped a hand between them and touched that sensitive part of her above where they were joined and Sophia felt herself fly higher, like a firework she'd once seen at Vauxhall, shooting into the sky. Her body trembled with the euphoria of it and she was lost. Her body remaining below while her soul flew away into the ether.

Some distant part of her felt his strokes quicken and Ben gave a throaty growl before she felt him stiffen against her. Then, he let out a long sigh and lowered himself on shaky arms to lie fully against her.

It was a moment before she came back to herself. And she was surprised to feel that they were both a little sweaty. Idly she stroked her hand over his naked back as he continued to catch his breath.

"I rather think that was better than advertised," she said with a touch of wonder. The books in her father's library had been rather flowery in their language and she found they hadn't quite captured the truly world-changing effects of what they'd just done. "Someone ought to write a pamphlet."

Ben lifted his head, his eyes full of mirth and a hint of satisfaction she'd not seen in them before. He was more handsome than she'd ever seen him.

"I rather think there are any number of pamphlets, my dear," he said with a crooked grin. "They just happen to be more common among naughty schoolboys than young ladies of delicate breeding. Otherwise I'm sure you'd have seen them."

"Humph," Sophia said unable to stop herself from ruffling his already disarranged curls. "I think it's preposterous that young men are allowed to see such things and young ladies are kept in ignorance."

"It's hardly something that's encouraged among lads," Ben said, moving so that she was in his lap and he wasn't crushing her. "In fact, at school it was soundly criticized. But I take your point. I imagine a number of young ladies would know better how to protect themselves from randy young lads if they knew what the act entailed."

"I was thinking more along the lines of knowing just how pleasurable it can be," she said with a sheepish smile. "Though there is sense in what you say as well. Either way, I wish I'd known before what I was missing."

He gave a playful groan. "So that you could be off doing this with other men?" he demanded, nipping her ear.

"So that I would have done this with you sooner," she said turning to kiss him. "It's maddening to think of all the months we could have been doing that but were instead sipping tea and chatting about village matters."

Ben gave a laugh that was as carefree as she'd ever heard from him. Perhaps she wasn't alone in the sense of euphoria their coupling had brought.

"I am quite glad you've agreed to marry me, Sophia, otherwise there's no telling what sort of wicked paths you'd lead me down."

"Yes," she agreed. "I will make an honest man of you to keep your reputation from being thoroughly ruined."

At that they must have both recalled the earlier discussion with the bishop, because Sophia saw his smile fade and she knew her own had done so as well.

"I know you said it didn't bother you," she said softly.

"But will it bother you very much for the bishop to keep you from advancing?"

He gathered her against him. There was a soft blanket hanging over the back of the settee and he pulled it over them both.

"I want to marry you, no matter what the Bishop of Chichester has to say about it," he said against her hair. "And the sooner the better."

She couldn't help the little sigh of relief that ran through her. Sophia had been prepared to give him up, but it would have been difficult. Still, she didn't wish to come between him and his calling. "You're sure?"

His laugh reverberated through her. "Sophia, do you know why and how I was called to the church?"

"Well, no," she said thoughtfully. "I suppose I just thought you . . . well, I don't know."

He stroked a hand down her bare arm. "I knew from an early age that as the second son, I'd be destined for either the church or the army. It's the tradition in the Lisle family. My Uncle Cedric is a celebrated hero of the Peninsular campaign, but another thing I knew from an early age was that I wasn't cut out for war. And by the time I went to university, Napoleon had been defeated."

"So, you chose the church by default?" Sophia asked, puzzled.

"Not exactly," he said. "It was more a matter of suitability. You see, I was always drawn to helping people. Freddie and Archer are both good with people too, but neither of them is particularly—" he searched for the right word, "—driven to help them, I suppose you'd say. I cannot go through life ignoring the suffering around us, you see. I must do something to help. Even if my assistance isn't necessarily welcomed, I'll at least know I've tried. Given all that, when the time came to choose a direction at university, the church was the logical choice."

She was silent for a moment, her heart full of affection for this dear man who had so much love for humanity.

He mistook her silence for censure, however. "I can see why that might be worrisome for you, I suppose. But I can assure you I would never neglect you, or our family for the sake of—"

She lifted her hand to his face and pulled him down for a kiss. "Of course I don't find it worrisome. What sort of monster would dislike the fact that her betrothed has a good heart?"

"I didn't think you were a monster," he protested. "Just that it was maybe—"

"Hush," she said against his mouth. "You're a dear man and I only hope I can live up to the example you set."

"I'm not a saint, Sophia," he said with a frown. "Far from it."

"For which I am most grateful," she said with a smile as she gestured to them lying together beneath the blanket.

"I want to marry you sooner rather than later," he said firmly.

"And I want to marry you," she said against his chest. "But I must solve this puzzle Lady Celeste has left for me first."

She both felt and heard his laugh. "Of course you do. And I wouldn't think of pulling you away from it. I'm just as invested in finding Framingham's killer as you are. And, in an odd way, I credit the conversation between Framingham and Morgan we overhead that morning on the cliffs with bringing us together."

It was true, she realized. They'd been drawn to one another before that. But it had taken that shared experience to thrust them together for more than the space of a few hours.

"I dislike owing a debt to Peter Morgan," she admitted. "But in this case there's no way around it."

Then, realizing the late hour, they reluctantly dressed and though Sophia objected to it, he wouldn't allow her to walk him downstairs.

"You need to rest," he said, kissing her nose. "And to get off your ankle."

She was loath to admit it, but he was right. It was also likely a good idea not to be seen by the household escorting her lover to the door looking as if she'd just been tumbled. "Fine," she agreed. "But tomorrow we must go see Ryder. It's time for him to admit his role in this."

At that he looked troubled. "I don't disagree, but tomorrow I have to go to London."

"Why?" she thought they'd just agreed that finding Framingham's killer was important.

"Because I need to get a special license," he said frankly. "We will concentrate on the murder of Framingham when I get back in a day or so. But I will not allow you to face any unnecessary censure as a result of your relationship with me. If that means we marry in haste, then so be it. And since the Bishop of Chichester is not particularly pleased with me at the moment, I will instead go to the Archbishop of Canterbury, who happens to be a friend of my father's."

She blew out a breath of frustration. She could argue, but she knew he would win. One thing she was becoming keenly aware of was that Ben Lisle would do whatever it took to protect her. "I suppose it can wait until you return," she said with a shrug. "I can look into the paintings a bit more too. Perhaps find out where they ended up."

He looked concerned. "Do not put yourself in danger," he said. "Please promise me."

As if to emphasize his words, he pulled her to him for a quick kiss.

"I promise," she said, pulling away before they got carried away again. "Now, shoo or your father will suspect me of kidnapping you for ransom."

He rolled his eyes at that. "I rather think he'll suspect we've been up to exactly what we've been up to," he said wryly.

Sophia felt her eyes widen. "I certainly hope not!"

She heard his laugher echo as he strode off toward the stairs.

Left alone in the studio, Sophia collapsed onto the settee and stared off into space.

She was going to marry a vicar, she thought with a grin. Did wonders never cease?

The next morning, after seeing his father off on his trip to visit Cam down the coast, Benedick packed a few things for a short trip into London and set out. It was only a day's journey by horseback and he arrived in town that evening exhausted but determined to meet with both the archbishop and the Earl of Mainwaring.

As he'd traveled, it had occurred to him that Mainwaring hadn't given Freddie the entire story about the forged paintings. Lady Celeste's letter to Sophia, along with the list of paintings that were lost in the Channel crossing, had made several things clear to him. First, that it was likely someone in the government had known from the start that the forgeries were—not coincidentally—copies of items from that list. And secondly, that Mainwaring had known, somehow, of Ben's friendship with Sophia and hoped to capitalize on it to find out what Lady Celeste had known about the forgeries. There was no way that the Home Office could have foreseen that he and Sophia find themselves betrothed, of course, but they were in the business of using connections to learn information.

The way the earl had used Freddie's relationship with his

brother to bring Ben into the investigation was a prime example of that.

If it was the case that Mainwaring had known just how much danger Sophia would be in as a result of her connection to Lady Celeste? Well, Ben would have a few choice words for the man. He had no issue with putting his own life on the line, because he'd made the decision to take part in the search for the forgers knowing the risk. But Sophia's position as one of Lady Celeste's heirs was not something she could choose. And as the only painter in the quartet, that meant she was automatically at risk from the men who had undertaken the scheme to fake the paintings that Lady Celeste's father had lost. She was the one most likely to recognize a forged painting when she saw it. And she was the one most likely to receive some word from Celeste about the forgery scheme.

After a bath and a change of clothes in his rooms at Pemberton House, the ducal mansion in Mayfair, he set out for the Mainwaring townhouse.

From the line of carriages leading up to the front entrance, and the lights blazing from the townhouse windows, Ben knew at once that the earl and countess were entertaining. His mother would be horrified to learn he intended to show up without an invitation, but given the closeness of the two families, and the importance of his errand, he ignored the niggle of guilt he felt.

Fortunately, he'd brought and worn evening clothes, so when he presented himself to the butler it was only with a slightly raised brow that the man escorted him to Mainwaring's study to wait for the earl, who was currently with his guests in the drawing room.

It took only a few minutes for Mainwaring, looking not particularly surprised to find Ben in his study, to arrive.

"Ben," said the earl as he stepped inside and shut the

door firmly behind him, "I might have known you'd come to beard me in my den at some point. Freddie told me you would have more questions about this forgery business."

The men shook hands and Ben noted that since his marriage, the earl had lost the restless look he'd once worn like a second skin.

"Freddie knows me too well," he responded once the two men had taken seats in the high-backed leather chairs that ranged before the fire. "And, of course, he can't have known at the time that Lady Celeste Beauchamp and her heirs would be so important to your investigation."

To his credit, Mainwaring didn't pretend to misunderstand the implication of Ben's words. "So you've discovered the list of paintings Lady Celeste's father lost in the Channel?"

"Miss Sophia Hastings found the list," Ben corrected. "Which you suspected would happen, I think?

A slight shrug lifted the earl's shoulders. "I knew from both the Marchioness of Kerr's and the Duchess of Maitland's experiences as Lady Celeste's heirs that there was a good chance Lady Celeste had left some sort of puzzle for Miss Hastings as well. It stood to reason that it involved the forgeries she'd been investigating for us before her death."

Ben blinked. "What did you say?"

"Don't tell me none of you has realized yet?" Mainwaring gave a soft laugh. "Given the sheer degree of intellect shared amongst the four Beauchamp House heiresses alone, I would have thought someone would have made the connection. Lady Celeste was one of ours."

It made a mad sort of sense, Ben realized, thinking over the events of the months since Lady Celeste's death. She'd left a series of quests for her heirs to investigate. Her own murder, of course, was personal and the perpetrator had had reasons for wanting her dead that had nothing to do with her work for the government. But the quest she'd sent the Duchess of Maitland on, and the task she'd left for Sophia, were both of interest to the Home Office.

"Did you know she'd left these bits of unfinished business for her heirs to deal with?" he asked carefully. If Maitland had knowingly allowed the Beauchamp House heiresses to put themselves in danger without guidance from the Home Office, he wasn't sure how he'd manage to keep his opinion to himself—longstanding family friendship or no.

"God no!" Mainwaring looked insulted at the very idea. "Celeste made those mad decisions on her own. I did guess that there were more to come after the business with the Duchess of Maitland, and so I sent Freddie to involve you before Miss Hastings got too heavily mixed up in this forgery business. Celeste was the one who realized they were using the list of her father's paintings, and so I left it to her to locate the major players. But she died before that could happen. She collected a few of the forgeries, but was unable to learn who was painting them. We've had our eye on Morgan, of course."

That was a relief, at least, Ben thought, relaxing a little. He'd been prepared to give his brother's friend a dressing down. But given that Lady Celeste seemed to have engineered much of this herself, he could hardly blame Mainwaring for her actions. He might be a spymaster, but he wasn't a mind reader.

"Miss Hastings is heavily involved now," he told the earl pointedly. "Mostly because we both overheard Morgan and the gallery owner Framingham arranging to rid themselves of the artist they'd been using to paint their forgeries. Though I imagine Freddie told you that."

"He did, indeed," Mainwaring agreed. "And of course we know about Framingham's murder now. Do you think Ryder is responsible? I believe he's the one who found the body."

Ben told him about what he and Sophia had witnessed in

the gallery the afternoon of the murder, not leaving out the scene between Ryder and Sophia he'd come upon.

The earl's brows rose in surprise when he was finished. "I knew he was a rough customer, but I hadn't realized his thuggery ran to threatening ladies as well. I wonder you didn't plant him a facer then and there."

"I considered it," Ben admitted. "But Miss Hastings reined in my temper. Not for the first time, where Ryder is concerned. Then, of course, we heard the commotion of him finding Framingham's body and the matter was put to the side."

"It sounds as though the lady has become quite the influence in your behavior, Ben," said Mainwaring with a smirk. "Watch out or you'll find yourself, a vicar, caught in the parson's mousetrap."

Ben rolled his eyes at the joke. "How long have you been waiting to use that line?"

"Since you took holy orders, actually," Mainwaring said with a grin. "Given that the swathe you cut through the ladies back in the day rivaled Freddie's, it wasn't unreasonable that you'd one day find yourself snared."

While it was true he hadn't been a saint in the years before he joined the church, Ben wasn't sure it was fair to say he'd been as profligate as Freddie. Still he couldn't exactly defend himself when there was a grain of truth in what the man said.

"As it happens," he said with a grin of his own, "Miss Hastings and I have agreed to make a match of it. Though you needn't look so pleased with yourself. If anyone is responsible for our betrothal, it's Peter Morgan and his insistence upon plotting the demise of his protegé in so public a location."

"Oh, come now," Mainwaring argued. "If I hadn't sent Freddie down to Little Seaford with instructions for you, do you really think you and Miss Hastings would have become so involved in this business?"

"Clearly you've never met the lady," Ben said, "Freddie or no Freddie she'd have found a way to look into the matter. I'm just grateful I was there to curb her impulse to confront Morgan and Ryder on her own."

At the mention of Ryder, Mainwaring raised a finger. "Speaking of Ryder, while I agree that he's a cretin, and up to his eyeballs in this business, I must warn you that the Home Office isn't sure that he's the only artist who's been involved in this business. In fact, we believe Morgan has a partnership with a group of artists. Which makes sense given that the forgeries are of works from artists from different eras and different styles. It would be rare for a single man to master so many different styles with the sort of skill necessary to paint such convincing fakes as these."

The hairs on the back of Ben's neck rose. "A group of artists? Do you have any idea who they might be?"

"There's a couple in the area," Mainwaring said with a shrug. "I believe they've turned a local manor house into a haven for artists? The Primbles?"

Chapter 24

"Primrose Green," Ben said, feeling like a fool for not realizing it before. The Primbles had been so ready to offer up Ryder as the forger amongst them. But if they were working with Morgan, then it would make sense for them to do so. Ryder was just one of many cogs in the wheel of this operation. As such, he was expendable.

"That's the place," Maitland agreed. "Celeste was friendly with the wife, in particular. And even confided about her father's lost collection in her. She never had proof the paintings were coming from Primrose Green, but it would have only taken a bit of investigation on the Primbles' part to get a list of the paintings from the insurance company. And Celeste hadn't told anyone else about the loss."

"Why wouldn't she tell Sophia about this?" Ben asked. "She gave her the list of paintings and told her about how she discovered the forgery scheme, but she left no word about the Primbles or the Home Office involvement in the investigation."

"I can only imagine that she was not in possession of all her faculties at the time she wrote the letter to Sophia," Maitland said with a frown. "Or that she hoped, out of misplaced loyalty to her friends the Primbles, that they were not responsible for the scheme. The last time I spoke to her she was still hoping Ryder was the only forger. Celeste was an intelligent woman, but even she was capable of being swayed by ties of friendship."

"And do you know anything about who murdered Framingham?" Ben asked, suddenly worried that he'd left Sophia in Little Seaford with only the household servants and her fellow heiresses as protection. If the Primbles were involved, they had a houseful of artists whose livelihoods were in danger if their crimes were discovered. Not to mention that Morgan and Ryder were still in the village. What had he been thinking to travel to London at this time?

"Northman has concluded it was likely a thief who was interrupted in the process of attempting to steal from the gallery," Maitland said with a snort. "It's ridiculous, of course, but then Northman is a fool. I think it very likely it was one of his fellow conspirators. Especially given that the man summoned you there to presumably tell you about the whole scheme. So, either Morgan, or the Primbles."

Ben stood.

"What's your hurry, man?" Mainwaring asked, frowning. "We'll have something to connect one of them to Framingham's murder soon. I'm sure of it."

"That's fine for you to say from the comfort of your home in London, Mainwaring," Ben said as he headed for the door. "But Sophia is in Little Seaford with only three other ladies and a houseful of servants to protect her from these people who have already killed once to hide their scheme. Forgive me if I don't share your sanguine view of the situation."

"Damn it," the earl muttered as he stood as well. "And Maitland and Kerr are in my drawing room. I think. But surely they won't dare to threaten Miss Hastings without provocation."

"Sophia promised me not to confront Ryder while I was gone," Ben said as he stopped for a brief moment in the doorway. "And she knows better than to speak to Morgan alone. But neither of us knew anything about the Primbles' involvement. For all I know she's invited them to dinner at Beauchamp House tonight."

"I knew it!" Gemma said, throwing her arms around her sister's neck upon the news that Sophia had accepted Benedick's proposal.

The sisters were in the library of Beauchamp House, along with Ivy and Daphne, the morning Ben departed for London. Sophia had wanted to give them her news the evening before but she'd been exhausted from the events of the day and had gone to bed early. But today, rested and ready to take on whatever the day brought to her, she'd come to the library after breakfast in her room to do a bit of research on the other artists in the list of lost paintings Celeste had left for her.

When she found Gemma and the others were already immersed in their own research projects in the library, she'd decided to share her news with them. She hadn't considered, however, just how many shrieks of joy and surprise the announcement would elicit.

"From the moment you met I saw sparks," Ivy said with a grin of satisfaction. "I can't wait to tell Quill. He discounted my ability to tell when couples are in love, but this is twice now I've done it."

"Who was your other success story?" Sophia asked, momentarily distracted. She tried to recall her first meeting with Ben and failed. It may have been when they went to discuss Daphne and Maitland's wedding plans, but she couldn't be sure. She'd have to ask him later.

"Daphne and Maitland, of course," Ivy said with a smug smile. "Quill will be quite put out. But I do have a bit of knowledge about the subject, given my study of love poetry."

Gemma frowned. "You can hardly be the only one to see that Maitland was smitten, Ivy, dear. He was gobsmacked from the moment he saw her."

"And he's not exactly one to hold his cards close to his chest," Daphne added with a smirk. "He's a terrible card player."

"Oh, I know Maitland was easy enough to see," Ivy retorted, "But Daphne herself was a different case altogether. And I could tell she was smitten as well. For all that she didn't let anyone know it."

"I was not!" Daphne objected, the telltale flush creeping up into her fair cheeks telling a different story. "I hardly noticed him."

"Dearest," Sophia said to the tall blonde with an affectionate smile, "you must know that's impossible. Your husband might be many things, but easy to ignore is not one of them. Even I noticed him. Any woman who wasn't dead or dying would. He is a handsome man."

By this time the other two had risen from their various study spots and gathered around the Hastings sisters.

"You are right about that, I suppose," Daphne said with a grin. "Maitland is quite good-looking. But so is your vicar."

"There's a reason the church is filled every Sunday since his arrival in the village, Sophia," Gemma agreed. "You've made yourself the most hated woman in Little Seaford by accepting him."

"This calls for a celebration," Ivy said with a grin. She went to the bell pull and when Greaves answered she requested a pot of tea and some celebratory cakes. "You are to congratulate Miss Hastings, Greaves. She has accepted a proposal of marriage from Lord Benedick."

Sophia had been afraid that her easy relationship with the butler might have been ruined by the situation with Lady Celeste's letter, but the man didn't seem to hold a grudge over the scolding she'd given him. And since she was no longer angry about the omission, given his reasons for keeping it from her, she was pleased to see they could go on without further awkwardness.

"I am very pleased for you, Miss Hastings," the butler said with a deep bow. "May I offer my best wishes for your happiness. Lord Benedick is a good man. I hope he will make you very happy."

Touched by the older man's words, Sophia went up on her toes and kissed him on the cheek. "Thank you, Mr. Greaves."

At that the butler turned bright red and murmured something about the tea and beat a hasty retreat.

Some minutes later, the heiresses were once more seated around a tea try and discussing one of Lady Celeste's letters.

Knowing that Greaves' role in keeping the letter away from her would likely poison them against the butler, Sophia had chosen to blame the delay in her receipt of Celeste's letter on her own failure to discover it amongst the documents in the studio.

"How extraordinary of Celeste to leave it up to chance for you to find her letter to you," Ivy said with a frown. "Though I suppose she was ill at the time she decided to do so."

"I think she must have been," Sophia said, sending a silent apology to the brilliant woman who had done so much to bring them together. "But the good news is that I have it now. And as a result we now know not only that the forgers are purposely recreating lost masterpieces, but also that they attempted to make it look as if Celeste was selling off a collection that her father had falsely claimed lost at sea. Whoever these people are, they are not only trying to profit from forged paintings, but they also sought to ruin Celeste's reputation."

"There are any number of people who must have been unhappy with Celeste and the way she chose to live her life," Gemma said, frowning. "She was outspoken on a number of sensitive topics. Even in Little Seaford she wasn't universally loved, though I believe she counted most of the local families as friends."

"With a few exceptions," Sophia reminded her. "I don't believe she got on very well with Peter Morgan, though by the time he arrived in the village she was already becoming ill. Her description of him in her letter to me is not flattering and she does seem to have suspected him of being involved in some way in the forgery scheme."

"It can hardly be a coincidence that the forged paintings found themselves into the homes of his cronies," Daphne pointed out. "The odds of that happening purely by chance are beyond even my calulatory abilities."

"No, it can't be just by chance," Sophia agreed. "He must be involved. And I think it very likely he had Framingham killed. Perhaps the art dealer was not comfortable with Morgan's scheme to have Ryder killed once he'd become a liability."

"But I don't understand why Ryder is still alive if Morgan had decided to get rid of him," Gemma said, frowning. "Even if he did say he wanted to wait until after the exhibition—presumably to show Ryder as an artist in his own right, and therefore hide his forgery—it would seem that the murder of Framingham made Ryder even more of a liability. He has to know that Morgan is the man behind Framingham's murder."

It was a conundrum, Sophia thought. Then, another possibility occurred to her.

"What if Ryder isn't the forger?" she asked excitedly. "What if we've been looking at the wrong artist this whole time?"

"Explain," Ivy said with a nod.

"It's just that Ben and I have assumed ever since we visited Primrose Green with Lord Frederick that it was Ryder who had forged the paintings. Which made some degree of sense given what we'd overheard Morgan and his accomplice—probably Framingham—say at the cliffs. Ryder is Morgan's protégé. He had plans for the man to be the star of the exhibition. After the exhibition, he would have served his purpose in making Morgan look good. The Primbles were full of stories about how unpleasant Ryder was and his skill at copying other artists. So, we put those facts together and agreed that Ryder was the likely culprit. But there's more than one artist in the area. And Primrose Green has at least a dozen."

"Are you saying the Primbles lied to you all?" Gemma asked, looking shocked.

"The only reason we were predisposed to believe them was Lady Celeste's supposed friendship with Evelyn Primble," Sophia said, "but if we work from what Celeste told us in her letter, about her father's paintings, who among her acquaintance in Little Seaford was she more likely to speak of about her father's lost treasure trove of valuable paintings?"

"Another artist," Ivy said with a look of understanding. "Celeste confided in her friend about the paintings her father lost and Evelyn took advantage of it."

"Celeste likely could find no proof that it was the Primbles," Sophia said. "If she had she most certainly would have put some clue about them in her letter to me. All I can guess is that she had a suspicion. She knew Morgan was involved without question, given it was his friends who'd bought the forgeries. But beyond that she didn't know."

"Poor Celeste," said Daphne with one of her rare bursts of emotion. "She trusted Evelyn Primble and was betrayed. Again."

The four were silent for a moment as they considered how

badly their benefactor had been treated by those in her life. Not only had she been murdered by someone who should have loved her, but her good name had been used to perpetrate a fraud within the very art world she held dear.

"We'll simply need to avenge her," Sophia said, her chin tilted in determination. "And I know just how we can do it."

Chapter 25

As it happened, Ben was able to meet with the archbishop just after he left Mainwaring's house. The man was taken aback to be summoned from his bed by his old friend's son, but he'd always had a soft spot for the Duke of Pemberton's boys and though he scolded over the reports he'd had from the Bishop of Chichester, the church leader signed the special license with a flourish.

"Tell your father he owes me a game of whist," he told Ben as he sent him on his way.

Sending a prayer of thanks that his father had happened to attend Eton with the future leader of the Anglican church, Ben returned to the Pemberton townhouse, intent on packing his bags for the journey back to Little Seaford.

He was met there by the Marquess of Kerr and the Duke of Maitland, who'd come as soon as their host had informed them of his presence in town.

"Why didn't you tell us what was going on?" Kerr demanded with a scowl. He'd become a friend during Ben's time in Little Seaford, and was clearly annoyed at being left out of the matter. "We can ride back with you in the morning."

"I planned on heading back to the village tonight," Ben said with a warning look. If they needed a night's sleep before traveling then they would do better to remain in London and travel at a more leisurely pace.

"Do you really think that's sensible?" Maitland asked, giving Ben a chiding look. "You've got bags under your eyes I could pack my entire wardrobe in. And your horse is likely exhausted from today's journey. It will do neither of you any good if you have an accident on the journey back."

Ben was about to argue, when Kerr added, "And Sophia is, in all likelihood, safe in her bed by now. If we set out early tomorrow we can arrive in time for luncheon."

He stared at them, thinking. He'd been charging around on the energy his fear for Sophia had given him. But as if it had been conjured out of pure ether, he suddenly felt the weight of fatigue descend upon him like a water-soaked blanket.

"Come, man," said Maitland. "She won't thank you for getting yourself killed. Get some rest before you take to the road again."

With a sigh, Ben scrubbed his hands over his face. "You're right. I'm in no condition for another long ride."

"We'll be here at first light," Kerr assured him, clapping him on the shoulder. "And try not to worry. If Sophia is anything like Ivy, she's up to any rig. Those four are the most determined ladies I've ever me. I'd stake them against Jackson at his best in a prizefight."

Ben had to smile at that. Kerr was probably right.

"Tomorrow," he agreed. "First light."

As promised, the men were on the road by the time the sun came up, Ben on a borrowed mount since his own had needed rest after the previous day's hard ride. After a few stops along the way, they made it into Little Seaford an hour or so after luncheon, and rather than go to the vicarage, Ben accompanied Kerr and Maitland to Beauchamp House.

To his relief, their arrival was met with all four of the ladies of the house pouring into the entryway from the drawing room where they'd been gathered.

"I thought you weren't due back for another few days," Ivy said, throwing herself into Kerr's arms.

As Daphne and Maitland enacted a similar scene a few feet away, Ben sought out Sophia, who pulled him into the drawing room so that their reunion could at least take place in some privacy. (Gemma, who had rolled her eyes at the embracing couples and muttered something about lovesick fools, had made her escape upstairs a few seconds earlier.)

Aware that he likely smelled of horse and the road, Ben nonetheless pulled Sophia into his arms as soon as the door closed behind them. It had been a day and a half since they'd seen one another, but it felt like much longer. And as he kissed her, he felt for the first time what his brother Archer had meant when he described his wife as "home." Sophia was his home. He knew that now as surely as he knew the sun rose in the east.

"I missed you," she said against his cheek as she pulled back a little. "Don't go away for that long again."

He laughed. "I'm not sure I can promise that. Especially given that I spent fourteen of the past twenty-four hours on a horse. A shorter trip to London from Little Seaford hasn't been made, I don't think."

They moved to a large chair where he sat down and pulled her into his lap. "I was afraid I'd come back to find you'd been kidnapped or worse by the Primbles." He rested his chin on the top of her head. "I have news."

She pulled away to look him in the face. "If it's to tell me you think the Primbles are behind the forgery scheme, then I have the same news."

Quickly, they each explained the conclusions they'd come to about the couple who ran the Primrose Green colony, and how they'd come about them.

"Lady Celeste was working for the Home Office?" Sophia asked when Ben was finished. "I should have guessed. This explains so much—not only about her knowledge of the forgery scheme, but also Daphne's search for the Jacobite Cipher and even her suspicions about her own murder. She had an analytical mind and it makes a great deal of sense to think the government would want to take advantage of that."

"It took me by surprise," Ben admitted. "Though I suppose I didn't know her as well as you did."

Sophia frowned at that. "I didn't know her."

"I think you did," he said gently. "You've made a study of her work. You've read her diaries. I think you know her as well as anyone she met during her lifetime. Excepting her family, of course."

That idea seemed to please her and Ben felt a warm glow at the notion.

She laid her cheek against his coat and then sat up again. "You need a bath, sir."

He saw the saucy grin and knew he was in trouble.

"Do I, Miss Hastings?" he drawled. "And how do you propose to make that happen?"

"You'll need to be very quiet," she said with a finger to her lips. "And it will involve a bit of subterfuge."

"Won't your fellow house-mates become suspicious if you suddenly disappear into your bedchamber?" he asked with a raised brow. "Not to mention that my horse is currently in your stables."

She looked disappointed at the news. "The housemates won't be a problem. We likely won't see Ivy and Kerr or Daphne and Maitland downstairs for days. But the horse is a problem."

"Would it make you feel any better if I told you I intended to stay at Beauchamp House to offer you my protection regardless?" he asked.

"Why? Am I in any more danger than I was before?" she asked with a frown. "The Primbles don't know we've realized they're the forgers."

"But they do know that Morgan's scheme with the bishop was unsuccessful," he said. "And I learned in London that Northman has determined Framingham's murder was the result of a robbery gone wrong."

"What?" Sophia asked, her eyes wide. "But that's absurd. Nothing was missing. And no robber would stab a man that many times just because he'd been found out."

"You have a more sensible take on the matter than our magistrate," Ben said wryly. "It's obvious to me that Framingham was killed by one of his conspirators. And to the Home Office, for that matter. But they will let Northman's determination stand for the moment because they don't wish to spook the actual killer. If he feels safe, then perhaps he'll make a mistake."

"Whether it was Morgan and his henchman or the Primbles," Sophia said, a furrow between her brows, "they'll think they've got away with it. I much prefer the notion of them quaking in their boots at the idea of being caught out."

"I know, my dear," he said, kissing her nose. "But we'll need just a few more days of playing along with their scheme before they're brought down for good."

"Oh, I know that," Sophia said with a shrug. "I've already determined the perfect way to make the Primbles confess. And once they're caught, it should be little enough trouble to make them turn on Morgan."

He should have known she'd have a plan. "You'd better tell me all."

She shook her head. "First, a bath. Then, I'll tell you everything."

"You know it's highly inappropriate for us to even discuss such things as bathing. Much less for me, a vicar, to contemplate creeping into your bedchamber to have my wicked way with you."

"You've got a special license in your pocket, haven't you?" she asked with a challenging look.

He patted his breast pocket. "Signed by the archbishop himself."

"Then unless you plan on abandoning me before we can marry, I don't see a problem."

The gossiping tabbies of Little Seaford might think differently, Ben thought wryly. But given that Morgan had already spread rumors about them, staying away from Sophia now would be like shutting the barn door after the horse had got out.

Even so . . .

"As much as I would love to let you have your wicked way with me in your lair, Wallflower," he said with genuine regret, "I cannot do further damage to either of our reputations. And now that Kerr and Maitland are returned I know you'll be safe."

Sophia grumbled under her breath. Something about vicars and propriety.

But he stood firm.

In more ways than one.

Reluctantly, he lifted her from his lap and stood, grateful his coat would cover the evidence of his arousal when he left the room.

Pulling her into his arms, he kissed her thoroughly.

When they were both breathless, he set her away from him. "Now, I must go. I'll come back for dinner if I may?"

The drowsy, just kissed look she gave him was almost enough to make him gainsay his own decision. But he steeled himself against it.

"Yes," she said, with a sigh. "Return for dinner. And we can discuss the plan for routing the Primbles and Morgan."

He left before his desire to pull her into his arms again overcame his good sense.

Once Ben was gone, Sophia went to the library in search of her sister. If she couldn't spend the afternoon in the arms of her betrothed, then she could use it to gather more evidence against the Primbles.

Gemma, as she'd suspected she would be, was curled up in a chair before the fire in the room all the heiresses had decided was their favorite in the house. When Sophia stepped inside, she looked up in surprise.

"I thought you'd be . . ." she seemed to search for the right word.

Sophia gave a shrug. "My vicar has a stronger sense of propriety than I have. And I daresay he has parish business to attend to, though he didn't mention it."

Her sister smiled. "He's a good man, your vicar."

It was a relief to hear her sister say the words. Sophia hadn't really discussed her relationship with Ben with her, and despite her own determination that she'd wed him, she did care what Gemma thought of him. She wouldn't have rejected him if Gemma had done so, of course, but it gave her a sense of inner peace to know that the one person in the world—aside from him—whose opinion truly mattered to her approved.

"He is," she agreed, lowering herself into the chair opposite. "And I have a difficult time believing he's as smitten with me as I am with him."

"Why?" Gemma asked, closing the scientific journal she'd been reading. "It's obvious to everyone that he's smitten. Has been since you first met months ago."

"How did everyone know this but me?" Sophia asked, shaking her head. "I had no idea. It certainly didn't occur to me until he sought me out at Morgan's ball."

"That's because until you injured your ankle you didn't

sit still long enough for him to speak to you," Gemma said
with a raised brow. "And you were always surrounded by
that gaggle of local gentlemen who were trying desperately
to catch your interest."

Sophia frowned at that. She hadn't attempted to draw
in those men. They simply appeared when she attended
a local entertainment. Had they really kept Ben from approaching her?

"Though, I'll add that he himself was busy dodging the
lures of every eligible lady in the village," Gemma said.
"You're both far too attractive for your own good."

"You make it sound like a liability," Sophia groused.
Though in truth, it sometimes was.

"Can you honestly say you don't sometimes wish to fade
into the wallpaper?" Gemma asked. "I've seen you juggling
gentleman at a ball. And I've seen the look you give when
they aren't paying attention."

It was true. Sophia did enjoy lively conversation and always had. But there were times when being the center of
attention grew tiresome.

"Then I must be thankful that my turned ankle allowed me
the chance to finally slow down." So many things would be
different if she'd decided not to take that walk on the shore.
"And to let Benedick catch me."

They were quiet for a moment in that comfortable way
between sisters.

Then Gemma asked, "What have you decided to do about
the Primbles?"

Suddenly, Sophia realized she hadn't shared Ben's news
about Lady Celeste with her sister. Quickly she filled Gemma
in on Celeste's work for the Home Office, and the role she'd
been playing to stop the forgery ring.

"I should have guessed it," Gemma said when she was
finished. "It did seem odd that one lady would be involved

in so many intrigues, but I suppose I thought she was just interested in many different things. The cipher that Daphne looked for made sense because Lady Celeste was herself interested in puzzles. And the forgeries were in her own village so of course as an artist she'd want to find an answer."

"Now that we know she was officially working with the Home Office, many things make sense," Sophia said. "The clues to her own murder she left for Ivy, the quest she left for Daphne relating to the cipher. And now the forgeries."

"But why didn't she implicate the Primbles in the letter she left you?" Gemma asked.

"We all have blind spots," Sophia said with a frown. "Even someone as brilliant as Lady Celeste."

Still, the fact that her benefactor hadn't named the Primbles specifically bothered her. There was something they were missing as it related to the forgeries. Something that would give them the insight they needed to catch the perpetrators of the fraud.

"I believe I'd like to take a turn in the garden," she said to Gemma. She'd been outdoors since her injury, but that had mostly been in the carriage, and it was no longer paining her now She needed fresh air to clear her head. "Would you like to join me?"

Gemma nodded, and stood up from her chair. "Come," she said, slipping her arm through Sophia's, "let's go see if the sea breeze will give us all the answers."

Moments later, the Hastings sisters were strolling through the garden, which had been designed by Lady Celeste herself. Though it was sunny for spring, there was a chilly breeze and it proved more than Gemma could bear.

"I'm going in to fetch my shawl," she told Sophia once they'd reached the far end of the stand of ornamental trees near the garden's edge. "Shall I bring yours as well?"

Sophia tucked a lock of hair that the wind had blown

loose behind her ear. "Yes, please," she said, taking a seat on a stone bench between two lemon trees. She'd brought her walking stick, thankfully, but she still needed occasional breaks for her weakened ankle. "And perhaps my pelisse. I'm not sure my wrap will be enough."

Gemma left with a promise to return in a few minutes. And Sophia, surrounded as she was by the scents of the garden mingled with the sea air, took a moment to simply appreciate her surroundings. It would have been difficult, back when she and her sister had been living with their parents in their respectable, but cramped townhouse in York, to imagine she'd find herself living on the coast in a house that boasted the most breathtakingly lovely library she could have imagined only a few months later. But here she was.

"I've always thought this was a lovely spot."

The voice startled her, and Sophia turned to see Greaves, his hands clasped behind his back staring out at the horizon beyond the boundary of the garden.

"Oh, Greaves," she said, pressing a hand to her chest. "You surprised me."

Something about the man's demeanor made her uncomfortable. But that was likely the residual effect of their quarrel over the letter from Lady Celeste.

"My apologies, Miss Hastings," the servant said with a bow. "That was not my intention."

"Has my sister been delayed?" she asked, wondering why the butler had made it to her side before Gemma.

"I'm afraid Miss Gemma will be unable to rejoin you here for the time being," he said with what sounded like sincere apology. "She's been detained."

"Detained how?" Sophia's heart began to beat faster, though she managed to keep her alarm from showing on her face. "Is she ill?"

"I was forced to give her a bit of sleeping draught in her

tea," Greaves said conversationally. "But she'll recover, I assure you. I simply needed her out of the way for a bit."

Sophia was regretting her decision to choose this particular part of the garden for her reflection. With Greaves blocking the path back to the house, and the open stretch of lawn leading to the chalk cliff, she had no options for escape. Not that her ankle would allow her to get far anyway.

"And why is that?" she asked, attempting to sound more authoritative than she felt. "Is there something you wish to tell me?"

To her horror, he stepped closer, and she saw that he'd been holding a bottle and a cloth behind his back. "Miss Hastings, you know I don't wish to harm you. So please, don't fight me."

But Sophia did fight. She tried to block him using her walking stick, but he must have been anticipating it because he ripped it from her hand and threw it aside. Then, with a strength she'd never have expected from the servant she'd come to hold in some affection over the past months, he grasped her by the arm and thrust the sweet smelling cloth in front of her face and she felt herself losing consciousness.

The last thing she heard before she faded was Greaves saying. "I'm that sorry, Miss Hastings. That sorry."

Chapter 26

Despite his attempt to stay away, after a bath, a shave and a change of clothes, Ben found himself on the road back to Beauchamp House some two hours after leaving Sophia and her invitation to visit her chambers.

He was a besotted fool, he thought, as he climbed the steps to the front door, but he didn't much care. As soon as this business with the forgers was over he would marry Sophia and they'd disappear for a bit where no one could find them.

He'd raised his hand to knock when the door was wrenched open from the inside and he found himself face to face with a stern-looking Lord Kerr.

"Good," he said without preamble, pulling Ben into the house and shutting the door behind him. "I was on my way to fetch you."

"What is it?" Ben asked, alarm coursing through him a the other man's manner. "Where is Sophia?"

He'd known he shouldn't have left her here, but his damned sense of propriety had made him go back to the vicarage.

"We don't know," Kerr said, his jaw tight with anger. "And we can't find Greaves either."

At this, Ben went cold. "Damn it."

"What is it?" Kerr asked. "Do you know something?"

Quickly, Ben explained about Greaves withholding the letter Lady Celeste had left for Sophia. "We both thought it odd, but Sophia was convinced he'd done it out of affection for her. To protect her from becoming involved the investigation into the forgeries. But it's possible that was just an excuse when she caught him out. His affection for her seemed genuine, but your guess is as good as mine whether it was an act."

Kerr swore under his breath. "I wish you'd told me about this before. This man has been here with all the ladies for days at a time. And we thought they were safe."

"And it would appear that they were safe," Ben retorted, thrusting a hand through his hair. "With the exception of Sophia."

Following the marquess into the drawing room, he found that the rest of the household—minus Sophia, of course—was gathered there. Gemma, her face pale, was lying on the settee looking much the worse for wear.

"I'm so sorry, Ben," she said when he entered the room. "I shouldn't have left her alone. But I only meant to be gone for a moment."

He hurried to her side. Sophia's sister looked enough like her that it was painful to look at her for a brief moment, then he got hold of himself and took charge. "Where were you? What happened?"

Gemma explained that they'd gone into the garden to get a breath of air and that she'd come inside to fetch their wraps. "When I stepped inside, Greaves was waiting with a tea tray. It had two cups. And he said he'd been on his way out to bring them to us, since it was chilly out. He insisted I drink mine there since I was shivering. And though I was in a hurry, I drank it so he'd let me go."

"And then what happened?" Ben prodded. He needed every bit of information Gemma could give him in order to find Sophia. "Did he say anything else?"

"I think he apologized," she said, shaking her head a little. "And when I started to tremble, he helped me to a chair and told me that Mr. Morgan would see to it that I was compensated."

Compensated? Ben stared. What could that possibly mean?

"I found her in the chair," Ivy offered, from where she stood by Kerr's side. "And she told me that Sophia was in the garden. When I went to look, she was gone. But her walking stick was there, tossed into the shrubbery."

"And there was no sign of where they'd gone?" Ben asked, his blood racing with fear. If Morgan, who had likely had Framingham murdered, was in involved, then there was no telling what he'd do to Sophia.

"None," Ivy said sadly. "But I think we can guess where he's taken her. If Greaves was working for Morgan, then they must be there."

"We need to search the man's rooms," Ben said forcefully, already striding for the door to head down the servants stairs.

"Wait," Maitland said, following. "I'll come with you."

Not waiting to see if he was behind him, Ben kept walking.

Greaves' rooms were small but tidy. He had a small bedroom that was modestly furnished, and a sitting room that was decorated with a far more sophisticated hand than Ben would have suspected of him.

In a place of prominence on the wall, however, was a framed painting that he recognized as one of the works lost in the Channel crossing.

He stepped closer and saw that on the table beside it was a wooden case, such as he'd seen in Sophia's studio, made to hold pigments and paints. An idea came to him. "Do you know if Greaves ever showed an interest in art before Sophia came to Beauchamp House?" he asked Maitland, who'd come into the room behind him.

The duke frowned. "He used to chat with my aunt about her own work," he said thoughtfully. "And I think I recall him saying once that he visited Primrose Green to take lessons on his off day."

They'd assumed because Ryder was the one Morgan had publicly taken under his wing that he must also be the artist the man had hired to forge the paintings. Then, when the Primbles came into the picture, it had seemed that they were the likely suspects since Celeste might have told Evelyn about her father's lost art. No one had considered that there was another person—living in Beauchamp House the whole time—who might also have known about the lost paintings. And whose skill with a brush might be every bit as good at copying as anyone at Primrose Green.

"We have to get to Morgan's mansion," he said, the possibility of why Greaves might take Sophia there sending a shiver of fear through him. "I think that's where he's taken her. And I believe I know why."

Whatever it was that Greaves had used to make her lose consciousness had left Sophia with a dry mouth and a groggy head. She became aware of both as she woke up in the back of a moving cart as it bumped over a bit of rough terrain. Her hands were bound, as were her ankles, and though her head wasn't covered, there was a blanket draped over her whole body that prevented her from seeing where they were headed.

The memory of Greaves overpowering her was disturbing enough, but more troubling was the fact that she had no notion of why he would do such a thing. As with most servants, he'd been good at being always at the ready without revealing much about his own personality. He had always, she'd known, had a soft spot for her. But to her shame, she'd accepted it as just another instance of her outward appearance bringing her undeserved praise. It hadn't occurred to her until he'd kept the letter from Lady Celeste, that his affection might run to something more sinister. Or that it could be a ruse to make her think he was more harmless than he was.

Her mind raced as she tried to remember just what he'd said about his reasons for hiding the letter. But nothing she could recall would have alerted her to the fact that he was planning to kidnap her. He'd said he was trying to keep her safe, and it had seemed at the time that he was sincere. Ben had even thought so.

At the thought of Ben, her gut clenched. What would he do when he discovered she was missing? She wished again that she'd been more forceful about making him stay that afternoon. If he'd been there, she would never have gone into the garden at all. Much less found herself bound and gagged in the back of a cart.

She heard the driver telling the horses to slow, and then the cart rolled to a stop. She waited in fear for Greaves to come for her, but rather than the butler, when the blanket was ripped away she saw two large footmen. One look at the blue and red livery they wore told her exactly where the butler had brought her.

They were at Morgan's mansion.

The larger of the footmen hauled her from the cart and when her ankle refused to hold her weight, he muttered a curse and tossed her over his shoulder like a sack of potatoes. She schooled herself against the indignity of being held against the man's body, especially when the memory of Ben cradling her against his chest was still fresh in her mind. As she bumped against his back, she tried to see details of the house and was strangely relieved to see that at the very least she was correct about the location. Bits of decor and wall hangings, familiar from the ball less than a week ago, told her she was indeed in Morgan's home.

Finally, after what felt like ages, the footmen, and Greaves, who had been walking behind them as if he were any guest being ushered in to see the master of the house, entered what looked from Sophia's upside-down perspective, to be the drawing room.

None too gently, the footman who was carrying her bent forward and deposited her, bottom down, into a chair. As he did so, her elbows went in opposite directions. And she realized that the rope knotted around her wrists wasn't as tight as it had been. Something about the bouncing journey from the cart to the house must have loosened it.

"This one can't stand," he said with a grunt to his master, who stood surveying the newcomers like so much driftwood coming on to shore. "Something wrong with her leg."

And having said his peace, he and his fellow left the room, and shut the door behind them. Clearly, Morgan must ask for many such odd tasks from his servants, she thought grimly. They didn't seem particularly upset or concerned that their master had just had them bring a kidnap victim into his home.

"What have you done, Greaves?" Morgan asked, looking from Sophia to the butler of Beauchamp House, who had come to stand beside her chair.

"I've brought the reason for all your troubles," Greaves said plainly. "It goes against the grain, but now, I want you to do me the courtesy of letting me leave unharmed."

"You damned fool," Morgan growled. "This is the last thing I needed. Do you know how many people will be looking for this woman? She's all but betrothed to the son of the Duke of Pemberton! I wanted her separated from him, but not like this. It's why I sent for the bloody bishop to chastise him. Now you'll lead the authorities right to my door."

"And you see how well your scheme to tell the bishop worked," Greaves returned, unrepentant. "Lord Benedick's kind never thinks authority applies to them. You know how the quality are. It's why I threw my lot in with you, sir. You represent the new way of doing things. Where men rise based on their talent and their determination, not by accident of birth."

"That's as may be, Greaves," Morgan said, his florid face looking, if anything, redder, "but you've got to play within the rules of the game. You can't simply kidnap their women and expect them to go away. We had a good scheme worked out. You're a talented artist, and I appreciate all you've done for us, but your time with this operation is at an end. This only proves it." He gestured to Sophia as if she were a prime example of the butler's failings. "Now I've got to rid myself of both of you. Which will only bring more suspicion my way if I don't take care of it the right way."

Artist? Sophia's brain teemed with the possibilities the industrialist's remark ignited. Was it possible that Greaves was the forger? It seemed impossible, though the man had always seemed to be interested in her work. And had spoken fondly about Lady Celeste's painting. She considered the matter as she continued her attempt to unravel the knot at her wrists.

At his words, Sophia saw Greaves stiffen. "What do you mean? I thought if I brought her to you it would make you see how important I am to you. You may think me too stupid to have realized it, but I know what you and Framingham were planning."

Morgan stopped in the middle of his path to the bell pull. "I'm not sure what you think you know, Greaves . . ."

Then, out of the corner of her eye, Sophia saw the butler bring a pistol from beneath his coat. "I know that you were planning to have me killed," he said coldly, leveling the gun at Morgan's chest. "And I know that I stopped Framingham before he could carry out your orders."

Chapter 27

At the sight of the gun, the color left Morgan's face. "Now see here, Greaves. It wasn't my idea. It was Framingham. He wanted to bring in Ryder because you were too close to the Hastings chit. He thought you wouldn't be able to keep your secret. Especially since we thought Lady Celeste must have left her some word."

Greaves laughed. The sound of it sent a chill down Sophia's spine. "As you can see," he said with a bitter laugh, "I am capable of overcoming my affection for the Hastings chit. Especially when it means a chance to save my own skin. It's remarkable what the threat of death will do to change a man's loyalties."

"What do you intend to do, then?" Morgan asked, looking from Sophia to Greaves. "It sounded as if you thought to buy your safety by bringing her here. Which I can assure you will do just that. I'll leave you be, man. Simply leave her here and go on your way. I'll make sure the authorities never know about your role in the forgery scheme."

But Greaves wasn't appeased by the man's about-face. "I'm afraid it's too late for that, Morgan," he said in a rare bit of discourtesy. "You've made it clear where you see me in the caste system and it is beneath you. You may preach to the masses that everyone is equal and deserves to rise to your level so long as they work hard, but it's all a lie. You care for nothing but your own skin. You set this whole forgery scheme in motion as a way to humiliate your competitors. There was money in it, sure, but you enjoyed knowing that they were paying you large sums for paintings they thought would bring them class, respectability, when in fact they were my paintings. Worth a fraction of what they paid."

"If you're so disgusted by the idea of tricking these rich idiots," Morgan asked with a sneer, "then why were you so eager to take your share of the profits?"

"Because I trusted you had a plan," Greaves said with a shake of his head. Sophia could see that he was just as disillusioned by Morgan as Morgan was contemptuous of him. "I thought you were a man with a vision for how society was supposed to work. I spent the better part of my life working in the houses of people born to rank and wealth. I saw no way out for me. But then you moved to Little Seaford. And I heard you speak about how it was time for a new sort of world. Where folks with determination and talent would run things for a change. And I started to think that my place wasn't fetching and carrying for the rich. It was out there, using my brush, like Miss Hastings here does, to show the world the truth."

Sophia couldn't help her gasp behind the gag.

"It's true, Miss Hastings," the butler said to her, his eyes sad. "I knew as soon as I saw your paintings that I could do the same with my work. But as much as I admire you, you're just another one of them who loves power and privilege. It's obvious by the company you keep. When you marry the vicar you'll be one of them."

So he thought to let Morgan kill her? She wanted to ask.

That was certainly a high price to pay for marrying into an aristocratic family, she thought.

"This way, you'll go before your flame is dimmed by marriage into that family," the butler said kindly.

He really thinks he's helping me, Sophia realized with a start. *That death would be preferable to seeing me marry Ben.*

At that moment, she managed to get her wrists free, and she schooled her features not to show her feeling of triumph. If she didn't get out of this alive, it wouldn't be from lack of trying on her part. She simply needed to wait for the right moment to make her move.

"This little scene is affecting," Morgan said with more bravado than he seemed to be feeling. Sophia could see that the hand that grasped the desk behind him was white from gripping so hard. "But I remind you, Greaves, that I've offered to let you go unharmed. Just leave the lady with me and take yourself off. There will be no repercussions. I give you my word."

"You think your word means a thing to me, Mr. Morgan?" the butler asked, his derision clear despite his polite use of the man's name. "You've proven again and again that you're loyal only to yourself and your own motives."

At that moment, she saw a face in the window of the French door just behind Morgan.

It was Benedick.

Thinking quickly, she decided to create a distraction. With the gag in her mouth it was difficult, but not impossible. Groaning as loudly as she could, she slumped back in her chair, hoping against hope that some remainder of Greaves' affection for her would bring him to her aid.

It worked. The butler glanced from Morgan and then, still holding the gun trained on the other man, he turned to see what was amiss with Sophia.

Waiting for her moment, when he leaned over her, she

brought her freed hands forward and pushed against his chest with all her might.

Ben, accompanied by Kerr and Maitland, decided that it would be easier to get into the Morgan mansion under the guise of paying a call than it would be to attempt to break in. So, Maitland and Kerr drove over in Maitland's curricle while Ben rode alongside them.

A few coins in the palm of a tinker on the road between Beauchamp House and the Morgan mansion told them that they were on the right track. Greaves had driven a cart with a blanket-covered load in the back about an hour earlier.

Ben planned to request a word with Morgan about his conversation with the bishop, which he reasoned must have been something the industrialist was expecting. That he'd brought his two aristocratic friends with him would, he hoped, seem like something a duke's son would do.

Thus it was that they arrived before the ostentatious manor house, with its overabundance of stone decorations and multiple mullioned windows, as a group. And when the three men presented themselves at the door, it was obvious from the look on the butler's face that the weight of the occasion was not lost on him.

"Your grace," the man said, his eyes wide, "my lords. It is an honor to welcome you to Morgan Manor."

Playing their roles to the hilt, Maitland lifted his quizzing glass, and Kerr gave the man a bored look.

"I should like to speak with Morgan immediately, sir," Maitland said with the air of one who was never gainsaid.

"It's a matter of some importance," Kerr said. "Come man, look lively."

"Mr. Morgan will know what it's about," Ben added. Then, with a speaking look, he added, "It involves a young lady."

At those words the butler blinked. He stared at the vicar

for a moment, and Ben was certain that the man had heard the rumors about himself and Sophia.

"Of course, of course." The butler said bowing. "Follow me."

He ushered them down a long hall and into a study that had been painstakingly decorated to resemble the centuries old book rooms in aristocratic ancestral homes. "I'll just let Mr. Morgan know he has visitors. May I bring you some refreshment?"

Maitland was already taking a cigar from the box on the desk and sniffing it. "Just get your master, man. We haven't got all day."

When the butler was finally gone, the three men dropped their poses of aristocratic impatience and moved to the window. They had no way of knowing where in the house Sophia was being held, but they would split up and search in different directions.

Ben had a feeling that Morgan would be just shameless enough to hold her in one of the more public rooms of the house. It was well known that his wife kept to her own apartments—staying as far away from her husband as she could—so there was no danger of anyone but servants coming upon the captive. And given that Morgan was known for demanding absolute loyalty from his staff, that wouldn't make a difference.

"I'll take this floor," he said to the other two men as they peered out the window to the grounds beyond. This side of the house boasted a balcony for every floor. And the views of the sea were something that Morgan was fond of boasting about. The construction of the house in this way was beneficial to their search since it meant that they could see into the rooms on this side of the house, at least, from the balconies.

"I'll go upstairs," Maitland agreed.

"That leaves me with the floor below," Kerr said with a nod.

"Be careful," Ben warned the other two men as they headed for the door. "Morgan is a bully, but he's a dangerous one. And we don't know yet what Greaves' full role in this is. Desperate men do desperate things."

The cousins nodded, then slipped out into the hallway beyond.

Ben turned and, opening the French door leading out to the balcony, he looked in either direction before stepping out and creeping along the outer wall of the house. He moved past two empty rooms before he peeked into a brightly lit drawing room.

The tableau before him made his heart stop.

Sophia, gagged and bound, was seated in a wing chair, just to the left of Greaves, who held a pistol pointed in the direction of a man who had his back to the windows. It was Morgan, Ben could tell. He'd know that arrogant pose anywhere.

He calculated how best to get inside and get the gun out of Greaves' hand. If he did the wrong thing, Sophia could get hurt. He didn't much care, at the moment, whether Morgan was harmed. He was responsible for this entire fiasco as far as Ben was concerned.

The moment Sophia saw him, he felt it in his gut. Her eyes widened and she glanced at Greaves, then at Morgan. To his surprise, she slid a hand out to show him that her hands were free. Then, just as quickly she pulled it back.

As he watched, Greaves spoke to her. He couldn't hear what the man said, but he knew it was an apology of sorts from the hangdog expression on the butler's face. Then, Morgan said something that made Greaves look coldly at him and raise the gun and point it more firmly at the man.

Sophia must have made a noise then, because Greaves turned to her, and taking advantage of the man's distraction, Ben turned the handle of the French door and slipped inside. Morgan had turned as if to run from the room. He stopped in his tracks upon seeing Ben in the room.

"Vicar!" he said, his surprise evident. "We have to stop this man. He's kidnapped Miss Hastings." Since Sophia had just launched herself at the butler, it wasn't a bad attempt at distraction, but it didn't work.

Ignoring the industrialist, Ben sprinted over to the where Greaves, lying on his back, was trying to evade Sophia's grasp. She was clinging to his head, her bound ankles and legs off to the side of the big man's body like a mermaid's tail.

"Miss Hastings, stop it!" the butler cried, his face a mask of pain as she twisted his ears. The pistol he'd been holding was lying a few feet away on the floor. "I'm trying not to harm you."

"You'd have done a better job of that if you'd not decided to kidnap her," Ben said, lifting Sophia off the man, then pulling him up into a sitting position.

Maitland came in from the hall door then. "I heard the shouting," he said, scanning the room. Seeing Ben tugging Greaves to his feet, he scowled. "Let me take him."

Not arguing, Ben let the duke take over subduing the butler, and moved to help Sophia, who was trying to untie the knot binding her ankles together.

He'd barely finished before she threw her arms around his neck and burst into tears. "I thought I'd never see you again," she snuffled against his neck.

Right there on the floor of Morgan's drawing room, Ben held her tightly and whispered soothing nonsense words into her hair until she calmed.

"I love you," he said, his voice trembling as he realized

how close he'd come to losing her. "I'm sorry I wouldn't stay. It was stupid. Priggish of me."

She gave a watery chuckle at that. "I love it when you're priggish. Don't you know that?"

He pulled her to him again. "And I love it when you're wanton, Wallflower."

Her kiss was every bit as enthusiastic as he could have hoped. And it held the promise of decades filled with more of the same.

"I found this one trying to escape out on the balcony."

The Marquess of Kerr's announcement from the French doors where Ben had made his entrance had them turning in that direction.

Kerr had Peter Morgan's arms held behind him, and marched him inside.

"You have no right to hold me," Morgan said with a scowl. "Unhand me."

Ignoring him, Kerr shoved the industrialist over to the where Maitland was finishing up the bonds on Greaves' hands.

"Here," Ben said, reluctantly unwrapping himself from Sophia. Rising, he carried the rope Greaves had used to tie her ankles and used it to bind Morgan.

Turning to his friends, he said, "Have you got these two under control? I'll send for the magistrate."

"Take your lady home," Maitland told him with a nod to Sophia. "I've already had a word with the servants. They might seem loyal to Morgan, but coin is even stronger."

"Thank you," he told the cousins. "I owe you."

"Just take care of Miss Hastings," Kerr said with a grin. "We take our duty to the Beauchamp House heiresses quite seriously."

He returned to Sophia's side. She was sitting on the floor where he'd left her a moment ago.

Without asking if she was able to stand, he pulled her to her feet then into his arms. "Let's go have that bath now, Wallflower."

"But I told you I like your attention to the proprieties," Sophia teased. "If the gossips hear about such a thing we'll be the talk of the village."

"We're already the talk of the village," he said as he made his way carefully down the main staircase. "But I have a feeling the capture of Peter Morgan will eclipse even our notoriety for a time. It's a small window and we have to take advantage of it."

The music of her laughter rang through the cold, marble-covered entryway of Morgan's monstrosity of a house.

Despite Ben's bold words about not caring about gossip, he had little choice but to accept when Kerr suggested they drop him at the vicarage on the way back to Beauchamp House.

Sophia hoped their earlier discussion coupled with the speaking look she gave him before he shut the carriage door behind him was enough to ensure that he doubled back later and found his way to her bedchamber. She wasn't even all that intent upon lovemaking—though of course she enjoyed that too—but instead craved the secure feeling of Ben's arms around her. Especially after the ordeal she'd suffered at the hands of Greaves, whom she'd trusted.

Once she'd bathed, and been fussed over by her maid, who was aghast and not a little overset by the news that Mr. Greaves had been the one to kidnap her, Sophia was seated at her dressing table when a noise at the window made her turn.

To her astonishment, she saw Ben step through the open casement.

"How on earth did you manage that?" she asked in astonishment as he shut the windowed door behind him.

Brushing off the front of his breeches, and then giving

the same treatment to his sleeves, which were, she saw, peppered with leaves, he said, "My brothers and I were quite competitive about tree climbing as boys. And fortunately the ornamental trees that line this side of the house are sturdy, and tall enough to give me enough height to grasp the edge of the balcony and pull up."

He stepped forward, and before she could ask any more questions, he pulled her into his arms and kissed her.

"Hello, Miss Hastings," he said in the low voice that never failed to send shivers down her spine. "I did tell you I'd see you again this evening, didn't I?"

"You did," she whispered against his mouth. Slipping her arms around his waist, she reveled in the warmth of his body against hers, the now familiar tingle of desire licking at her insides.

"I'll always keep my promises to you, Sophia," he said in a low voice, his hands caressing her through the fabric of her night rail. She'd been disappointed with the practical nature of her night clothes when deciding on what to wear earlier. But whether it was Ben's proximity or the knowledge that very soon clothing would be forgotten altogether, she soon ceased to care.

She lifted her mouth to meet his, and it felt like the most natural thing in the world to kiss him. To be the one who took his mouth, who opened hers and slipped her tongue against the seam of his lips. And, ever patient, he let her, responding to her overtures with answering heat, but not taking over as she experimented with taking the lead.

Stroking her tongue against his, she soon lost track of who kissed whom, and before long, her hands were tugging at his waistcoat. "Take these off," she muttered against his mouth, surprising a breathy laugh from him.

Without speaking, he lifted her into his arms—and in an echo of the way he'd carried her from the beach only days earlier, he carried her to the bed, which had been turned down, and deposited her gently on the cool sheets.

He made swift work of removing his coat and while he bent to remove his boots, Sophia grasped the bottom of her gown and lifted it over her head. When she turned back from tossing it to the side, she found he was watching her.

His own shirt was gone as well, and for a moment they stared, taking one another in.

It was somehow more exciting to see the muscles and smooth skin she'd already felt beneath her hands. There had been that day in her studio, but this was different. She was far enough away to be able to take it all in. The curling dark gold hair that tapered from between his pectoral muscles— she'd learned about those while studying anatomy for painting—down into a narrow line that disappeared into his breeches.

And beneath that trail, well . . . Sophia swallowed. She might have felt him inside of her once before, but the proud erection there seemed larger than she'd remembered it.

While she watched, Ben—never looking away from her— unbuttoned his falls and shucked out of the breeches.

When he stood naked before her, Sophia felt as if she'd run a mile. Beautiful. It was the first word that came to mind, though not one normally used to describe men.

She must have spoken aloud because almost as soon as she thought it, his lips curled in a knowing smile. "Thank you, my dear," he said as he stalked toward her.

Suddenly overcome with shyness, Sophia scrambled to get beneath the bedclothes. She thought perhaps he'd tease her for it, but Ben slid beneath them too, perhaps sensing that she was less self-assured than she'd at first seemed.

When he took her in his arms, and she felt the over-whelming sensation of skin on skin, she exhaled with such relief that it almost brought her to tears. She clung to him, then, and despite her excitement and arousal, she also felt the fear and rage and disappointment of the ordeal in Morgan's house that evening again.

She must have cried out, because Ben pulled her closer, and made soothing noises as he stroked over her back. "It's all right, Sophia," he whispered against her hair. "You're safe now. I have you."

They lay there together like that for a few moments, just holding onto one another, drawing the most elemental sort of comfort from simply touching. And when he kissed her, the embrace turned fiery again and soon his mouth left hers and trailed down over her jaw and into the hollow just below her ear, where his hot breath made her shiver.

While he kissed her, she let her hands rove over him, stroking down his hard chest, where she stroked a finger over his tight nipples—first one, then the other—and then lower, gliding over the trail of hair she'd only gazed at before.

But before she could stroke the part of him that pressed impatiently against her stomach, his hand circled her wrist and brought her hand up to rest on his shoulder. "Not yet," he said as his tongue flicked out over the tip of her breast. "Later."

She wanted to object, but the feel of his mouth, which was now hot and wet and covering her nipple, made rational thought impossible, and she moved both hands to clutch his shoulders as he gave the same treatment to the other side.

"So soft," he whispered against her skin, the vibration of his deep voice against her skin giving her another reason to shiver.

As he caressed her, Sophia's hips had begun to shift restlessly, and that part of her where she needed him most ached. When she felt his fingers there, she almost cried out with relief.

"Yes, please," she said, her head thrashing a little as he teased at her entrance. "Please, Ben, please."

But instead of giving her what she wanted, he pulled away. "What are you—?"

She stopped in mid-question as she felt him slide down the bed and nudge her legs wider with his shoulders.

His mouth was on her before she could even understand what was happening. And the sensation of his hot mouth on the sensitive skin of her core was enough to make her cry out.

It was almost too much to bear. Sophia had never known anything like it, not even the intimacy she'd shared with him in her studio that day. It was as if her whole being had been set alight but the fire made her whole rather than destroying her.

Her hips moved of their own volition now, and when he slipped two fingers inside her while his mouth sucked one particularly sensitive spot, it was simply too much to endure. With a sharp gasp of relief, she felt herself tumble over the precipice, her being suffused with indescribable joy. And for a moment, it felt as if she left the mortal world and reached the heavens.

The feel of Sophia's body climaxing around his fingers was something Ben wouldn't soon forget. He'd guessed this kind of lovemaking would be something she'd take to, but he hadn't been prepared for his own response to her joy in it.

As it was, he was rock hard and though he'd have liked to give her more time to recover, he could barely keep himself from spilling before he moved to brace himself over her and lift her knee to his hip.

"Yes," she said, lifting her arms to him and pulling his mouth down to kiss him. "Yes, now."

And he wasted no time pressing himself into her. By the time he was fully seated his arms were trembling with the effort it took to keep from hammering into her like an untutored youth. When he opened his eyes, however, he saw that Sophia's were open, watching him. It was unlike anything he'd ever felt, this connection. And when he pulled out and then thrust back in, she whimpered. The noise snipped the last remaining thread of control he had, and he could hold back no longer. With a strangled noise, he pulled both her knees up and tilted her hips, which in turn made Sophia gasp at the deeper contact.

Once, twice, three times he pushed into her and on the fourth stroke he felt her clench around him and cry out as her crisis took her. Then, it was only a matter of a dozen or so more before he felt himself fly over the edge with a groan.

He came back to himself and realized he was likely crushing her with his dead weight. But when he made to move to the side, Sophia protested. "Stay," she said clutching him to her. "I like it."

Her shifting hips made him groan at the friction. Clearly his long deprived carnal side was not yet slaked. Even so, he was mindful of her ordeal earlier and reluctantly moved to her side.

When she'd settled against him, their bodies still touching from head to toe, he turned to rub his nose against hers. "We couldn't stay like that forever, you know," he said earnestly. "It would be dashed difficult to wear clothing. And I feel sure my congregation would not approve at all."

As he'd intended, she giggled.

There was something so intoxicating about being here with her like this. He'd been with other women, of course. As a student at university—before he decided on holy orders— he'd behaved like any other randy young man. But in the years since, he'd of necessity curbed his physical desires and channeled them into other activities.

Being with Sophia, though, was different from anything he'd experienced before.

He understood the sacrament of matrimony now in a way

he hadn't before. They might not yet be wed in the church's eyes, but they were man and wife all the same.

"Does it bother you?" she asked, interrupting his reverie. "That we've anticipated our vows?"

"Did it feel as if I was regretting anything just now?" he asked, tilting his head so he could meet her eyes, which were shadowed now with concern.

"No," she said softly, "but sometimes in the moment . . ."

"I don't regret anything I've done with you, Sophia," he said firmly, "because if I know anything about the joy given us to enjoy on earth, then you are the Lord's own gift to me. How can our joy in one another be a sin? We haven't yet wed in the church, but in our hearts we are and have been since that day in your studio."

She exhaled, and Ben felt her physically relax against him. "I felt that too," she said, tucking her face into his neck. "But I was afraid I had sullied you somehow. I've never been particularly devout. And I thought perhaps my own sins might . . . might ruin you."

He touched her face, forcing her to look him in the eye again. "No one is without sin. Not me, not you. No one. I don't need a wife who is perfect. I need a wife who will love me despite my imperfections. Who will let me love her despite hers."

"Did you just tell me I'm not perfect, Ben?" she asked with a mock frown.

"What? Me?" He shook his head. "I suppose I did. But will it make you feel better if I point out my own imperfections?"

She laid her head on his chest and stroked her hand over his chest absently. "I don't think that's necessary. After all, you had to learn all those skills you so aptly demonstrated a few moments ago somewhere."

He stifled a laugh. "Yes, you see. Not so perfect after all. And for all that you seem to think that taking holy orders turned me into some sort of saint, I'm only a man. With the same desires and faults as other men."

As if to prove his point, his body chose that moment to respond to the soft strokes she slid over his chest.

"Thank heavens for that," she said softly. Then, leaning up to kiss him, she said in a tone that made his chest ache, "I love you, Ben. So much more than I thought possible."

"I love you, Sophia," he returned. "Let me show you how much."

There was no more conversation for a long while.

Chapter 28

"I can't believe Greaves was the forger all along," Ivy said the next morning as she buttered her toast.

The four heiresses were at breakfast alone. Maitland and Kerr had gone to speak to Squire Northman about the events of the day before, and Ben had, reluctantly, left Sophia's bed at dawn to return to the vicarage, where he had parish business to attend to.

Their night together had been a revelation for Sophia and she had found herself wondering how she could possibly have gone through her life before without him. Ben was kind and funny and warm, and when she was in his arms she felt as if they were invincible. Alone, apart, they were strong. But together? They could do anything.

Even bring down a forgery scheme that had flummoxed the Home Office for almost a year.

"The clues were there," Sophia said with a shake of her head. "We just didn't know to look for them."

"Maitland told me that Lady Celeste took a real interest in Greaves' painting," Daphne said, looking sad. "She told him once that Greaves had real talent, but no imagination. Which is why he was so good at copying masterpieces, I suppose."

"I must confess that it never occurred to me," Sophia

admitted, her own feelings of guilt still lingering despite Ben's reassurances that she was not to blame. "He took an interest in my work, but I thought that was all it was. I had no notion that he had ambitions of his own. And I was far too wedded to the notion that Ryder and then the Primbles must be responsible for the forgeries. I fell into the habit of seeing what he wished me to see. A servant."

"He fooled us all," Gemma said, patting her hand. "Even Lady Celeste. When I think of how brilliant she was, how much she managed to foresee before her untimely death, it's maddening to think of how she missed the turncoat living under her very own roof."

"I wonder what the authorities will do to him," Ivy said with a shiver. "If he did in fact kill Mr. Framingham, then it's likely he'll face hanging."

"We'll know more when the men come back from seeing the magistrate," Sophia said. "I suppose the Home Office will need to speak to both Greaves and Morgan before anything can go forward. Ben said that they had suspicions that the money from the forgeries was being sent by Morgan to a group of Bonapartists."

"What on Earth for?" Gemma asked, aghast. "Haven't we spent enough years at war? Why would they wish for such carnage again?"

It was the same question Sophia had asked Ben, whose response had been galling.

"Because in addition to cotton mills," she told them, "Morgan also owns several factories which manufacture supplies for the military."

Daphne said a word that was not appropriate for mixed company.

"For once," Ivy said to her, "I agree with you. What a horrid man. To think that he would try to foment war simply for the purposes of lining his own pockets."

"It's despicable," Sophia agreed. "I just shudder to think what would have happened if Ben and I hadn't overheard his conversation with Framingham at the ball. We might never have become interested in the forgeries at all."

Ben had told her last night that the industrialist's crimes hadn't stopped at treason either. She'd been horrified to learn what Morgan had done to Mrs. Debenham. As if his other crimes weren't disgusting enough, he'd attempted to intimidate the widow into a liaison.

"Speaking of," Gemma said with a frown. "Why did Greaves give you the letter from Lady Celeste? Surely it would have been in his best interest to keep that information from you as long as possible."

Sophia shrugged. "I'm not really sure. All I can think is that he knew I was looking into the matter anyway. And that Lady Celeste's letter cast suspicions on the Primbles since she and Evelyn were such good friends. I wondered if he had read the letter before he gave it to me. I decided he must have. The seal did look odd. He must have melted it then re-sealed it. Lady Celeste had several seals in her study. It would have been easy enough for Greaves to get hold of it and melt some wax."

"It's all so hard to believe," Ivy said. "Such a great many mysteries left behind by Lady Celeste. And even though they were all left unsolved, I cannot think we would have even known about them if she hadn't gone to such lengths to leave us the clues."

"She was a remarkable woman," Sophia agreed.

"And so are you, Sophia," said Gemma with a smile. "I can't wait to see your paintings at the exhibition next week."

"Now that Morgan is out of the way you'll be able to show them without objection, right?" Daphne asked.

"I believe so," Sophia said. "I shall have to speak to the Primbles, of course, though I believe they will allow it. It was always Morgan's attempts to influence the committee that stood in my way."

Just then, the sound of the front door alerted them to the fact that the gentlemen had returned.

Daphne and Ivy rose and went to investigate, leaving Gemma and Sophia at the table.

"I am happy for you," Gemma told her sister with a grin. "Even if knowing Lord Benedick spent the night here has stripped away my last vestige of maidenly innocence."

"Oh, please," Sophia said with roll of her eyes. "You are as prone to fits of virginal blushes as I am."

"You wound me," Gemma replied before ruining the effect by sticking out her tongue.

Their teasing was interrupted by the entrance of Serena, who was followed closely behind by Ben whose cheekbones were suspiciously pink.

"Gemma," said Serena in a suspiciously calm voice, "would you leave the three of us alone for a moment?"

Gemma bit back a giggle, before giving her sister a wide-eyed look. Aloud she said, "Of course."

When she was gone, Serena shut the door behind her and Ben went to sit beside Sophia. Under the table, he took her hand in his and laced their fingers together. Exhaling gustily, Serena took the chair opposite the couple and poured herself a cup of tea. "I believe we had a wager, Sophia," she said in a suspiciously calm voice.

Sophia relaxed a little, and squeezed Ben's hand. "We did. Any of my paintings you want."

After taking a sip of tea, Serena settled her cup back on its saucer. She turned her attention to the vicar and shook her head. "I thought if I could count on anyone to conduct himself with propriety, Lord Benedick, it would be the vicar. I hope the two of you are satisfied. I've now proven myself to be the least effective chaperone in Sussex. Possibly all of England."

"Don't say that, dearest," Sophia said with a frown. "It's a silly antiquated notion in any event. I'm my own person and responsible for my own actions. One hardly expects you to sit with a shotgun outside our bedchambers."

Clearing his throat, Ben added, "I take full responsibility for the lapse in propriety, Lady Serena. And I promise you that we will be wed as soon as possible by special license.

"Don't you dare take responsibility for me, Ben," Sophia said hotly, pulling her hand from his. "You hardly forced yourself on me."

"But I should have been strong enough to resist," he countered in a heated whisper. "Let me take the blame."

"I certainly will n—"

"Children, please!" Serena said sharply. "It doesn't matter which of you seduced the other. What matters is that you marry soon enough to preserve both your reputations. Which I am happy to learn is your plan, Lord Benedick. In that, at least, we are in agreement."

"I am pleased to hear you approve, Lady Serena," Ben said with a nod. "And I can assure you, in your role as guardian, that I love Sophia and will do my utmost to make her happy."

"Why must you be so sweet," Sophia said pettishly. "I wasn't finished being cross with you over your high-handedness."

She kissed him on the cheek to take away the sting of her words, and then slipped her hand back into his.

"Completely without remorse," Serena said with a laugh. "I don't know why I'm surprised since neither my cousin and Ivy, nor my brother and Daphne showed an inkling of regret either."

"It's difficult to feel sorry when you can't stop smiling," Sophia said grinning.

"Come give me a hug, then," Serena said, opening her arms, and Sophia and Ben rose and crossed to the other side of the table to exchange embraces with Lady Serena.

"I'm pleased for you, my dear," she told Sophia as she held her close. "Be happy, that is all I ask."

To Ben, she said, "I will keep you to your promise, you know."

Then, giving them one last shake of the head, she told Sophia. "Instead of one of your paintings that is already finished, I have a special request."

"Anything," Sophia said, blinking back tears of joy and gratitude.

"I should like a portrait of Jem, if you feel up to it. I know as the baronet, he should have an official portrait, but I should feel better knowing his likeness is in the hands of someone who knows and loves him."

"I would be honored," Sophia said, clasping her hand to her chest. "Truly."

"Good," Serena responded with a smile. "Now I'll leave you alone. But please recall that servants are quite observant and that the walls in this house are not quite as thick as everyone seems to think."

With that closing remark, she left them, shutting the door behind her.

Almost as soon as the door clicked shut, both Sophia and Ben burst into peals of laughter. When Sophia grasped onto his arm to hold herself up, he pulled her close and soon their giggles turned into kisses.

"I missed you," he said in a low voice that played over her spine like a bow on a violin string, echoing his fingers doing the same thing. "It took every ounce of strength to leave you sleeping this morning and go back to the vicarage."

"I missed you too," she said, tucking her head into the crook of his neck. "Were you able to send for the vicar in Bexhill?"

"Yes," he said with a broad smile. "I asked him to come tomorrow. Unless something unforeseen happens, by dinnertime tomorrow we'll be wed."

Sophia gave a squeal of excitement. "I can't wait."

"You're sure you don't wish to wait for our families?" he asked, his tone serious. "I'm eager to say our vows too, but I am happy to wait if you wish it."

Kissing her on the nose, he added, "I will do whatever you wish."

"You will?" she asked, her voice going soft.

"Perhaps you haven't noticed yet, Miss Hastings," he said with mock solemnity, "but I am utterly devoted to you."

"You are?"

To prove how charmed she was by this, she took his mouth and it was some minutes before they spoke again.

"Miss Hastings, please," Ben said with mock severity when they came up for air. "Whatever will the neighbors think?"

"That I'm pleased at the idea of marrying you?" she asked, feeling her heart swell with so much love she could hardly bear it. "Because I am."

"So, is that a no on waiting for our families?" he asked a moment later.

"We can celebrate with them later," Sophia said, her whole being suffused with love. "For now I want you all to myself."

If his kiss was any indication, Ben most heartily approved of the notion.

Epilogue

"I don't know, Miss Hastings," said the mayor with a shake of his head. Then, catching his mistake, he said, "I mean Lady Benedick. I do apologize. It's hard for me to remember your good news. What I mean is that, I don't know, Lady Benedick, how I feel about this painting. If you'll pardon me for the admission. It just doesn't seem proper."

They were standing in the empty exhibition hall, where Sophia's painting, *Fallen,* was hanging high on the wall above a landscape by one of the Primrose Green artists and beside a mediocre still life of some fruit by the butcher's wife. It was hardly the most illustrious showing for an artist of Sophia's caliber. But given the work that she'd had to put forth in order to get it here, she wasn't complaining.

Now, in the quiet before the doors were opened to the local populace, she had come to take one last look and had found the mayor standing transfixed before it.

"I agree that the subject matter is rather difficult, Mr. Mayor," she said carefully. She preferred not to receive criticism of her works directly from the mouths of her audience. It was much easier to make the decision about whether or not to pay attention when it came in the form of a newspaper column or a magazine review. "But I think anything that makes people think must be accounted a good thing, do you not?"

He turned to her, his bushy brows furrowed. "I . . ." Then, as if the sun had suddenly clarified things he laughed. "Goodness me, no. I don't mean the dead lady there." He pointed a beefy finger to the figure of the dead prostitute at the edge of the painting. "I meant that we should divide 'em up by type. Your painting is very good. But it's got people in it. I think we ought to have a section for people and a section for fruits and a section for trees and the like."

She turned to look at him, arrested by his placid acceptance of the fact that her painting—an indictment on the disposable manner in which men in the upper classes treated women—upset many of the proprieties laid out by polite society, and instead was troubled that it was placed between fruit and a stand of trees.

"I'm afraid that's not up to me," she said, relieved to be able to say so. "You should bring it up with Mrs. Primble. I believe she's over there by the refreshment table."

With a nod, the mayor shambled off to share his concern with the chair of the committee. She gave one last look upward, and was startled to feel a hand at the small of her back. As caresses went, it was subtle, and likely no one would have seen it given its speed. But she knew who it was without turning.

"Lady Benedick, have I told you today that you're talented beyond measure?" Ben asked from where he stood just close enough behind her so that she could feel his warmth.

"I believe you told me that this morning," she said, remembering just how much his praise of that talent in particular had pleased her. She was still a relative novice, but she was eager to gain more proficiency. And he seemed quite happy with the frequency with which she insisted upon practicing.

"And so I did," his voice got that roughness that told her he was remembering that morning's activities too. "And so you are. Talented at any number of things."

"Why, thank you, Vicar," she said with a coy smile.

"Minx," he said with an answering grin.

Then, changing the subject, he asked, "What was the mayor saying to you? He looked very concerned. I was worried he might be upset by your work."

When she told him what the mayor's pressing concern had been, he threw his head back and laughed.

"It's not that funny," she said with a chiding tone.

"Oh, I disagree," he said, reaching out to squeeze her hand. "I've been dreading this day for you. Because I know how talented you are, and how exquisite your work is. But I didn't trust the good people of Little Seaford to appreciate it. So, imagine my relief when the worst our mayor has to say about it is that it's been misplaced."

Her heart constricted. "You've been worried for me?" She fell in love with him all over again in that moment.

"Of course I have," he said, with a frown. "I want every minute of your every day to be a pleasure. I know that's not possible. But I want it for you nonetheless."

Not caring who saw them, she wrapped her arms around his neck and kissed him.

Since it was a public venue—and no matter how they might feel about one another, they did have a certain level of propriety to maintain—she quickly withdrew and settled for slipping her arm into his for the moment.

"I almost forgot," he said when they'd stepped further down the line of paintings. Reaching into his coat, he withdrew a letter. "This came for you, and Serena asked me to give it to you."

Recognizing Aunt Dahlia's handwriting, Sophia quickly unfolded the missive and scanned the crabbed writing for the highlights. But one line in particular leapt out at her and she gasped.

At almost the same moment, there was a commotion at the door to the exhibition hall.

"I am well able to walk on my own, young man," said Miss Dahlia Hastings, still dressed for travel as she entered the large room flanked by the Duke of Maitland and Daphne. "I am hardly so old and infirm that I cannot cross a threshold without assistance. Now, tell me where I can find my nieces, if you please."

Suppressing a laugh, Sophia pulled Ben toward where a sheepish-looking Maitland waited with Daphne and Aunt Dahlia.

"You did seem to stumble when you climbed down from the carriage," Daphne said in her blunt fashion. "I think maybe you are wrong about yourself."

"Aunt Dahlia," Sophia said before her aunt could respond in her own blistering fashion to the duchess, "What a surprise. I only just now received your letter."

The old woman's face softened for just a fraction when she saw her niece. "Finally," she said with a nod. "Someone with sense. I am happy to see you, my dear child."

Ignoring the hand her aunt offered, Sophia hugged her. Aunt Dahlia might not be particularly demonstrative, but she was not opposed to affection. "It's good to see you. I have news."

Stepping back a little stiffly, her aunt pinned her with a narrow gaze. "If you mean the news that you have up and married a vicar without so much as a by-your-leave, young lady," she said with a scowl, "I've already heard it. It was the first thing your sister told me when I saw her at Celeste's house. Your parents will be none too pleased, I can tell you. Your Mama was hoping—despite your attempts to dissuade her—on a viscount at the least. Still, you might have married a blacksmith as you threatened to do. I'll never forget the look on her face."

Sophia took the opportunity to speak while her aunt drew breath.

"There was no time to let them know, you see, and—"

But her aunt had already turned to Ben, who bowed over her wrinkled, beringed hand. "Miss Hastings," he said with the typical Lisle charm, "I am so pleased to meet the strong lady who helped shape my dear Sophia into the jewel she is today."

Turning to Sophia, Aunt Dahlia said in a stage whisper, "I can see why you rushed this one to the altar, my gel. Vicar or no, he's a charmer, isn't he?"

Sophia exchanged a mirth-filled glance with her husband.

"But make no mistake, young man," Dahlia said to him, "you've married one of the most intelligent, principled, talented young ladies in this great nation. And custom and propriety be damned, if you prove to be a rapscallion I will help her leave you behind. Duke's son or no."

Instead of arguing, Ben kept his expression grave and only said, "Yes, ma'am. If I prove to be a rapscallion I shall do all I can to help you."

Dahlia gave a bark of laughter. "Impertinent, too, I see? Well, I suppose you'll rub along well enough together then."

Then, as if she'd done what she came to do, she turned to Maitland and Daphne, who had waited behind her like retainers. "You may take me back to Beauchamp House now. I've seen m'niece and it's clear she won't be able to leave this place for a while." She gestured to the doorway where curious exhibition goers were beginning to trickle in.

"I shall see you and your vicar at dinner, Sophia," she said with a regal nod before turning to offer her arm to a bemused Maitland, who pulled a face, but escorted her out as his gentlemanly training dictated.

"Why do I feel like I've just survived a typhoon?" Ben asked as he and Sophia watched them leave.

"Because you have," Sophia said with a shake of her head. "You most assuredly have."

"I see where you get your backbone from," he said with a grin. "Will you be like that at her age? Shall I prepare myself to be ordered about?"

"Most assuredly," she nodded. "Prepare yourself."

"I'm prepared for anything so long as you're with me," he told her, turning to face her fully, taking her hands in his. "Together, we are unstoppable."

"I love you, Reverend Lord Benedick Lisle." She looked up into his dear, handsome, sweet face, her heart full with love for him.

"Not as much as I love you, Lady Benedick," he said kissing her nose. "And just so you know, I also have a deep appreciation for your intellect and your work as an artist. Just in case that gives you some sort of extra appreciation for me."

"I don't need any extras from you, Ben." She pulled him down, until his mouth was hovering a breath from hers. "You're perfect just as you are."

His eyes softened, in that way they only did when he was looking at her.

"So are you, Wallflower," he said closing the distance between them. "So much more than perfect."

Acknowledgments

As always, huge thanks to my editor Holly Ingraham for steering my crazy plots in the right direction, and trusting me to go off the map sometimes; Holly Root, agent extraordinaire, who keeps me focused on the business side of things and is always there when I need a voice of reason and a read on this crazy publishing world; my friend and now third set of eyes, Lindsey Faber, who makes sure my timelines don't go off the rails and my word echo problem is under control; the art and production departments of St. Martin's Press who give me gorgeous covers and lovely typesetting; Vanessa Kelly who listens to me whine and shares my love of this discrete corner of English history; my pets for keeping me company during long days at the laptop; my family who keeps me afloat when the vagaries of everyday life threaten to consume; and last, but not least, my readers, whose appreciation for my mystery/romance mashups will never cease to amaze me. Thank you all for keeping this writing gig weird and fun.

One for
the Rogue

*For Holly, who took a chance on an unpub-
lished author and opened up a whole new world
of possibilities.*

Chapter 1

The hushed sounds of the quiet house accompanied Miss Gemma Hastings as she crept from her bedchamber through the hallways of Beauchamp House.

She wasn't doing anything wrong. She was a woman grown and come the end of the year she'd be the owner of the estate on the south coast of Sussex. But her emotional memory of being chastised for her nighttime rambles as a child seemed to override her brain's sense of righteousness.

As one of the four heiresses named in the will of Lady Celeste Beauchamp, chosen for their intellectual capabilities to spend a year in residence at the house, which boasted one of the most impressive libraries in England, Gemma had enjoyed the freedom leaving her parents' house in Manchester had given her. But even so, she had moments when their expectations and mundane disappointments threatened to shadow her new life of independence.

Shaking off the anxiety, she pulled her dressing gown more tightly about her and lifted her candle higher to light the way to Lady Celeste's—now her—workroom and gallery.

Insomnia had been her constant companion from an early age. One of her first memories was of lying beside her elder sister Sophia—whose skill with a paintbrush had earned her a place at Beauchamp House as well—and asking for one more story to relieve the desperation of sleeplessness. Poor Sophia had begged her to go to sleep, but Gemma knew that she asked the impossible. Her brain simply would not shut off no matter how much she wished it to. Unfortunately, it was still the case at times.

Now, of course, Sophia was likely fast asleep beside her husband Benedick, the local vicar. The thought made Gemma glance toward the windows overlooking the back gardens of Beauchamp House and beyond the winter-barren trees and shrubs toward the direction of the vicarage.

She'd expected pitch darkness, but to her surprise, she saw a light bobbing far beyond the area surrounding the house and near where she knew from frequent walks the bluffs overlooking the bit of shore belonging to the Beauchamp property lay.

"Who the devil is that?" she asked aloud, but the only response was the creak of a board beneath her feet. Not only was it two o'clock at night, but it was also a cold, bleak November night. No one of sense would be outside at that moment.

Her trip to the workroom forgotten, she quickly retraced her steps to her bedchamber and hastily pulled on the woolen gown she'd worn that day, her sturdy boots, and her warmest cloak.

Minutes later she was pushing through the kitchen door leading into the gardens with a lantern lifted from its hook on the wall. The cold struck her face like a slap. The wind had picked up since she'd dared to go down to the shore earlier in the day—or rather yesterday, she supposed.

It was darker than she'd first thought, but when the moon came out from behind the clouds, it bathed the garden and the landscape beyond in light. And sure enough, she saw a dark figure carrying a light in the distance.

In the months since the heiresses—comprised of Gemma,

Sophia, classics scholar Ivy and mathematician Daphne—had come to Beauchamp House, there had been several dangerous incidents, including murder and kidnappings, which should have given Gemma pause, but she had no intention of putting herself in danger. She would stay at a safe distance from whoever it was that trespassed on Beauchamp House land.

As the only one of the heiresses to have thus far been unable to interpret the letter Lady Celeste had left for her, she was eager for some sort of distraction. Her trek to the workroom had been intended as another search of the artifacts and fossils for some clue to the "greatest find" Lady Celeste had hidden away for her.

My own endeavors in geology were sadly lacking when compared with yours, but because I so admire your self-taught insight into the bone and stone remnants left to us by Mother Nature, I have in turn left to you my greatest fossil-hunting find. It lies where earth and sea and sky take hands and dance together in the wind, where once the terrible lizards roamed and giants walked amongst the—

Unfortunately, her benefactress had left the letter unfinished, no doubt because of the ravages of illness that had taken her life. So unlike the other heiresses, who had been left puzzles and quests to fulfill, Gemma had a half-finished letter alluding to a great find but giving only vague clues as to where it might be found. Gemma, who was not poetic at the best of times, had spent the months since her arrival at Beauchamp House staring at the inked lines, trying to make herself understand the hidden meaning there.

Thus far, she'd only managed to work out that the fossil was located somewhere along the shore. But the stretch of beach below Beauchamp House was too wide to dig up in its entirety, and besides that, why would Lady Celeste bury a fossil she'd already unearthed?

But Lady Celeste's fossil was not foremost in her mind as

she hurried through the windy night. There was no reason for anyone to be on the Beauchamp House property in this weather and at this hour. She had to assume that they were here for nefarious purposes.

Wishing she'd brought some sort of weapon with her, she glanced around at the shrubs and trees of the carefully planned natural gardens and sighed at the fastidiousness of Jenkins, the gardener, who was far too conscientious to leave a convenient branch for her to use as a weapon.

The lantern would have to do.

Opening its window, she snuffed the flame and continued along the path toward the cliff's edge where she saw the dark figure step into the copse of trees near the sea stairs leading to the shore below.

When he emerged on the other side, he lifted his torch higher and she was able to see his face clearly in the light.

"Cameron Lisle!" she cried out in anger. "I should have known it was you."

Lord Cameron Lisle had done many foolish things in his lifetime.

There was the time he'd—on a dare from his brother Freddie—climbed onto the roof of the stables at Lisle Hall and removed the weather vane.

He'd also once ventured into a cave in Cornwall in search of what a smuggler had referred to as "odd bones" and almost been swept out to sea on the tide.

But wandering along the cliff's edge near Beauchamp House in the dead of night in pursuit of Sir Everard Healy was by far the most chuckleheaded endeavor he'd ever undertaken.

He tightened the scarf around his neck and lifted his lantern higher as he watched the other man—nimble for someone of his age and size—creep toward the sea stairs.

At the shout from behind them, from the Beauchamp House gardens if he wasn't mistaken, Cam stifled a groan.

He might have known Gemma Hastings would find a way to ruin this for him.

Secluding himself behind a tree, he watched his quarry glance over his shoulder in alarm before turning to run back in the direction of his carriage on the road beyond the wood.

"What are you doing here?" Gemma demanded, her tramping footsteps drowned out in the din of the wind. "At this hour, too?"

Turning to fully face his accuser, he saw that she brandished an unlit lantern like a cudgel, as if ready to swing it at his head at any moment.

"I might ask you the same questions," he said hotly. She'd very likely frightened Sir Everard so badly he'd not venture this way again, which meant Cam, in turn, would never learn what it was the man was after. "A lady has no business outdoors at this hour. And certainly not in this weather."

He'd hoped she'd rise to the bait and argue with him over the appropriateness of her presence here, but instead she *ignored* that and went for the thing he wished to avoid talking about.

"Who were you following?" Gemma demanded, her eyes narrow. "I saw another light near the stairs."

"That was likely a reflection," he said dismissively, hoping again that she'd get angry and change the subject. "You ladies are so fanciful."

On their first meeting, not long before her sister Sophia married his brother Benedick, she'd flown into the boughs when she learned he was the editor of the *Annals of Natural History*, and assumed it had been because she was a female. But, clever man that he was, he'd assured her it was only because her article was not interesting. Things had not gone well after that. Not only had Gemma ripped up at him, but so had Sophia and Benedick.

Now, however, she seemed determined to ignore his blatant misogyny in favor of pressing him for details he didn't wish to disclose.

Dash it all.

"Why are you here at all?" She demanded, pulling her cloak more tightly around her. "Sophia didn't tell me you were visiting them at the vicarage."

Recognizing that no amount of evasion would satisfy her curiosity, he sighed. "I'll tell you, but let's go inside. I don't want to be blamed for you catching your death."

She looked as if she'd like to argue, but finally nodded and began walking back in the direction of the house.

With one last glance over his shoulder into the darkness, he followed.

The drawing room off the terrace leading into the gardens was lit as brightly as a ballroom in the height of the season. Which should have been Cam's first clue that he'd made a huge mistake in following Gemma back to the house.

"I vow, you young people are far too spoilt with your blooming health and imperviousness to cold," Miss Dahlia Hastings said from her chair before the fire, where she sat with a book opened on her lap as if she'd just put it down. "Even sitting here near the French doors sent me scurrying for the fire. It is really too tiresome of you, Gemma, to make me do it."

The older lady, who had been paying an extended visit at Beauchamp House lowered her spectacles so that she might get a better look at Cam. When she recognized him, however, she gave a bark of laughter. "I thought perhaps you'd been up to no good, Gemma, but if it's young Cam you've been outdoors with in the dead of night I have no fear for your virtue."

Cam wasn't sure whether to be insulted or relieved at the assessment.

Beside him, Gemma unfastened her cloak and draped it over a chair before moving to stand before the fire.

"I didn't go to meet Cam, Aunt," she said over her shoulder. "I saw a light near the cliffs and went to investigate."

Deciding that silence was likely his best defense, Cam removed his greatcoat, gloves, and scarf and moved to stand as far away from Gemma as possible but still within the range of the fire's warmth.

"Your window doesn't overlook the cliffs, my gel." Aunt Dahlia fixed her niece with a speaking look. "You weren't in the collection rooms again, surely?"

At the mention of the collections, Gemma scowled at her aunt and tilted her head none-too-subtly in Cam's direction. Clearly she didn't wish to discuss the room where Lady Celeste's fossil collection was housed in front of him.

But Dahlia seemed not to have noticed. "You've wasted far too much energy searching for that blast—"

"Aunt," Gemma interrupted her. "We'll speak of it later."

Her aunt looked as if she wished to argue, but at Gemma's steely glare, she threw up her hands.

And, to Cam's dismay, turned her attention upon him. "So, what were you doing out on the cliffs at this hour of night, young Lord Cameron? For that matter, why are you in this county? I had it from Sophia only yesterday that you were expected to be away at a gathering of geologists for the next week or so."

"What?" Gemma demanded with a scowl. "She didn't tell me that."

"Likely because you wear that same expression whenever he's mentioned," Dahlia told her without any delicacy for either of their feelings.

It would appear, Cam thought, that Gemma still held a grudge over the rejected submission, then. Good to know.

"I do not," Gemma protested. Then, as if realizing that

wasn't entirely believable, she corrected. "At least not anymore."

"Then who was it you were grousing about yest—?"

"Aunt."

To Cam's amusement, color rose in her cheeks.

"I have that effect on many ladies," he said with an attempt at levity.

As he'd hoped, it removed the sting of embarrassment and replaced it with annoyance.

She raised a brow. "That I believe."

Her honey blonde hair was mussed from where the cloak's hood had caught on it, and with her cheeks flushed from the fire she was in looks. It had never been Gemma's lack of beauty that made her the most frustrating female of his acquaintance. Her sister Sophia was probably the one who would be considered prettier. But he found he preferred Gemma's taller, more athletic build to her sister's petite one.

He let himself imagine what it would have been like if they had been outdoors for lascivious purposes. Then, in horror, stopped. Clearly the cold had addled his wits.

Fortunately, Miss Dahlia Hastings was still bent on questioning them and since his thoughts had warmed him up, he was able to step away from the fire and proximity to Gemma and moved to the sideboard where he knew they kept a decanter of brandy.

"Well, young man?" the sexagenarian demanded. "What were you up to out there? Especially if you were meant to be somewhere else."

He used up as much time as he could pouring three glasses, then handing them round. It was cold enough he guessed that both ladies would appreciate the heat of the alcohol.

"I am . . . or rather, was, at a gathering of naturalists," he admitted. "But it's not in some far-flung locale, it's in this neighborhood in fact, at Pearson Close."

Both aunt and niece made noises of understanding.

"That explains why I wasn't invited," Gemma said with a shake of her head. "Is Pearson as violently distrustful of women as is rumored?"

This last she addressed to Cam, who shrugged. "I haven't seen him around any, but then again, he doesn't even have female servants, so there must be something to it."

"I suppose it's not that unusual to have an all-male gathering of fossil hunters," she continued. "The Royal Society doesn't admit women, after all. But even so, having such a gathering so close to home and not even being extended the courtesy of an invitation is quite angry-making."

"If it is any consolation," Cam told her, taking a seat opposite the chair she'd just dropped into, "so far the symposium has been quite dull. I had thought it might be entertaining since Pearson is said to know most of the major collectors, but most of the men there are only collectors with no real understanding of the science behind their finds."

"And was this meeting so dull that you were moved to walk along the chalk cliffs in gale force winds?" Aunt Dahlia asked, her expression revealing her skepticism at such a notion.

"Yes, you did promise to tell me," Gemma reminded him.

Both women sipped their brandy and turned similar, expectant looks upon him. If he hadn't known it already, their expressions would have confirmed their familial relationship.

"You won't like it," Cam said with a sigh.

But when no staying hand was raised against his speaking further, he knew he had to go on.

"I was following one of my fellow naturalists from Pearson Close," he told them. "And I have no notion of why he came here or what he was searching for. But I intend to find out."

Gemma wasn't sure whether she believed him or not.

It would be easy enough for Cam to blame his presence

on Beauchamp property on following someone else. Especially if he wished to hide his own nefarious purposes.

Yet, Gemma was sure she'd seen another light beyond where he'd stood.

It was too much of a coincidence that she suspected Lady Celeste had left her a find of great significance on the very beach where this second man had been headed.

Could someone else know about the fossil her benefactress had left for her?

She studied Cam for a moment before she spoke. His looks were a bit more rugged than his brother—her brother-in-law—Benedick's. Whereas Ben's features were refined, almost ethereal, Cameron's were blunter, with less symmetry. And his build was more solid, as if he'd spent more time physically laboring. Which, she thought, he likely had since he was rumored to prefer extracting his own fossils from the earth. Even without his brother's male beauty, he was still handsome—Gemma had to admit it—and to her mind, it was the slightly bolder, craggy elements that made him the better-looking one.

Though she'd never say so.

Aloud she asked, "Who was it you followed? I—I mean *we,* all four heiresses, have a right to know who attempts to trespass on our property."

"So that you might go and confront him and make him flee the county before we even know what he's up to?" Cam asked with a raised brow. "I think not."

"You are the most infuriating man," she said crossly. "How are we to protect ourselves if we don't know why he was even here?"

"Might I make a suggestion?" asked Aunt Dahlia in a deceptively sweet tone.

Gemma knew her aunt far too well to believe that meekness.

But Cam was not so familiar with her wiles.

"By all means, Miss Hastings," he said with a nod of deference. "Perhaps you can talk some sense into your niece."

"I don't know about the two of you," the older lady said with a speaking look, "but I will be traveling back to Manchester in the morning and I need my sleep. So I suggest you table this discussion until tomorrow. I will be sorry to miss your—no doubt, entertaining—argument over why and why not Gemma deserves to know this man's identity, but I am quite sure she'll send me an entertaining letter detailing all of it."

Gemma opened her mouth to object, but closed it when Dahlia raised her brows.

And to her disappointment, Cam seemed too well mannered to object to her aunt's suggestion.

"I am sorry to hear you're leaving so soon, Miss Hastings," he said over Dahlia's hand as he took his leave of her. "I wish you a safe journey. And I shall endeavor to make our row as colorful as possible so that you might be entertained by a missive about it in the future."

Gemma rose to see him to the door, but Cam shook his head, then shrugged into his greatcoat and pulled on his gloves and scarf. "I'll just go out the way I came in. I'll send word if I'm unable to call in the morning, Miss Gemma."

And with a jaunty salute, he stepped out onto the terrace and closed the French doors behind him.

"You might have allowed me to question him further," Gemma complained to her aunt after a minute. "I've all but convinced myself that whoever it was out there was searching for the fossil Lady Celeste left for me."

"If I knew Celeste at all," Aunt Dahlia, who had been well acquainted with the lady in their youth, said, "then I have little doubt that she hid it well enough that you need not fear someone stumbling over it in the dark. Or that she would breathe a word of it to someone else. If there was one quality Celeste was endowed with in large quantities, it was discretion."

"But that's just it, Aunt," Gemma protested. "The very fact that this man was trying to walk the beach in the middle of the night—and not just any man, but a fossil-hunter—must mean he knows something's there."

She crossed her arms against the sudden chill that ran through her. "Not to mention that for the past week or so I've had the distinct feeling of being watched."

Dahlia's dark brows—a contrast to her white hair—drew together. "You never said that. At least not to me."

Gemma shrugged. "I didn't wish to alarm anyone. And besides I've had no real evidence of anything. Just a feeling."

"You aren't prone to flights of fancy, my dear," her aunt said. "Promise me you'll speak to Serena about this tomorrow. And your sister. After what's happened to the other heiresses over the past months, it would be foolish to ignore your instincts."

Gemma nodded. Suddenly she wished Dahlia wasn't leaving. Having her here for the past month had been a great comfort in the wake of Sophia's marriage and Ivy and Daphne's absence. Once Dahlia was gone, there would be only herself and Serena. And as much as she loved the widow, Serena didn't enjoy spirited academic debate like the others did.

"You might also mention the matter to Lord Cameron," Dahlia said, interrupting Gemma's thoughts. "As much as you pretend to despise him, he's not as bad as all that. He did tell you he'd been following someone tonight. And he may have heard gossip amongst the gentlemen at Pearson Close about fossils hereabouts. Or perhaps the Beauchamp Collection itself. They might deny women the opportunity to join their clubs and societies, but they are happy enough to sweep in after the ladies have done the hard work and claim credit for it."

"In case you've forgotten," Gemma said wryly, "Lord Cameron is one of them. He's editor of one of the most important journals in the field of geology and has never once published more than a letter from a female geologist."

"I didn't say your objections to him were wrong," Dahlia said mildly. "Just that he may not be the worst of the lot. And he obviously has a great deal of affection for his brother and Sophia. That must account for something."

Gemma wasn't quite convinced but she didn't argue. "I will consider speaking to him about it. It's likely that whoever it was he followed tonight is the same person who's been watching the house."

"Good," Dahlia said with a nod.

Something in her tone made Gemma look closer. "Never say you're telling me to set my cap at him," she said with a horrified expression.

"Heavens no," Dahlia said with a laugh. "My opinion of marriage has changed not at all, despite the fact that your sister seems happy enough with her vicar. I want more for you, though, my girl. You have the potential to break down barriers. To succeed where those of us who came before you, like Celeste and I, failed."

It was something her aunt, who had been a part of the Hastings household in Manchester since both Gemma and her sister Sophia were small children, had told them again and again. She'd made sure her nieces, whose parents were loving but largely uninterested in their progeny, were educated and took them herself on outings to museums and the theatre and anywhere else she thought they might find food for the mind.

Her reaction to Sophia's marriage had been unexpectedly cheerful considering she had openly advocated against the institution for years. But, she'd decided since the deed was done—and she did like Benedick, Sophia's husband, a great deal—that she would not protest it.

And, after all, there was still Gemma to fulfill the spinster's dreams of the life of the mind.

Dahlia's own dreams had been crushed by the fact that her brother controlled her purse strings and had required her to live under his roof. But Gemma, as one of the Beauchamp House heiresses, had no such restrictions.

She was endowed with the funds and the independence that Dahlia had lacked, and Gemma felt the weight of her aunt's expectations upon her in a way that Sophia never had.

"I wasn't so sure when I first arrived," her aunt continued, "but now I'm certain that you've got the recognition we've always dreamed up within your grasp. Once you find whatever it is that Celeste left for you, I have no doubt you'll be able to show those closed-minded men of the Royal Society how wrong they are to deny you entrance. I can't wait to read the announcement in the papers."

Gemma wished she shared her aunt's optimism about her prospects, but decided not to air her doubts just now. It was quite late, after all, and they both had to rise early to get Dahlia on the road.

"Neither of us will do anything unless we get to bed soon," she said, helping her aunt to her feet. "I can't believe you're leaving us already. It feels as if you only just arrived."

Slipping her arm around Gemma's waist, Dahlia allowed her niece to help her from the room and up the stairs. "You must promise to write me as soon as Sophia is increasing. I know she'll want to wait but I trust you to keep me informed. And tell her I can be here in a week's time if she needs me."

For someone who was so against the notion of marriage, Dahlia was very much in favor of infants, Gemma thought with a smile.

Aloud she said, "I promise. And of course I'll write regardless."

They reached the door to Dahlia's bedchamber and she gave her niece an impulsive hug. "I've enjoyed these weeks here with you girls," she said. "I am so grateful to Celeste for giving you this opportunity. I only pray you won't make the same mistakes I made and squander it."

Before Gemma could ask what she meant, she turned, and shut the door firmly behind her.

Chapter 2

Despite the lateness of his return to Pearson Close the night before, Cam was awake and dressed at a relatively early hour.

"I may be driving to Beauchamp House later this morning," he told his valet, Sims, who was arranging Cam's shaving things on the dressing table while Cam tied his cravat himself. "Ask James to be ready with the curricle."

"Yes, my lord," Sims said with a nod. The man had been with Cam since he was a youth, and though he may have wished for an employer who preferred a more flamboyant—or at the very least more fastidious—mode of dress, they rubbed along well together.

"Ask for some hot bricks," Cam added, remembering how cold it had been last night without them. Instead of bothering with the curricle he'd chosen to ride out to the cliff and had arrived back at Pearson Close shivering. "I don't think the cold will let up anytime soon."

Leaving the valet to finish tidying his bedchamber, Cam made his way downstairs toward the breakfast room.

Before he set out for Beauchamp House, he'd first question Sir Everard a bit to see if he could learn anything more about why the man had been trespassing on Beauchamp House land last night.

So far the gathering of fossil hunters at the home of Mr. Lancelot Pearson, a fossil collector known for his reclusive nature, had been less intellectually stimulating than he'd hoped it would be.

For one thing, though there were a few collectors of note among the guests, like Mr. Roderick Templeton, Viscount Paley, and Sir Andrew Reynolds, the rest were enthusiastic but not particularly knowledgeable about the theories and science that tried to make sense of the origins and development of the creatures whose fossilized remains they collected.

It would have been far more enjoyable if his own friends in the collecting world, like Joshua Darnley, a physician who lived with his wife and children in Leaming, or Adrian Freemantle, a Cambridge don, had been able to make the journey. But both men were restricted from such gatherings by the demands of their respective professions. He'd met both men through their membership in the Royal Society and counted them among his closest friends, aside from his brothers, of course. Adrian would have made quick work of the worst offenses against logic and sense at the current gathering. Sir Everard Healy, whom Cam had at first thought was one of the more thoughtful men at the meeting, would have infuriated his scholarly friend. Not only was the baronet rather fond of the sound of his own voice, but he also managed not to take in anyone else's arguments. Just banged on with his own ill-informed opinions like a discordant drum.

It was, perhaps, dislike which had prompted Cam to follow him the evening before, but he'd learned long ago to trust his instincts about people and their motives. And something about Sir Everard made him suspicious. That he'd been unable to catch the man in anything more nefarious than a midnight trip to the shore didn't mean Cam had given up his instinct to find out what the other man was up to.

He entered the breakfast room to find Sir Everard himself

holding forth on his theories relating to the *proteosaurus*, a marine lizard that had been found just down the coast in Lyme Regis by the celebrated fossil collector Mary Anning.

Like her father before her, Mary made her living by selling the fossils and bones and oddities she found embedded in the chalk cliffs and sand near her home. It was dangerous work, and often required the help of local laborers and even tethering herself to the shore to keep from being swept out to sea by the powerful waves.

No doubt Gemma would have something to say about that despite the fact Mary had taught herself French so that she could read the work of Cuvier, and could likely more knowledgeably discuss a fossil's origins than most men, she was effectively ignored so that men like Sir Everard could pontificate about the fossils she'd discovered.

Gemma wasn't wrong, he thought as he listened to Sir Everard posit—wrongly in Cam's opinion—that the fossil in question was related far more closely to the crocodile than Cuvier had theorized. The world of geology, and fossil hunting in particular, were male-dominated. And when he saw men like Sir Everard gaining acclaim while Gemma and women like Mary Anning were denied entry into the Royal Society, it rather made Gemma's point for her.

When Cam had filled his plate from the sideboard he turned toward the table.

"Ah, Lord Cameron," said Pearson, a plate of kippers and eggs before him, as Cam took a seat on the other side of the table. "You must tell us what you think of this *proteosaurus* Sir Everard is discussing. I must say, I had thought Cuvier had the right of it, but Sir Everard makes a good argument."

Indicating to the footman behind him that he'd like coffee, Cam made himself busy with his cutlery to give himself time to avoid the question. He had no wish to insult his host, but nor did he wish to give Sir Everard the idea that Cam agreed with his assessment.

Fortunately, Lord Paley, seated on his other side, chose that moment to speak up. "I rather think Lord Cameron might be one of those fellows who is better able to articulate himself after he's had coffee or tea."

To Cam's relief, Pearson laughed. "Fair enough, old fellow. Fair enough."

When their host turned his attention back to the other men, Cam spoke to Paley in a low voice. "I appreciate the help, there. I was afraid I'd be forced to give my true opinion of Sir Everard and that would be a bad thing for all of us, I think."

"I merely thought that if I found the fellow tedious," said Paley in an equally low voice, "someone of your stature in the collecting world must find him insufferable."

Cam wasn't sure if he should be flattered or wary at the compliment. It was true he was well known in the collecting world, in part because of his role as editor of the *Annals*. But he was hardly of stature. "I rather think tedium is evident to most people whether they are well regarded or not."

"Fair enough," said the other man, raising his cup of tea. "Though our host seems to hang on his every word, doesn't he?"

Cam took a bite of his eggs before speaking. "I suspect he's just trying to be a good host. Given his usual preference for solitude I'd imagine a gathering like this would be a bit challenging."

Paley laughed. "You are determined to be kind when I am determined to be quite the opposite, Lord Cameron."

Cam laughed too. "I did sound a bit priggish, didn't I? Let's just say I am trying to be agreeable in the face of some challenges."

By the time Cam finished his breakfast, both Pearson and

Templeton had left to look at something in Pearson's collection, leaving Cam and Paley with Sir Everard, who for some reason, seemed keen to speak to them.

Or rather, keen to speak to Cam.

Pushing his plate forward, the large man got up from his chair and came to sit across from the two men.

"You're related to one of the Beauchamp House heiresses by marriage, aren't you, Lord Cameron?" he asked without preamble.

"I am," said Cam, careful not to let on his interest at Sir Everard's question. He'd thought he would have to be the one to broach the topic of Beauchamp House. Clearly he'd underestimated the other man's boldness. "My brother, the vicar hereabouts, married Miss Sophia Hastings a couple of months ago."

"There's another, though, isn't there?" Sir Everard pressed. "Another Hastings sister at Beauchamp, I mean. Calls herself a geologist, I believe?"

Cam felt himself bristle on Gemma's behalf at the other man's dismissive tone. "Miss Gemma Hastings is a geologist, yes," he said in a deceptively calm tone. He was rather surprised at his reaction to the man's condescension, but there was something particularly vile about such a dullard belittling Gemma's place in their field of study.

"You are acquainted with the chit, then?" the older man pressed. "Able to wrangle an invitation to the house, I mean?"

Cam blinked. Was this man actually attempting to garner an invitation to Beauchamp House after effectively calling one of its mistresses a pretender? He'd known the baronet was bold given his attempt to search the shore last night, but he hadn't thought him presumptuous enough to inveigle an invitation through Cam's familial connection.

"I believe I could arrange something, yes," Cam said after

a minute. "You'll wish to see the Beauchamp House collection, I suppose?"

Sir Everard nodded. "Yes, of course. It would be foolish to come this close to such a renowned collection and miss out on seeing it for myself. Despite her lack of any true understanding of the science behind it, I've heard Lady Celeste had a rare knack for choosing important items to keep for herself."

"I say," Lord Paley interjected before Cam could reply, "you wouldn't mind if I were to tag along, would you? I've long wished to see Lady Celeste Beauchamp's artifacts. What a spot of luck that you're connected to the house, Lord Cameron."

Not bothering to comment on Sir Everard's dismissal of Lady Celeste's intellect, Cam nodded to both men. "I should be able to garner invitations for you both. I know Miss Gemma will be quite pleased to show us the finer points of Lady Celeste's collection."

In a fit of pique, he added, "She's quite knowledgeable about the study of fossils and their origins herself, you know. I've read some of her work and it's sound analysis."

He'd rejected it for the *Annals*, but they didn't need to know that. It wasn't because her analysis was flawed but because he'd seen a similar argument in a different publication not long before he read hers. It wasn't her fault that she'd arrived at the logical conclusion.

But if he expected Sir Everard to look chastened and apologize, he was doomed to disappointment.

Ignoring the mention of Gemma completely, the baronet grinned. "Excellent. Excellent."

And to both Cam and Paley's astonishment, his task complete, Sir Everard left the breakfast room.

"I thought you two would come to blows," Lord Paley

said with a laugh once Sir Everard was gone. "You're not involved with the Hastings chit, are you?"

"What?" To his embarrassment, Cam's voice went unnaturally high. "Why would you ask that?"

"Calm yourself, man," said Paley with a laugh. "I simply noted your defense of the lady. But if you tell me it was only annoyance at Sir Everard's snide tone, I will believe you, of course."

"Of course that's all it was," Cam echoed him. "And I dislike hearing anyone I consider a friend disparaged in such a way. Lady Celeste was said to be one of the great minds of her generation, lady or no. And Miss Gemma was handpicked by Lady Celeste to oversee her collection and use it for her studies. It's infuriating to hear someone as foolish as Sir Everard demean them, that's all."

Lord Paley nodded, looking thoughtful.

"I'll just go write a note to send round to Beauchamp inquiring whether the three of us, or anyone else who might wish to join us, might come view the collection tomorrow."

He stood and gave a slight bow.

Cam wasn't sure if it was the viscount's watchful eye he was trying to escape or his own reaction to hearing Gemma's intellect dismissed. Either way, he needed a moment to himself.

The skies above Beauchamp House were gray with clouds and the wind had Gemma's hair, unruly at the best of times, flying around her face as she and Sophia stood on the drive bidding Aunt Dahlia goodbye.

"You're sure you won't just stay through the holidays?" she asked her aunt for what must have been the hundredth time. "There's no need for you to go back north. Especially in this weather. Travel will be must better in the spring."

"When the rain will make the roads impassable?" her

aunt asked with a raised brow. "Don't fuss, Gemma. I wish to go back to Manchester. I have responsibilities with the Ladies' Lecture Society and I've neglected them for a month already."

"Perhaps we could help you form something similar here," Sophia, hugging her cloak more tightly around her, offered. "I could suggest any number of ladies in the neighborhood who might be interested. In fact, Benedick might also—"

Aunt Dahlia pounded her heavy walking stick into the shell drive. "Enough! I must go and that's that. I've loved this time with you girls, but my life is there."

She hugged each of the sisters, taking the sting from her words. "I can't begin to tell you how proud I am of you both. Sophia, I had hoped you would devote yourself exclusively to your painting, but if you must marry, then Lord Benedick is as fine a choice as you can have made."

Turning to Gemma, she smiled. "And Gemma, your work here, cataloging and studying the collection Celeste left for you, will be of the greatest scientific importance. If Celeste did leave you something, then you must find it and make your mark. It will be in the analysis of fossils that you distinguish yourself. Poor Mary Anning's analysis is ignored because men have taken her finds and imposed their own theories on them. Celeste has left you an opportunity to be the first to study her fossils. Do not squander it."

She didn't mention their conversation the night before about the importance of remaining unmarried, but Gemma heard the warning anyway.

"Yes, aunt," she said obediently.

And then the sisters were watching their aunt and her maid climb into the large and comfortable traveling carriage that had come with the house. Gemma had seen to it that they were supplied with a basket of food, hot bricks for their feet, and heavy carriage blankets.

To her surprise, Gemma felt tears spring to her eyes as she watched the horses take off at the signal from the coachman and begin the journey.

"Come," Sophia said, slipping her arm through hers. "Let's get inside before we both turn into icicles."

She must have sensed her sister's distress because she didn't comment when Gemma surreptitiously wiped her eyes.

Inside, after removing their coats, scarves, and gloves, they repaired to the breakfast room, where Serena was sipping a cup of tea.

"I take it Miss Hastings has departed?" she asked, no doubt taking in the sisters' glum expressions.

"She has," Gemma said as she spooned eggs onto her plate at the sideboard. Despite her mood, she was ravenous. Cold weather always left her hungry. For good measure she added two pieces of toast to her meal before taking a seat beside Serena.

"I know you'll miss her," said the widow, who, as the niece of Lady Celeste, had been chosen to act as chaperone for the four heiresses over the course of their year in the manor house. "But, I've had a letter this morning that might cheer you up."

"Do tell," Sophia said as she took a seat opposite them. "We could use a bit of good news."

"Ivy and Daphne have decided to return to Beauchamp House for the rest of the year," Serena said, handing Gemma the letter that had been folded on the table beside her teacup. "Ivy wrote that she and Daphne crossed paths at a dinner party in town and that they'd both lamented what Daphne called 'the hair-witted conversation to be had at *ton* entertainments.'"

Sophia stifled a giggle while Gemma scanned the note. "It would seem that Maitland's slang has begun to influence her."

The letter was penned in Ivy's tidy penmanship, and was

dated a week previously. "They'll be here soon, according to this. She says they're leaving tomorrow."

Sophia clapped her hands. "Just the thing we needed to distract us from Aunt Dahlia's departure. I hadn't realized how much I missed them while they'd been in London, but I can't help but feel their absence every time I come to the house now."

"Gemma and I rub along together well enough," Serena said with a nod, "but we've felt the loss of all three of you since your marriages have taken you away from the house."

"Things have changed so much since we first arrived," Gemma said. "There have been so many dangers and adventures. And weddings. It's hard to believe it's been under a year."

"There's still time for more adventures," Sophia said with a grin. "And weddings for that matter. Are there any gentlemen on your dance card, sister?"

"You know me better than that," Gemma said firmly. "I intend to remain unwed, like Aunt Dahlia and Lady Celeste."

"You won't hear any argument from me," Serena said. Her late husband had been an unpleasant, sometimes brutish man. "I fully support your decision. Though of course I am happy for Sophia and Ivy and Daphne. It simply isn't for everyone."

"I cannot afford to let anything distract me from my studies," Gemma said with a shrug. "I have a responsibility to the women who came before me. I cannot let them down."

Sophia tilted her head. "I hope you won't let Aunt's views on the matter pressure you too much. It is possible to have both a loving relationship and a fulfilling career in your chosen field of interest. Men do it often enough, certainly."

"But men are able to ignore the mundane tasks of running the household and caring for children," Gemma retorted.

"Our own Mama should show you that not all ladies are tasked with those duties either," Sophia said with a raised brow.

Their parents had been largely absent from both Gemma and Sophia's lives, so wrapped up in one another that they were uninterested in their children except insofar as they could be held up as reflections of themselves. The raising of the sisters, and much of their education, had been left to Dahlia, who had seen to it that they were educated far better than the daughters of their parents' middle class peers.

"Yes," Gemma responded, "and look how she imposed on Aunt Dahlia to afford herself that luxury."

"I won't argue with you," Sophia said after a moment. "But I do wish you wouldn't close the door on marriage before you've even had a chance to see if you might find a man who would suit you. It will sound silly to you, I fear, but I didn't know life could be so content until I met Benedick."

"It doesn't sound silly," Gemma said softly. It actually sounded wonderful. Gemma couldn't remember a time before she felt this nagging in her gut. That said she had more to do. More to see. More to learn. Thus far she'd found nothing and no one who'd managed to quiet that sense of hunger. And she wasn't sure she ever would.

Aloud, she continued. "It sounds wonderful. I'm happy for you. Truly."

That kind of fulfillment might not be intended for her, but she was happy beyond words that her sister—and Ivy and Daphne—had found it.

They'd moved on to less fraught conversation when the footman, Edward, appeared with a note. "This came for Miss Gemma from Pearson Close."

As Gemma took it from him, she felt the scrutiny of her sister and chaperone.

"Why are you receiving clandestine letters from the mysterious master of Pearson Close, I wonder?" Sophia said thoughtfully.

"It's hardly clandestine when it's delivered in full sight of the two of you," Gemma said tartly as she unfolded the missive. Scanning the words, she continued. "It's from Lord Cameron. He asks if he might bring Viscount Paley and Sir Everard Healey round tomorrow to see the collection."

"Of course," Sophia nodded. "I'd forgotten he was staying at the Close this week for Mr. Pearson's gathering of fossil collectors."

"You could have told me, you know," Gemma chided her sister. "I wouldn't have been angry. Not very angry, at any rate."

Serena, however, was focused on something else. "I know I've supported you in your decision not to marry, but I do think you should take this opportunity to put your best foot forward among these men, your scholarly peers."

Gemma felt a prickle of unease. "I wasn't intending to put my worst foot forward."

"Of course you're intelligent and can hold a conversation with them," Serena said kindly. "But perhaps we can take this opportunity to ensure that your attire is as confident as your knowledge of geology."

Gemma looked down at her gown, a practical gray woolen that was warm and didn't show dirt when she was cleaning artifacts in the collection. "What's wrong with my attire?"

"Nothing is wrong with it, dearest," said Sophia in the tone Gemma recognized as her managing voice. "But men are shallow creatures and I fear they will take you more seriously if you take a bit of time to make yourself pleasing to the eye. And I must admit I've been longing to see you in some colors."

"That's just because you're an artist," Gemma said with a scowl. But she had to admit, though she'd never say so aloud, there was a certain appeal to the notion of making a certain fossil-hunting gentleman of her acquaintance look at her in a different way. Not that she intended to let anything come of it, but it would give her a certain satisfaction to see something in his eyes when he looked at her besides exasperation.

"Fine," she told the other ladies. "I will allow you to dress me tomorrow. But I will not allow you to have Tilly curl my hair. The last time you convinced me to try it, Sophia, I had the stench of burning hair in my nostrils for weeks."

The incident had happened when the heiresses embarked on one of their first social outings not long after their arrival at Beauchamp House. Against her better judgment, Gemma had allowed her sister to talk her into trying something new with her coiffure. It hadn't been a pleasant experience.

Her hair was fine and straight and frankly, the time and effort it took to coax curls out of it was not worth it to her.

"She's gotten much better since then," Serena said with a laugh.

"We promise," Sophia said, placing her hand over her heart. "This is going to be fun."

"I'm glad you're amused," Gemma said with a roll of her eyes. Though inside, she was looking forward to tomorrow.

And not just the discussion of geology, either.

Chapter 3

"Ouch." Gemma made a face as Serena's maid, Tilly, stuck a pin into the coil of curls she was transforming from a blowsy fright into the sort of elegant style Serena herself would be happy to wear.

"Now, Miss Gemma," the maid scolded, "You know I'm as careful as an ewe with a newborn lamb with you."

"She's always been thus, Tilly," Sophia, the traitor, said from her comfortable chair to the side of her sister's dressing table.

If she weren't attempting to convince the gentlemen from Pearson Close of her fitness for their company, Gemma would never have put this much effort into her attire. But Sophia and Serena had convinced her that perhaps her intellect alone was not enough to prove her bona fides to them. As much as it pained her to admit it, men seemed to care as much about a lady's looks—perhaps more—than they did for the sharpness of her mind.

"You are here for moral support," she reminded Sophia tartly. "Taking Tilly's side against me is not that."

"We're all on the same side, miss," said the maid reproachfully as she twisted another lock of hair into a coil. "I'm as intent on you showing those gents your smarts as anyone. It's about time someone took us females serious-like."

"Seriously, Tilly," Gemma reminded her automatically. She'd taught the girl to read soon after the heiresses arrived at Beauchamp House and now they were working on her spoken language. Tilly had ambitions beyond life in service and Gemma was as invested as she was in making her dream of becoming an educator come true.

"Seriously," the girl repeated. "Seriously."

The sisters exchanged a smile in the mirror before Sophia responded to Gemma's earlier rebuke. "I am here to ensure that you are as fine as a five pence when you go downstairs to greet your peers. It is frustrating, I know, that ladies are expected to be well turned out as well as intelligent amongst these sorts, but it is the way of things. Think of it as catching more flies with honey."

Gemma frowned. "I've never liked that expression. I do not wish to catch flies in the first place."

"Do not be so literal," Sophia said, her exasperation evident in her tone. "You take my point. Otherwise we wouldn't be here right now."

Turning her attention to Tilly, she asked, "Which of the gowns I sent over did you settle on? The blue or the green?"

"The blue brings out her eyes very well, Lady Benedick," the maid said before stepping back from the dressing table.

"There, Miss Gemma, all finished."

Gemma, who had closed her eyes to the image in the glass, now opened them and was surprised at what she saw.

She'd never been particularly careful about her looks. Indeed, she could often be found with a pencil tucked into her messily coiled braid when she was in the library scouring the latest journals from the world of natural science. It had been a trial to her mother when she and Sophia still lived in

Manchester. Aunt Dahlia had thought it a foolish concern. And unlike Sophia, who as the eldest, and the most intent on pleasing her elders, and who made an effort with both her appearance and her studies, Gemma had decided to please herself. Only when Sophia had insisted she pay lip service at the very least to society's expectations, had she allowed herself to be pinned and coiffed and laced. But it had never felt comfortable. And certainly didn't give her the sort of confidence it gave her sister.

Still, staring at the tidy, even elegant hairstyle she now wore, gave her a little glow of satisfaction.

Was this why Sophia had always made such a fuss over her hair then?

"Let those boors ignore your thoughts on the *icthy*-whatever now," Sophia said with grin from behind her.

"*Ichthysaurus*," Gemma said automatically, correcting her sister just as she'd corrected Tilly earlier.

"Come on, miss, and let's get you into the blue velvet. It's nearly ten thirty and the gentlemen are arriving at eleven."

Dressing was not nearly the ordeal as the hairdressing had been, but once Gemma was buttoned into the long sleeved velvet, as beautifully made as it was practical, with a bright white fichu for warmth at the neck and finely embroidered red roses at the hem, she was once again feeling an uncustomary surge of pleasure at her appearance.

"If we aren't careful, all of this elegance will go to my head and I will never have another thought for fossils or science," she said wryly as she surveyed herself in the pier glass.

Careful not to wrinkle the gown, Sophia gave her a quick hug. "I've always tried to tell you, it's possible to care about one's coiffure and gown and whatever academic interest one has. You need not trade one for the other. Indeed, I think of my pretty gowns as armor. Maybe now you will view them in the same way?"

"That all depends on how this morning's tour of the collection goes," Gemma said with a rueful smile. "But I do admit that it's nice to be pleased with my appearance in the glass rather than feeling as if I'll disappoint you."

Sophia blinked, her eyes narrowed with concern. "Dearest, you could never disappoint me. Not in a lifetime. I might tease you about your windblown hair and dirty hands, but you must know I don't mean it."

This time the hug she gave her was unmindful of the gown and Gemma felt a wave of affection for her sister wash over her. She'd missed her in these months since she'd married and moved just down the road.

"I know it," she told Sophia, returning the hug. "I simply wish to please you. That's all. And it feels as if a great deal of the time what pleases us is at cross-purposes."

"I am on your side," Sophia said. "Always."

"And I'm on yours," Gemma said, her smile wide. "Now, let's go downstairs and show Serena how well I can look when I'm made to care about it."

They found Lady Serena in the sitting room with a bit of darning, and her gasp when Gemma entered the room was what she'd hoped for.

"Gemma," she said, beaming, "you look as fine as I've ever seen you. I hope these gentlemen are able to listen to your scientific talk without being distracted by your radiance."

This was something that hadn't occurred to Gemma and she turned to her sister with alarm. "Will they do that? I do not wish them to be inattentive because of my hair and a silly gown. I will go upstairs and change at once."

But Sophia held her fast by the arm. "She's only teasing, my dear. Do not, I pray, go destroy all of Tilly's hard work because of a jest."

Serena, her expression contrite, hastened to reassure her as well. "I know we say that gentlemen have very short spans of attention, but I feel sure they will be able to manage. Aunt Celeste was forever complaining about the way that lady scholars insisted upon being dowds to be taken seriously, too."

"You never told me that," Gemma said with a pang of distress. "I thought she was a devotee of sensible dress."

"Only when it came to practicality," Serena said with a shrug. "She was quite fond of pretty things, and I vow had more hats than any lady has a right to. But for those occasions when it was necessary to wear a less-than-fashionable gown—while digging in the sand and soil for fossils, for example—she did so."

Gemma had been here for nearly a year and she still didn't feel as if she truly knew everything there was to know about the woman who had bequeathed her estate to four strangers.

"So, if you needed it," Sophia said with a grin, "you now know that Lady Celeste would have approved of your gown."

The idea pleased Gemma, though she was not quite comfortable discussing it aloud. Instead she turned to the subject of the luncheon menu. In addition to touring Lady Celeste's collection, the gentlemen from Pearson Close would also be sitting down to a light luncheon afterward. The idea had been Serena's, who had thought it would be an opportunity for Gemma to have further conversation with them about her favorite subject rather than sending them on their way as soon as they'd seen the fossils.

Without Serena and Sophia, and even Tilly, Gemma was quite certain she'd have been able to conduct herself passably with her fellow fossil-hunters, but she would without doubt have done so without making much of an impression. At the very least, this way she had learned how much she appreciated having embroidered roses on her gown.

And that was something for which she'd be eternally grateful.

"Lady Celeste Beauchamp was rumored to have quite a collection," said Sir Everard as he, Lord Paley, and Cam rode in the Pearson Close coach over the somewhat bumpy road to Beauchamp House. "I appreciate the invitation, Lord Cameron. I had thought to make a trek there myself before I left the area, but it's much better to get in the door with a relation by my side."

Perhaps realizing how that sounded, he amended, "To ease the introductions, of course. I find that having a male relation along makes the ladies much more comfortable in social situations."

Cam rather thought the ladies of Beauchamp House would have some arguments with the assertion but decided to let the comment pass. After all, this trip had afforded him the opportunity to learn more about what Sir Everard's motives were in both his midnight visit to the beach and the more conventional but no less suspicious visit to the collection. The man was after something, and Cam wanted to know what.

His own motives for this curiosity were not clear to him either. Logic would dictate that the familial connection between his family and Gemma's made it incumbent upon him to protect her from whatever harm Sir Everard posed to her, and by extension, the Beauchamp House collection. But he could just as easily have informed his brother of the man's suspicious activity and gone on about his own business.

Honesty meant admitting that as a collector himself, he wanted to know what it was Sir Everard thought to find on the cliffside property and how he might make use of it in his own studies. Fossil hunters were a competitive lot and there was a certain sense of anticipation at the idea of snatching an important find out from under the other man's nose.

That, however, would also mean snatching whatever it was from beneath Gemma's nose. And there was the rub. If she were a man he'd have no misgivings about it. Obviously he wouldn't steal it. He wasn't that competitive. But honor dictated he give her the opportunity to reject this mysterious prize (which he still didn't know was actually a prize) before making his own claim upon it.

Life was far less complicated when one wasn't bending over backward to please a woman. His brothers might all be cozily trussed up in the bonds of matrimony, but he, thank you very much, would prefer to keep his life simple.

Or at the very least, he would choose a bride who was sweet and biddable and did as she was told. Not someone like Gemma Hastings, who was quick-tempered and didn't have a mild bone in her body.

"I have heard your brother's wife is a very refined lady," said Lord Paley, interrupting Cam's brooding. "I believe the Hastings family is from Manchester?"

Wondering where this conversational gambit was headed, Cam nodded. "I believe they are, yes. Her father is some sort of merchant, I believe? But Sophia and her sister Gemma are both well mannered and intelligent."

"I look forward to meeting them both," the viscount said with an approving tone. "With the added inducement of the collection amassed by Lady Celeste and the estate, I should think Miss Hastings has quite a few suitors vying for her hand."

It was said with the hint of a question in the tone. As if he were asking for Cam's assessment of the situation.

Before Cam could respond, however, Sir Everard broke in. "Never say you've got your eye on the Beauchamp fortune, Paley? If the chit is pretty enough, perhaps I'll make an attempt on her as well."

Cam felt his temper rising at the words. "Do not forget,

Sir Everard, that the lady in question is related to me by marriage. I won't have you speak of her with such disrespect."

The other man threw up his hands. "Of course. Of course, old man. No offense intended. I, of course, misspoke."

"Of course," Cam said with a lightness he didn't feel. Aside from his distrust of the man in general, he also added a disgust for his attitude toward ladies to the marks against him. He hoped whatever it was that brought the fellow to Beauchamp House would prove to be worth the time he'd have to spend in his company.

"Besides," Sir Everard continued, "even if Miss Hastings turns out to be a fright, it's the Beauchamp Lizard I'm really after."

Despite the fact that he'd been waiting for just such an admission from the man, Cam was still surprised by Sir Everard's bald declaration.

Trying to maintain a sense of calm he didn't feel, Cam asked casually, "What's the Beauchamp Lizard?"

"Lady Celeste was said to have found it on the cliffs below her house," Sir Everard said, his eyes bright with excitement. "If it makes up part of the collection, I mean to make an offer to Miss Hastings for it. She's the owner of the collection now, is she not?"

"But what *is* it?" Cam asked again. For a man who liked the sound of his own voice, Sir Everard could be dashed skimpy on details when he wished to be. He still couldn't figure out why, if it had already been unearthed, the other man had been trying to visit the place where it had come from. In the middle of the night.

Though it made some sort of sense to think that if one valuable fossil had been found in a place, others might also be had there. Assuming it was a fossil he spoke of.

"You don't actually believe it exists?" Paley asked, his tone dismissive.

Then, perhaps noting that Cam was still looking at them as if they had branches growing from their ears, he took pity on him.

"About a dozen years ago," Paley said, "a rumor ran through the collecting community hereabouts that Lady Celeste Beauchamp had found the skull of what had to be one of the largest of the ancient lizards to be unearthed in this part of England. But almost as quickly as the rumor spread, it was squelched by the lady herself who said it was all a misunderstanding. That it was only a horse skull that had been buried on the beach."

"It's quite easy to tell a horse skull from that of a lizard," Cam said with a frown. "Why would she make that mistake? Lady Celeste was not a novice. She traveled to Paris to see Cuvier's collections and has a quite thorough bit of scholarship in the library at Beauchamp House."

"That's just it," Sir Everard said with a gleam in his eye. "What if she wasn't mistaken? She was a canny enough sort. Perhaps she wished to protect herself from prying eyes. What if she simply hid the Lizard in her own collection, in plain sight? If I spy it among the contents I mean to purchase it without having Miss Hastings any wiser. If, of course, I don't decide to marry the girl and have the entire collection."

"Isn't it a little early to be speaking of marriage?" Paley asked with a moue of distaste. "You haven't even met the lady properly yet."

"If the collection is as fine as it's rumored to be, Paley, it doesn't matter if she's covered in scales under her petticoats," the other man retorted.

Then, perhaps recalling that Cam was a sort of relation to the lady in question, he turned a narrow eyed gaze on him. "I hope I can count on your discretion, Lord Cameron? I know you wish to purchase the spinal column I outbid you for in that London auction last month."

Cam gave a mental curse. It had been a particularly galling

defeat at the auction held on behalf of Mary Anning and her family. He'd seen the fossilized spinal skeleton the year before as part of Lord Lawler's collection and hadn't had the ready cash to purchase it then. But when he was ready to do so at the auction, Sir Everard had bid almost five times the fossil's worth. Cam was a devoted collector, but even he wasn't prepared to pay a year's allowance from his father for one artifact, no matter how important it might be. When Sir Everard had indicated to him that he might be willing to part with it for a far more reasonable sum, Cam had been thrilled, though outwardly noncommittal. The other man's words now indicated that Cam's motives hadn't been as inscrutable as he'd hoped.

Now he calculated how serious Sir Everard was about his prize versus the likelihood that this Beauchamp Lizard even existed. How likely was it that Lady Celeste had found a lizard skull of such importance and chosen not to share it with the world? Thinking of what he knew of Lady Celeste's character and how she prized scholarship, he doubted it.

"I will be silent as the grave," he said with an inclination of his head to the other man. "I do not believe you'll find the skull in her collection, but if you do, I will say nothing."

He felt a pang of conscience at promising to keep quiet about something Gemma had a right to know about. But if it wasn't in the collection, then he could speak freely to her. And, despite his impatience with her at times, he had enough faith in her abilities as a geologist to know that if there was a skull as fine as the one Sir Everard described in the collection, then she would have noticed it.

"Excellent," said Sir Everard, who actually rubbed his hands together like the villain in a melodrama Cam had once seen on the stage.

Cam was suddenly grateful he knew what it was the baronet

had been looking for on the shore now so that he needn't spend more time in his company.

A few minutes later, they were welcomed into the entry hall of Beauchamp House by the newly appointed butler, George, or rather Stephens, who had been elevated from the position of first footman after the unfortunate dismissal of his predecessor.

"Lord Cameron," said the young man with gravity. "The ladies are expecting you in the drawing room."

Cam and the other men handed over their coats, hats, and gloves, then were ushered upstairs to the drawing room where the warm fire was welcome after the chill of the ground floor.

As they were announced he saw Sophia, Lady Serena and another, unfamiliar lady rise to welcome them.

"Gentlemen," said Lady Serena, the portrait of elegance and grace, "we are so pleased you were able to come today." Cam had long thought her to be one of the loveliest women he'd ever met. Though he had no particular attraction to her, it was someone with that sort of grace and charm that he wished for in a bride. She had also proven herself to be quite practical as a chaperone to the four heiresses, a quality he also found impressive. Not all ladies could claim that for themselves.

Of course, three of her charges had been married rather hastily, but nobody was perfect.

But who was the third lady? And where the devil was Gemma?

"Lady Serena," said Lord Paley into the lull left by Cam's silence, executing a perfect bow. "What a pleasure to see you again. I believe we've met in London once or twice."

"Indeed we have, Lord Paley," said Serena, offering the man her hand.

Turning she gestured to Sophia and the stranger. "May I present my friends Lady Benedick Lisle, and her sister, Miss Hastings?"

Cam felt his breath catch.

This lovely creature was Gemma?

He'd known she wasn't a hideous monster, of course. Any man with a pair of eyes could see that she was attractive enough. But in that blue velvet gown that accentuated her small bosom and hinted at curves he'd never noticed before, coupled with an elegant chignon and a healthy glow in her cheeks, she was extraordinarily beautiful.

Something his two companions didn't fail to note.

Beside him, he felt Sir Everard's elbow in his rib. "Well, well, well. The Hastings chit cleaned up into a beauty, didn't she? Perhaps I won't need to purchase the Lizard after all, eh?"

Paley was bowing over Gemma's hand and Cam noted that he lingered longer than was strictly appropriate.

It wasn't that he was jealous, Cam assured himself. He simply didn't wish for Gemma to be overly bothered by the blandishments of the two men. After all, she had pronounced her desire to remain unwed any number of times.

Bringing the men here had been a mistake. He would be sure to apologize to her later.

"I must admit," Sir Everard said smoothly, "I was quite pleased at Lord Cameron's invitation. I have long heard about the extraordinary collection dear Lady Celeste amassed before her untimely death. But I hadn't realized her most impressive find was you, Miss Hastings."

To Cam's annoyance, Gemma actually blushed at the baronet's flattery. What on earth was wrong with her? Where was the Gemma who would normally send this fool packing for being so presumptuous?

Perhaps recognizing the danger Sir Everard posed, Sophia stepped forward and slipped her arm through his, "I quite agree with you about my sister, Sir Everard. But I hope you won't mind escorting me as we tour the collection? Precedence, you know. Lord Paley will escort Lady Serena, and dear Gemma will be with Lord Cameron. I do hope you'll explain it to me. I've never had a head for such things, as Gemma will tell you."

Despite his disappointment, Sir Everard couldn't resist a captive audience and with a show of gallantry allowed Sophia to slide her arm through his and lead him away.

Paley, meanwhile, looked delighted to be paired off with Lady Serena. "I hope you'll tell me more about your aunt, Lady Serena," he said with an easy smile. "I've heard so many intriguing tales, but I can only imagine yours are far more interesting."

They followed the other pair, leaving Cam and Gemma standing some three feet from one another.

She did not look pleased. He, on the other hand, was relieved. At least he needn't strain himself to make sure the other two men didn't say something untoward. That he had no fears for Sophia or Serena didn't occur to him.

"Shall we?" he asked, offering Gemma his arm with a flourish.

Chapter 4

What on earth had Serena and Sophia been playing at?

Gemma took Cam's arm with what she knew was a lack of grace, but she was too annoyed for niceties.

Hadn't the whole point of having him bring some of the gentlemen from Pearson Close been to ensure she'd be able to speak with them? She was treated to Lord Cameron's company on an all too frequent basis. If they were going to discuss the latest news in the fossil-hunting world, it would have happened by now.

(It had not.)

"A penny for them," said her companion as they climbed the stairs toward the gallery where Lady Celeste had displayed her most prized finds. "If I didn't know better, I'd say you were not best pleased with my company."

Leave it to Cameron to state the obvious. A true gentleman would have ignored her pique.

Still, she hadn't missed the appreciation in his eyes when he first entered the drawing room. And it was hardly his fault that Sophia and Serena had schemed to place them together.

Her innate sense of fairness made her relax a bit and the smile she gave him was genuine.

"Of course not. I am merely trying to recall which of Lady Celeste's treasures will be the most intriguing to Lord Paley and Sir Everard."

"I've never seen the collection either," he reminded her. "What might I want to see?"

And just like that she was annoyed again.

"It's not from want of opportunity," she reminded him tartly. "You've been to visit your brother any number of times since his marriage and have never once come to Beauchamp House to see it."

"Perhaps you've forgotten the occasion of our first meeting," he reminded her, "but I have not. I know we seemed to make up the quarrel once my brother and Sophia arrived that day, but I left with the impression you were not fond of me. I thought it would be . . . unwelcome for me to ask you to show me."

That assertion made Gemma stop in her tracks, in the center of the carpeted hall.

So much for keeping her temper.

Removing her arm from his, she turned to face him.

"You are a gentleman who has traveled the world in search of natural artifacts," she said in a low voice so they wouldn't be overheard. "You have dined with royalty and no doubt wooed ladies on three continents. Am I really to believe that you were afraid to ask me to show you a few fossils that, despite my appreciation for them, are hardly the sort of groundbreaking discoveries you've seen before? Because I was intemperate enough to argue with you at our first meeting when you mistook me for a not very bright gentleman? Truly?"

As she spoke, his cheekbones reddened. As did his ears.

His voice was equally low when he responded, stepping closer so that she could hear him. "I've met seasoned diplomats who would have difficulty knowing how to handle you in a mood, Miss Hastings. And I do not know from whom you have got your information, but I'm hardly a penny dreadful explorer who digs fossils with one hand and woos ladies with the other. I have traveled, yes. I have seen some of the important specimens, but that doesn't mean I have no interest in others. As you well know, there are bones and fossils that have been in collections for decades that are only now revealing their place in the history of our world. So please do not paint me as some sort of snobbish Lothario with more hair than wit."

Gemma swallowed at his words, and tried to maintain her composure.

There was some truth in what he said. Though she was hardly going to admit that now. Not when he was standing so close and she could see the dark ring of blue that circled his pupils.

And definitely not when her eyes were drawn to the lines that framed his mouth as he spoke.

When had Lord Cameron Lisle become so handsome? The thought made her frown, which he took as a response to his words and so continued.

"As for our first meeting, I explained myself already, but I will repeat, I thought the article was written by a man. But that doesn't mean I ever mistook you for one. And far from thinking the author of the piece not bright, I thought it was well reasoned but unsuitable for the journal at that time. The very fact that you are still holding a grudge after so many months should be reason enough to show why I have not importuned you to show me the collection. You are the sister of my brother's new wife. I cannot insult you without sowing discord in my family. And as you know, I value my family above all things."

They stood close enough that anyone who came upon them might suspect a different conversation altogether.

"There you two are."

At the sound of Sophia's voice, they both stepped back with almost comical haste.

Sophia looked between them for a moment, as if trying to determine what sort of confrontation she'd just missed.

Knowing how easily her sister could read her, Gemma didn't dare meet her eyes.

"Sir Everard and Lord Paley are eager to hear your descriptions of the collection, dearest."

The glance Sophia gave Cam was speculative. Gemma knew well enough what sort of quizzing she'd face after the men were gone and resigned herself to it. At least she'd have the morning to devise some sort of explanation.

Because right now, she wasn't quite sure what had just happened.

That went well.

The ironic thought reverberated in Cam's head as he trailed the sisters into what looked to be a workroom, judging by the wide table and neatly arranged tools along the wall behind it.

It was a familiar sort of room for anyone who had spent time cleaning and examining bones and stones.

But he couldn't help but notice the feminine touches. A floral chintz covered pair of chairs with a tea table between them in one corner. A small bookshelf with frequently consulted resources on the history of the Sussex coast and its soil, the proceedings of the Royal Society, and if he wasn't mistaken, a couple of Cuvier's works. Sir Everard must have missed that, or they'd have been treated to his stubbornly incorrect opinions on the Frenchman and his theories.

Lady Celeste, Cam knew from what Sophia had told him, had been a highly intelligent lady with many interests. He'd been reluctant to think she could possibly have been as well read and knowledgeable as reputed. In part because he was a believer in the old adage that a jack of all trades was master of none.

And yet, the workroom did more to convince him of the lady's genuine interest and knowledge in geology than the most ardent defender could.

"The bookshelf is my doing," Gemma was saying to Sir Everard, who had taken her arm, Cam noted grimly.

So much for the order of precedence.

"Lady Celeste's library is quite impressive," Gemma continued. "But I wished to have my own books here so that I might use them to help understand and authenticate my finds."

Sir Everard's eyes narrowed as he tried to make out the titles on the shelf, but fortunately he was forestalled from comment by Paley.

"I see you are mindful of creature comforts as well, Miss Hastings," he said with an approving nod to the chairs. Despite his earlier declaration of interest in Gemma, Cam noted, Paley's arm was still threaded through Lady Serena's.

Interesting.

"I'm afraid those were here when I arrived at Beauchamp House," Gemma admitted with a laugh. "I would never have been bold enough to remove such lovely furniture from one of the other rooms. Especially to a room like this where they might become soiled. But I believe Lady Celeste had these made for this room particularly. I readily admit, I do retreat to them sometimes when long hours standing over the worktable have my back in knots. She thought of everything, you see."

"My aunt was nothing if not practical," Serena noted with a smile. "And as she got older, she had no reservations about providing for her own ease. And I do believe many of the improvements here in Beauchamp House were undertaken with the heiresses in mind."

"What a pity you weren't here long enough to take advantage, Lady Benedick," said Sir Everard with a laugh. "Though I suppose what you've missed, your sister gains."

Gemma stiffened. "I may be the only one of the four to be in residence at the moment, Sir Everard, but that doesn't mean that I would keep my sister or the others from enjoying the House now that they're married. On the contrary. They are free to come and go as they please. And after a few days together none of us was prepared to hold the others to the strict terms of the bequest."

"But as the last heiress it will become yours, will it not?" Sir Everard pressed her.

"If I remain unwed until the first of February, yes," Gemma said coolly. "But as I said, it is not something about which any of us is overly concerned. And I have no intention of marrying anytime soon."

Or at all. Cam could almost hear her add.

Certainly she had no interest in marrying a man of Sir Everard's ilk.

At least he thought not.

If he'd learned anything at all from today's events it was that he didn't know nearly as much about Miss Gemma Hastings as he'd thought.

"Now, is there anything else in this room you wish to see?"

Sir Everard might be pompous, but even he recognized a maneuver to change the subject in Gemma's words.

"Tell us about this specimen here, Miss Hastings," Sir Everard said, with a gesture to a long fossil lying in the center of a dark blue cloth.

"A particularly fine spinal column from a sea lizard," Gemma said, removing her arm from his and carefully taking up the fossilized bones in her hands. "I found it on the shore just below the bluffs here. I keep returning—especially after storms and particularly strong tides—to see if the rest will reveal itself, but so far I've had no luck. As you know, there can be years between discoveries in the same location. So I try to be patient."

"Might there be a skull in the collection that could be paired with it?"

Sir Everard's tone was casual but Cam knew exactly what the other man was digging for.

Oblivious to the subtext of the baronet's question, Gemma shook her head. "Alas, no. That was my first thought, too. But there is nothing of this size in the main collection. But there are several boxes of Lady Celeste's finds in the attic that I haven't yet had a chance to search through. Perhaps I might find some other part there."

At the mention of boxes, Cam saw Sir Everard's eyes light up. Of course he'd find that interesting given his interest in the no-doubt apocryphal Beauchamp Lizard. He could see the other man working up the nerve to ask for a look in the attics, but before he could do so Gemma made it unnecessary.

"Lady Celeste put her most impressive finds in her collection here, in the gallery, so I have no doubt that the boxes contain little more than ammonites and some smaller bits. But it will be amusing to see what she found interesting enough to keep nonetheless."

But Cam had underestimated the baronet's determination to leave no fossil unturned.

"If you would like," Sir Everard said with a patronizing smile, "I will have one of my servants itemize the contents of the boxes for you. I cannot think you should wish to worry yourself over such trivial matters when there are finds like this to be had."

Paley, who had been watching the exchange with interest, spoke up. "I'm sure it would be far more convenient for Miss Hastings to have the boxes out of her way altogether. I'm always looking to expand my own collection. What if I were to purchase the boxes from you, Miss Hastings?" He then named a sum that had Cam's eyebrows rising into his hairline. Gemma herself looked a little shocked as well.

Before she could respond, Serena spoke. "Until the year is completed, the sale of any part of Lady Celeste's estate is strictly forbidden, Lord Paley. And I will let Gemma speak for herself, Sir Everard, but I think you would have better luck convincing the Avon River to flow in the opposite direction, Sir Everard."

"I'm afraid she's right," Gemma said with a smile. "I wouldn't part with any of Lady Celeste's findings for the world. Even if it were legally possible. I've been looking forward to examining each and every item in the boxes myself for months now, but there's been so much excitement. I hope now that the weather has turned cold I will be able to lock myself indoors to do the job properly."

"They understand, of course," Cam said for his companions. Though it was plain from the expression on Sir Everard's face that he did not, in fact, understand.

It was more difficult to read Paley, since he was by far the more polite of the two.

Either way, they would not be leaving here today with any lizard, Beauchamp or otherwise.

For Gemma's sake, Cam was pleased.

Chapter 5

The tour of Lady Celeste's gallery was far less exciting that Gemma had imagined it would be.

First of all, she got the feeling that Sir Everard was looking for some item in particular. Over and over again he asked her whether these were all of Lady Celeste's most important finds. And if perhaps they shouldn't go up to the attics to retrieve the boxes she'd mentioned so that they might see if there might be some hidden treasures among them.

Then, Lord Paley had been so overly solicitous that she'd got the impression he didn't take her seriously as a scientist, or even a collector. And more than once she caught him speaking to her bosom. She had to admit that the blue velvet gown did show it to advantage, but perhaps it had been a mistake to believe Serena and Sophia's insistence that looking her best was the way to have these gentlemen give her the respect that was her due as a fossil-hunter.

And finally, Cam, who had been so heated in his defense when they'd been alone in the hallway earlier, spoke very little as she removed item after item from the stands upon which Lady Celeste had placed them. He'd asked questions, of course. He'd wondered aloud if a femur, which Celeste had noted to be that of a large mammal found close to Lyme, might be similar to one Cuvier had described. His questions and remarks were always insightful and despite her earlier pique, she found herself grateful for his presence. If she'd had only Sir Everard and Lord Paley to show round it might have felt like an entirely wasted morning.

Thus it was with some relief when Lady Serena announced that it was time for luncheon.

"I owe you an apology, Miss Hastings," Cam said as they followed the others downstairs toward the dining room. "Though I'd read your work and knew you were not unintelligent, I must admit I thought you were not quite equipped to understand the collection you'd inherited."

Before she could complain, he held up a staying hand. "I was wrong, Miss Hastings," he said, his voice tinged with the ring of sincerity. "I should have known better."

Gemma blinked. Of all the things she might have expected of this day, an apology from Cam was not one of them.

She paused in her descent of the stairs and faced him. "I must admit it gives me some sense of validation to hear you admit to your earlier prejudice," she said with a nod. "I only wish we could have had this conversation earlier so that for our siblings' sake we could have got on better."

He nodded in agreement, a single dark curl glancing over his brow. To her surprise, she had to fight the urge to brush it back.

What on earth was the matter with her?

"The blame for that can fall on me," Cam said, obviously unaware of Gemma's tender impulse. "But I hope that we can now be friends."

"I would like that," Gemma said and was surprised to find she meant it. Would wonders never cease?

Their newfound amity was something she was eager to explore, but to her disappointment, however, she was seated beside Sir Everard for the meal, and as he wished to discuss the boxes yet again it was not the most scintillating of conversations.

"You must tell us what you intend to do once your year of residence at Beauchamp House is at an end," Lord Paley, who was seated on her right, said. "I cannot think a young lady as lively as you will be content to remain buried in the country, no matter how its proximity to the shore might tempt you to dig for fossils. I hope you will come to town for the season."

If he had asked her to save the first waltz at Daphne's ball, Gemma thought wryly, Lord Paley could not have announced his interest more plainly. He was not an unattractive man. He was perhaps a bit older than she would have considered in a husband. But with his tall athletic frame, and silvering dark hair, he was handsome in his way. But she felt not an ounce of attraction to him, though his interest in the collection had been genuine. And he clearly knew nothing of her at all if he thought she'd dislike being here in Sussex for any duration.

She contemplated for a moment how best to respond.

But Cam spoke before she could.

"I do not believe Miss Hastings considers an extended stay in a house with a fine library, and proximity to the shore to be as much of a hardship as most ladies of your acquaintance, Paley," Cam said with a raised brow. "Lively though she may be."

This last made Gemma's eyes widen. Perhaps he did understand her better now.

Realizing his mistake, Lord Paley backtracked a little.

"I didn't mean to imply that Miss Hastings was anything but an original," Lord Paley said hastily, his concern evident in his drawn brows. "And she's not like any other young lady I've met. But that is why I believe London would benefit from your presence, Miss Hastings. A lady with your gift for conversation and intellect must need stimulation." He laughed wryly. "Even I am not content to spend all my days amongst my collection."

It was prettily said, and Gemma unbent a little. He was a well-meaning man. Just not the one who could make her give up her vow to remain unwed.

"I am often in my sister's company," she said aloud. "And I find that she and her husband, Reverend Lord Benedick, are quite intelligent enough to keep me from withering into a husk from boredom. Not to mention Lady Serena," she gestured to their hostess, who had watched the interplay avidly but didn't intervene, perhaps knowing Gemma could take care of herself.

Lord Paley turned to Lady Serena with an abashed look. "Lady Serena, pray forgive me. I didn't mean to give offense. Of course Miss Hastings has you to keep her in good conversation."

If Gemma didn't know her chaperone could fend for herself, she might have leapt to her rescue. But it was entirely unnecessary. Serena could very likely conduct witty repartee in her sleep.

"Think nothing of it," the widow said, her blue-gray eyes lit with laughter. "I will readily admit I am the last person Gemma would come to for conversation about her work. I know nothing of fossils and what's more, I have little interest in them. It's not that I don't appreciate them and what they tell us of the past, but I do not enjoy interacting with the small lizards my son likes to smuggle into the nursery when his nanny isn't looking. I most certainly do not wish to entertain the notion of an enormous one with large teeth."

Everyone laughed, as she'd intended, and the brief tension was broken.

This allowed Serena to steer the conversation toward less uncomfortable topics and when the meal was at an end, the gentlemen declined to take tea and were soon in the entrance hall preparing to leave.

Only when the door had closed behind them and the ladies were safely back in Serena's sitting room did Gemma let out the breath she'd been holding in.

"If I ever agree to welcoming more than one unwed gentleman to luncheon again," she told her sister and chaperone, "I pray you will dose me with laudanum and send me to bed for a week."

The drive back to Pearson Close was far less congenial than the drive there had been. For one thing, Sir Everard was fuming at the fact there had been no sign of the Beauchamp Lizard in the collection, and Gemma, perhaps guessing that he had been the one out on the shore the other night, had been less than encouraging at the idea of opening the attics of the house to the man.

Cam had been relieved, of course, because as he'd suspected, the Lizard was just a myth. He had no need of lying to Gemma because of his promise to Sir Everard. For some reason that mattered more to him now than it had when he'd actually made the promise.

It had nothing, he assured himself, to do with the way she'd looked in the blue velvet gown she'd worn for their tour. He was just feeling companionable because of the time they'd spent in conversation that morning.

Thus it was that they arrived at Pearson Close far less convivial than they'd been when they set out and the three men split up to find their own entertainment as soon as they stepped inside.

Curious about the typography of the land hereabouts, Cam retired to the library, where he searched out whatever he could find about this part of the Sussex coast, and the geographical composition of the area.

He was poring over a study of the local soil composition in a large chair near the fire, when he heard a door behind him open with a thud.

"I've several studies and essays on all sorts of important finds that would be perfect for *The Natural Scientist*," he heard Sir Everard say in that boastful way he had of making his every accomplishment sound like the most consequential thing anyone had done in the history of the planet.

The other man, who was no doubt Roderick Templeton, the editor of the aforementioned journal, made an interested but noncommittal sound before he undoubtedly made his escape.

Unable to do the same, Cam prepared himself for conversation as Sir Everard approached the fire and lowered himself into the chair beside his.

"Lord Cameron," said the baronet with a nod before leaning over to see what Cam was reading. "I see you're investigating the local soil. I piqued your interest in the Beauchamp Lizard, didn't I?"

Rather than respond to the question, Cam asked instead, "You really thought it would be in the collection, didn't you?"

"I hoped," said Sir Everard. "But I won't give up. I am confident it's there somewhere. Though I have another notion of where I might find it."

"And where is that?" Cam asked, curious despite himself.

Sir Everard leaned forward, as if fearful of being overheard. "I think it's on the shore."

Cam frowned. "What do you mean?"

"I think she reburied it."

So that's why he'd attempted to go down to the bottom of the cliff the other night. He thought Lady Celeste had put the skull back into the ground where she'd found it.

"What makes you think that?" he asked, careful not to show his interest. The least hint of competition from him and Sir Everard would stop talking altogether. He was that sort of man.

"It's just a theory," Sir Everard said, "but what better place to hide it but in plain sight? There were the rumors that it was just a horse skull. Well, what if Celeste really believed that? I think her reputation was probably exaggerated and she really did think she'd made a mistake. And what better way to hide a mistake than to put it right back where you found it?"

"So you think that she found an important lizard skull, then convinced herself it was a horse skull and hid it to save herself from embarrassment?" Cam wasn't sure if he thought the notion was more condescending or fantastical.

"Ladies are very proud when it comes to their intellectual prowess," Sir Everard assured him with the air of a man who had encountered legions of bluestockings in his time. Cam was far more convinced he'd had several discussions *about* bluestockings that he'd mistaken for actual social intercourse with the species.

"They can't bear the slightest bit of scrutiny, y'see," Sir Everard continued. "It turns their minds when they're questioned. So, of course if someone suggested what Lady Celeste found was a horse skull, she'd turn right around and put it back. Stands to reason. Much better to hide it than to expose herself to the examinations of actual geologists and collectors, who have educated themselves about the subject for decades. I think she got scared and hid it away."

It was amazing to Cam that this man could walk about with the weight of the self-importance he bore on his shoulders.

From everything he'd heard about Lady Celeste, she was not only Sir Everard's intellectual superior, she was the last person in the world who would fear public scrutiny of her work or her finds. She'd made a point of building her home and its collections into a one-of-a-kind place where her hand-chosen heiresses could make names for themselves in the intellectual world.

That woman would not, at least not in Cam's estimation, mistake a horse skull for a lizard skull, or the other way round.

"I mean to visit the shore below the Beauchamp House cliffs," Sir Everard continued.

Cam was about to protest, but realized that it would be better to be with him when he made his trip than not.

"I might have a way for you to get there without going onto Beauchamp House land," he said aloud. He knew there was access to the little beach from a path leading from the vicarage. They could pay a call on Benedick and go down to the shore afterwards. It wouldn't hurt to have Ben along with them just in case Sir Everard did find something.

Cam wasn't sure of many things, but he knew he'd be damned before he let this buffoon steal a fossil that was meant to belong to Gemma.

Or, he reminded himself, Beauchamp House.

Sir Everard's round face split into a grin. "I knew making your acquaintance would come in handy, old man."

The next morning, after a good night's sleep, Gemma viewed the visit from the gentlemen the day before in a somewhat more philosophical way than she had last night. At the very least, she reasoned, she'd come to a sort of cessation of conflict with Cam. And if she'd not received the sort of acceptance of her place in the community of fossil-hunters from Sir Everard and Lord Paley, at least she had been able to hold her own in conversation with them. Which was no small thing.

After a quick breakfast, she went back upstairs and donned one of the gowns Sophia had been so disparaging of before. Because honestly, digging in the earth was not the time to worry about fashion, Gemma thought as she tied her thick boots. Adding a wide-brimmed bonnet, to shelter her from the wind, she retrieved her bag of hand trowels and other tools for unearthing stones and bones and the like, and made her way downstairs.

Despite the bonnet, she found the wind was strong enough to need the added protection of her cloak hood. And as she neared the sea stairs, she wondered if she shouldn't tear a page out of Mary Anning's book and lash herself to the railing of the stone steps.

But now that she was out here in the brisk air, the salt and spray foam in her nostrils, she couldn't bear to go back now.

Carefully, she made her way down the stairs in the cliff-side and saw at once that, as she'd hoped, the storm had brought forth debris from the sea, but had also eaten away some of the chalk from the cliff. She'd need to get closer, of course, but there were some promising protrusions from the sloping of the chalk into the sea.

Using her broad walking stick to steady her against the wind, and as a means of propelling her forward, she made her way across the narrow strip of pebbled beach toward the far edge of the crescent-shaped piece of land. There, the pebbles jutted against the chalk where the cliff came out to meet the sea.

She saw her target as soon as she got a closer look up at the upper slope. There, emerging from the chalk in a manner eerily like a headstone from this angle, she saw what was likely just a stone. But something in her gut told her that it needed to be looked at more closely.

Though she had felt eerily as if she were being observed in the past week or so, today there was no sense of it. So without a backward glance, she began the slow, steady climb up to where the jagged object—stone or bone—awaited her.

By the time she reached it, she was breathing heavily from the exertion of moving against the wind against the steep incline. But finally, she was there, and ignoring the hazards of dirt to her cloak, she stabbed her walking stick into the chalk like a spear and collapsed onto the ground beside her find.

Despite the cold, she had to remove her gloves to touch it with her bare hands. And the more she felt, the more she saw, the more she knew in her heart that this was a truly important find.

It was a fossil, not a bone. And she wouldn't be able to tell for sure until it was unearthed completely, but it was a skull. If she didn't miss her guess, a rather large one.

Pulling her gloves back on, she retrieved a hand trowel from her tool bag and carefully removed as much chalk from around the base as she could. But she'd worked for no more than ten minutes or so before she knew she'd need help with it. It would take a great deal of time to dig it out. And it would be too large for her to carry up the sea stairs.

It went against her every instinct to leave it here, but given that this bit of shore was on Beauchamp House property, it would be all right for the time it took her to fetch Stephens and Edward from the house.

She rested her hand atop the fossil, which had likely been here for hundreds of thousands of years, bid it a silent adieu and made her careful way back down the cliff.

As soon as she stepped through the French doors on the terrace, she sensed the change in the house. A laugh from the drawing room—definitely male, and belonging to the Duke of Maitland if she weren't mistaken—had her discarding her cloak, bag and stick and setting off at a pace far too unlady-like for someone of her age.

When she burst into the drawing room she found that—as she'd hoped—the Marquess of Kerr and his Marchioness, the former Ivy Wareham, and the Duke of Maitland and his Duchess, the former Lady Daphne Forsyth, were seated around the tea tray with Lady Serena—who was the duke's sister—and her seven-year-old son Jeremy, making up the rest of the party.

"Gemma!" cried Ivy from the table before rising to greet her with a hug. "It's so good to see you. I take it you were out digging, you madwoman. Are you aware of what the temperature is?"

Daphne had risen and Gemma was astonished when the normally standoffish mathematician hugged her as well. "It's been too long. You have no idea what sort of nonsense the people in town talk about. I'd forgotten during my time here with you all. But it's nothing but rot and gammon all the day long."

Gemma grinned at her use of slang. At her look, Daphne raised her brows. "Maitland has been teaching me cant. I find it allows one to speak with the necessary vehemence some situations call for."

"Hullo, Gemma," the duke said, waving from his seat at the tea table. "You must wait until she's really in a temper. The slang becomes almost as incomprehensible as in the crowd outside a Bermondsey boxing match. It's truly impressive."

"I acquired the most fascinating dictionary by Francis Grose," Daphne said with enthusiasm. "Were you aware that *boxing the Jesuit* is way to describe male—"

"I'm sure you can educate your friends on that very colorful definition when poor Kerr isn't here to expire from embarrassment, my dear," the duke said with a glance at the marquess, his cousin and Ivy's husband, who did indeed appear as if his neckcloth had suddenly shrunk three sizes.

"I'm sure he knows what it is," Daphne said patiently. "It's something all men do, you told me yourself that—"

And now it was the duke's turn to redden. "Perhaps, Kerr we'd best take young Jeremy to the nursery to see if he can beat us at soldiers."

Jeremy frowned, certain he was being removed from the most interesting conversation. But the prospect of soldiers with his favorite uncle and cousin was distraction enough.

"It's good to see you, Gemma," said Lord Kerr, clasping her shoulder as he passed on his way out the door.

Maitland, Jeremy on his shoulders, leaned in to kiss the top of Daphne's head. "I'd say be good, but I know what kind of mischief you get up to away from one another. Together, you're a menace."

When they were gone, Serena rose as well. "I'll go send a note round to Sophia. She'll be furious if I don't let her know you're here."

Alone, the three ladies moved to the tea table. Fortunately, there was still some in the pot, so Gemma found an empty cup and poured.

"It's good to be back," Ivy said, sitting back in her chair with satisfaction. "I'd used different words but Daphne is right about the level of discourse in town. And everyone is so bent on showing up everyone else. It's competition, but for silly things like who has the most invitations, or who throws the most lavish party. None of it is at all meaningful. And it's all so—"

"False," Daphne finished for her. "I disliked it before I came to Beauchamp House, of course. When I was gambling for my father, to keep him in waistcoats and brandy, I was able to ignore it, but now that I've known friendship, the interactions with people in town seem that much more tiresome. Especially since I had the great misfortune to marry one of the most eligible peers in the country. I ask Maitland every day why he couldn't have been a common laborer, but he hasn't given me a satisfactory answer yet. It's all very trying."

Gemma bit back a grin. It was such a relief to see them. She still had Sophia and Serena here, of course, but Ivy and

Daphne were the only ones who had no guardianship role over her. Sophia would always feel like her elder because she was, well, her elder sister. And Serena was her chaperone. But these two had never been anything but her friends. And something in her relaxed at knowing they were here.

"So, you were out digging," Ivy asked before biting into one of cook's lemon cakes. "Did you find anything?"

At her word's Gemma's eyes widened. "Oh my goodness, I almost forgot!"

Quickly she told them about the fossil she'd found in the chalk. She didn't mention her hope that it was important. She didn't want to bring bad luck on herself before she had more information about it. It never did one any good to count one's chickens, after all.

"Well, what are you here with us for?" Daphne asked her with a frown. "We will be here for the foreseeable future. Go gather the footmen and collect your fish head, or whatever it is."

Laughing, Gemma left them to do just that. Perhaps by the time she finished, Sophia would be there too and they could have a proper heiress reunion.

Since Paley was the only other member of the Pearson Close guests who knew about the Beauchamp Lizard, and Cam didn't relish spending more time than he had to with Sir Everard, Cam invited the viscount to join them on their ostensible visit to the vicarage.

He'd been afraid Lord Paley would have found something else to do but to his relief, the viscount agreed to the jaunt with some alacrity.

"I should like to see the cliffs from another angle," he said with a smile. "Topography, you know, the second favorite interest of the fossil hunter."

The three men set off in the late morning in the hopes that the sun might have warmed things up, but to no avail.

Benedick's welcome was warm, however, and he ushered the three men into his study with the promise of brandy, which he dispensed with the efficiency of a churchman used to handing out beverages, albeit tamer ones.

"I hope you found the ladies at Beauchamp House well yesterday," Ben said once the visitors had settled into his study. "I don't mind telling you—though my wife would not like it—she was quite happy to know that a few of the collectors and scholars from the Pearson Close party had come to call on Gemma. The sisters are quite close, and Sophia felt the slight of her sister's lack of invitation as sharply as Gemma did."

Sir Everard looked nonplussed. "I cannot imagine it was ever a possibility. Especially given Pearson's abhorrence for female company."

Before Cam could step into the breach, Lord Paley spoke up. "I found Miss Hastings to be quite knowledgeable about natural science and especially the history of the soil and fossils recovered from this area. Your wife must be very proud of her."

He then went on to extol the virtues of Gemma's beauty and fashion sense, the latter description causing a line to appear between Ben's brow.

"I believe she had a new gown for the occasion," Cam responded to his brother's questioning look. He didn't add that the way she'd dressed her hair had drawn every male eye to the soft skin at the nape of her neck, or that despite its modest long sleeves and high neck, the gown had shown her bosom to advantage.

"Ah, that must be it," Ben said, ever the diplomat. "Well, I am pleased you were able to tour Lady Celeste's collection in any event."

"Speaking of Lady Celeste," said Sir Everard, "I wonder if you can recall her ever mentioning a particularly fine fossil she found on the beach below Beauchamp House?"

Cam fought the urge to roll his eyes. This fellow had a one-track mind.

Ben shook his head. "I'm afraid I didn't come to Little Seaford until after her death. And the vicar who was here before me left rather hastily after some bad business earlier in the year.

"Speaking of the shore," he continued, "As part of that investigation into Lady Celeste's death, a door was discovered in the cellar of this house leading out to the shore. I've not had much call to use it, certainly not at this time of year, but it's a unique feature for a vicarage, don't you think?"

"You've never told me about a secret door," Cam complained.

"This is the most I've seen you since I came to this village," Ben responded with a raised brow. "And that includes the month you spent in Lyme this summer."

But Sir Everard wasn't interested in the brothers' conflict. "Is the door still accessible, Lord Benedick?"

Cam and Ben both glanced at the window, which showed the skies were darker and the wind was whipping the boughs of the bare elm on the other side.

"It is," Benedick said with a nod, "though I don't know that I would recommend a walk on the shore at the moment. There was a storm last evening too so there may be obstructions to an easy jaunt. Perhaps you can come back next summer when . . ."

"What is a bit of weather when there may be fossils dredged up from the storm there on the shore as we speak?" Sir Everard said, getting to his feet. "I will go even if you three will not. A true collector does not allow a triviality like that stand between him and the possibility of the perfect specimen."

"These are new boots," Paley said with a sigh even as he too rose from his chair.

Clearly fashionable garments should be added to the list of items that would not hold back a true collector, Cam thought wryly.

And since there was no way he would allow the other two men to comb the shore for finds while he lingered behind, he too got to his feet.

Ben looked at the trio with a sigh of resignation. "Let me get my coat. And I'll have my man make sure there is hot tea and coffee waiting for us when we return. One moment."

He hurried downstairs, leaving the three collectors alone.

"You know where the cellar is, do you not?" Sir Everard's tone indicated that he expected to be led there. Immediately.

It would be rude for them to set off without Ben, but on the other hand, the sooner Sir Everard saw the shore, the sooner he could be rid of the fellow.

"Follow me."

By the time they stepped through the cellar door leading into a short stone passageway, Ben had joined them, as had his butler and footman, who carried hot bricks and a flask of brandy. It was an odd parade, but Cam supposed they'd all seen odder ones. Collectors often found themselves going out in inclement weather and strange circumstances. The hope of a rare find was greater than self-preservation at times.

As soon as the men emerged from the door onto the shore, which was bordered on one side by an angry-looking sea and on the other by steep chalk cliffs, it was evident that last night's storm had done more than simply dredge things up.

The far end of the cliffs, where the beach first began to bow inward from the water's edge, had begun to erode away from the overhang above. And in one spot in particular there appeared to be a large stone sticking out of the chalk, like a hand waving for help.

"There," shouted Sir Everard before he all but sprinted over the pebble beach toward the mudslide.

It was a good way to twist an ankle, but even so, Cam jogged after him, followed by Lord Paley and Benedick.

By the time Cam reached the base of the cliff from which the stone protruded, Sir Everard had already begun to climb against the wind and through the sucking mud toward what would likely turn out to be a piece of wood. Not willing to risk his own safety by stepping into what might be unstable ground, Cam examined the trail that the other man's boots had left as he'd climbed.

Was that the mark of a walking stick, he wondered, leaning down to take a closer look at what looked to be a hole in the mud.

"He is particularly eager," Ben said as he and Paley reached Cam's side. "I should think he'd wait until better weather if he wanted to search this bit of cliff."

This would be the time to tell his brother about the Beauchamp Lizard, but with Lord Paley there to listen in, and perhaps tell what he'd overheard to Sir Everard, he dared not. And there was the added issue that anything he told Ben would most assuredly make it back to Sophia and therefore Gemma.

"It is a skull, I believe," shouted Sir Everard from his higher vantage point. "I do not have my tools. We'll need to dig with our hands."

It was clear from his "we" that he meant the three other men should come up and assist him. An idea which Cam didn't think particularly sound given the fact that the mud might give out from beneath them without warning. But Lord Paley and even Ben began to make the careful climb upwards, so not wishing to be the odd man out, he went after them.

Soon they were all sunk boot-deep into the mud around

the piece and having decided to ruin their gloves rather than lose fingers in the cold, began to dig.

They were almost to the point where they might be able to shift the piece to loosen the mud's hold on it, when a shout came floating on the wind.

Cam thought he might have imagined it, but then he heard it again, this time more incensed and sounding very much like Miss Gemma Hastings.

"What are you doing?" she shouted. And when he dared to look over his shoulder, he saw her, bundled up in a large coat, her scarf wound tightly round her neck, and a walking stick in one hand, a case of tools in the other. "Step away from there at once!"

Whether she shouted from anger or because they would not have been able to hear her otherwise, he didn't know. But from her expression, he suspected it was the former.

Behind her, he saw George, the footman-turned-butler, with a pry bar in his hand.

And suddenly he realized that the mark he'd seen in the mud had been from a walking stick.

Gemma's walking stick.

"This is Miss Hastings' find," he told Sir Everard. "I saw the mark of her walking stick but didn't make the connection until now."

Sir Everard, who was elbow deep in mud and struggling to loosen the earth around the fossil, grunted. Then, as if realizing what Cam had said, he shook his head. "That's impossible. There's no way a lady can have got this far up the slope. I found this myself. You saw me do it."

"I demand you come down here at once." Her voice was closer now, and yes, it was definitely anger he'd first heard there. She was livid if he didn't miss his guess.

And at the moment he couldn't blame her.

"Sir Everard," he said, trying to sound reasonable, though he was feeling anything but. "This is Beauchamp House land. Surely you can recognize that even if you were the first to discover this piece, by rights it should go to the owner of the house."

"You know that won't hold up in court, Lord Cameron," the big man said with a huff of exertion. "Besides, I came here to find the Beauchamp Lizard. If this is something similar I won't let it out of my grasp. You know how important something like this can be for a collector's reputation."

He did know, which was why he wanted Gemma to have it. She'd obviously been here while they were at the vicarage.

"This is wrong," he said firmly. "I beg you will reconsider."

"Sir Everard," said Lord Paley, who had risen from his crouch beside the hole the men had managed to dig around the fossil. "If Lord Cameron is right, then the fossil belongs to the lady. I cannot think you would abandon your honor simply to enrich your own collection."

But Sir Everard's expression was mulish. "I mean to have it. And none of you will stop me from getting it."

Chapter 6

Gemma stood her booted feet braced against the wind that threatened to knock her over with its force as she waited for some response from the men on the slope. It would be difficult to hold a conversation, it was true, given the sound of the wind, but at least one of them had heard her. She'd seen clearly enough the look of understanding on Cam's face as he'd turned to her.

"George," she said to the butler, "come with me. We must get my skull away from them."

"But Miss Hastings," he argued, "I can't just take it away. They're gentlemen. And Lord Benedick is there. He's a vicar. It ain't—isn't—right."

He'd been trying to correct his grammar since rising from footman to butler, and if she weren't fuming, Gemma would have smiled at the correction. It had taken a month of lessons, but his speech was improving by the minute.

But she *was* fuming. All because of the gentlemen assembled.

Perhaps excepting Ben, who cared as much for fossils as his wife did.

"George, that is my fossilized skull." She turned to look him in the eye as she spoke. "I would not mind if Lord

Benedick were to take it, because he would most likely give it to me. But the rest are not to be trusted." She didn't even bother to mention Lord Cameron because her disappointment in him was keen. She'd thought they'd come to some kind of understanding today. That he'd at long last recognized her as a fellow scientist. But his attitude had been as ephemeral as the waves washing onto the shore beside her.

She almost jumped out of her skin when the man himself appeared beside George.

His approach had been hushed by the wind, she realized.

A glance at him revealed that he'd been just as immersed in the mud on the cliff as the others had been. Even his neckcloth was spattered with the stuff.

"I have tried to convince Sir Everard to give up his claim on the fossil," he told her without preamble, "but he refuses."

Ben, looking equally bedraggled, came up beside his brother. "The man is a little unhinged, I'm afraid," he said in a low voice. "He keeps going on about lizards and Lady Celeste."

"It is the skull of a marine lizard," Gemma said with a frown. "Others have been found hereabouts but this one is much larger than any I've seen or heard of. Which is why it is so important that I'm able to claim it for my own collection. It is *my* find."

"I know how important it is," Lord Cameron said with more sympathy than Gemma thought he'd offer her. "But, for what it's worth, I don't think he'll be able to shift it out of that mud today. The weather is too damp to get a grip on it and without the proper tools, it will be impossible."

"Which is why I brought these," Gemma said raising her case of digging tools.

They turned to look at the slope, and saw Lord Paley throw his hands into the air and began the slow descent down to the rock-covered shore. When he reached their huddle, he too was exasperated. "I tried to convince him that he should leave it to you, Miss Hastings," he said, frowning as he tightened his muddy scarf around his neck. "But he is like a dog with a . . . well, a bone, I suppose."

The play on words made them all laugh, defusing the situation a bit.

They were silent for a few moments as they tried to figure out what to do.

"What if we allow him to think you've capitulated?" Cam asked thoughtfully. "He obviously has no intention of leaving the field to you at the moment. But he cannot stay here all night, and he'll need help to remove it. You can tell him you've decided to let him have it. Then once he's gone, we'll come back and remove it."

"I do not like to advocate telling falsehoods," Ben said his brows drawn, "but in this instance, I think it may be the only way you will get your fossil, Gemma. For it is quite plain that Sir Everard will not give up the field until he's convinced you won't take it from him."

Gemma didn't like the idea of lying to get what rightfully belonged to her. "How can I be sure he won't send someone to get it in the meantime?"

"We'll be going back to Pearson Close with him," said Lord Paley. "I will ensure that he doesn't send anyone back. I give you my word."

"You and I will come at first light to retrieve it," he said, turning back to her. "Long before Sir Everard has a chance to dispatch anyone or to come here again himself. But you'll have to leave it for now, if only to prove to Sir Everard now that you've given up the fight."

She looked through the dimming light toward where the baronet still tried to shift the fossil. As if he felt her gaze on him, he looked up then and gave her a defiant stare.

She'd known she disliked him during his visit, but she'd

not guessed just how much contempt he felt for her. Clearly his flattery and interest had been a ruse to get close to the collection.

"All right," she said, finally, turning back to the others. "I'll do it. Tell him I have no intention of claiming it, and that he may come back tomorrow to get it. But I hope you will be prepared to protect me tomorrow when he discovers it's gone."

"The prior claim is yours, Miss Hastings," Lord Paley assured her. "And besides. Are not ladies allowed the prerogative of changing their minds?"

She didn't bother to tell him the myriad of ways in which such an assumption made life in male-dominated fields more difficult for ladies.

At this point, she'd fought for her scholarly sisters enough for one day.

"I think it would probably be better if you were not here when we convince him to leave with us." Cam's expression was that of a man who knows he will be contradicted.

But Gemma was tired of conflict. "I'll go back to the house. But I'm trusting you to ensure he doesn't stay, or find some way to remove the skull before I have a chance to come back."

"I give you my word," Cam said, echoing Lord Paley. Despite their previous arguments, Gemma believed him.

"Come, my dear." Lord Benedick gestured to her. "I'll escort you back to the house while these two deal with the tantrum Sir Everard is likely to have when they make him depart."

With one last look over her shoulder to where the baronet stood hunched over the skull, Gemma allowed her brother-in-law to lead her away.

Behind her she heard Lord Cameron say in a low voice, "This might get ugly."

She didn't linger to hear how the other man responded.

For the first time in a long while, she let someone else handle things.

If possible, the carriage ride back to Pearson Close was more uncomfortable than the scene at the cliff had been.

Cam and Paley were silent as Sir Everard raged about their failure to intervene on his behalf. "You may as well have been stone statues," he said with disgust. "If the skull is gone when I arrive tomorrow, you mark my words, I will sue."

Mentally, Cam ran through the list of solicitors who might defend Gemma against the baronet's baseless claims. Because now, more than ever, he intended to remove the fossil and get it into her hands as quickly as possible. Sir Everard was not only a bully, but his determination to effectively rob Gemma of what—whether it was the Beauchamp Lizard or not—by rights belonged to her, or to the Beauchamp House estate, had solidified Cam's determination to thwart him. Not only was he the worst possible representative of the fossil-collecting community as a whole—and Cam had little doubt he'd use the fossil to puff himself up as far more influential than he actually was—but he was simply a small-minded boor.

Fortunately for Cam and Paley, when they returned to Pearson Close, the baronet chose not to tell all and sundry about his having been thwarted by a scheming harpy (his term) because his fear that someone else would swoop in and take the fossil was greater than his need for consolation. Or maybe, Cam thought cynically, he wasn't sure which side his fellow collectors would take. Lady Celeste's reputation had been impeccable among the fossil-collecting community, and there were many among Pearson's guests who had admired her.

Acquaintance with Sir Everard, however, did much to reveal the illusory nature of his accomplishments.

Mindful that servants' gossip could ruin the plan to save the fossil from Sir Everard, Cam made his way to the Pearson stables after dinner to request his mount be ready before sunup, and swore the man to secrecy.

Later, as he lay in bed staring up at the damask canopy, he considered the idea of using this time spent with Gemma to assess her as a potential bride.

There was something attractive about the idea of marrying someone who would be able to understand his passion for collecting as well as trying to place the things he found within the scientific history of the earth.

And she was lovely. It would not be a hardship to bed her, of that he was certain.

But it was these things that also made him wary of her.

He'd long ago come to the conclusion that he needed the sort of wife who was affectionate but not particularly dependent on him for her happiness.

When he was a youth he'd seen just how destructive it could be when a husband was distant—or in his father's case—was unfaithful. He had seen the light go out of his mother's eyes in the space of a few months. And though she'd seemed to recover later, Cam couldn't help but feel that it would have been better if the Duke and Duchess of Pemberton had maintained some distance from another from the start. That way his mother would never have had to be hurt at all.

Cam had no intention to commit infidelity, but thought it better, since he was his father's son, not to put himself in a situation where it would even matter. Unbidden the memory of Gemma's animation yesterday when she was talking about the collection came to his mind. She was lit from within. So passionate. He simply could not be responsible for snuffing that light.

No matter how much he was drawn to her.

His decision made, he turned on his side and tried to sleep.

"It simply doesn't make sense to risk your neck on the cliff stairs when there is a perfectly functional corridor through the wine cellar," Serena said as she and Gemma breakfasted the next morning at a far earlier hour than was their custom.

Both the chaperone and Sophia had been incensed on Gemma's behalf the day before when they learned of Sir Everard's attempt to steal the lizard fossil. Sophia had even offered to come along with her when she returned to retrieve it, but Gemma, knowing just how much her sister detested getting up early, had assured her it would not be necessary.

Serena, however, had at the very least insisted on being there when Gemma set out with Cam, Stephens and the foot man Edward.

And true to her word, she had been at the breakfast table when Gemma came down.

Her suggestion that the excavation party should use the secret passageway had been a surprise, however.

Gemma was not particularly fond of enclosed spaces and had not been through the tunnel more than once or twice because of it. "I will give Stephens and Edward, and even Lord Cameron, leave to use the passageway. But I will be using the cliff stairs."

At Serena's scowl of frustration, she continued, "Despite the harshness of the wind, the view of the sea as one descends the stairs is one of my favorite things about Beauchamp House's location. I won't deny myself unless I absolutely must."

The chaperone looked as if she'd like to argue further, but perhaps seeing Gemma's expression, she sighed. "I won't press the point," Serena said. "But, I do think it might be easier to remove your bone without being seen by having George and William carry it up through the passageway."

It was something Gemma hadn't considered. "That is sensible. Especially considering that Sir Everard may very well arrive while we are there. Cam's note said that he and Lord Paley were able to convince him to leave it until some of the others from Pearson Close could accompany him and witness his triumph."

That bit of persuasion had made Gemma laugh aloud since it was perfectly calculated to appeal to the man's self-regard.

"But," she continued, "he may very well decide when he awakens this morning that he simply cannot wait."

Too nervous to eat any more of her eggs, she pushed the plate away and took a last gulp of tea just as Cam entered the breakfast room.

"I thought I'd find you dressed and waiting on the front step for me," he teased, and Gemma was charmed despite herself.

Once again, he was dressed for warmth as well as style, and his many caped greatcoat, which he hadn't bothered to remove given they'd be departing soon, had somehow been scrubbed clean of yesterday's mud. Gemma felt a pang for his poor valet—her own maid had upbraided her roundly last evening when she came in.

"I'll be only a few moments," she said rising from the table. "I have to get my gloves but I'll be right down."

Cam watched as she hurried from the room.

He'd only been half-joking.

He really had expected to find her tapping her foot while she waited for him at the door. He supposed he should be relieved that she'd relaxed enough to sit down to breakfast given just how nervous she'd been last evening about leaving her precious skull behind overnight.

Having been forced to wait for help to retrieve his own discoveries before, he could sympathize. It was one of the reasons he'd volunteered to point Sir Everard in the other direction, and to come back and assist her today.

And there was something about Sir Everard that he didn't trust. It would be just like the fellow to agree to wait until later today, then double back before anyone was the wiser.

Of course, that's what he and Gemma were doing, but since Gemma was the rightful owner of the skull, theirs was the lesser sin.

"I appreciate the way you're helping her," Lady Serena said as she poured him a cup of tea and gestured for him to have a seat.

She was really a stunningly beautiful lady, he thought not for the first time.

It was unfortunate he didn't feel the same kind of attraction for her as he did for her wholly unsuitable charge.

"I know Gemma appreciates your assistance as well," Lady Serena continued, breaking him out of his reverie.

He turned his attention to the widow. "Given that Sir Everard wouldn't have known about the little beach here without my having brought it to his notice," he said aloud, "it's the least I could do."

She nodded, her blue eyes shining with approval. "She will never say it aloud, but your acceptance of her into the scholarly fold, as it were, means the world to her. Gemma is quite proud, but I know she craves what we all want—to be taken seriously."

He was silent for a moment, trying to figure out whether he should confess that his attitude toward her work had changed.

"I'm ready," the subject of their discussion said from the doorway.

Cam looked to see if she had overheard any of their conversation but Gemma seemed unaware.

"You'd best be off, then," Serena said with a smile. "Gemma, dear, be sure to bring Lord Cameron back when you're finished. We owe him a hot drink and a seat by the fire at the very least."

"Of course," the heiress said with a roll of her eyes. "Though I'm quite sure he's endured far more uncomfortable weather than a Sussex seaside winter."

After a quick bow to his hostess, Cam offered Gemma his arm and escorted her to where George waited in the entry hall with her coat.

"William and I will be along shortly, Miss Hastings," said the butler as he allowed Cam to take her fur-lined pelisse from him.

He held it for her as she slid her arms in first one sleeve then the other, resisting the temptation to run his hands over the shoulders to smooth out the fabric. At least, that's what he told himself was the origin of the impulse.

Her gown today was far less tempting than the blue velvet from the other day—a dark gray wool that had been chosen for warmth and not fashion—but it was becoming and reminded him once again that there was a rather tempting body to go with the sharp mind.

Unaware of her escort's thoughts, Gemma pulled away as soon as her coat was on and donned her bonnet, speaking to the butler as she did so.

"Now, George, do not forget to bring a litter to assist you with carrying the skull through the tunnel. It's quite large, and though I do not doubt you'd be able to carry it in your arms, I do not wish you to risk dropping it. It is quite precious and we dare not risk it sustaining any blemishes."

"Yes, Miss Gemma," the butler said with a nod. "William has already found the one we used when Miss Ivy was stricken and it will do the trick."

With one last glance behind her, as if she were afraid of

forgetting something, Gemma finally turned to Cam. "Let's be off then."

And rather than go out the front door—or the passage-way he knew led directly to the shore—she led him toward the first floor and the drawing room with French doors leading into the gardens behind the house.

Chapter 7

As she led Cam through the gardens, which, with the exception of the evergreens, were as plain as a lady of the previous century without powder and patch, she waited for him to comment on their route. Surely he knew about the cellar passageway and wondered why they were taking the stairs, precarious in the best of weather.

But he surprised her.

"I am sorry for the way our first meeting went," he said, and Gemma had to shake her head a little to see if she'd heard him right.

"In the autumn," he clarified as if there were more than one first meeting to choose from. "I should have been more diplomatic about the rejection of your findings. Less dismissive."

Aside from the fact that her nose was in danger of falling off from cold, Gemma was also feeling some trepidation about seeing her marine lizard fossil again. What if it were not, in fact, as spectacular as she'd thought it was. What if it were simply the skull of a horse, killed in a shipwreck hundreds of years ago?

She was not concerned about her companion's bad behavior from months ago.

Still . . .

"I accept your apology.. I can assure you I've not thought of it since." A lie, but she was hardly going to spill out her heart to him now. It wasn't the time for it, and besides that, she didn't wish to show vulnerability at the moment when he finally seemed to take her seriously.

"Well, I have," he said, halting in his tracks and putting a hand on her arm. "It was foolish of me. You've shown yourself to be a serious scholar and I didn't take you seriously. It was badly done of me. I simply wish you to know that I have changed my opinion."

She chafed to get down to the shore, but sensed that he needed to say his piece.

Then a troubling thought occurred to her.

"This has nothing to do with the way I was dressed yesterday, has it? Because I can assure you, I was just as knowledgeable the day before as I was with my hair dressed and my bosom on display."

She'd expected perhaps he would respond with stuttering outrage, but she ought to have known better.

He laughed. "No, Miss Hastings, it has nothing to do with your gown. Or your very agreeable bosom."

She felt her cheeks redden with heat. "Agreeable bosom indeed."

"You're the one who brought it up," he said, then snickered for some reason she didn't quite understand.

"What's so funny?" She didn't like not being in on the joke.

"Oh no," he said, taking her arm in his and beginning their trek again. "I've already said 'bosom' in a lady's hearing. I won't compound the issue by explaining what is a highly inappropriate jest."

"You're the most frustrating man," she said in a harassed tone. "How am I to know anything if everything is kept from me?"

But he would not relent no matter how she pressed him.

"If we're to be discussing bosoms and the like," she said finally, in a grudging tone, "then I suppose we might be excused for using one another's Christian names."

"In for a penny, in for a pound?" he asked wryly. "I suppose it makes sense."

"Then, Cameron," she said regally, "let us proceed. I am freezing and I wish to ensure that my fossil has endured no damage in this wind."

"It would be my pleasure, Gemma." His voice sent a frisson of something up her spine. A feeling that intensified when he said her name.

What had she got herself into?

Trying to ignore her new awareness of him, she returned her focus to the ground beneath her feet.

When they reached the sea stairs, the wind was such that further conversation was impossible. And she wasn't too disappointed in that. Such moments as they'd just shared were dangerous. Especially for a woman who had no intention of ever entangling herself with a man, as she was. Yes, it was possible for lady scholars to marry without sacrificing their studies, but such things were rare. And rather than risk having her goals subsumed by those of her husband, she'd rather not jeopardize them in the first place. Remaining unwed had been the best course for her Aunt Dahlia, after all. And Lady Celeste. Though, to be sure, Lady Celeste's solitude had not been her choice.

Still, it was better to nip whatever it was she felt in Cam's presence in the bud.

Anything else would risk danger.

Further thoughts on the matter, however, were impossible, as the climb down the stairs was far more treacherous than it had been the day before. At this hour, a thin sheet of ice had formed along the treads, and she was grateful for the railing and Cameron's grip on the back of her coat. By unspoken agreement, they made their way slowly, one step at a time.

They were but halfway, however, when she glanced over at the area where the fossil had been and gasped, stopping.

Lord Cameron had to pull up short to keep from running her over.

"What is—" He broke off when he looked over and saw what had alarmed her.

Cursing the ice that slowed their progress, she and Cam went as fast as they could without endangering their own necks. When they finally reached the beach below, Cam began to run, his caped greatcoat flapping behind him.

Hurrying as fast as her skirts would allow, Gemma thought at first that the red near the victim's head was a kerchief of some sort. But as she got closer, she realized it was something far worse.

"Don't come too close," Cam said over his shoulder. "You don't need to see this."

"But perhaps I can—"

"Gemma," his voice was sharp, and something about it told her he was feeling some intense emotion. "Please don't argue with me. I would like to unsee it if I could."

She blinked at that. And stopped where she stood, several yards from the fallen man.

"But who is it?" she pressed, turning to face the other direction.

"It's Sir Everard," Cam said tensely. "He's quite cold so he's likely been out here for hours."

Unspoken was the realization that the baronet must have doubted Gemma's word just as much as she'd doubted his.

And the fool had risked his life by coming to get the fossil on his own.

"The magistrate is away for the holidays," she said

suddenly, thinking back to how they'd handled things when Daphne and Maitland discovered a dead body in the library.

The hysterical thought arose that they should write some sort of process guidelines for such occurrences to keep on hand in Beauchamp House. Especially given the number of accidents and mysterious deaths that had happened here in the past year.

"He may have left someone in charge in his absence," Cam said, bringing her attention back to the present matter. "Perhaps we can send one of the footmen to check at Northman's house. I'm sure he has a secretary at the least."

A shout from the other side of the beach alerted them to the arrival of George and William.

"I'll go back to the house with William and see to it," she said. "And I know it's not important since a man has lost his life, but is the fossil there? I didn't see it when I first looked because of all the—"

"No," he responded before she could finish. "It's not here. The marine lizard skull has been removed. It's gone. And it's very likely the reason why Sir Everard was killed."

As it happened, the Northmans had not yet left for their holiday travel and so it was the squire himself who entered the drawing room some two hours later.

"I thought it must be a mistake when I got your message, Miss Hastings," he said without preamble, "for I thought the likelihood of there being another murder at Beauchamp House was nigh impossible. But clearly, I was wrong."

"You might have a bit of courtesy, Northman," Cam said with a scowl from where he sat beside Gemma on the settee. "A man lost his life."

Given that Sir Everard was dead, he'd decided to leave the guarding of the body to William and had gone indoors not long after Gemma left him. He'd found her in the drawing room with Serena, her eyes suspiciously red as if she'd been weeping. Without waiting to be asked, he'd told George to send for Ben and Sophia. He might not know Gemma all that well, but at a time like this, she'd want to have her family around her.

Now, with Northman barreling in like a bull in a china shop, he was doubly glad he'd called them. Ben's diplomacy would clearly be needed if they were to get through this interview without Cam throttling the squire with his own neckcloth.

"We're obviously quite disturbed, Squire," Ben said, rising from his seat beside Sophia. "It's a dreadful business and we'd like to get it settled as quickly as possible."

"I can speak for myself," Gemma interjected with a frown. "I realize it's another odd occurrence at Beauchamp House, Squire Northman," she said, "but as none of the other deaths could be blamed on the inhabitants of this house, I don't see the point of your criticism. It's hardly our fault that we've been targets for such goings-on. And I can assure you I had nothing to do with Sir Everard's death. Which you will learn as soon as you look into the matter. I could hardly know that Sir Everard planned to return to the shore in the night."

The magistrate made a begrudging noise. Then, he frowned.

"You said 'return,' Miss Hastings," he pointed out. "Was he here before? What was your relationship to this Sir Everard. Your footman told me only that he'd been staying at Pearson Close."

Serena who had been sitting at the tea tray, brought him a steaming cup and he took it from her. At her insistence, he lowered himself into a chair near the fire. But the hospitality didn't dim his curiosity.

"Well, Miss Hastings?" he prompted. "You'd best tell me what you know or I'll find out some other way."

Cam stiffened at the man's tone. He had all but accused her of intending to lie.

He opened his mouth to object, but stopped when he felt a hand on his arm. He glanced up and saw that Gemma was frowning. She shook her head in a silent plea for him to stand down. Reluctantly he gave her a small nod and waited for her to speak.

"Sir Everard was one of three gentlemen from the party at Pearson Close," she began with an admirable degree of calm, "to pay a visit to view Lady Celeste's collection of fossils and bones two days ago. Lord Cameron, Lord Paley and Sir Everard."

She was perched on the edge of the settee and the vibrations from a tapping foot beat a tattoo beneath them.

At the mention of Cam, the man's brows drew together. The magistrate's gaze settled on him speculatively.

"What's the nature of this party at Pearson's place, then?" he asked, addressing Cam. "I'd heard he had a group of gentlemen there but not much more. I wouldn't have thought a visit to see a bunch of old stones would prove a temptation away from card games and cigars."

Clearly, Northman couldn't imagine a reason for men to gather that didn't bear some resemblance to White's or Brooks'.

"It is a symposium of sorts," he explained. "Where collectors and scholars of geology might discuss important developments in the discipline, recent finds, that sort of thing."

"So, you sit around and talk about bones and soil and whatnot?" Northman didn't bother hiding his skepticism. "Seems a dull way to spend a house party, if you ask me. But then, I didn't much care for that sort of thing at university either."

Ignoring the man's dismissal of geology, Cam continued, "When I learned of Miss Hastings' interest in fossils, I offered to bring some of the other gentlemen to see Lady Celeste's collection. I thought it would give her an opportunity to share in some of the same sorts of conversation on offer at Pearson Close."

As soon as he finished he realized his mistake.

If Gemma's slight intake of breath wasn't enough to alert him, of course.

"Why would a lady wish to attend a party like that at Pearson Close?" Northman clearly had a guess. And it wasn't one that reflected well on Gemma. "I shouldn't think that sort of gathering would interest a lady no matter how much of a bluestocking she might be. Though all those gentlemen gathered together in one place without any other ladies to offer competition might be just the thing for a spinster who had already seen her three closest allies wed before her."

"Now see here," Gemma said with a scowl. "I had no interest in—"

Cam cut her off before she could finish that thought. It was one thing for Northman to speculate, but quite another for her to put his thoughts into words.

"It is precisely *because* she was not able to attend the symposium that I brought these gentlemen to visit her," Cam said. "To talk," he emphasized. "About fossils."

The words hung in the air.

"It was all perfectly proper," Serena assured the magistrate after a minute. "Sophia and I were here to chaperone and Gemma was able to show the gentlemen all of Lady Celeste's collection and discuss fossils and collecting without fear for her reputation. And if you think she welcomed them here with an eye toward securing one of them for a betrothal, well, you don't know Gemma very well. That was the farthest thing from her mind."

Cam would vow it hadn't been the farthest thing from Serena and Sophia's minds, however. But they were discussing Gemma at the moment. And though she might have been flattered by Sir Everard's and Paley's compliments, he doubted sincerely she'd considered either of them as potential matches.

"So, we know why this Sir Everard was here in the first place," Northman said thoughtfully, "but why did he come back? And why the dev—er, deuce, would he wish to go out onto the shore in this weather?"

This time, Gemma gave him a brief summary of their contretemps yesterday, complete with her plans to come back this morning with Cam to retrieve her skull.

"You went back to Pearson Close with him?" Northman asked Cam. "And you didn't tell him about Miss Hastings and her plans to go back?"

"Of course not. I gave her my word," Cam said with a frown. "As did Paley."

"She gave Sir Everard her word but she didn't mean to keep it, did she?" Northman had turned his gaze on Gemma, who sat up straighter. Cam could practically feel the indignation oozing from her pores.

"He tried to steal my discovery," she said with ill-disguised hauteur. "And I didn't give my word, I didn't have to. He dismissed my claims as if I didn't even exist. As far as he was concerned, my prior claim didn't matter. My leaving was enough to convince him he'd won. He was horrid."

"Seems to me, Miss Hastings, that you had a very good reason to wish Sir Everard dead."

The room fell silent as everyone stared at the magistrate.

"I don't think you understand my sister very well, Mr. Northman," said Sophia coming to stand behind the sofa at Gemma's back. "She has difficulty killing flies. It would be impossible for her to inflict physical harm on another person. Even one as odious as Sir Everard."

"And how would she have known he would return in the

middle of the night?" Serena said calmly. "He wasn't supposed to return until later today."

"I think you've got the wrong end of the stick, Squire," Ben said, coming to stand beside his wife. "Gemma didn't do this."

Beside him, Cam felt Gemma relax a little at the defense. He wanted to offer a consoling touch but now was hardly the time. Not when all eyes were on her.

Northman, however, had turned his gaze on *him* and Cam couldn't help but feel the weight of the man's speculation.

"You could have killed him, though, couldn't you, Lord Cameron?" Northman asked thoughtfully. "Mayhap you didn't care for the way the man insulted your lady. And since you were also in attendance at Pearson's house party, you might very well have heard him leaving in the middle of the night to return to Beauchamp House's bit of shore. It would have been easy enough to follow him here and beat him with his own pry bar."

"That's ridiculous," Cam said sharply. "I had no reason to wish Sir Everard dead. I thought he was out of order to refuse Miss Hastings' claim but that was hardly enough reason for me to murder the fellow. We had a plan to come back this morning and I had no reason to think it wouldn't work."

"We don't even like each other," Gemma assured the magistrate, focusing on the man's designation of her as Cam's "lady."

When he turned and widened his eyes at her, she shrugged. "It's true. We've done nothing but bicker since we met. I'd sooner expect you to murder *me* than murder on my behalf."

She turned back to the magistrate. "Neither of us killed Sir Everard, Mr. Northman," Gemma said firmly. "Not me, and certainly not Lord Cameron."

Northman didn't look particularly convinced, but rose

from his chair. "I will have my men remove the body to the doctor's in town so that he may examine it. Perhaps that will give us more information about the circumstances of the fellow's demise."

There was one detail about the body that Cam hadn't shared with Gemma, and despite knowing she would resent the omission, he said aloud, "There is one more thing about the body, Mr. Northman." Reaching into his coat pocket, he retrieved the note he'd managed to secrete there while Gemma's back was turned. "This was beside the corpse. A warning, I believe."

He felt Gemma stiffen beside him. "Let me see that!" she said sharply. "Why didn't you show me?"

But Northman had already taken the page—torn from a diary or journal it would appear based on the jagged edge. The magistrate stared down at it and frowned. "You should have told me about this first thing," he said to Cam.

"I'm telling you now."

Gemma made a noise of impatience and Northman turned a cryptic gaze toward her. He proffered the page and she all but snatched it from his hand.

Cam knew what it said, but seeing the color drain from Gemma's face made him realize that whatever his response had been, hers was compounded by the fact that she was its target.

"*Stop looking for it or you'll be next,*" she read aloud in a voice that was uncharacteristically shaken.

"Who else knows about this fossil?" Northman asked pointedly. "Besides you lot? And Lord Paley?"

"I have no notion of who Sir Everard might have told," Cam said with a shake of his head. "He seemed reluctant to speak about it last evening for fear of someone attempting to take it, but to be honest, I have little trust in his discretion. He was a boastful man and I would think it next to impossible for him to keep such a discovery to himself."

The magistrate nodded. To Gemma and Cam he said, "Don't either of you leave the county. And since I know the other ladies in this house have fancied themselves to be amateur Bow Street Runners, I will warn you, especially Miss Hastings, not to interfere in my investigation. Leave this business to men who know what they're about. It ain't seemly for a lady to get mixed up in this sort of thing."

Before Gemma could argue, Serena stepped forward and put her arm around Gemma's waist. "I promise you, Mr. Northman, I will see to it that Gemma stays out of trouble."

Northman made a sound that sounded suspiciously like a snort.

To Cam, he said, "I'll be round to Pearson Close later this afternoon to interview the rest of the guests. I'll thank you not to warn them ahead of time so that they all agree on the same story."

It was far more canny than Cam would have given the man credit for. He nodded.

And with that, the Squire left, shutting the door behind him.

"I cannot believe we're being forced to deal with that horrible man yet again," Serena said, rubbing her forehead. "I love you girls dearly, but could you not have avoided getting involved in murder for this one year?"

Gemma, who seemed to have recovered from her shock over the threat, gave the chaperone an impulsive hug. "I promise none of us did it on purpose. And hopefully this particular misdeed will be solved with little discomfort for you."

"I'm more concerned about your safety, Gemma," Sophia said, lines of worry between her brows. "Whoever killed Sir Everard seems intent on warning you against searching for the fossil. I know it's a waste of breath, but I do hope you'll heed that warning."

"But if I simply step away and allow this—this murderer—to steal without any sort of a fight, then what's to stop him from killing the next time he wants something?" Something about the determination in Gemma's tone made Cam's chest tighten. An image of her body in place of Sir Everard's rose in his mind's eye and he clenched his jaw.

"Northman will find the culprit," he told her with a surety he didn't feel. "You must at least let the man do his job." Seeing her skeptical response, he continued, "Or, if you are not content to wait for Northman, let me look into the matter. I'm sure I can find out whoever he told about the fossil."

But instead of gratitude he saw impatience in her eyes. "I am not a child to be placated with promises of sweets. I'm perfectly capable of finding the fossil on my own and when I do—"

She stopped at Sophia's hand on her arm. "Dearest, you've obviously had a trying morning. Perhaps it would be better to discuss this later, when you're feeling less distressed."

At her sister's words, Gemma's mulish expression deflated a bit. "I'm sorry. It's just that I'm so frustrated. That awful man tried to take what I am convinced is the bequest Lady Celeste left for me, and now some other terrible person has killed him and in the process stolen my fossil."

She sighed. "And I sound like a monster for speaking so of a dead man. What a wretched person I am."

"We needn't attribute saintly characteristics to the dead," Ben said quietly, laying a hand on her arm. "There's no shame in recalling them as they were. Nor is there glory in praising them undeservedly."

Cam was struck, as he always was, by his brother's ability to say the right thing at the right time.

It was a skill he had never mastered and he was grateful for Ben's presence here today.

"I'll go down and sit with William for a bit, I think," the vicar continued. "It can't be an easy task to watch over a body in this weather."

Ben was also a master of understatement, Cam thought on a smothered laugh.

Before the vicar left, however, he gave Gemma a hug. Then laid his hand on Cam's shoulder.

"I'm here if you need to talk," he said quietly. "Both of you."

Sophia took her husband's arm. "I'm coming with you."

With a sigh, Serena rose and said, "I'll go see if cook will send some tea out to them."

She was careful to leave the door open, however, something Cam noted with a mixture of amusement and resignation.

He was hardly going to attempt a seduction so soon after finding a corpse.

Or at any time with this particular lady, for that matter.

But Gemma's first words once they were alone told him she was thinking of anything but seduction.

"Where the devil is my fossil?"

Chapter 8

Gemma felt Cam's eyes on her as she paced from the window to the fireplace and back again.

But she couldn't help herself. It was impossible to sit still while the most important fossil she'd ever come across was missing. A fossil that had very likely been the cause of a man's murder.

"Where is it?" she asked again. "Did the killer take it? Or did someone else happen upon it before Sir Everard even returned to the cliff?"

She stopped, some of her frenetic energy dissipating at the memory of the dead man. He'd not endeared himself to her, but he hadn't deserved to have his life cut short for being boorish. What if he had family?

At that thought, she collapsed into the chair Serena had so recently vacated.

She couldn't imagine what she'd do if something happened to Sophia. Or anyone she'd come to know and love since her arrival in Sussex, for that matter.

"It seems unlikely that anyone would stumble upon that stretch of shore in the middle of the night by chance." Cam leaned forward in the chair opposite hers, his elbows on his knees. "We must assume that the killer, very likely someone Sir Everard brought with him, took it."

She nodded. It did seem the most logical explanation.

"If he brought an accomplice," she said, "it must have been someone from Pearson Close. One of the other collectors."

"Or his valet," Cam said thoughtfully. "He did say that Chambers often assisted him in his excavations."

"Then we must speak to this man," Gemma said, her spirits rising at the thought of some occupation to help her find the skull. "I have no intention of allowing a murderer to make off with my skull."

But Cam was already shaking his head.

"You heard what Northman said. He expressly warned you against looking into the matter yourself."

Gemma waved that objection away. "He warned me against investigating the murder. Not the missing skull."

"If you won't listen to Northman's caution, then listen to the killer's," Cam argued, his expression turning forbidding. "If you need reminding, Sir Everard was bludgeoned to death with his own digging tools. I cannot allow you to put yourself at risk for a similar fate. I won't."

"You aren't the one who decides what I may and may not do," she said with a glare.

"Now is not the time for stubbornness, Gemma," Cam said, thrusting his hands through his hair, as if to keep from gripping her by the arms. "Just let me search for it. I promise to report on it to you as soon as I learn anything."

But she shook her head. "Either you assist me, or I search alone," she said firmly.

She watched as he slid his hands down his face in exasperation.

"I know you think it's sheer bullheadedness on my part," she said, taking pity on him, "but you have to understand that I've spent the better part of a year at Beauchamp House with little hope of finding out where Lady Celeste hid my inheritance."

At his questioning look, she continued. "All of the others had detailed instructions and quests outlined for them. Puzzles and mysteries to solve. But Lady Celeste left my letter unfinished." Gemma felt her eyes well. "She died before she could complete it. That's what the note from the solicitor said that accompanied it. So, if she did indeed leave this skull for me—and I am convinced now that she did—then l must be the one to find it."

Cam's expression softened and he took her hand. "I know it must be incredibly frustrating for you, but I cannot believe Lady Celeste would wish you to risk your life to find this fossil."

"No," Gemma said quietly, "But nor would she expect me to simply cede the field to someone else.

"I must be the one to conduct the search, Cam," she said. "And if you insist, then you may help me."

"Help you?" Cam shook his head. "I most certainly will not. You don't need to be mixed up in this business. A man was murdered, Gemma. It's not a jaunt to the shore to dig for stones."

"That's why you'll be there." Really, who would have guessed Lord Cameron Lisle was such a prig?

"To protect me," she clarified, just in case he hadn't figured it out. "It's really quite brilliant. You'll assist me, and I'll find the stone."

"It's not brilliant at all," he countered. "If something were to happen to you, Sophia would be livid. And when Sophia is unhappy, Benedick is unhappy. I do not relish a thrashing from my brother the vicar, Gemma."

"Oh come now. You can't tell me you're afraid of your own brother, can you?"

That was a bridge too far, apparently.

"I'm not afraid of Ben," Cam said in the voice of a man who needed very much to assert his bravery. "I am simply not willing to risk jeopardizing my relationship with him by helping you put yourself in the path of a killer."

"But I'm sure it would be perfectly rational if you had been the one to discover the skull first." Gemma rolled her eyes. "Why is it when a man wishes to pursue something, it's a noble cause that everyone should rejoice over, but if a woman wants to embark on a search for her own property, it's far too dangerous and she should stay at home and . . . and . . ." she searched for the perfect womanly activity to illustrate her point.

"Knit? Cook? Sew? Polish her fossil collection?" Cam asked.

If anything, his attempt at levity made her even angrier. "Any of those things," she said heatedly, stomping her foot for good measure. "And I will not sit still this time. I will not let my discovery be taken from me."

To her shame, tears sprang into her eyes. She'd worked so hard to gain recognition in the world of geology, and the excitement she'd felt when she caught sight of the skull protruding from the mud had been like nothing she'd ever felt before. She'd felt in her bones the importance of it. How dare that . . . that man . . . attempt to steal it from her.

She gulped back a sob and before she knew what was happening, Cam was on his knees before her, pulling her into his arms and flipping them so that he was in the chair and she was in his lap.

It was utterly improper, but at the moment she didn't care for such niceties. Not when he was so warm and strong and it felt so good to be held close.

"Hush now," he whispered, his breath tickling her ear. "Hush. I'll help you. I'll help you find your skull."

She pulled away a little to look him in the eyes and found something there that made her stomach give a flip. "You will?" she asked, her voice hoarse with tears.

"I will," he said, and his eyes glanced down at her mouth.

Without conscious thought, she closed her eyes and whispered, "Thank you."

Then, in what at the time she'd doubtless considered a gesture of gratitude, she kissed him.

What the devil was he about?

Cam tried to form a coherent thought, but Gemma Hastings in his arms with her mouth pressed against his was far too overwhelming to allow anything to cross his mind but disbelief followed by sheer exhilaration.

It was clear from the tentative nature of the caress that she wasn't practiced in the art of seduction, but her mouth was sweet and he let her explore a bit before leaning into her, opening his mouth a little, to tease her.

That surprised a soft "oh" from her as she opened her own mouth and he nipped her lower lip before tasting her with his tongue.

She clung tighter, and he felt her hands slip up and around his neck. He smiled against her as she tilted her head and took to the art of kissing as she did everything else.

With unabashed enthusiasm.

Soon they were exchanging bits of dialogue in a conversation only they could understand.

When she made a noise of satisfaction as he caressed her breast, it sent a lick of fire through his veins.

"Gemma, do you know where my . . . ?"

No two people could have leapt away from a kiss faster than they did.

Though her eyes were still hazy with passion, Gemma had jumped to her feet and turned her back to him.

Cam, meanwhile rose, grateful for the length of his coat.

But they hadn't been hasty enough to hide what they'd been up to.

Lady Serena had seen far more than she should have, if her expression was anything to go by.

Damn it.

He'd even made note of the open door.

"Lord Cameron," Serena said coolly. "I would like to have a word with Gemma alone, please."

He bowed. "Of course, Lady Serena. Miss Hastings, I will speak to you later, if I may?"

Having turned back to face him, Gemma nodded. Her lips were a little swollen from his kisses and he felt a mix of protectiveness and anxiety at the sight.

He'd been afraid of angering Ben by putting her in danger.

Little had he realized he was far more dangerous to her than Sir Everard's murderer was.

"Of all my charges, Gemma," Serena said in an exasperated tone as she shut the door, "you are the last one I'd expect to find in such a scandalous position. What were you thinking?"

Gemma could hardly argue with her. She was just as surprised as her chaperone was by what had just happened. She'd never have guessed she'd be caught in anyone's arms. Much less Lord Cameron Lisle's.

"I was upset," she explained, and to her own ears it sounded like a weak excuse. "He was comforting me."

"With his tongue?" Serena asked with a disbelieving laugh.

"I know what you saw wasn't precisely proper," Gemma said, "but it's hardly the worst behavior you've seen from the Beauchamp House heiresses."

"And why should the others' behavior matter?" Serena countered. "You are responsible for your own actions. And

I'm afraid that I cannot simply forget what I saw and let this slip by. I am assuredly the most lax chaperone in all of England, if not Europe. But never let it be said that I do not hold my charges accountable."

"It isn't your fault," Gemma protested. "As you say, I'm responsible for myself and so was Ivy. She's the only one really who ignored the proprieties."

"Do not try to tell me that Daphne and Sophia didn't anticipate their vows," Serena said with a shake of her head, "for I will not believe you. But they are beside the point. We are speaking of you."

Gemma swallowed. She'd never thought to be on the receiving end of Serena's look of disappointment. It didn't feel good at all.

"Do you love him?" Serena asked, her expression grave.

It was a simple question, but had no simple answer.

Gemma hadn't even liked Cam until this week. Could she grow to love him? Perhaps. But that was not part of her plan. And she'd certainly never thought to kiss him.

"I don't know," she answered. "Not yet."

Serena sighed and took Gemma's hands in hers. "I must write to your parents about this. There's no other option. I am acting as your parent while you are here."

"But what about Sophia?" Gemma asked. Though the idea of Sophia learning what had happened was more alarming than having her parents find out, if she were being honest. "She's a married woman now. Why cannot she be the one to decide?"

Serena thought about it. "I suppose that will be acceptable. Though you must agree to abide by her decision."

"Of course," Gemma said with a nod. She trusted Sophia. And though she'd married a vicar, she hadn't changed her opinions on the strictures that society placed on women.

She would understand that Gemma shouldn't be forced into marriage because of a few kisses.

No matter how toe curling and wonderful those kisses had been.

She wondered what Cam was thinking right now.

Was he just as alarmed as she was at the prospect of a betrothal?

Surely he was, she reasoned. He had no more wish to marry her than she had to marry him.

Why did that bother her so much?

Just then a knock sounded at the door and Sophia stepped in and shut it behind her.

"Cam told me I was needed in here." Her eyes were troubled as she glanced from Serena to Gemma. "What's amiss?"

Serena gave Gemma an encouraging smile and said, "I'll leave you two to discuss this alone."

To Gemma she said, "I trust you to make the right decision."

Then she was gone and Sophia looked alarmed. "What's going on? Has something happened?"

Deciding that plain speaking was best, Gemma said, "Serena caught me kissing Cam."

It was clear from her sister's expression that Gemma confessing she'd been in on the Gunpowder plot with Guy Fawkes would have come as less of a surprise.

"What?" Sophia blinked. "I have to sit down."

She collapsed onto the settee.

Gemma sat down beside her. "I know it's unexpected. But the important thing is that it was only the one time. Really just a slight indiscretion. Nothing to concern ourselves about."

There, she thought. That should convince Sophia to let this whole matter pass without any sort of betrothal nonsense.

"A slight indiscretion is treading on someone's toes on the

ballroom floor," her sister said with a frown. "A slight indiscretion is bumping into someone accidentally. Being found kissing one's brother-in-law is not a slight indiscretion."

"Oh please, Soph," Gemma argued. "We all know how silly and hypocritical the rules about how ladies should behave are. And only Serena knows. There's no reason for it to go any farther."

"I know," Sophia returned. "And I'm sure Ben knows too because Cameron is very likely telling him at this very moment."

Gemma blinked. "What? Why would he do that?"

"Because he's an honorable man, Gemma," Sophia said with a look of disbelief. "I know you have had your disagreements with him, but Cam is not the sort of man who would shirk his duty. You are an unmarried lady. He is an unmarried man. There is every reason for him to do the right thing."

"Marry me, you mean?" Gemma could hardly believe her sister was uttering these platitudes. "What happened to the Sophia who was ready to storm the patriarchy and show her art no matter what the cost to her reputation?"

"She is still here, my dear," her sister assured her. "But there is a time and a place for resisting society's strictures, and since I've married Benedick I've seen far too many examples of what can happen when a lady is ruined. It isn't a happy existence."

"Oh come. I will hardly be ruined because of a few kisses," Gemma chided.

"All it takes is the whisper of scandal and you will not be received anywhere."

"I've always planned to pursue my studies and remain unwed," Gemma said defiantly. "I will be independent like Aunt Dahlia and Lady Celeste."

"My dear," Sophia's voice was sympathetic. "Aunt Dahlia

lives on the kindness of our parents. And Lady Celeste, despite this magnificent house and library she built, was dreadfully lonely."

It was Gemma's turn to blink.

"You would be financially secure, of course, thanks to the inheritance from Lady Celeste," Sophia said. "But you wouldn't be able to be received by Ivy or Daphne without damaging their reputations. And I would have to see you in secret lest word get back to the church hierarchy and endanger Benedick's position."

Gemma stared at her.

"All because of a few kisses." This time it was a statement rather than a question.

"Is it really such a dismal prospect?" Sophia asked softly, taking her sister's hand.

Gemma reflected on the matter.

Cameron was, at the very least, a gifted fossil-hunter.

He was also an honorable man, who clearly bore a great deal of affection for his family.

In agreeing to help her find the lizard skull, he'd also proved himself to be a loyal friend.

And there was no question about his kissing skills, which were, so far as Gemma could tell, exceptional.

"Perhaps not dismal," she admitted aloud.

"Maybe instead of a hasty wedding," Sophia said slipping an arm around her, "we can arrange a betrothal. If at the end of a few weeks you are still against the match, you can agree to go your separate ways. That will silence any rumors of overfamiliarity between you, and will give you a bit of time to get to know one another better."

"Won't that be odd? If we choose to break things off, I mean?" Gemma asked, frowning. "We will still have to see one another from time to time because of our family connection."

"More odd than being married to someone you do not wish to be married to?" Sophia asked wryly.

"I see your point," Gemma said with a nod.

The sisters sat in silence for a moment. Then, Sophia turned to her. "So, tell me all about it. Was it a good kiss?"

Gemma grinned. "Very good."

Very good, indeed.

Chapter 9

"You did what?"

Cam had expected his brother to be angry, but he had perhaps underestimated the degree to which Ben would express this anger.

"Now, Ben," he said, raising his hands in a surrendering motion. "You needn't lose your temper. It's not seemly for a vicar to engage in fisticuffs."

Though Cam knew it took a great deal to raise his brother's ire, it would appear that this was one of those occasions.

"There is every reason for me to lose my temper, you lout," Ben said through clenched teeth. "There are millions of women in the world for you to seduce. But who do you decide to lay hands on at the first opportunity? My sister-in-law. I knew you were a rake, Cam, but I thought even you would draw the line at my wife's sister."

They were in the empty library, where Cam had pulled him so that they wouldn't be overheard. Which was a good thing, considering that Benedick was shouting the dashed roof off.

"It was badly done of me," he said, attempting to cool things down with a preemptive admission of guilt.

Which he then ruined by giving excuses. "But you weren't

there. She was crying, dammit, and I only meant to comfort her a bit. And then she kissed me, if you want to know the—"

He was stopped in mid-sentence by the very strong punch of Ben's fist against his jaw.

It was unexpected, and knocked him to the carpet.

For a minute, he had no thoughts beyond the pain in his face.

Followed closely by satisfaction. If he could have punched himself in the jaw he'd have done it as soon as he stepped out of the drawing room.

He moved his lower jaw from side to side. Though it hurt like the devil, it wasn't broken.

Looking up he saw his brother looking down at him with exasperation. "I shouldn't have done that," he said. "It isn't vicarly."

"Feel better?"

"Not as much as I'd hoped," Ben admitted. He reached down and offered him a hand. "I think there's some brandy hidden in here."

On his feet again, Cam walked over to one of the large over-stuffed chairs that faced the fire. The rest of the furniture was more suited to ladies but she must have had some gentlemen guests—or anticipated them—to have furnished her library with chairs obviously built for the comfort of large bodies.

He sat, then leaned his head back and lifted his forearm to cover his eyes and sighed. He'd awakened this morning feeling like the veriest saint. He was going to help Gemma, who only days ago had been a thorn in his side. It was selfless of him. Yes, he'd be double crossing Sir Everard, whom he'd come to loathe, in the process, but that was beside the point.

And now Sir Everard was dead, Gemma's fossil was missing, and he was facing the prospect of a hasty wedding.

Because there was no way his brother was going to let him off the hook for this.

What a difference a few hours could make.

"Here," he opened his eyes to see his brother offering a generously filled glass of brandy.

He put his arm down and took it. "It's not poisoned, is it?"

"Not my style," said Ben, taking the chair opposite. He extended and flexed the fingers of his right hand as he sipped from the glass in his left.

Cam took a swig of the brandy and was pleased to find it was quality. No cheap liquor for Lady Celeste either. The more he learned of her the more he respected her. She'd been clever enough to choose Gemma after all.

At the thought of her, he couldn't help but remember her mouth on his. Her sweet curves pressed against him as if she couldn't get enough. He couldn't either. But he didn't mention it, of course. He had no wish for a black eye to go with his bruised jaw.

He would have liked to avoid the subject altogether, but that was not going to happen while Ben was drawing breath.

"I barely know the girl, Ben," he said aloud. And even as he said the words he felt their inadequacy. Couples who knew one another far less than they did were married every day.

"You should have thought about that before you kissed her, idiot," his brother said without any of his usual carefully worded tact. "What were you thinking?"

Then, recalling perhaps why he'd punched Cam in the first place, he held up his hand. "In general terms, please. I don't want to break my hand."

Cam shook his head. "It was the heat of the moment," he said wryly. "It wasn't planned. I wasn't trying to seduce her. Hell, I didn't even mean to kiss her."

"You must be attracted to her," Ben pressed. "I mean, if you weren't—and I am going to believe that she kissed you, just for the sake of argument—then you wouldn't have kissed her back."

"Of course, I'm attracted to her," Cam said. Really, his brother was such a simpleton at times. "She's lovely. Maddening as hell, but lovely."

"So, why is the idea of marriage such a problem?"

Cam leaned back in his chair and sighed. "I have been thinking about settling down, but hadn't made up my mind yet. And I'd certainly not thought to choose someone like Gemma. For all that she's beautiful she's the opposite of what a wife should be."

"What should a wife be, then?" Ben asked, tilting his head with puzzlement.

"Don't be an ass," Cam said, feeling his ears go a little red. "You know what I mean. We all have an idea of what we'd like in a bride. I'm simply saying that Gemma is not what I envisioned."

"And I'm asking what you envisioned," Ben said patiently.

"Someone more . . ." Cam struggled to put the idea into words. "Someone more like Lady Serena. Beautiful, calm, sweet. She would make the perfect wife."

"Oh!"

He glanced at the door and saw Gemma there her mouth agape. But she quickly regained her composure.

"I'm sorry, I didn't mean to interrupt. I'll leave you to your conversation."

With that she was gone.

"Now who's an ass?" Ben asked.

Cam, already on his feet, didn't argue.

For once, he was in full agreement with his brother.

Cam passed Sophia in the hallway but when she tried to stop him, he waved her off. "I have to find Gemma," he said as he brushed past her.

"She's in the fossil workroom," she called after him.

He cursed himself for a fool, though to be honest, he wasn't sure why he was so worried about what Gemma had overheard. Didn't she deserve to know the truth? She wanted a marriage between them no more than he did. She didn't even like him. She'd made that perfectly clear in their every interaction since that disastrous first introduction.

True, they had reached a detente of sorts since then, but it was hardly a complete change of opinions.

As he neared the double doors of the fossil gallery, he felt an unusual flutter of nerves. Which he immediately repressed.

He had likely hurt her feelings. That was all. Once he explained his reasons for saying what he had, they would have a good laugh about it. She was a woman of sense. She would understand.

He'd approached the gallery from the far side of the house, so the workroom was on the other side from where they'd entered only yesterday.

And though there was no sign of Gemma in the gallery itself, he could hear a scrubbing sound from the workroom.

When he reached the door to that chamber, it was to see her wearing an apron over her gown and standing at the worktable, using fine brushes to clean the dirt from what looked to be a stack of ammonites.

"What are you doing?" he asked, though it would have been obvious even to young Jeremy, Lady Serena's lad, what she was doing.

"I'd like for you to go, please," she said firmly, not raising her eyes from the task at hand. "I'll figure out what to do about my fossil on my own. Think no more about what happened earlier. My sister won't force me into a marriage neither of us wants. And . . ." she paused. He saw her jaw clench before she went on. "Lady Serena will not force me either. So, you'll be free to court her if that's what you wish."

That was quite a speech.

It was the utter lack of intonation that told him just how hurt she was by what she'd overheard.

He really was an ass.

"Gemma," he said, "let me explain."

She didn't look up, but kept on brushing, occasionally changing to a firmer one when the softer was inadequate. "There's nothing to explain. I am quite aware of my own shortcomings. I walk like a man, I sometimes talk like one. I'm not nearly as pretty as my sister or Serena. And you're right. She would make a far better wife than I would. Nothing you said was untrue. It's just been a long day. I've never seen a dead body."

Seeing that she would not be rising to speak to him face-to-face, he bent so that he could see her face. "Gemma," he said softly, "I have no intention of wooing Lady Serena. Or anyone really. At least I hadn't. Until what happened between us."

She stopped scrubbing and glanced over at him. "You needn't be kind to me. We've always spoken honestly with one another. Do not, I pray, start wrapping things up in cotton wool now. What happened was a mistake. Neither of us should be forced to pay for it with our freedom."

He'd been thinking much the same, but hearing it from her lips made him want to dig in his heels. "Unexpected, perhaps, but not a mistake, surely."

"Cam," she said, a little desperately. "Stop. I understand you feel guilty about hurting me, but there's really no need for it. I know the truth now, and that's far better than muddling along with some farce of a betrothal that would fall apart later. It was only a kiss."

"Only a very good kiss," he said, reaching out to touch her cheek. "Do you think it's like that with everyone?"

"Since I've never kissed anyone else, I'm sure I don't know," she said primly. She didn't look up at him.

Then, with a sigh, she looked up at him. Her cheeks were pink, and her eyes were red. Whether from her tears earlier or more recently, he couldn't know. But he felt a stab of guilt over it just the same.

She'd never looked more appealing.

Cam closed his eyes at the thought. Dammit, he was only here to apologize. Not notice her appeal.

"Well?" she asked, her tone impatient.

He said the first thing that came to him. "What made you come here? To the workroom, I mean?"

She looked surprised at the question, but shrugged. "It's where I'm most comfortable. And cleaning fossils helps me think."

"Think?" He really was the most imbecilic man in the nation, he thought with an inward sigh.

But she seemed to find this amusing. Or something . . .

"Yes, Cam, think. I know you've heard of it, though I feel sure you are of the opinion that ladies don't engage in the practice very often."

"That's not fair," he said scowling. "I never said anything of the sort. And I thought we were friends."

"Perhaps not in so many words," she admitted. "But it's quite clear to me now that what I'd thought was a friendship between us was only some foolish misunderstanding on my part."

She shook her head a little. "I don't blame you. Serena is lovely. And the perfect sort of proper lady a man would wish for in a wife. If I were a man, I'd marry her myself."

He didn't laugh at her joke. This was far worse than he'd thought.

He took her hand. "Gemma, I think you are just as lovely as your sister or Serena. What's more, you're intelligent and brave. But even you must admit that we would likely kill one another before the bridal trip was over."

He said the words and meant them, but a small part of him protested the notion. They might be at loggerheads frequently, but there would certainly be passion. And as he'd told her, that wasn't something that happened every day.

Gemma smiled at that. "I think I could restrain myself. Annoying though you may be."

He smiled too. It would be much easier to come to some sort of solution if he didn't want to kiss that dimple that appeared only when she smiled.

"What will we do, then?" she asked. "It's plain as a pikestaff that we cannot simply go on as before. Serena and Sophia, while not ready to force us into marrying, at the very least expect a betrothal to protect my reputation."

It was what he'd come to realize too. He had no wish to ruin her reputation, or to see her cut off from her family and friends because of his mistake. He might not have kissed her first, but he'd not pulled away. And for all that she considered herself a full participant, he was a gentleman and had more experience in these matters. He should have stopped it before it got out of hand.

"I think we should, at the very least, enter into a betrothal," he said. "You may cry off in a month or so. Once we've had a chance to squelch any rumors. For we both know that even if Serena told no one about what she saw, servants talk and they might have overheard something. I wouldn't be surprised if they were remarking upon the fact that we've been in this room together alone for an extended period of time."

At that, Gemma muttered a curse and scrambled to her feet, pulling her hand away from his in the process.

He felt strangely bereft at the loss. But he, too, got to his feet.

"We really will have to do this, then?" she asked with a moue of distaste. "I am not very good at pretense. My face is far too quick to reveal my thoughts."

"Will it be so distasteful, then?" Good lord, he was turning into some sort of mooning schoolboy. If he didn't stop himself he'd be writing her poetry and composing ballads to sing up at her window.

She narrowed her eyes, and looked at him for a moment. And he felt as if she were trying to see into his soul.

"Perhaps not so distasteful," she admitted. "Mayhap we can use this as an opportunity for my education."

He nodded. "I would be happy to teach you more about geology. I've brought some of the latest journals from France with me and . . ."

When she moved closer and slipped her hands over his shoulders, he felt a frisson of alarm. And desire, if he were being entirely honest.

"I do not need you to teach me about fossils, Cam," she said with a raised brow. "But as I mentioned, you were the first person I'd kissed. And as I mean to remain unwed, I would hate to miss out on the opportunity to experience all the pleasures to be had from life."

His eyes went wide with alarm. "Oh no. Gemma, this is not a good idea." He tried to remove her hands from his shoulders, but his traitorous brain slipped his arms about her waist instead.

"I think it's a very good idea," she said, leaning forward to touch his nose with hers. "If we're to be betrothed, why not behave as other betrothed couples do?"

"I . . . Gemma, we can't . . ." If Ben found out about this he was going to do more than plant him a facer.

But when her lips met his, Cam couldn't think about what-ifs and consequences. His only thoughts were for the warm woman in his arms and just how much he wanted her.

When he began to kiss her back, Gemma felt as if she'd scaled the chalk cliffs in one leap. Her heart beat faster, her breath caught in her throat and she felt a pulse deep in her belly. Whatever their reasons for this betrothal, she knew one thing with every sinew of her body: they were very good together.

She'd been upset at what she'd overheard. What woman with any sort of self-respect wouldn't? He'd practically come right out and said Serena was his preferred choice. And though she'd understood it—Serena was by far the most beautiful and accomplished lady of her acquaintance—the comparison had hurt. Because she knew she wasn't nearly as sensible a choice as Serena was.

His explanation had stung, but it would have hurt more if he'd lied. And though she wasn't quite sure whether his compliments of her were genuine, it had been kind of him to say so.

But whether he thought she was the perfect choice for a bride, he most certainly agreed that there was something else between them. His confession that it wasn't as combustible with everyone had been very flattering.

And as he licked into her mouth and pulled her closer to his hard body, she couldn't deny that she was pleased that she made him feel this way. Even if their betrothal ended in a few months, she would use this time to learn everything she could about what went on between men and women. And if she ended up with a broken heart—because she knew she could very easily fall in love with him no matter how much of a dolt he could be—then she would have at least known the pleasure of holding him in her arms.

"Again?"

This time the interruption came from Sophia, who was looking exasperated as she stood in the door to the workroom.

"If you're going to be behaving this scandalously, it's obvious that we should get the two of you married sooner rather than later."

Pulling away from Cam far more slowly than she'd done

earlier when Serena found them, Gemma slipped her arm through his. "First things first, Sophia," she said with a grin. "You must wish us happy on our betrothal."

And in the flurry of congratulations, Gemma sent up a silent prayer that she'd made the right decision. Because she knew in her heart of hearts that this might be her undoing.

Chapter 10

Gemma and Cam celebrated their betrothal over luncheon with Lady Serena, Sophia and Ben.

And for a temporary measure meant only to protect Gemma's reputation, it felt damned real to Cam.

So real, in fact, that when, instead of discussing wedding details with her sister and chaperone, Gemma announced that she was ready to go to Pearson Close, he laughed. He couldn't help it.

They'd both been up since before dawn, had seen a dead body, been interrogated by the local magistrate, and been compromised into a false betrothal.

Any other lady would have taken to her bedchamber with smelling salts.

But, as he'd realized months ago, Gemma was not like any other lady.

"I'm serious," Gemma said frowning even as she slipped her arm through his as they left the dining room. "We must go examine Sir Everard's belongings before Mr. Northman does. I fear he may have already got there ahead of us, but it's worth a try, at the very least. There may be some clue to who killed him, and therefore who has my fossil."

Cam stopped to look at her, not unaware of his brother smirking behind them. Ben was likely pleased to see another man having to contend with the mad starts of a Hastings sister.

He'd always been happier when he had company.

To Gemma he said, "I know I agreed to help you find your fossil, but—"

"Yes," Gemma interrupted, "and the best way to do that is to see if there's anything in Sir Everard's things that will give us a clue. It might not go amiss if we interview his valet. Did you not say he often helped his master in his endeavors? He will likely object to our examining Sir Everard's papers. You will have to distract him, somehow." She beamed at him as if he were a prized pupil. "I have faith in you, though, Cam. You can be quite persuasive when you want to be."

Before he could reply, she said, "I'll just go fetch my coat and hat. I'll only be a moment."

With that, she hurried up the stairs.

Cam felt as if he'd just been knocked over by a gale force wind.

"So, I see you've been given your orders," Ben said wryly, clapping him on the shoulder. "Welcome to my world."

"Thanks so much for your help," Cam said with a glare.

"Come now," Ben said cheerfully. "The Hastings sisters may know their own minds, but they make up for it in other ways. Sophia hardly ever orders me around like that anymore. At least, not when I've been doing my best to keep her happy."

"So you just do her bidding?" Cam asked aghast. He'd be dashed if he would allow himself to be led around by the nose.

"I wouldn't quite put it like that," Ben said with a shrug. "I try to do what will make her happy. And she does the same for me. But sometimes we both fail. In which case, we argue, then make up. To be honest, the making up is the best part sometimes."

"You're a very strange fellow," Cam told his brother.

"You should hear Archer," Ben said with a shake of his head. "He's been married longer than any of us. He knows far more about dealing with a wife. Though of course, every lady is different."

This was a whole world that Cam hadn't even known existed, he realized. He was almost sad he'd not be welcomed into this husbands' club.

But only almost.

Tillie was buttoning her into a long-sleeved persimmon-colored velvet when a knock heralded the arrival of Ivy, followed close behind by Daphne.

Seeing that they were wide-eyed and obviously wished to discuss the morning's events, she said to the maid, "I can manage the rest, Tillie. Thank you."

With a nod, the girl slipped from the room.

"It would appear that we chose the wrong morning to sleep in," Ivy said with a shake of her head and she came forward and gave Gemma a fierce hug. "What an awful thing for you to see. And then to be imposed upon by Lord Cameron like that. Do you wish me to tell Kerr to have a word with him? Or perhaps both he and Maitland. I know he is Lord Benedick's brother, but that can be no excuse for his behavior."

"No matter how many facers Lord Benedick plants on him with his fives," Daphne added staunchly.

Despite herself, Gemma laughed. "There's no need to send your husbands to talk sense into Cam," she told her friends. "Though I am grateful for the offer. And contrary to what you must think, Ben and Sophia aren't forcing me into anything. It's to be a temporary betrothal until some time has passed.

For propriety's sake. I would have dispensed with the whole thing, but Sophia, rightly pointed out to me that a ruined reputation might mean that I would be cut off from my friends and family."

She took them each by the hand. "I couldn't bear it if you were unable to receive me because of my own foolishness."

"We would never do that to you," said Ivy fiercely, her eyes stern behind her spectacles. "Not even if Kerr ordered it of me."

"And I wouldn't wish to put you in that position," Gemma said. "Though I do appreciate the loyalty."

"And what of Lord Cameron?" Daphne asked, her blue eyes searching. "Was the thrashing the vicar delivered sufficient or should we have it followed up on by Maitland and Kerr?"

"He didn't deserve a thrashing at all," Gemma said with a shake of her head. "I was a willing participant in the kiss, and if Serena hadn't walked in on us, no one would have been any the wiser."

"Oh poor Serena," said Ivy with a shake of her head. "I believe she hoped you, at least, would manage to finish out the year without compromising yourself."

"One cannot compromise oneself, Ivy," said Daphne with a shake of her head. "Unless one were to do the female equivalent of boxing the Jesuit in public, I suppose, but really that's simply outside the realm of anything Gemma would be likely to—"

Deciding she'd best get back downstairs before Cam left without her, Gemma cut Daphne off mid-thought. "I'm sorry to go before we have time to speak more candidly about this, but I'm afraid Lord Cameron is waiting for me downstairs and we must be off."

Ivy's eyes narrowed. "That's a new gown, isn't it?"

"Where are you going?" Daphne demanded.

Gemma picked up the hat Tillie had left out for her and busied herself pinning it to her hair. "We are going to question Sir Everard's valet at Pearson Close."

"You're investigating the murder, aren't you?" Ivy asked, wide-eyed. "Poor Serena."

Before they could begin questioning her further, Gemma kissed them each on the cheek and fled.

But not before she heard Daphne call out, "Good luck."

She wasn't sure whether her friend referred to Cam, or the search for the murderer. She'd take the luck for either.

When Gemma finally reappeared, she'd changed into another formfitting velvet. This one was a dull red color and was partially covered by a pelisse of the same shade. The color accentuated the peaches and cream of her complexion and was set off by a jaunty hat adorned with a cluster of flowers he couldn't identify. None of it seems particularly practical for the current weather but as they would be indoors most of the time, it didn't seem to be an issue.

And he had to admit, she was in fine looks.

"I took the liberty of having your curricle brought round," Gemma told him as she stepped forward. "I hope you don't mind."

He looked up to see what Ben thought of this but he was gone.

The coward.

"Certainly not," he said aloud. "I suppose we should go if we're to get there before Northman."

He gathered his coat and hat and gloves from George and soon he was lifting Gemma into his curricle. It wasn't the most practical of vehicles in this weather, but with the bonnet up and the hot bricks and carriage blankets William brought them, it would be bearable.

Once they were on the road, Gemma turned to him and asked, "How shall we get me into the house?"

"Dash it," Cam said, "I forgot about Pearson's ridiculous no females rule. Perhaps I should go alone. I'll turn back."

He made as if to direct the horses to do just that but Gemma put a hand on his arm. "Don't do that. We can figure something out. Just give me a minute."

Reluctantly he did as she asked, though he wasn't particularly hopeful of their prospects. It wasn't as if they could dress her in men's clothing and sneak her in that way.

"What were Mr. Pearson's plans for today?" Gemma asked. "Did anyone plan on going out for some reason? Perhaps a trip to the pub?"

But he shook his head. One of the most disappointing aspects of the house party had been Pearson's reluctance to introduce his guests to the local attractions. Which was a shame given the proximity to Lyme and other well-known fossil grounds. And there had been no question of a large group traveling to see the collection at Beauchamp House. Pearson, of course, disapproved of Lady Celeste and her decision to leave her estate to four ladies.

"As far as I know, everyone was intending to remain at the house," he said aloud. "Though I suppose with the news of what happened to Sir Everard, there will be some who wish to go into town to get more details. Or perhaps leave altogether."

"Perhaps that will be our cover story, then," Gemma said with a nod. "We're coming to bring the sad news. It did happen at my home. And you're my betrothed so there's no surprise in our coming together."

"Northman warned us not to tell them before he could," Cam reminded her. "And Pearson doesn't even allow female servants in his house. How do you expect to get past the butler?"

"It isn't our fault that Northman is taking so long," Gemma said innocently. "And the butler can hardly toss me out on my ear with my handsome fiancé—who is a guest of his master—at my side, can he?"

"Handsome, eh?" He gave her a sideways look and she blushed and refused to meet his eyes.

"You know perfectly well you're handsome, you devil." The single dimple he liked so well made an appearance.

"But I didn't know you thought so," he said softly, holding the reins in his other hand so that he could slip his arm through hers. "I'm quite flattered."

"Don't let it go to your head," she said tartly, though there was a hint of breathlessness in her voice. "I still think you're stubborn as a mule."

He barked out a laugh.

"That sentiment is mutual, Miss Hastings," he said grinning.

He was still smiling like a fool when the curricle approached Pearson Close.

A groom stepped forward to take the reins and when Cam asked if he'd seen Northman that morning the man shook his head.

"No visitors at all today, my lord."

Relieved that one obstacle had been avoided, he leapt down and moved to assist Gemma from the vehicle. He'd halfheartedly decided to keep things platonic between them while they were here so as not to antagonize Pearson, but that went the way of the marine lizards when she slid down the front of his body as he lifted her to the ground. He clenched his jaw at the teasing contact, and frowned at her. But Gemma's only response was an innocent lift of her brows.

She wasn't going to give an inch, he realized.

But really, had he expected anything less?

Of course not.

Laughing softly at his own foolishness, he took her arm and they walked together up the front steps.

When they reached the door, it opened before Cam could lift the gargoyle knocker.

Fanshawe blinked when he saw Gemma at his side.

"Lord Cameron," he said solemnly. Then, looking down his nose at Gemma, he intoned, "I hope you know your companion will not be allowed inside. Mr. Pearson has very strict rules about females.."

"Oh, I only wish to remain in the entry hall," Gemma assured him. "I'm Miss Gemma Hastings, by the way. And we've come to speak with Sir Everard's valet."

At the mention of Sir Everard, the butler's face turned, if possible, even more dour. "Why would you wish to do that?"

"We have some news to give him," Gemma said solemnly. "It's about his master. Something very unfortunate has happened. I'm afraid he won't be returning to Pearson Close."

Fanshawe's mouth dropped open, his usual impassive expression erased in his shock. "Do you mean to say that Sir Everard is dead, Miss?"

"I'm afraid he is," Gemma said.. "And I discovered his body, I wanted to be the one to tell his valet. What's his name? Chambers, is it?"

The butler was still taking in the news that one of the houseguests was deceased. "I don't know, Miss. This seems most irregular. And there's been no news of it from—"

"It's a most irregular matter, Mr. Fanshawe," she said, cutting him off, and Cam watched as the older man struggled to decide whether he should allow her in or not.

"I assure you, Fanshawe," Cam said, "it's all above board. I can confirm the dreadful news about Sir Everard. And while my betrothed speaks to Chambers I'll just go gather my things. I'm removing to my brother's house for the duration."

It was the perfect solution. He would let Gemma speak to Chambers downstairs—with Fanshawe in attendance so that she wouldn't be endangered on the off chance Chambers was the one who'd killed his master—while he nipped up to search Sir Everard's rooms.

Fanshawe, however, was focused on the other news now. "Miss Hastings," he said, looking mortified. "If I'd known you were the betrothed of Lord Cameron I would not have been so . . ."

"Think nothing of it, Mr. Fanshawe," she said with a wave of her hand. "We only just got engaged this morning. You did nothing wrong." She clung to Cam's arm like a limpet and looked up at him with such adoration he felt like a puppy in the hands of a toddler.

"Indeed," was his only response. "Now, Fanshawe, if you'll just take Gemma to see Chambers now?"

They watched as the man struggled to decide what he should do. Finally, with the utmost reluctance, he gestured them inside.

Once they were in the entry hall, he frowned at them. "I'll just go see if he is available. I'm afraid Mr. Chambers likes a tipple and with Sir Everard's absence he's been indulging himself." His bushy brows drew together as he frowned at Gemma. "Wait here."

Before they could respond, he had disappeared through the door leading to the kitchens and servants quarters.

Just as Cam was about to remark on Chambers' intoxication, Gemma was sprinting toward the staircase.

"What are you doing?" Cam hissed, hurrying after her. "Get back here."

"You get up here," she said in a low voice, over her shoulder, as she hurried up the carpeted stairs. "If we don't get to Sir Everard's bedchamber before Fanshawe emerges with Chambers we'll lose our chance."

She meant, of course that she'd lose *her* chance to search the baronet's rooms. But by now he'd realized it was impossible to change Gemma's mind once she had decided a course of action. So, mindful that they didn't want to be caught out by the butler, Cam hurried to catch up with her.

Chapter 11

Though she would very much have liked to take a detour into Mr. Pearson's collections room, mindful of the reason for their presence in the house, Gemma let Cam lead her toward what had been Sir Everard's room during his stay at Pearson Close.

"I can't believe you've got me into this," he said under his breath as they hurried down the hall.

"You really are far more circumspect than your swashbuckling reputation had led me to believe," Gemma said, careful to keep her voice just above a whisper. "I would have thought a little housebreaking was child's play for an adventurer like yourself."

Cam snorted. Or was that a growl? It was so hard to tell when he was dragging her alongside him.

"Contrary to what you may have heard," he said, his harassed tone all too clear, "I am not a common thief, nor am I accustomed to circumventing the authorities."

She almost tripped when he stopped short before a door near the end of the corridor.

"This is Sir Everard's room?" she asked in a low voice.

When he didn't immediately respond, she realized how unnecessary her question had been.

"Sorry," she muttered. "Nervous."

Cam turned to look at her, and she was surprised when he gave her a rueful smile. "Me too," he said.

Then placing his ear against the door, to see if there was any movement within, he listened for a moment. Seemingly satisfied, he depressed the thumb latch and in one swift move, hustled them both through the open door.

The room was dim thanks to the gray skies outside and the lack of any indoor illumination. Cam found a candle near the door, lit it and gave it to Gemma. Then he moved with admirable stealth to the lamp on the writing desk and lit it as well.

With light it was easy to see that Sir Everard's valet was perhaps not the most adept at his chosen occupation. The floor was strewn with clothing and papers and all sorts of items that a gentleman of a certain social status would bring along on a week's long stay.

"Someone has been here before us," Cam said with a frown.

"Or Sir Everard was a very untidy person," Gemma offered, scanning the disarray. "Though I believe yours is the more accurate assessment. Even a valet with a penchant for drink would not dare leave his master's rooms like this."

"He might if he knew his master wasn't coming back," Cam said.

"We can discuss it later," she said. "Fanshawe has likely found him by now. I'll take the desk, you look through the papers on the floor."

Cam didn't argue, but knelt amongst the papers nearest the bed. Gemma moved to the desk and began scanning the documents strewn across the surface.

Most of what she found were scientific papers that had been disordered to such a point that it was impossible to tell which page went with which study without the kind of careful examination for which they had no time. So she just began stacking them in a tidy pile.

"Any luck?" Cam asked from the floor, not looking up from his own task.

"They're geological studies and scientific papers," she said as she worked, "but they're so disorganized it's impossible to tell which page goes with which study."

"We might have time to—"

The sound of voices in the hallway stopped him mid-sentence.

"Fiddlesticks," Gemma said crossly. "I hoped we'd have more time than this."

She finished pulling pages into a stack and clutched it to her chest.

Cam, likewise, got to his feet holding a similar sheaf.

"What do we do?" Gemma asked, looking with alarm at the door as the voices got closer.

It had been her idea to brazen their way into Sir Everard's bedchamber but her scheme hadn't got much farther than that.

Cam, however, was already at her side, pushing her into the adjoining dressing room.

They had just managed to shut the door when she heard the bedchamber door open and hit the wall.

"I might have known she was up to no good," she heard Fanshawe say in an aggrieved tone as she and Cam huddled together on the other side of the dressing room door. "But I hadn't thought Lord Cameron would be in on her scheme."

"All the ladies up at Beauchamp House are trouble," Squire Northman muttered in response.

Gemma let out a little huff of anger at that unfair bit of criticism, and Cam clapped a hand over her mouth. When she glared at him, he widened his eyes and put a finger to his lips. She got the message and indicated that he could remove his hand. Which he did, but not without another gesture for her to keep quiet.

Really it was too unfair that she had to remain quiet while her character was being unfairly maligned.

Unfortunately, this interchange was too late to keep the men on the other side of the door from hearing her initial outburst.

"Who's that?" Fanshawe demanded, causing Cam to swear silently.

Then, before she even knew what was happening, Gemma was propelled backward against the window and being thoroughly kissed. But though the kiss was breathtaking, she wasn't too overcome to notice Cam removing the stack of pages from her hands. Nor did she miss the way he fiddled with the window behind her. She felt a burst of freezing air on her back, then almost as quickly as it happened, it was gone.

Her attention was diverted again, however when Cam pressed the full length of his body against hers, and she was lost in the heat and strength of him. She slipped her arms up around his neck and slid her fingers through the silky hair at his nape.

For several moments she forgot where she was and was lost to the sensations his every touch sent coursing through her.

She was opening her mouth wider to welcome him in when the door to the dressing room burst open.

"Lord Cameron!"

Fanshawe's pronunciation of the name drew out every syllable in a very good impersonation of a scolding nanny.

Though she'd known their intrusion was coming, it still managed to make Gemma jump in surprise.

Cam, however, was unfazed. Not hurrying to move away from her, he pulled back and rubbed his nose against hers, before kissing her softly one last time.

Then he put his mouth at her ear and whispered, "Follow my lead."

Gemma was too bleary-eyed to argue and allowed him to pull away then bring her against his side.

"What is the meaning of this, Lord Cameron?" Fanshawe demanded. "I did you a courtesy by fetching Chambers, but I didn't intend to allow the lady above stairs. You know that Mr. Pearson does not hold with females of any sort in this house."

"Fanshawe, don't be such a prig," Cam said with a laconic drawl. "The lady is my betrothed and . . . well . . ."

Northman, who had been watching them through eyes narrowed with suspicion raised his brows. "She wasn't your betrothed when I visited Beauchamp House earlier this morning, Lord Cameron."

Cam's laugh was so utterly knowing and just-between-us-lads that Gemma wanted to pinch him. It was only thanks to their audience that she did not.

"You know how it is, old man," he said with a shrug. "A bit of danger goes a long way toward changing a lady's mind."

"That's all well and good, Lord Cameron," said the magistrate, "but what has that to do with your presence in Sir Everard's dressing room? Which just so happens to be connected to a dead man's disarrayed bedchamber?"

Gemma was having a very difficult time not answering the man's questions. Subterfuge was not her forte. But Cam was not a stupid man. He had some sort of endgame in mind for this and she had to let him follow his plan.

"They wished to speak with Sir Everard's valet," Fanshawe told him before Cam could answer. "But the fact that he's nowhere to be found, coupled with the untimely death of Sir Everard leads me to believe they knew all along he wasn't here and merely wished to divert my attention so they could pilfer through Sir Everard's things."

Cam laughed softly. "Do you hear that, dearest?" he asked Gemma. "They think we came here to steal from Sir Everard."

Gemma laughed, but it sounded hollow to her own ears.

Before she could say anything, however, Cam continued. "I hope you won't think too badly of me," he said to the other two men. "But I'm afraid, we came here for a far less nefarious reason."

"Well, we haven't got all day, man," said Northman with a scowl. "Spit it out."

Gemma felt Cam squeeze her hip, and she read it as a warning. What on earth was he going to say?

"Well, you know how it is, lads," he said sheepishly. "Beauchamp House is thick with chaperones. And it's dashed cold outside at the moment. So we thought of Sir Everard's rooms, which are unoccupied at the moment and . . ."

Gemma felt her face turn scarlet. Cameron was going to pay for this. She wasn't sure how yet. But she would make it something truly painful for him. And preferably involving bees. There would be no bees about until summer, of course, but didn't they say revenge was best served cold?

"And why, might I ask were your own rooms not adequate to your needs, Lord Cameron?" asked Northman, his mouth tight.

Not wanting to be seen as some passive party to this charade, Gemma jumped in before Cam could. If she were going to be painted as the sort of hussy who would accompany her betrothed to another house so that they could be amorous, she would dashed well make herself a participant with agency.

"It was my idea, Squire Northman," she said, snuggling

closer to Cam. In a low voice, as if she were afraid of being overheard, she said, "I thought it might be more exciting."

To her satisfaction, Squire Northman, who was perhaps the most imperturbable man of her acquaintance, blushed to the roots of his sparse hair.

Beside her, Gemma felt Cam shake with laughter. Take that, she thought smugly.

"That is . . ." Northman, began, then fell into a coughing fit. When he had regained his voice, he continued, "I'll just ask you two to leave Pearson Close for the time being. Though I must ask you, for investigative purposes, was this room ransacked when you arrived?"

"Oh yes," Gemma said in a mournful tone. "I suspect poor Sir Everard's valet is to blame. If he's really run off as Mr. Fanshawe said."

They stood in an uncomfortable silence for a moment before Northman regained his composure and pulled himself up to his full height.

"Be off with you, then," he said sourly. "And do not speak of what you found here in this room to anyone else."

"And of course I must ask that you and Mr. Fanshawe keep our little secret, too, Squire," Gemma said with a bat of her eyelashes. "We are betrothed, but I shouldn't like my sister or her husband the vicar to learn of our little . . . adventure."

"Go, Miss Hastings," Northman said in a tone of desperation. "And Lord Cameron, I advise you to be more sensible when it comes to following the whims of your lady. She's going to get you both into a great deal of trouble."

Without pausing to reply, Cam slipped an arm around Gemma's waist and escorted her to the door as quickly as they could go without running.

Before they reached the hall, Gemma thought she heard the Squire say, "Dear God, I do not envy Lord Cameron the chase she's likely to give him."

They were downstairs and bundled up in their outerwear in minutes.

It wasn't until they were settled back in the curricle that Cam finally spoke.

"More exciting?" he almost shouted. "Are you mad?"

Chapter 12

Cam wasn't sure whether he wanted to kiss Gemma or spank her.

"I'm not a child, Cam," she said with a roll of her eyes, which alerted him to the fact he'd spoken the thought aloud. "I do know what happens between men and women."

"But that isn't . . ." he searched for the right words. "That is to say, that sort of . . ."

Gemma sighed, and patted him on the hand. "I know this has upset your sense of propriety," she told him kindly, "but we had best not sit here in the drive of Pearson Close or Mr. Northman will suspect our reasons for being here weren't quite as carnal as I made them out to be."

Cam blinked. Then realized she was right.

But rather than turning toward the main road that led to Beauchamp House, he directed the horses in the other direction.

"Where are we going?" Gemma asked, looking far more suspicious than a woman who had just admitted to taking her betrothed to someone else's rooms because it stimulated her had a right to be.

"So now you don't trust me?" Cam asked with a raised brow.

"That was pretend and you know it," she said haughtily.

"It wasn't pretend when you put your tongue in my m—"

"Lord Cameron," she said in a not unconvincing impersonation of Fanshawe, "I was playing a part. Nothing more. Pray do not refer to it again."

He had a very good idea of just how much—or little—of a part she'd been playing, but they would save that argument for another time.

"I dropped the papers out the window," he said smugly. "When we were . . . you know."

She didn't remark on his inability to name what it was they'd been engaged in, for which he was thankful.

"Oh! I wondered what you were doing," she said with what sounded like awe. "That was a brilliant idea. I'm sorry for doubting you."

"Do not praise me yet," he said ruefully. "I dropped two sheaves of papers out of a third story window. The odds of them not having scattered all over the garden are very low."

"Do not be such a pessimist," Gemma chided him. "At least we have them."

"I am a realist," he responded as he brought the curricle to a halt on the path he'd seen tradesmen take to the kitchens at Pearson Close.

Cam tied the horses to a tree branch, then stepped around to grasp Gemma by the waist and lift her down from the vehicle.

He was grateful he'd instructed the grooms yesterday to give his matched pair a rest. He had no doubt that this pair of carriage horses they kept in Beauchamp House stables would be far more amenable to remaining tied up outdoors in this weather. The grays would have broken the reins or injured themselves at such an indignity.

Just as temperamental as the grays, but equally as valuable he'd come to realize, was the lady in his arms at the moment.

When she got her feet beneath her, he saw a spark of

desire in her eyes, but then she'd shaken it off and pushed him away.

"Come on," she ordered, stomping forward over the shell-covered path.

"Yes, ma'am," he said in an undertone as he followed her.

It was just as well that she was keeping the focus, he reflected as he caught up to her.

He'd forgot for a time that their betrothal and everything that went with it was only temporary. It wouldn't do to mistake lust and friendship for anything more permanent.

Once he was walking beside her, he was careful to keep them to the edge of the wood so that they would be less visible from the house. But it was slow going thanks to the mud and ice. The hems of Gemma's garments were soon filthy, but she didn't complain once.

"Which window?" Gemma asked as they neared the path alongside the house.

Cam had calculated the location based on his view out his own window, and its proximity to Sir Everard's rooms. But it had been the papers contrasting with the dark green of the holly bushes growing beneath the windows that gave him the precise location. Fortunately the wind had been blowing toward the side of the house rather than crossways, so the pages were in a relatively tidy pile.

Unfortunately, aforementioned holly bushes were well over seven feet tall. A height neither of them could boast even on their toes.

"You'll have to boost me up," Gemma said frowning up at the top of the hedge. "Make a step with your hands. Like so."

She threaded her fingers together and proffered them in the way she wanted him to do it.

Cam shook his head. "That won't work."

"Why not?" she demanded. "I'll get the height I need."

"But you've got nothing to hold on to," he argued. "You'll have to climb onto my shoulders."

He said it with an air of apology.

"I certainly will not," Gemma said emphatically. "Not in this gown."

She glanced around them, as if looking for some alternative means of getting the papers.

"Gemma," Cam said in a soothing tone, "It's the only way. You need enough time to be able to gather them all and I certainly can't climb onto your back."

"But it's . . . it's . . . it's unseemly," she finally finished.

"Where is the lady who confessed to enjoying lovemaking more in the bedchambers of other people?" he asked wryly.

"That was different," she hissed. "That didn't entail you putting your head up my skirt."

"If you're doing it right it does," he said with a shrug.

"I hate you," she said hotly.

"I know you do," he said. "But it's the only way."

Even as he spoke, he knelt and held out his hand to help her climb up.

Gemma scowled. Then when he didn't relent, she gave a very unladylike curse.

"Do not look," she ordered. He did his best to obey, but it was impossible not to peek just a little.

From the corner of his eye he watched as she gathered her skirts between her legs, then lifted them so high her garters were showing.

Her legs were long and slender, and he was forced to think about the mineral composition of his latest soil samples in order to suppress the image of those legs over his shoulders in a very different circumstance than the present one.

The frigid temperature did the rest.

"If you ever tell anyone about this I will murder you,"

Gemma said tightly as she climbed onto his shoulders. "With a rusty knife."

"You have my word," he said, reaching up to grasp her by first one stockinged leg, then the other.

Despite his attempts at distraction, it was impossible to ignore the fact that if he were to turn his head just a fraction he'd be able to kiss the soft skin of her inner thigh. He closed his eyes and counted to ten.

"Stand up," Gemma ordered, pulling on his hair. "It's cold."

He felt a shiver run through her and cursed himself.

Without reply, he stood to his full height and walked slowly so that she was close enough to the top of the neatly trimmed holly bushes.

"A little to the right," she instructed him, and Cam did as she asked.

"Here."

It took much less time than he'd have expected, probably because she was cold and when he offered to rub her legs to make them warmer she'd told him to go to the devil.

Finally, when she had them all, she handed the sheaf of papers down to him and ordered him to kneel so she could climb off. He wasn't even completely on his knee when she hopped off and dropped her skirts down and began smoothing them.

With an imperious hand she indicated that he should hand her the papers.

He did so, deciding that she had earned the right to order him about for a little while.

Without a word to him, she set off back toward where they'd tied up the curricle and horses.

"We will not speak of this again," she said firmly as he came up beside her.

"Was it so bad?" he asked. "It only took a quarter hour at most."

"You take off your breeches and climb up on someone else's shoulders in the freezing cold where anyone might happen upon you at any minute, and tell me how much it matters that it only lasted a quarter hour."

"You have a point," he said.

Then, he heard her sniff. And had that been a wobble in her voice?

She tried to hurry forward, but he stopped her with a hand on her arm.

"Gemma," he said gently, "are you all right?"

She didn't turn but he could see that her shoulders, normally proud and strong, were sagging.

"Cameron, my day has consisted of finding a dead body, discovering that the fossil I hoped would help me establish myself as a legitimate scholar missing, kissing my brother-in-law, being hurried into a betrothal with said brother-in-law, breaking into a dead man's bedchamber, pretending I enjoy lovemaking in other people's homes, and exposing my lower limbs in the outdoors in the freezing cold where anyone might see them. I am most assuredly not all right."

Her voice broke on that last, and Cam muttered a curse and lifted her into his arms.

She clutched the papers to her chest, but didn't protest him carrying her because she was shivering too badly to speak.

"I'm an idiot," he said to himself. If she caught her death of a cold from this he'd never forgive himself.

The walk to the curricle was brief, thankfully, and when he climbed in after untethering the horses, he shrugged out of his greatcoat.

"What are you doing?" she demanded through chattering teeth. "It's freezing."

"For once in your life, do not argue." He wrapped the coat, still warm from his body, around her, and turned to rouse the horses.

"There's room enough for a family of four beneath this coat," she said after they'd gone a few hundred feet. "You must be cold too."

Realizing that she would very likely argue until he succumbed, he allowed her to drape the coat over his upper body, too. Before they were halfway back to Beauchamp House, she'd snuggled up against his side and fallen fast asleep.

Cam shook his head ruefully.

If he didn't watch it he was going to find himself married to her.

He was no longer entirely sure that would be a bad thing.

Chapter 13

Gemma came awake with an abrupt jolt when the curricle stopped.

She realized with a start that she was cuddled up against Cam's side like an ivy vine twining around an arbor. She pulled away, trying to be casual about it, but given that he was about two inches away it was doubtful he'd failed to notice.

"We're here," he said unnecessarily.

Fortunately William appeared at the side of the vehicle then, and she hastily scrambled to climb down with his assistance instead of Cam's.

But to her dismay he was there just as she gained her footing and offered her his arm.

When she hesitated, his lifted brow was all it took to spur her into accepting his escort.

"I've got the papers here," he said as they walked. "I thought perhaps we should wait until tomorrow to go over them. You need to get warmed up after . . ."

"After exposing my legs like a common strumpet?" she asked bitterly. She truly wanted to recover her fossil, but this afternoon's escapade had perhaps been too bold even for her.

"I didn't see anything," he said with a haste that told her he had in fact seen everything.

When they reached the door, it swung inward and George ushered them inside with a tutting noise. She must have looked more bedraggled than she realized, Gemma thought with an inward sigh.

"This mud will be the death of us, Miss Gemma," said the butler with a shake of his head. "I'll see to it that Tillie takes good care of this."

She looked down and realized that, indeed, her lovely persimmon velvet was thoroughly spattered. Which reminded her of something else.

"I know I've resisted it, but I suppose you'd best choose a ladies maid for me from among the staff, George," she said. "Or perhaps Serena won't mind sharing Tillie with me for a few days until one can be hired on? Either way, one of them should be able to salvage it."

To his credit, the butler's eyes only widened for a half-second before he nodded and said he would do so at once.

"Look at me nattering on about household business while you wait," she said, realizing that Cam had been standing silently behind her. "Let George take your things. I'm sure Maitland or Kerr have something you can change into while yours are cleaned."

But to her surprise—and disappointment, she realized—he shook his head.

"I won't be staying. You need some rest, and if I'm to reach the vicarage in time for supper, I should leave now."

Gemma frowned and turned to look at him. She'd been embarrassed by her behavior in the curricle, but somehow she'd thought he'd take his evening meal here.

"I wish to discuss the best course of action in our search for your fossil with Benedick," he said. "He's a bit of a nuisance as brothers go, but he's not entirely useless."

"You're frozen to the bone, he added. "Get warm and get some rest. I'll see you tomorrow."

This last he said with such gentleness she felt her chest squeeze.

Perhaps it was better if he left now. If she wasn't careful, she'd become so attached to him she wouldn't be able to break their engagement when the time came.

"Then I'll see you tomorrow," she said with what she hoped sounded like lofty unconcern. "We can go over Sir Everard's papers."

"Yes," he said with a nod.

They stood awkwardly for a moment. How did one take leave of the man who'd had a close up view of one's naked thighs, she wondered. That wasn't even accounting for the kissing.

To her shock, when she offered him her hand, Cam pulled her closer and kissed her on the mouth.

"You didn't see that, Stephens," he said to the butler.

"See what, my lord?"

"Until tomorrow," Cam said to Gemma.

And then he was gone.

She stood dumbfounded for a moment. When Stephens coughed slightly, she realized it had been longer than she'd realized.

"Send up a bath please, Stephens," she said over her shoulder as she hurried up the stairs. At least one reason for her shivers could be taken care of.

An hour later, Cam was seated in Benedick's study. Fortunately, they were of a size, so he'd been able to borrow a mud-free, dry set of clothes. He'd need to send for his things tomorrow. Any pretense of normalcy at Pearson Close had been lost with Sir Everard's murder and Cam would rather be here, close to Beauchamp House in case Gemma had need of him.

Good lord, he was a fool.

"Already regretting your actions of the day?" Benedick asked with one of his omniscient vicar looks. Cam knew there was no actual all-knowingness behind them, but it was an effective tool in his brother's repertoire of expressions that annoyed Cam.

"Not at all," he replied blithely, despite his very real misgivings. "We'll dissolve the betrothal a few months from now and all will be well. Gemma wishes to marry me as little as I wish to marry her."

"I can't imagine she's eager to give up ownership of Beauchamp House so soon after inheriting it," Benedick agreed. "Especially after she's been the one heiress to escape the parson's mousetrap over the course of the year. I can't say I blame her for being reluctant."

That was one aspect of the situation Cam hadn't considered.

"I know it's the law that her property would become mine, but I'm not a monster. I'm sure I could have my solicitor draw something up if it came to that," he said with a frown. "She knows I wouldn't do anything with her property without consulting her first."

"Does she?" Benedick wondered thoughtfully.

"Of course she does," Cam said with a vehemence he immediately regretted. So much for appearing calm and collected.

"Does she?" Ben asked again. "It's not difficult to believe she might not know that. You don't know one another that well, do you?"

Rather than protest that they knew one another quite well, in fact, Cam instead tried for nonchalance. He set one booted ankle on his knee and leaned back in his chair.

The picture of calm.

"It isn't important," he said. "We've agreed not to go through with it."

Why did the room, which earlier had seemed a comfortable temperature, despite the cold outdoors, seem blisteringly hot?

He resisted the urge to run a finger beneath his cravat.

"Hmmm." Benedick got up to stoke the fire and Cam had a tiny fantasy of leaping to his feet and throwing all the windows open. But he remained where he was.

"I thought the two of you were better suited than we'd realized," Ben said once he'd stood upright again. "But you know best, of course. I don't know where you'll find another woman who would be content with your collection of dead things and stones."

That surprised a laugh out of Cam. "But I know very well where I can find a wife who will not put up a fuss about anything. Much less my fossil collection. Gemma would no doubt object to everything but the fossils."

"Oh, and where is this magical place where uncomplaining wives are so readily available?" Ben asked, sitting on the edge of his desk. "For I must save up the name and tell everyone at Brooks' when next I'm in town."

"Come now, Ben," Cam said to his brother with a roll of his eyes. "You know as well as I do that young ladies willing to marry into a ducal family are thick on the ground in London during the season. I could likely find a half dozen willing to wed me in the course of one trip to Almack's."

"You seem to assume that these ladies have no minds of their own," Ben said with a shake of his head. "I think you may be mistaken in that."

"And you seem to have become accustomed to having the sort of wife who doesn't know her place," Cam said. Even as he said the words he knew he was being rude.

But Ben had never been quick to anger. "If I were a different sort of man," he said dryly, "I'd call you out for that. Fortunately for you, I only inflict physical harm on one person per day. And it's too damned cold out to duel."

It was his brother's sangfroid that made Cam feel the worst. He deserved a thrashing.

"That was badly done of me," he admitted, dropping the pose of calm and leaning forward to set his brandy glass down. "I don't know what I want, Ben, and that's the honest truth."

"I know you're uneasy in your mind," his brother replied. He'd also never been the sort to say 'I told you so.' "But perhaps this time you spend together searching for Gemma's missing fossil will give you the answers you seek."

"It's proximity that I'm afraid of," Cam said, thrusting a hand through his hair. "I fear the more time we're together, the more opportunities I'll have to compromise her beyond the point where either of us can call off the match."

Perhaps not the best thing to tell the brother who was also a sort of guardian for the lady in question. But Cam had no one else to confide in. And as Ben knew Gemma better than he did, maybe he'd have some notion of what to do.

"What does your heart say?" Benedick asked.

Cam laughed bitterly. "I don't know that I have a heart. I've spent most of my adult life pleasing only myself and seeking to fulfill only my ambitions in the quest for the next discovery. I'd always thought finding a wife would be another extension of that."

"What do you feel when you're with her?"

Cam sighed. "Did you hear what I said? I don't feel anything."

"You must feel something or you'd not be so miserable."

He hated it when Ben was right.

"I feel something," Cam amended grudgingly. "Lust, affection, protectiveness perhaps." He thought back to that moment in the curricle when she'd slept, curled up next to him like an exhausted kitten. He'd wanted to carry her up to her bedchamber at Beauchamp House and tuck her in. Then climb in and sleep next to her.

On top of the counterpane.

He was clearly losing his mind.

"And you don't think you would feel any of those things for a wife?" Ben asked, unaware of the thoughts racing through his brother's mind.

"I don't want that sort of marriage, Ben," he said, his frustration at the situation and his happily married brother overtaking him. "I'm not cut out for that sort of thing. The rest of you can be blissful with your willful wives. But I don't want the sort of thing our parents have. It's nothing but a sham."

He hadn't meant to say that.

That day he'd seen his father leaving the house of a local widow had shattered his understanding of the Duke and Duchess of Pemberton's marriage. Of what a happy marriage looked like. They might seem happy on the surface, but the rot that lay beneath had spoiled all such facades for Cam. Ben might think his union with Sophia was destined to remain blissful, but Cam knew that it was an illusion at best.

Far from protesting Cam's confession, however, Benedick instead said, "You aren't seriously telling me you won't allow yourself to be happy because Papa had a mistress when we were young? Are you?"

Cam looked up at his brother and saw that he was indeed serious.

"You knew?"

Chapter 14

Gemma luxuriated in her deliciously hot bath for far longer than was sensible, and her fingers and toes were wrinkled by the time she climbed out and was bundled into a thick towel.

She was wearing a flannel nightdress and seated at the dressing table brushing out her hair, having sent Tillie away with instructions to bring her a tray in her room for dinner, when Serena knocked on the door.

"Is something amiss?" Gemma asked, turning away from the glass to better see her.

"I was about to ask you the same thing," Serena said with a tilt of her head. "I don't think you've asked for a tray in your room in all the time you've lived here."

Gemma let out the breath she'd been holding. She'd been afraid someone had sent word of what she and Cam had got up to at Pearson Close that afternoon.

"If you must know," she admitted, "I'm exhausted. What with finding Sir Everard's body, then questioning the others at the house party, and of course the cold on top of it all, I simply want to climb into my bed and sleep for days."

"It's funny you should say you were questioning people at Pearson Close," Serena said as she sat down on the bench at the foot of Gemma's canopied bed, "because I shouldn't think that would be a particularly muddy activity."

Gemma bit back a curse. Of course Tillie would tell Serena about the state of Gemma's gown. Though in her defense, it also could have been George.

Thinking to evade more questions, Gemma decided to confess to part of what had happened. "We liberated some of Sir Everard's papers from his bedchamber and we . . . may have dropped them out the window to avoid being caught taking them out the front door." This last she said in a rush, as if saying it faster would make it sound less scandalous.

Of course that wasn't possible with Serena, who was above all things proper, and would never expose her legs to a gentleman in the course of theft.

"Oh Gemma." The disappointment and exasperation in her chaperone's voice was enough to make Gemma want to scream.

"We needed the papers, Serena," she said with more vehemence than she'd intended. In a more moderate tone, she said, "I need them to find out where my fossil is. And to find out who killed Sir Everard."

"I was hoping you would listen to Mr. Northman's warnings to stay out of the investigation into Sir Everard's murder," Serena said with a sigh. "I do not know why my aunt was so intent upon giving you all quests that led you into danger. It was most inconsiderate of her."

"But she didn't arrange to have Sir Everard murdered," Gemma protested. "Indeed, I'm the only one of the four who hasn't been left some sort of puzzle to solve by Lady Celeste." This was something she'd only admitted to Cam before now. Somehow telling him made it easier to reveal her conclusions to Serena now.

"Of course she didn't," Serena said, her neatly coiffed reddish blond hair glowing like a penny in the candlelight.

Really, it was no wonder Cam thought of her as the perfect wife. She truly was.

"I fear, however, that the other ladies' adventures have made you take Sir Everard's death as some sort of puzzle for you to solve. Even though it's obvious my aunt died before she could concoct some kind of scheme for you."

It was the same conclusion Gemma had come to regarding herself and Lady Celeste. But it smarted to hear Serena say it.

"I don't think I'm trying to make something out of Sir Everard's death." She might agree that Lady Celeste hadn't left her something besides the house, but she was certainly not making more of Sir Everard's death than it deserved. "Whoever killed him stole my fossil. I cannot simply sit by and allow that thief to get away with my discovery."

Serena rubbed her temples. "Gemma, dear Gemma," she sighed. "Please, just let Mr. Northman do his job. He is the local magistrate. He is tasked with finding Sir Everard's killer. Not you."

"Why are you so against me searching for my fossil?" Gemma asked. It was unlike Serena to be so disagreeable. She'd not objected to Ivy and Daphne getting into dangerous situations. Nor Sophia, if it came to that.

Then, something dreadful crossed her mind.

"You're trying to keep me away from Cam," she said with burgeoning horror. "Are you . . . jealous?"

Of course. She was an idiot not to see it sooner. Serena had been far more upset that morning on finding them in the drawing room than Gemma had ever seen her in her capacity as a chaperone.

"What?" Serena looked gratifyingly shocked at the idea.

"No, you may rest easy on that point. I have no designs on Lord Cameron or any gentleman, for that matter. I do not intend to marry ever again."

That response was far more of a relief than Gemma was comfortable with, but she set that aside to pore over later.

"Then what is it?" she asked, trying and failing to come up with an alternative explanation. "Why are you trying to hold me back?"

"Have you looked at your neck in the glass?" Serena asked pointedly.

Alarmed, Gemma reached up to touch her neck. "No, why?"

"Perhaps you should, then we'll talk," her chaperone said with a frown.

Turning back around to examine herself in the glass, Gemma was all set to tell Serena she must be mad, when she saw it. A purple mark just below her left ear.

Unbidden, the memory of Cam's mouth on that precise spot while they'd "pretended" in Sir Everard's dressing room.

She turned back around and knew her cheeks were scarlet. "So?" She was trying for nonchalance, but knew her blushing ruined it.

Sighing, Serena stepped forward and knelt before her. "My dear girl, you are playing a dangerous game, and I fear that you're going to find yourself in a difficult situation when the time comes for you to end this betrothal."

"I'm not a child," Gemma protested. She did feel a bit out of her depth with Cam, but since they had agreed their—whatever it was they had together—would end soon, she wasn't overly worried about it. "I know what I'm about."

"Gemma," the widow said with an intensity that made Gemma uncomfortable, "I know what it can be like to be married in haste to man with a temper."

She blinked. Was that what so bothered her?

"I know Cam can be passionate about things," she said with a frown, "but he's not really as angry as he seems."

"What about the day you met?" Serena asked, her blue eyes dark with concern. "He was shouting."

"So was I," Gemma said patiently. "In fact, I was shouting the loudest. Because he was being a dismissive lout."

"Precisely," Serena said. "Dismissive. He had to be pressed into asking for your hand. And then he did so only after he said something that made you rush away in tears."

It seemed like a million years since that morning when she'd run away to the workroom to scrub the floors. But suddenly she realized how that scene would look to someone from the outside. Someone who had endured the heartache of being married to a man with little kindness and a great deal of cruelty.

She hugged her chaperone, who had become like another sister over the course of the year. "I can assure you that what happened this morning was as much about me listening in on a conversation that wasn't meant for me as it was about Cam." She didn't tell her that it had been about her. That was a confession for another time—perhaps never.

"But he has such a temper, Gemma," said Serena as she pulled away. "I don't want you to find yourself in the same kind of situation I was in. I won't let you. I won't see you forced into a marriage, even if your sister and the vicar try to make you do it."

The notion of Sophia and Ben forcing her to do anything was laughable, but Gemma didn't let out the giggle that hovered at the back of her throat.

"I know you mean well, Serena," she said with a smile, "but please trust me when I say that no one will force me to do anything I don't wish to do. And despite what you might think about Cam and me, we are no more likely to marry now than we were this morning when you discovered us kissing."

"You didn't get mud all over your gown simply by retrieving papers, Gemma."

Thinking of the trek through the back garden of Pearson Close, Gemma contradicted her. "I actually did. And you must know that one can get a mark on one's neck just as easily in a warm drawing room as rolling about in the mud."

At that Serena deflated a little. "I suppose that's right."

Taking pity on her, Gemma patted her on the shoulder. "I promise you that if worst comes to worst and I'm forced to marry Lord Cameron . . ." Even as she said it, she felt disloyal in some way. As if Cam would care that she'd described matrimony with him thus. He very likely thought of it in the same way. "If I'm forced to marry Lord Cameron," she continued, "I will not be in the same situation you found yourself in. I know you think he's a hotheaded rogue, but he's not nearly as much of a bear as he seems."

But the furrow between Serena's brows didn't disappear as Gemma had hoped.

"I'll trust you in this," she said with a worried nod. "But please know that you only need to say the word and I will see to it that you're taken away from him for as long as needed to keep you safe."

Knowing that the words were heartfelt, Gemma thanked her sincerely. "You've been a good friend to all of us," she told her and was surprised to feel the sting of tears in her eyes.

"I've enjoyed this year with you girls far more than I could have imagined," Serena said with a smile. "I'm so proud of all of you. Your bravery and boldness have given me hope that one day I will be able to carve out a place for Jem and me."

"I think you already have," Gemma said, somewhat puzzled by the other lady's words. To her mind, Serena was far more settled than she was.

"Not yet," the other lady said, rising from the floor. "But soon. Very soon, I think."

Benedick leaned back in his chair. "I suppose it makes some sort of sense. You always did put Papa on a pedestal. At least more than the rest of us did. Even Rhys, and he practically worshipped him when were children." He referred to their elder brother, the heir to the Pemberton dukedom.

"I thought I was the only one," Cam shook his head in amazement. "All this time and we never talked about it. Not once."

"We knew it would hurt you," Benedick said. "For all your bluster, you were always the one who fell hardest when you lost one of your heroes."

Cam considered it. He supposed he had been easy to disappoint in those days. Not like now, when he'd built up a protective armor around himself. "You said 'we.' Who else knew?"

"It was Freddie and Archer who first figured it out," Benedick said. "They were in the village to buy Christmas presents one year and saw Papa leaving Mrs. Gill's little cottage. It wasn't hard to put two and two together. They told me, of course." Ben had been the one the other boys had confided in, even in those days. "And Rhys overheard us. You were off gathering stones, if I recall correctly. And we all agreed we wouldn't spoil the holidays for you."

"This was the year Mama was ill. wasn't it?"

Part of what had so pained Cam about his father's betrayal was that his mother had spent much of the year suffering from some mysterious ailment that he'd never really understood.

"You mean the year she miscarried," Benedick said. "They were always very careful not to tell us what was actually wrong. But I'd seen her increasing enough times at that point to know what it looked like."

Cam took in this news. "Miscarriage. Of course."

"It was one of those unspoken things that men, especially sons, didn't discuss," Benedick said. "Certainly Papa didn't tell us about it. He made some vague noises about lady problems. And then he never mentioned it again."

"Knowing this makes Papa's actions all that much worse," Cam said darkly. "That he was straying while she was ill."

He knew that it was common among members of the ton, both husbands and wives, to take lovers. But his parents' devotion to one another had been something he saw as a mark of their goodness. He'd been sixteen that year and his time at school had by that time exposed him to the unhappy home lives of his peers. Learning that his own parents were just as unfaithful as the rest of them had torn away his last veil of innocence. About his own family and the world in general.

"You're still thinking about it as your sixteen-year-old self," Benedick said gently. "Perhaps you should consider something else."

"I don't follow." Cam pinched the bridge of his nose. Maybe he should have saved this discussion for another day. This one had already been filled with more than enough excitement.

"Mama was ill from a miscarriage," Benedick said patiently. "Papa wanted to save her from illness."

The last stone in the wall fell into place. "Oh."

"One doesn't really wish to consider the fact that one's parents have ever . . ."

To Cam's relief his brother didn't name the activity that he never ever wished to have associated with his parents.

But the explanation made sense. One of the things that had so crushed him about his father's infidelity was the fact that he had—hypocritically, Cam thought—seemed as devoted a husband as ever.

"There are not very many alternatives when a lady's health can be endangered by another babe," his brother said. "There are ways to prevent it, of course, but I doubt either one of them knew much about—"

The idea of his parents discussing French letters or vinegar-soaked sponges was too much for Cam to take.

"No need to go into detail," he said raising a hand against Benedick's words. "I understand your meaning."

"So, you also understand that the situation was far more complicated than any of us could have guessed at the time." It wasn't a question.

Cam nodded. "I suppose so."

"Marriage is complicated," Benedick said with the air of a man who had learned so the hard way. "There are negotiations and intimacies that a few hours of pleasure with a mistress can't prepare you for."

"So you would take a mistress if for some reason Sophia was unable to endure your attentions?"

"We aren't speaking of Sophia and me," his brother said with a frown. "But we are speaking of Mama and Papa. And they did what they thought best in their own marriage. It's not for us to judge what decisions they made. Especially given that they took pains to ensure that we didn't know anything was amiss."

If their father had been seen by three of his sons leaving his mistress's house the pains hadn't been all that great, Cam thought. But he took his brother's point.

"I suppose I was too quick to judge," he admitted. He tried to imagine himself in his father's position—and of course it was Gemma he thought of as his wife. Would he be able to go to another woman when he was married to another? If it meant keeping Gemma alive, he knew he would do whatever it took. Though a part of him wondered why his father simply hadn't been abstinent altogether.

"I don't mean to say that Papa was a saint," Benedick said. "But nor was he a monster."

Suddenly Cam was exhausted.

"I hope you don't mind if I stay here tonight," he said. He hadn't yet bothered to ask, and he wanted nothing more than to sleep now.

"I would have insisted if you didn't ask," Benedick said with a smile. "You're always welcome in my home, brother. Even when you're behaving like a fool."

Rising to his feet, Cam stretched his shoulders and remembered the weight of Gemma on them. If Ben only knew what foolish things he'd got up to today.

But he only said, "I fear that's the only way I behave these days."

Rising from his own chair, Benedick clapped him on the shoulder. "Welcome to the club, old man."

Thus it was, that for the second time in the space of as many days, Cam found himself—though the surroundings were different—unable to sleep thanks to one Miss Gemma Hastings.

And not, to his great disappointment, for reasons having to do with the kind of pleasurable activity to which he would rather attribute his insomnia.

Benedick's revelations about the actual reason for the rift he'd seen in his parents' marriage had made him reevaluate everything he thought he knew about the nature of marriage itself and his own ability to embark upon the sort of relationship he saw between his brothers and their wives.

It was undeniable now that the connection he felt for Gemma, however unexpected, was more than simple lust—though there was an element of that, as well. But he felt an impulse where she was concerned, one he'd never had with any woman before, to protect her. Not just from the blackguard who'd threatened her. But from any number of things—small and large.

He'd found himself more worried than was reasonable at how chilled she'd become during their clandestine document-gathering outside Pearson Close. It had taken every bit of self-control he had to stop from taking George aside to ensure that her bath was hot enough and was sent up to her sooner rather than later. Not out of a need to control her, but simply because he wanted to ensure that she didn't take ill.

Cam could count on the fingers of one hand when he'd felt more than a superficial concern for the health of anyone outside his immediate family.

Was that love? He regretted that he'd not thought to ask Benedick when they'd spoken earlier. But he hadn't failed to notice that his brother seemed to pay attention to his wife's comfort—from ensuring he brought her fresh flowers on occasion, to building up the fire when she entered a room because he knew she was cold-natured. Cam hadn't been around Gemma enough to learn her preferences for such things. But he had little trouble believing that a bit more time in her company would have him performing similar tasks.

Ben didn't know it, but his revelation that their father had strayed not because he didn't love their mother, but because he did, had changed everything.

There was no way to know the exact circumstances, but he had little trouble at all imagining the duke taking a mistress at the duchess's behest. Indeed, it made far more sense than the idea that Pemberton, who was besotted with his wife, would have ever done such a thing on his own.

It had been immature on his part to believe it was his father's infidelity that had seemed to so distress his mother, but Cam realized now that his understanding of the world—

and everyone's, he supposed—was comprised of experiences and feelings beginning in childhood. It had taken hearing about the scene he'd witnessed in a different context to show him the effect his incorrect assumption had had on his views of marriage.

What, he wondered, would Gemma think of his change of attitude? She still believed their betrothal was a temporary thing that could easily be set aside once enough time had passed. Then, there was her belief that she needed to remain unwed in order to prove to the world, and perhaps to herself, that she took geology and fossil-collecting seriously.

That might prove to be a more difficult task than upending his misunderstandings about marriage, he thought grimly, lifting his forearm to cover his eyes.

He took a moment to question whether he was up to the task, Then realized with a laugh, that he had no choice. Gemma might not think their betrothal was real, but he was quickly coming to recognize that there was no other woman he wanted to wed.

And that, he reflected, was the real consequence of what he'd learned from Benedick. Not that he could contemplate marriage.

But that he could contemplate—and desire—marriage to her.

He'd simply have to prove to her that marriage between them wouldn't mean she'd have to give up her passion for fossils.

He wondered suddenly how the Duke of Maitland managed it. The Duchess was also one of the heiresses, and from everything Cam had heard was a brilliant mathematician and had not, as far as he knew, abandoned her field of study. Perhaps he should have a word with the duke and see if he had any suggestions.

If nothing else, he could speak to someone other than his brother—who could be a bit insufferably smug at times about the happiness of his marriage.

The matter settled, at least for now, he forced himself to empty his mind and sleep.

Chapter 15

Despite yesterday's excitement, Gemma awoke the next morning with a renewed desire to find her stolen fossil. She was also determined, no matter what happened, not to let herself get caught up in whatever it was that lay between her and Cam. She would keep her hands to herself, and if he tried to touch her, she would politely, but firmly, tell him she wanted no part of his seduction. At least until she found her fossil.

There would be time enough for carnality later. Thus it was that when Lord Cameron entered the library some two hours after she had risen and dressed and breakfasted, she greeted his bow with a polite but distant nod. That he too seemed to be a bit reticent should have pleased her, but instead made her chest tight.

It was all well and good to be the one doing the resisting, but not quite as pleasant to be resisted.

Still, she would try to be grateful for the lack of temptation. Though honestly, he had only to be himself to tempt her. She knew all too well now how soft his windswept dark curls were beneath her fingers, and just how enticing the scent of sandalwood and male skin was when he held her close.

"I see you have already started without me," Cam said, apparently oblivious to her Cam-inspired fever dream.

He gestured to the pages strewn across the wide oak library table. "Have you had any luck?"

Resuming her seat, and indicating that he should take one as well, she waited before responding. When he chose the chair next to hers rather than the one across the table, she sighed inwardly but outwardly ignored it.

"I've only been trying to put the different studies in order," she said, indicating the seven piles she'd formed thus far. "So far sorted out these individual essays, but without any sort of numbering it's been slow going."

He was once again dressed in country breeches and boots and looked far too well rested for someone who had endured the same day as she had yesterday. It had taken three cups of tea to truly awaken her and even that hadn't completely erased the circles beneath her eyes.

"I suppose we have whoever ransacked Sir Everard's rooms to thank for that," Cam said with a frown. "But you've made good progress."

Gemma shrugged at the compliment. It was hardly higher maths.

"I don't quite understand why he would travel with all of these scientific papers in his bag," she said aloud, trying to ignore the warmth of him sitting beside her. "Is that customary? And some of the papers are duplicates in differing hands."

"I don't know that it's all that strange," Cam said, lifting one stack to flip through the pages. "If he were planning to show them to one of the other men at the house party, for instance, it would make sense."

"But why the different hands?" she asked. "This essay for instance. It's word for word the same study. And both scripts are perfectly legible so it isn't as if he was recopying poor penmanship to be read more easily."

Cam frowned. "Let me see that." Wordlessly she handed the duplicate essays to him.

Silently, he scanned first one set of pages, then the other.

"There's something about this turn of phrase here," he said, pointing to a passage about the soil around a quarry in Northumbria.

"What about it?" she asked.

"I'm not sure," he said, thoughtful. "It seems familiar somehow."

"Maybe you've read it in a different one of Sir Everard's papers," she said. Then, with a speaking look, added, "When you published one of them in your scientific journal."

"Ha-ha," he said with a fake smile. Then, turning serious, he said, "For your information, I've never published him. But the quality of this is far better than the pieces he submitted and were rejected."

"Writers do improve," she said wryly. "Maybe he listened to your critique, or had someone else assist him."

At that he laughed in earnest. "Can you honestly imagine Sir Everard listening to anyone's suggestions for improvement?"

Gemma thought about the man she'd met a few days earlier. "No. Not remotely."

"I wish I could recall where I'd seen that phrasing," he said again. "I can't help but feel it will solve part of this particular puzzle."

"Let's put it aside for the moment," she said, taking the pages from him and placing them back where they'd been plucked from.

He nodded, though it was obvious that he was still troubled by his inability to recall where he'd seen the words.

By agreement, they split the rest of the disordered pages and began sorting them into their own individual stacks.

They worked in silence for nearly half an hour before there was a knock on the door.

Looking up, Gemma saw Serena in the doorway.

Was that relief in her eyes at finding them working rather than in one another's arms? Thinking back to their discussion the night before, Gemma realized it was. She'd confided her plans to keep from becoming further entangled with Cam this morning at breakfast, but clearly she hadn't been all that convincing.

Before she could say anything, however, Serena ushered in Lord Paley.

Gemma exchanged a look of alarm with Cam. They were elbow deep in stolen papers and it was quite possible Paley was in a position to recognize Sir Everard's writing.

She made as if to gather them up into one stack, but Cam shook his head slightly. Attempting to tamp down her nerves, she dropped her hands back down onto the table and tried to look innocent.

"Look who's come to call, Gemma," Serena said, entirely unaware of the distress signals her charge was sending with her eyes. "Wasn't it kind of Lord Paley to call to ascertain your well-being after yesterday's contretemps?"

In truth, yesterday had been such a disaster that Gemma had trouble guessing which of her embarrassments Serena could be referring to..

Then, she recalled that Lord Paley would only have known about the death of Sir Everard and her discovery of his body, and was somewhat relieved.

"Indeed," she said with what she hoped was a welcoming smile despite her nerves over the papers, "very kind."

Stepping forward, Lord Paley offered her a posy of violets. "I see I'm not your first visitor, however, Miss Hastings." His gaze flickered over to Cam, and she was surprised to read enmity there. Were not the two men friendly, then? It could hardly be jealousy. She barely knew the man.

Taking the flowers from him, she buried her nose in them to stall for time. "These are lovely. Thank you so much."

He must have found a shop that bought from a hothouse, Gemma thought. Which meant the man—or his valet more likely—had gone to a deal of trouble to secure these.

"Paley," said Cam, coming to stand beside her. He didn't touch her, or in any overt way indicate that they were anything more than what they seemed. Sister and brother-in-law. Or friends.

And yet, she felt the ownership he projected around her as clearly as if he'd marked a circle around her like a wolf in the wild.

Far from backing down, however, Lord Paley simply bowed. "Lord Cameron. I see that your familial concern has brought you here this morning as well. How admirable of you to look in on Miss Hastings."

"Not so familial as all that," Cam returned with a smile that showed far too many teeth.

Serena looked alarmed, and Gemma felt her worry about the newcomer finding the stolen papers was eclipsed by annoyance at both men.

"Perhaps we should call for some tea," Serena said with forced brightness, moving to the bellpull.

Resigned, Gemma raised her arm to indicate the quartet of chairs before the fire. "Why don't we have a seat.?"

She felt Cam following close behind her. So close she had to resist the urge to stop short just to make him bump into her.

Men were such absurd creatures, she thought in disgust.

Though on the bright side, she would have little difficulty resisting Cam in his present mood, which must be counted as a positive.

"I heard about what happened with Sir Everard yesterday, Miss Hastings," said Lord Paley, taking Gemma's hand as they came to a stop before the fire. "What a horrific scene for you to come upon. I hope you are not too overset."

"A dreadful business," she agreed stiffly, taking her hand

back and indicating that he should be seated. "I hope we'll find out soon who is responsible for poor Sir Everard's murder."

She took one of the chairs, while Lord Paley sat opposite her. Cam meanwhile moved a third chair closer to Gemma's.

When she turned to look at him with a frown, he ignored her and leaned back, stretching his long legs out before him like a king getting comfortable on his throne.

"Indeed," said Lord Paley said, perching on the edge of his own chair so that he was only inches from Gemma. His expression was troubled and she could tell that he was genuinely upset. "I knew Sir Everard was frustrated by the way we insisted he leave the fossil to return to the next day, but I had no notion he'd come back in the dead of night. It was a risk, both because of the inclement weather and the mud, but also, as he learned to his detriment, because of thieves."

"None of us could have foreseen what happened," Gemma said firmly. "Only the man who murdered him knows why it happened."

"But Lord Cameron and I did ride back to Pearson Close with him," the viscount continued, his mouth twisted with dismay. "I wanted to assure you that he said nothing in my presence about retur—"

Cam cut him off. "Nor in mine, Paley," he said with a scowl. "Of course if he had I would have told Miss Hastings at once."

Clearly reading the tension between the two men, Serena intervened from where she stood near the fire. "Of course, neither of you knew of Sir Everard's plans," she said smoothly. "I assure you, Lord Paley, we know who our friends are. And you may rest easy that none of us suspects you had any knowledge of Sir Everard's scheme."

The thought had crossed Gemma's mind, but she was hardly going to contradict Serena now. Especially not with Cam and Lord Paley at daggers drawn.

"Well, that is a relief, Lady Serena," Paley said emphatically. "I couldn't bear it if either of you suspected me of being in cahoots with a man like Sir Everard."

The footman came to the door then and Serena stepped aside to speak to him about the tea.

"It's interesting you should come in person to reassure Miss Hastings," Cam said once the chaperone was gone. "I should think a note would have sufficed."

"And I find it intriguing that you spend so much time in this house given that your brother lives only a few miles down the road and you are ostensibly still a guest at Pearson Close." Lord Paley didn't look away from Cam's steady gaze. "You didn't come back to Pearson Close last evening, did you?"

"Are you my keeper, sir, that you pay such close attention to my comings and goings?" Cam asked, with a tilt of his head.

"No," Paley said through clenched teeth, "but I do pay attention when a gentleman is careless with a lady's reputation. Especially when they are newly betrothed and he leads her into indiscretion in someone else's home."

Gemma's eyes widened. "What do you mean?" she demanded. But she had a sinking suspicion she knew exactly what he meant.

When he turned to her, Lord Paley's gaze softened. "I do not wish to cause you alarm, Miss Hastings. On the contrary. But I, unfortunately, occupy the room next to Sir Everard's at Pearson Close and couldn't help but overhear some of what . . ."

Cam rose to his feet. "If you were a gentleman you would stop speaking right this moment."

"If you were a gentleman you would not expose your lady to such scandal," Lord Paley shot back, leaping to his feet, his fists clenched.

"You were goading me on purpose," Cam said bitterly. "You knew all along about our betrothal."

"I wanted to see if it was truth or a fiction you made up on the spot to excuse your bad behavior." Lord Paley's words were as sharp as cut glass.

"I'll show you bad behavior," Cam said, stepping forward with menace.

"No," Gemma hurrying to push between them. "Lord Paley, I appreciate the sentiment, however, I—"

"Stay out of this, Gemma," Cam said in a low voice without taking his eyes off Paley. "This is not your concern."

"Of course it's my concern, you nodcock," she said in a sharp tone. "Who do you imagine you're arguing about?"

If she'd expected Lord Paley to see more sense than Cam, however, she was very much mistaken.

"Miss Hastings, he's right," he said in an apologetic tone. "You have already suffered enough indignity and—"

"What is going on?" demanded Serena in a surprisingly authoritative tone.

As Gemma watched, her chaperone came rushing forward and, in a manner only the mother of a small boy could manage, ordered, "Gentlemen, I must insist that you both sit back down and stop this nonsense this instant."

When they didn't, Serena stepped over to where they stood nose to nose and tried to push in between them. When that didn't work, she turned to Gemma. "Go get George and William and tell them that we'll need them to bring the ash buckets."

Without waiting to ask why, Gemma began to hurry to the door.

She was almost there when she heard Cam. "Stop, Gemma. You won't need them."

Turning back, she saw that the two men had stepped back from one another and had relaxed their militant poses.

"I apologize, Lady Serena," said Paley, looking sheepish. "That was unforgivable of me. I should have discussed this matter with Lord Cameron somewhere else. Away from where we would disturb you two ladies."

Gemma put her hands on her hips. "So that you could fight over my honor without my involvement at all, you mean? I hardly think that's an improvement, my lord."

Lord Paley blinked at her vehement tone.

"Yes," she told him with a sour look. "Contrary to what men believe, ladies do not wish to be fought over like a bone between curs. And this lady most certainly does not wish it when the so-called scandal was of her own making."

"There's no need to—"

But before Cam could finish, she cut him off. "And you, sir. I don't know what makes you think that I am your personal responsibility, but you are not my blood relation and our connection is tenuous at best. Pray do not involve yourself in feuds with other men on my behalf. I am perfectly capable of taking care of myself, or if I wish it I will ask my sister's husband to intervene for me."

When he opened his mouth as if to respond, she held up a staying hand. Turning to Serena, she said, "I will go see what's become of the tea tray. While I am gone, I would ask that you see to it that these two cloth-heads reach some kind of peace. Otherwise I am perfectly happy for both of them to take themselves off."

With that, she stepped into the hallway and slid the pocket doors closed behind her.

Chapter 16

The only sound in the library after Gemma's departure was the popping of the fire.

Cam watched as Serena looked from him to Paley, then back again.

"Well, gentlemen," she said with a regal nod, "I'm going to see if Gemma needs my help."

And without bothering to give them any parting wisdom, she left the room, sliding the doors shut behind her.

When Cam looked up it was to find that Paley still stood with his feet braced apart, as if expecting to ward off a blow.

"Oh stand down, man." Cam strode to where the brandy was kept and poured two generous glasses. "It would cost more than my life is worth if I challenged you. I have little doubt Gemma would follow us onto the field and shoot both of us and leave without a backward glance. And we'd deserve it."

But Paley was still skeptical. "What's your claim on her? She doesn't seem particularly ready to claim you."

"It's complicated," Cam told the other man, handing him a glass. "I still have some persuading to do."

"An understatement, surely," Paley took one of the fireside chairs and didn't seem particularly interested in leaving, much to Cam's dismay. "And it doesn't seem as if Miss Hastings is one who does anything not of her own volition."

That was certainly correct, Cam thought. But aloud he said, "In time, I believe we'll come to an understanding."

"Then why not let me take a run at her?" the viscount asked blandly.

"She is not a fence to be jumped, Paley." He was offended on Gemma's behalf. "We are betrothed. Let that put an end to your meddling."

"I suppose that will have to do," Lord Paley said thoughtfully. "But if anything should happen . . ."

"It won't," Cam ground out. He took the seat opposite and the two men sat in tense silence for a moment, sipping their brandy and thinking.

"I couldn't help but notice when I came in that you were looking at papers," Paley said. "I don't suppose those are Sir Everard's?"

Since Paley had admitted to knowing they'd been in the baronet's rooms, it wasn't too great a logical leap.

"Yes," Cam said. He wasn't going to volunteer information unless absolutely necessary—especially since they had no idea who had killed Sir Everard and stolen the fossil.

When Cam didn't say anything else, Paley made a noise of frustration. "I'm not your enemy. I ask because Sir Everard stole something from me and I wish to know if you might have found it."

At the mention of theft, Cam went on alert, though he was careful not to show it. "We only took papers," he said casually. "No objects or fossils or the like."

"It's papers I'm looking for," Paley said with a scowl. "Sir Everard stole several papers from my home and I have reason to believe he brought them with him to Sussex in order to give them to Roderick Templeton."

Templeton was one of the men at Pearson's house party and published one of the newer, more influential scientific magazines.

"What makes you think Sir Everard brought them?" Cam asked. Though Paley's stolen papers could explain why the documents from Sir Everard's room were in two different hands. It was possible, of course, that Sir Everard had hired an amanuensis to copy them out. But there was usually some mark from the scribe on the pages they wrote, and he and Gemma hadn't yet found any.

"As soon as the pages went missing I sent correspondence to the editors of all the major journals inquiring whether they'd received any proposals on these particular topics," Paley explained. "Templeton sent word a month ago that he'd received an offer of one such paper from Sir Everard. We arranged for Templeton to tell Sir Everard to meet him at Pearson Close with the paper."

"That's quite the supposition," Cam said thoughtfully. "Why would you imagine someone had stolen them? Perhaps you merely misplaced them?"

"Because my home was burgled," Paley said with a scowl. "That's when I noticed the pages were missing. And only someone with an interest in geology and fossils would have found them at all interesting. The papers were only valuable insofar as they could be published."

"What were the titles?" Cam asked, curious despite himself.

"One was called 'Thoughts on a Pebble from the Sandstone of the Tilgate Forest in Sussex'," Paley said.

It was a mouthful. Which was precisely what Cam had thought when he'd seen it at the top of one of the pages currently in a tidy stack on the library table.

"Would you be willing to write out something to prove the piece is in your hand?" he asked without confirming they had the essay.

The other man put his brandy down on a side table and sat up. "You've found it." It wasn't a question.

"There is one such paper amongst the items we found," Cam admitted. "But if you have someone else copy out your pages then I'm afraid I won't be able to give it to you without some corroboration from Templeton."

Paley laughed. "Oh, I write them out myself. Because I didn't trust anyone else with the task." He shook his head in disgust. "I was focused on the wrong thief, obviously."

There was a pot of ink, pen and foolscap on one of the other library tables and Cam watched as Paley wrote out the full title of the article he claimed he'd composed.

When he was finished, he sanded the page and handed it to Cam.

"Well?" Paley asked as Cam looked at the title page they'd found among Sir Everard's papers and compared it to the new version.

"I'm no expert, but I'd say these were written by the same person."

His relief evident, Paley crossed to where Cam was standing at the wide table with Sir Everard's documents on it. "May I?"

Cam indicated that he was welcome to study them, and took a moment to think.

It was not all that much of a surprise, given Sir Everard's attempt to steal Gemma's fossil, that he would have also stolen Lord Paley's intellectual work to publish as his own. He'd often found that once a man began to practice deception, it became a way of life.

But one thing puzzled him. "Surely Sir Everard didn't break into your home himself? He didn't strike me as the sort of fellow who could move about a house in the middle of the night on cat-feet."

Looking up from his study of the documents, Paley said

with a scowl, "He hired a man to serve as my footman. I'd noticed some older pieces in my collection had disappeared a few months earlier. I thought I'd misplaced them until I caught the fellow at it. I made an inventory of my entire collection, and my papers, and discovered the Pebble write-up was missing."

"The footman told you who'd hired him?"

Paley shook his head. "He didn't know, but most of the major collectors in England are known to me, and it was hardly a leap to think it was one of them. Then I hit on the idea of writing to the editors."

"I'm the editor of a prominent natural science magazine," Cam challenged.

The other man shrugged. "To be honest, I didn't think you'd respond. You're well known for ignoring the magazine in favor of traveling to find fossils. I didn't want my suspicions in the hands of some underling who would gossip about it."

It was on the tip of Cam's tongue to argue that his personal secretary, who was in fact the one who did the most work on the magazine, would never gossip about such a thing. But then he realized how damning the other man's assessment was.

"I like to be there to find my own fossils," he said, hearing the defensiveness in his voice but unable to stop it.

"Which is admirable," Paley said with a raised brow. "But you must then accept that you will not be the best person to respond to letters like mine."

There was more he could say on the subject, but Cam chose instead to change it altogether.

"It's there, then?" He indicated the table of documents.

"It is," Paley said with a smile. "He was able to take some that I'd written years ago and decided not to publish, as well. The man was a fraud, pure and simple. I have little doubt that the rest of the publications credited to him are also someone else's."

"Why go to the trouble, though?" Cam asked. "If he wasn't interested in the work, why bother with it at all?"

"I don't know," Paley said. "It's hard to know what motivates others without knowing them quite well. And I certainly didn't claim friendship with the fellow. Though we did meet a few times over the years."

The doors of the library opened then and Serena and Gemma stepped inside followed by a housemaid carrying a large tea tray.

"Lovely," Gemma said with an approving nod as she looked them over—presumably to ensure that neither was injured. "It appears that you have worked out some sort of compromise."

Then as she realized that Paley had some of the documents in his hand, her eyes flew to Cam's.

"A compromise indeed," he said. "And some clarification on the extent of Sir Everard's crimes."

"You can tell us all about it over tea," Serena said in the voice she normally reserved for her son Jeremy.

Knowing to obey orders when he heard them, Cam moved to the seating area, Paley close behind him.

Though she'd left the two men together insisting they come to a compromise, Gemma had not, in fact, been at all sure one was possible. Especially once Serena reached her side in the kitchens.

"I hope they don't actually come to blows," the widow said with a troubled look.

"I'm sure they won't," Gemma assured her with a confidence she didn't feel. "If for no other reason than they both know I will be extremely put out if they do. And for the moment at least, they both are intent on pleasing me."

"Never say you are enjoying the fact that they're fighting over you." Serena only looked as if she were partly joking.

"No. Of course not." Gemma wasn't that far gone, at least. "But if their foolish rivalry keeps them from coming to fisticuffs then I am all for it."

"And what will you do when they expect that you'll choose one of them at some point?"

"Are you not the one who only last evening tried to convince me to break things off with Cam because of his temper?"

"That was before I realized he holds you in genuine affection," Serena said. "He was serious about fighting for you, Gemma. I think he really does l—"

Gemma put a finger over Serena's lips before she could finish. "Do not say it. I am already too close to abandoning all of my plans and deciding to take this betrothal seriously. I need no more encouragement. Especially not with the idea that he is thinking the same thing. One of us must be strong, And if Cam cannot be trusted to be the strong one, then it will have to be me."

"But if you lo—"

"Shhh." Gemma stamped her foot. "Do not say it. Please, Serena."

Her chaperone looked at her in amusement. "All right. I won't say it. But that isn't enough to make it untrue."

For the time being, Gemma thought firmly, it would have to be.

"Let's go tell cook to get the tea ready," she said, deciding a change of subject was necessary.

Some thirty minutes later, they were both seated in the library again, enjoying the sandwiches and cakes cook had included along with a steaming pot of fragrant tea.

And to Gemma's relief, the men had settled their differences.

"It's wrong to speak ill of the dead, Miss Hastings," said

Lord Paley apologetically, "but I fear you weren't the only one Sir Everard stole from."

Quickly, Lord Paley explained what he knew about Sir Everard's scheme to steal artifacts and papers from other collectors.

"At least, I'm sure he tried to," Paley assured them. "I spoke with a few of the others at Pearson Close last evening and they all reported having missed items from their own collections in the past year. No one had lost important papers, but they all intend to search their documents when Mr. Northman allows them to go home."

"It's extraordinary," Gemma said. "How can one person so utterly fool a group of collectors and scholars into trusting him? And not only that, but holding him up as some sort of model of wisdom? It would be laughable if it weren't so utterly deplorable."

"I suppose we're all too trusting," Cam said, taking a bite of cake. When he was finished, he continued. "We take men at their word and don't question them."

"Especially men," Gemma said scowling. It was really too frustrating to see how easily Sir Everard had fooled the major players in the world of fossil collecting. She had little doubt if Sir Everard had been Lady Evelina, there would have been a very different outcome.

"You aren't wrong," Cam said with a note of apology. "I daresay he'd not got as far as he did without the inherent trust of other men."

Gemma was taken aback. "Do you really believe that now?"

"I do," said Cam. "And you've opened my eyes to the uphill climb that ladies must face in the scholarly world."

She looked at him through narrowed eyes. Was he serious? she wondered. Or was this another way to score points over Lord Paley? He looked sincere enough, however, and she felt her heart melt a little.

"Thank you," she said, trying and failing to keep the admiration from her voice.

Lord Paley clearing his throat alerted her to the fact that she and Cam had been staring moonily at one another for several long seconds.

Dash it.

"Well, I mean to say," she said hastily, "that is most interesting, Lord Cameron."

"I see now I was mistaken earlier," Lord Paley said wryly.

Gemma frowned, not knowing what he meant. But before she could speak up, he was speaking.

"There is something else I thought you should know," he said. "In fact, it was my primary reason for coming here today, but we got a bit distracted."

Distracted. What everyone called almost getting into a duel these days, Gemma thought with an inward sigh.

"The evening before Sir Everard was killed," the viscount said, "after we'd returned from our tour of the collection here at Beauchamp House, and his false discovery of your fossil on the shore, Miss Hastings, he confided to a few of us that he was quite convinced that the skull was part of the Beauchamp Lizard."

He turned to Cam. "I believe you'd already gone to bed, Lord Cameron."

"What is the Beauchamp Lizard?" Gemma said, not waiting for Cam to comment.

To her surprise, Lord Paley looked at Cam.

Cam, whose jaw was set and whose cheekbones were tinged with red.

"What is the Beauchamp Lizard?" she repeated, beginning to feel a bubble of anger welling in her chest.

Lord Paley looked apologetic. "I thought Lord Cameron would have told you by now or I wouldn't have mentioned it, Miss H—"

"Someone had better tell me what the Beauchamp Lizard is," said Gemma angrily, "or I won't be answerable for my actions."

"It's not as dire as you imagine, Gemma," Cam said hastily. "I doubt the thing ever even existed."

She didn't miss the furious glance he gave Paley before he went on. "According to Sir Everard, Lady Celeste found a large lizard fossil on the shore just below Beauchamp House some twenty or so years ago. And it came to be known as the Beauchamp Lizard."

"And when, pray, did you learn about this?" she asked him coldly. "And when did you intend to tell me about it?"

She tried to tamp down the sense of hurt she felt at being kept in the dark about something that, by rights as the heiress who shared Lady Celeste's love of fossils, she should have known from her first day at Beauchamp House. She felt betrayed both by her benefactress and by Cam.

"To be honest, I haven't really given it much thought since Sir Everard turned up dead," Cam said, thrusting a hand through his hair.

She unbent a little at that. It *had* been an eventful couple of days.

Turning back to Lord Paley, she asked, "Where is it? And why would Sir Everard think that the skull I found had anything to do with the Beauchamp Lizard?"

"As to the first, I have no idea. And as for the latter, I asked him that very same thing, Miss Hastings, I assure you." Lord Paley was warming to his topic. "But he assured me that it bore all the hallmarks of the Lizard, which he claimed to have seen years ago when he and his father had come to Sussex to visit Lady Celeste."

"If he'd been to the house before," Cam asked with a frown, "why wouldn't he mention it when he came to visit this time?"

"I can only imagine because he didn't wish anyone to know he had some prior knowledge of the Lizard," Paley said. "And of course, it would have removed his reason for touring the collection if he'd been here before."

"So that's what he was looking for," Gemma said with a start. "I got the feeling the entire time we were examining the collections that he was searching for something in particular amongst the shelves. And he wanted to go through the boxes in the attics."

She turned to Lord Paley with wide eyes. "As did you, my lord."

Now it was Paley's turn to redden. "Sir Everard might have mentioned the Beauchamp Lizard on the drive here, and I became caught up in the fever to see it. Especially if it was as impressive as Sir Everard claimed it was."

Gemma shook her head. It would appear that she was surrounded by mendacious men.

Getting back to the matter at hand, she asked, "What made him think that my fossil was the Lizard?"

"He claimed that there had been several attempts at theft not long after she found it," Paley said. "And that his father suggested she bury it to keep it safe."

"But surely one whose sense of right and wrong was as flexible as Sir Everard's would have come here to retrieve it long ago." Cam said, his expression puzzled.

"He said without knowing where or if Lady Celeste had buried it, he hadn't the time or inclination to go digging for it. Of course, that was before he had the good fortune to come upon it after you'd done much of the hard work, Miss Hastings," Lord Paley said. "I don't know whether to believe the story or not, but the fact that he was murdered in the process of taking the fossil from where you found it tells me that someone among the guests at Pearson Hall he told did believe it was the Beauchamp Lizard. And likely killed him for it."

It was too fantastical to be believed, but Gemma had learned over the past year that when it came to Lady Celeste, the most outlandish turned out to be the most accurate. And she would be just the sort of person to hide a thing in plain sight.

"You will know far more about Lady Celeste's inclinations and actions than I will," Lord Paley continued, "but I do know that it was wrong for Sir Everard to steal your discovery whether it was the Beauchamp Lizard or not. And I knew I had to warn you that your benefactress's most celebrated fossil might very well be the same skull you'd unearthed."

"Now," he continued, "I must be off. I do apologize for our earlier contretemps, Lady Serena," he said with a bow to the chaperone. "I misunderstood the relationship between Miss Hastings and Lord Cameron."

Before Gemma could protest this last, he'd bid them both goodbye and had accepted Serena's offer to show him out.

When they were gone, Gemma was unsure which of her multiple annoyances with Cam to confront him with first.

"A penny for them," Cam said after a few moments of gathering her thoughts.

Deciding to start with the most troublesome, she said, "you should have told me about the Beauchamp Lizard. I had a right to know. Especially since Lady Celeste didn't see fit to tell me about it."

He sighed. "I know. I am sorry. I honestly didn't consider that the fossil Sir Everard told us about on the ride here that day could be one and the same as the fossil you'd found on the shore. I did know he was trying to determine if it was in the house during the tour. But when he didn't find it there, I thought no more of it."

She wanted to believe him. Really she did. But a fossil find as big as this particular one was said to be would go a long way toward elevating its finder's reputation in the world of collecting. And even someone as celebrated as Cam couldn't simply rest on his laurels.

Rather than discuss something she had no way of knowing for certain at the moment, she turned to the next most troublesome issue Lord Paley had raised.

"I don't know what he meant about our relationship," she said with a shake of her head. "Clearly, Lord Paley has a very active imagination. And even if—"

She broke off with a squeal as Cam leapt up from his chair, gathered her in his arms, and turned to sit in her chair. All in the course of a few quick seconds.

"What are you doing?" she demanded, though once he'd settled again she made no move to escape him. "I'm quite cross with you. I have no intention of allowing you to kiss me again."

"I'm taking advantage of your chaperone's absence," he said, nuzzling her neck. "It's what fiancés do. It's science, I'm sure of it."

She closed her eyes against the feel of his hot mouth against the sensitive skin. "It's not science," she said in a credibly schoolmarmish tone, considering the shivers coursing through her. "And I haven't forgiven you yet."

"Haven't you?" he asked, pulling back a little and looking into her eyes. "Because I am sorry, Gemma. Very, very sorry."

At the sincerity in his eyes, she felt her stomach flip.

"Are you?" she asked in a voice barely above a whisper. And suddenly she knew she was asking for more than just an apology.

"I am," he said, kissing her softly. "Please forgive me, Gemma."

Closing her eyes, she let him tell her without words that he regretted his actions.

When they were both breathless, she said with mock

severity, "If this is your way of proving to me that our relationship is . . ."

She trailed off when she felt his hand close over her breast.

"Yes?" he asked, amusement in his voice. "If our relationship is. . . . what?"

"Whatever," she said on a moan as he stroked his thumb over her. "This isn't fair," she muttered as she found his mouth.

"I don't play fair," Cam said as he opened his lips to her. "I play to win."

Chapter 17

"To win?" Gemma shifted so that she was astride his lap. Then she could kiss him more fully, stroking her tongue into his mouth in the way she'd learned he liked best. Pulling away a little, she asked, "And what if instead of competition, we engage in a meeting of equals?"

While she waited for her words to filter through the lust, she stroked her hands over his chest, which she had to admit she was very curious to see without all of his coats in the way.

"What are you proposing?" he asked, his blue eyes suddenly suspicious.

It was a notion she'd come up with last night, thinking about how much she'd wanted to continue what they'd started in Pearson Close. She knew it wasn't precisely the most proper way to go about things, but then propriety wasn't something she'd ever been all that invested in. She'd ended up betrothed to Cam because of a few stolen kisses. All for propriety's sake.

When their temporary engagement was at an end, she'd realized, she would very likely never be this close to a man again. She had little doubt she would receive offers once it became widely known she was the sole heir to Lady Celeste's estate. But she'd made up her mind that she would not give up her inheritance to a man simply for the sake of being wed. Her plans to go through life alone, as her Aunt Dahlia had done, hadn't changed.

"After we go our separate ways," she said, leaning back on her heels so that she could look him in the eye, "I will have no other opportunities for these kinds of—"

One of his dark brows rose. "Interactions?" he supplied.

"Yes," she said with an approving nod. "I have decided that I'll model my life after those of my Aunt Dahlia and Lady Celeste. I'll live a solitary life of scholarship. Without the distraction of this sort of thing."

He made a skeptical sound. "While I admit this sort of thing can be very distracting," he admitted, "I do not think you can know what your aunt and Lady Celeste actually got up to. Their reputations were unblemished, but who's to say they didn't take lovers?"

This was a possibility Gemma hadn't considered. But it was true that one could never truly know how a person's private life was conducted. In truth, however, it was beside the point. "Whether they did or not," she said with what she hoped was dispassion, "I will endeavor to remain unentangled."

"And what has this to do with me?" he asked. To his credit, he was not looking at her as if she had maggots in her head. Which was another reason why she was certain he was the perfect man to assist her with her scheme.

"Once our betrothal is at an end," she explained, "I'll no longer have any opportunities like this. So I wish to take advantage of our proximity while I may. And I hope it will be agreeable to you as well. An experiment of sorts."

"So, we're back to this, are we? You wish to use me to experiment?" he asked, brow furrowed now as if he were trying to understand her proposition.

"Yes," she said with relief. It was one thing to hit upon a notion, but it was another thing entirely to be forced to explain it. "I will have you as my lover for the duration of our betrothal but at the end of it, we'll go our separate ways as we agreed upon before."

Now he was frowning. "Gemma, it is no small thing for a gentleman to set aside the morality he's been brought up to follow from boyhood. Not for me, at any rate."

She felt the sting of disappointment. She had known there was the possibility that trying to formalize the caresses and pleasure they'd thus far engaged in as the opportunity arose would ruin things. But she'd never been one to find comfort in serendipity. She liked a bit of order and agreement in her world.

Unable to speak, she began to turn so that she might stand. But soon found herself held firmly.

When she wouldn't look up at him—how could she?—he lifted her chin.

"I haven't said no," he said in a husky voice. "But I have some conditions."

Another thing she hadn't considered was counterarguments.

"And they are?" she said, trying to sound unconcerned.

"I want your agreement that if there is a child, you'll marry me without argument," he said, his expression deadly serious.

Gemma blinked. "There are ways to prevent it," she said finally, knowing her face was scarlet. Ladies were not supposed to know about ways to prevent pregnancy, of course. It was another means to keep them in their place. But Aunt Dahlia had taught both Gemma and her sister about them.

A circumstance that suddenly had her reevaluating Cam's suggestion that perhaps Aunt Dahlia hadn't been as celibate as Gemma had imagined.

Cam must have considered it too because he didn't look

particularly scandalized. "All right," he said with a nod. "If you need my help procuring them . . ."

She shook her head.

"Another condition," he said, "is that if at the end of our betrothal in a few months you find you've changed your mind, you'll let me know. I am not against the idea of a marriage between us."

"You aren't?" she asked with a frown. "But I thought—"

"Opinions change," he said with a shrug.

When he didn't elaborate, she pressed, "What else?"

So far, he'd surprised her with all of his conditions. She could only imagine the others would be equally as shocking and she wanted to get this part over with.

"You'll agree not to put yourself in danger while we search for your fossil," he said firmly.

"What has that to do with my proposal?" she asked, puzzled. "I consider the two to be entirely separate."

"I'm not foolish enough to think you'll follow my orders any other way," he said. "And I'm not finished with this one—if you should happen to endanger yourself, you'll agree to marry me. No arguments, no wheedling. As soon as I discover you've put your life at risk, the betrothal becomes real."

"That is most irregular," she objected.

"And proposing that we become lovers for the duration of a pretend betrothal is entirely aboveboard?" he asked. There was that brow again, she thought with a scowl.

"Fine," she said with a roll of her eyes. "But you must promise not to lure me into dangerous situations so that you can force me into wedlock."

"I am a gentleman, Gemma," he said. "I keep my word."

"So we're agreed then?" she asked. "I agree to all of your conditions, and you agree to mine?"

"It would appear that we are," he said, and she noted that his eyes had darted to her lips.

Leaning into him, she pressed those lips against his.

"Sealed with a kiss," she said softly. She made to pull away, but he deepened the meeting of mouths. By the time she pulled away, they were both a little breathless.

"I'll figure out a way to get to your rooms tonight," he said, allowing her to pull away and stand.

That brought her up short. "Here?" she asked, and realized it sounded rather like a squeak.

"You've given me a three-month limit," he said with a shrug. "I mean to use every day of them."

Gemma blinked. What had she got herself into?

She'd just smoothed out her gown, and Cam had patted down his hair, which looked just as if she'd been running her fingers through it, when Serena entered the room, followed by Sophia and Benedick.

"I hear you've had a bit of excitement," Benedick said. And Gemma couldn't help the guilty glance she turned Cam's way.

"Lord Paley, he means," Sophia said, reading far more into the exchange than Gemma had wanted her to. Her sister knew her far too well.

"Yes, of course," Gemma nodded. "It was quite the scene. But Lord Cameron did the right thing and he and Lord Paley came to an agreement."

"I agreed to let him live," Cam agreed with a nod.

At her scowl, he shrugged. "And we may have discussed some things about Sir Everard and learned a great deal of new information about that fellow's activities. I don't think anyone will be surprised to learn that he was just as much of a scoundrel in other parts of the collecting world as he was with Gemma's fossil."

Serena excused herself to check on Jeremy, and the two couples moved to the seats before the fire.

"What else had Sir Everard been up to?" Benedick asked, oblivious to the glances being exchanged between his wife and her sister.

Gemma, however, was very much aware of her sister's searching look. As Cam explained what they'd learned from Lord Paley, Gemma shook her head slightly to warn her off. The look Sophia gave her—lips pursed and brow furrowed—indicated that she would revisit the subject later.

Which was fine with Gemma. As long as they didn't discuss the fact that she and Cam had agreed to engage in an affair in front of his brother the vicar, she was content.

My, how her standard for contentment had changed this week, she thought wryly.

Then she turned her attention to the subject of Sir Everard.

But beneath her concentration on that matter, a little hum of excitement ran through her.

Tonight, it seemed to repeat. Tonight he would come to her.

Just then, Cam caught her eye. And she knew he was thinking the same thing.

Despite his distraction over his assignation later with Gemma, Cam was able to concentrate on the matter of Sir Everard and her missing fossil as soon as he saw that his brother wasn't as oblivious as he'd seemed.

This, Ben had conveyed with only a slight narrowing of his eyes. Anyone else would have missed it, but Cam had spent his entire boyhood learning his brothers' silent cues. And if he wasn't mistaken, his brother the vicar had not missed the heated look Cam had just exchanged with Gemma.

Fortunately, Sophia was there too, and was more interested in discussing Sir Everard than her husband seemed to be.

"Do you believe Sir Everard's suspicion that your fossil was, in fact, this Beauchamp Lizard?" she asked Gemma, who also seemed able to concentrate on the matter at hand. "If he was a fraud about his own abilities as a scholar, I mean, who's to say he wasn't simply wrong and intended to pass off your fossil as Lady Celeste's?"

"I'm not as familiar with Sir Everard's work as Cam is, I fear," Gemma said with a shrug. "I do know that my first instinct on seeing the skull fossil was that it could be quite exciting. But I didn't have the time to examine it properly, or to compare it against other important finds in this area to see if it bore any relationship to them."

"I have been acquainted with Sir Everard for some years," Cam said, "but I never found him to be the scientific equal of some of the other prominent members of our circle. I had no notion he was such a fraudster but nor did I think him a genius. I think to know whether it is, in fact, Lady Celeste's lizard, we'll need to find some sketch or description of it."

"She never wrote about it in any of the scholarly periodicals?" Sophia asked. Cam supposed her knowledge of the natural science world came from being Gemma's sister. It spoke well of their relationship. His brothers, whom he held in great affection, had never bothered to learn any of the details of his passion for collecting.

"I have examined all of the scientific papers and books in this library," Gemma said, gesturing to one wall of books and bound documents, "and I've never seen any mention of it. I suppose there may have been something in her diaries, but when we made a point of reading through them, we weren't looking for scientific things." As Cam understood it, when the heiresses had first come to Beauchamp Hall they'd undertaken to read through all of Lady Celeste's personal journals in an effort to find their benefactress's killer.

"It sounds as if we have some light reading in our future,"

said Ben, stretching out his shoulders as if in preparation for some physical endeavor.

But Gemma, who was wearing the expression Cam had come to recognize as the precursor to an outlandish idea, shook her head. "I don't think we'll need to go to the journals yet."

She turned to her sister, "Do you recall how I used to make you draw the items I found whenever I went fossil collecting?"

"How could I forget?" asked Sophia with a sigh. "I was never more pleased than when I stumbled on the idea to teach you to sketch them yourself. I know artists are supposed to enjoy drawing in and of itself, but stones are deadly dull as subjects go."

Cam knew at once what Gemma was getting at. "You think Lady Celeste must have some sort of collecting journal or sketchbook."

It wasn't a bad notion. Most collectors, wanting to have a way of showing their best finds without lugging them cross-country in a trunk or valise kept some kind of descriptive record. Lady Celeste's collection, as he'd seen on the tour, was quite extensive and if she'd been as active in the collecting community as she was said to have been, she would have had sketches.

"It's a logical idea," he agreed. "Especially if she intended to hide it. She'd want to know precisely what it looked like without needing to remove it from its hiding place each time she wanted to see it."

"I don't understand why she would have buried it, though," Ben said. "If Sir Everard's tale was even true."

Cam did, though. "Collectors are all a little mad about their finds," he explained. "And I've seen them do all sorts of things to stop other collectors, or worse thieves, from making off with their most prized discoveries. As schemes go, burying it in the cliffs where she found it wasn't all that bad. After all, she'd already found it there. Why would someone search there again?"

"But it's quite common to search the same place again if it yielded something important earlier," Gemma argued.

"Yes, but she owned that particular bit of beach," Cam said. "She would have no fear of someone else coming onto her property to dig there. At least, no one but you."

That made her eyes widen. "You don't think she buried it there for me to find, surely?" Despite the negative way she'd asked the question, it was obvious that she found the notion tempting. It must weigh on her that she'd not been left a specific quest as her fellow heiresses had been.

"You'll have to figure out if your fossil was, in fact, this Beauchamp Lizard," Sophia reminded them. "So you have to find the sketches. Then you'll know more about her motives."

"Agreed," Gemma said. "You don't happen to recall seeing anything like that in your studio, do you?"

"Alas, I do not," Sophia responded. "I should think you'd have the most luck in the collection, or the workroom."

But Gemma shook her head. "I've inventoried everything in both rooms and there was nothing like that. I'm afraid there's only one place where they can be. I feel foolish for not considering it earlier."

"The attics?" Sophia asked.

Gemma gave a quick nod. "I think that's our only option now."

"We'll discuss our strategy over luncheon," Ben said, rising to his feet.

"We wrangled an invitation as soon as we saw Serena," Sophia explained, linking arms with her sister. "It's too cold to go back to the vicarage without sustenance."

"Why do I get the feeling you pressed for that invitation so that you wouldn't miss any gossip," Gemma said with skepticism in her tone.

"You are free to draw whatever conclusion you wish," her sister returned tartly. "I get luncheon either way."

Walking behind the sisters, Cam glanced at his brother.

"How's your jaw?" Ben asked. "I may have hit you harder than I originally intended."

"Nice of you to say that now that the damage is done," Cam said, his hand going to the bruise.

But if he wanted an apology, he would be doomed to disappointment.

"I didn't say you didn't deserve it," Ben said. Though he was a vicar, he was still an elder brother with all the arrogance that came with it.

Cam didn't argue. But he felt Ben's gaze on him.

"What?"

They'd just reached the hallway in time to see Gemma and Sophia's skirts disappearing around the corner.

"Why do I get the sensation that I owe you another thrashing?"

Thinking back to his earlier discussion with Gemma, Cam reflected that he was probably owed more than a few thrashings for what they'd agreed to embark upon. But at the end of it, he had every intention of making said thrashing unnecessary. His brother could hardly fault him for touching his own wife.

He'd simply need to convince Gemma to take on the role.

"I don't know what you mean," he said to Ben, adopting his most innocent air.

"You're such a terrible liar," Ben said, shaking his head in disgust. "I thought we taught you better."

"I must admit, it never fails to amuse when my brother the vicar reminds me that he is a better liar than I am," Cam said.

"Don't change the subject."

To Cam's surprise, Ben stopped in front of him and looked him in the eye. "Let's speak frankly, shall we?"

At Cam's nod, he continued. "I want your word that if things go too far, you'll marry her."

"Of course I will." Cam was a bit offended that there was even a question of it.

"Do not look so put out," Ben said. "You're the one who told me you never wished to marry."

"Perhaps I've changed my mind," Cam said in a grudging tone. He hadn't had any intention of telling his brother that his revelations of the reasons for their father's infidelity had shifted something inside of him. Whatever impediment he'd harbored that stopped him from considering happy ever after for himself was gone.

That took Ben aback, he was perversely happy to see.

"Have you indeed?"

"I just said so, didn't I?"

Ben examined his face for a moment before, apparently, satisfied by what he saw there, clapping him on the shoulder. "I'm glad to hear it."

"Don't be so pleased yet," Cam said. "I haven't convinced Gemma to go along with it."

But this didn't worry his brother in the least, it would seem.

Grinning, he grabbed Cam in a one-armed hug. "You're a Lisle boy, Cam," he said with all the arrogance that statement entailed. "I have every confidence in your powers of persuasion."

That made one of them, Cam thought wryly.

For now, it would have to be enough.

Chapter 18

Luncheon was a jolly affair, and Gemma found herself un-expectedly pleased at the fact that for once, she wasn't the only heiress at the table without a gentleman of her own there with her.

She also, much to her chagrin, was more concerned about how her friends felt about Cam. It wasn't that she needed them to approve of him. They'd met him when he was here in the summer and seemed to like him well enough. But they'd not seen him as a potential match for her then. And however false she might tell herself their betrothal was, her earlier conversation with Cam—and his insistence that if there was a child she'd agree to marry him—had her considering how he would fit into her world. And, far more than her parents, her fellow heiresses were important to her.

The thought of her parents gave her a pang of guilt over what Aunt Dahlia would make over all of this. Her insistence before she left Little Seaford that Gemma owed it to the female scholars who had come before her to use this opportunity to make her mark had been forgotten in the wake of what had happened since Sir Everard's murder.

But now, the memory of her beloved aunt's warning gave

her pause. No longer hungry, she pushed her plate back and took a sip of wine.

To her discomfort, it was Cam, seated beside her, who noticed her change in mood. "Not hungry?" he asked, in a quiet voice only she could hear.

"Just tired," he said with a smile she knew seemed false. She'd never been very good at hiding her emotions.

He slipped a hand beneath the table and took hers. "If you've changed your mind about . . . um . . . tonight," he said, "I won't hold it against you. It's been a hectic week. Perhaps we should take it a bit more slowly."

The relief she felt was profound and it must have shown in her expression because he squeezed her hand, then let it go.

"That would be for the best," she said. "I don't want it to seem like I don't know my own mind. Because I do, but . . ."

"You needn't apologize, Gemma," he said with a rueful smile. "I'm not an ogre."

The rest of the meal passed without any further chance for private conversation, and to Gemma's surprise, when the meal was concluded, rather than staying so that he might search the attics with her, Cam excused himself.

"I noticed that my gelding is having a bit of trouble with his right foreleg," he said easily, "so I need to see what your stablemaster recommends."

To Gemma's further surprise—though on reflection it shouldn't have surprised her at all—Kerr and Maitland, and even Ben, who was not known to be particularly horse mad, were at his side in seconds, offering up their own suggestions.

"Send word if you find something useful in the attics," Cam said with a nod. To Gemma's disappointment, his farewell was only verbal and if she wasn't mistaken, he had made it a point not to meet her eyes.

Was he really so upset that she'd rescinded her invitation to her bedchamber for that evening that he'd run away?

She stood staring at the door that had just closed behind them, dumbfounded.

"Is there a problem?" Ivy asked, stepping up beside her.

"Tea," said Daphne from her other side.

"We just had luncheon," Gemma said, laughing despite her mood.

"It will be dessert," Sophia said, taking her by the hand and leading her toward the library where they'd always done their best thinking.

Maitland had examined the foreleg of Cam's bay gelding, Romulus, for no more than a minute before he looked up at him in disappointment.

"There's nothing wrong with his foreleg at all, is there?"

"It was a ruse," Cam said sheepishly. "I'm sorry to deny you the torn ligament you were hoping for."

"Woman trouble," said Kerr with a nod. "I surmised as much. Especially given that tête-a-tête between the two of you at the luncheon table."

"What have you done?" Ben asked his brother in exasperation.

"Now, vicar, now's not the time for recriminations," said Maitland, clapping Ben on the shoulder. "It's obvious to anyone with eyes that the fellow is in love."

Cam felt color rise in his face. To his relief, Kerr spoke before he had to. "Don't put him on the spot. What this calls for is a pint."

"Too cold to walk," Maitland said with a shiver.

"Then isn't it convenient we're in a stable with more than a few carriages in it?" the marquess asked drolly.

"Come on," he told Cam and the others. "The sooner we

get to the village, the sooner we can warm up and solve all of young Lord Cameron's romantic troubles in the process."

Having removed her slippers and tucked her feet beneath her in her favorite library chair, a cup of tea warming her hands, Gemma felt some of the tension that had threatened to overwhelm her earlier dissipate.

"It's good to be together again like this," she said aloud as she took in the sight of her sister and Ivy and Daphne similarly disposed in chairs of their own.

"Do you wish to talk about what it is that's bothering you?" asked Ivy gently. "I promise you whatever you say will not go farther than this room."

Before she could stop herself, Gemma looked at Sophia.

Her sister shook her head. "I know you think that I tell Ben everything, but if you tell me something in confidence, I keep it. I give you my word. You are my oldest friend, Gemma. As well as my sister."

Gemma felt a pang of shame at even questioning Sophia's loyalty. But that was an indication of just how much this business with Sir Everard and Cam and the Lizard had overset her. "Of course," she said. "I just don't know what to think. Of myself as much as anyone else."

"Has Lord Cameron done something to make you doubt yourself?" Ivy asked gently.

"Not as such," Gemma said with a sigh. "Not intentionally, I mean."

"How then?" Daphne asked.

"I just never considered before—not seriously at any rate— the idea that I would ever marry," Gemma said. "Indeed, I promised Aunt Dahlia that I wouldn't. So that I wouldn't squander the opportunity that being selected to come here has given me."

Three sets of eyes stared at her.

"Do you think that we've squandered our opportunities?" Sophia asked, aghast. "That by marrying we've thrown away what Lady Celeste gave us? Does Aunt Dahlia think that of me?"

"Of course I don't think that," Gemma said, frustrated that she'd worded her concern so badly. "Of course, you've all chosen husbands who will support you in your studies. But even you must admit that gentlemen like that are a rarity."

"Has Lord Cameron done something that makes you think he wouldn't be as supportive as our husbands?" Ivy asked.

"No, nothing like that," Gemma said with a shake of her head. "If anything, he's been as eager as I am to find the stolen fossil."

"Then what is it?" Sophia asked, gently. "Has he pressed you for more than you're willing to give him?"

It took a moment for her to get her sister's meaning but when she did, Gemma shook her head. "No! Not at all. If anything I've been more . . . that is to say . . ."

"Of course you have," Daphne said with a nod that seemed almost proud. "You're a healthy woman of childbearing years with an interest in a handsome man."

Gemma hid her laugh behind a cough. "Yes, well, it's nothing about Cam's behavior that worries me. It's more my own fear of disappointing Aunt Dahlia, and I suppose myself, that is of concern."

"You can't make such an important decision as who to love," Sophia said, "or even whether or not to marry, based on anyone's opinion but your own."

"But this is Aunt Dahlia, Soph," Gemma protested. "She is the one who took me to see my first collection of fossils. Who saw to it that our governesses had more than a passing knowledge of geology. Without her guidance I would never have considered it possible I could study fossils, much less make it my primary focus in life."

"Dearest," Sophia said with a sympathetic smile, "you must understand that however much you might wish to please Aunt Dahlia, she would never wish you to give up something you truly wanted just to please her. And, though I love and respect her, I think it's unfair that she put such a burden on you."

It was a relief to hear what she'd even feared to think to herself said aloud.

"I don't want to disappoint her," she said softly. "And though I do think I've grown very fond of Cam, how do I know if choosing to marry him will not do precisely what she thinks and keep me from making a place for myself in geology?"

"Have you tried asking him whether he would support your work?" Ivy asked thoughtfully. "Because it seems to me that some frank discussion between the two of you might set your mind to rest. Or at the very least let you know whether to continue with the betrothal."

"That would seem to be a sensible thing to do, wouldn't it?" Gemma asked wryly.

"Whatever you decide," Sophia said, "you must do it for you. Not for Aunt Dahlia. Not for me and Ben. Not for Lady Celeste. This is your life. If nothing else, Lady Celeste's bequest gave us each the independence needed to make decisions for ourselves."

Gemma nodded. "Thank you," she said with a smile. "All of you."

Suddenly she felt much less anxiety about all of it. She still had work to do, and a difficult conversation to have with Cam, but at least she knew now that her decision was her own.

The tavern in Little Seaford was not particularly busy at this hour of the day, and the Lisle brothers, accompanied by Kerr and Maitland, were soon seated in the taproom with tankards of ale before them while the icy wind whistled against the windows.

"So, young Cam," said Maitland after a generous swig of ale, "tell Uncle Maitland all about it."

Resisting the urge to roll his eyes, Cam reminded himself that he'd asked them for their help. Even so, he thought, seeing Kerr and Ben exchange gleeful looks, it was at a cost.

"I want to know," he said, deciding to just come right out with it, "how to go about reassuring Gemma that marrying me won't mean she has to give up her ambitions as a geologist."

Maitland frowned. "I should imagine you just tell her," the duke said with a shrug.

Cam sighed. "I thought perhaps, since the duchess seems to have kept up with her mathematics since your marriage that you might have some suggestions. Or perhaps you would, Kerr. I believe Lady Kerr is a classicist?"

Before Kerr could respond, Maitland guffawed. "If you think Daphne's maths work is anywhere in my purview, old man, then you know very little of marriage. Or Daphne."

When Cam turned to Kerr, the marquess gave him a sheepish grin. "Our wives have minds of their own, and we knew that when we married them. I don't know about Maitland, but it was understood that Ivy would continue to pursue her work."

Maitland nodded.

Benedick, who had been silent so far, added, "Sophia was afraid that her painting would affect my ability to move up in the church hierarchy. It took some persuading to prove to her that I cared more for her than becoming a bishop. But I did manage it."

Cam took a swallow of ale.

"If you don't mind my saying so," Kerr said with a twist of his lips, "perhaps it's not just marriage that's what frightens

Gemma, but marriage to another fossil-hunter. The three of us are not in competition with our wives."

That was something that hadn't occurred to Cam. Which was foolish since it was what had caused their very first disagreement. He, a fellow geologist, had rejected her geology paper for his journal.

"Can it really be that simple?" he asked with a shake of his head. "She's just afraid I'll try to eclipse her?"

"You must admit," Ben said, "it's not easy for ladies in any area that's dominated by men to make a name for themselves. Perhaps she's afraid that marrying you will bring her under suspicion from the rest of the collecting world who might suggest she was trying to climb up the ladder by marrying someone on a higher rung, so to speak."

"That's ridiculous," Cam said, angry at the idea anyone would think such a thing.

"It's how the world works," Kerr said. "Like it or not, marriages are made every day for more mercenary reasons than professional acclaim."

"I suppose so," he admitted, thinking of Sir Everard's, and even Paley's, speculation about the Beauchamp fortune and how much Gemma was worth.

"Whatever misgivings she has," Maitland said, his normally sunny expression muted with sympathy, "you have to show her that you care more about her than your fossils and whatnot."

His words pierced Cam like a knife.

He couldn't remember a time when he hadn't been obsessed with collecting objects from the natural world.

"Don't look so morose," Ben said gently. "You don't have to give them up altogether. Just prove to her that she's more important than the fossils are."

"How do I do that?" Cam asked, relieved, but only just.

"Give her your most treasured fossil," Maitland said without batting an eye.

"My collection isn't here with me," Cam said with a scowl.

"You brought some with you though, didn't you?" the duke asked, with a gimlet eye. "You collector chaps can't leave the house without bringing your best bits along."

Cam thought about the highly polished cherry trunk in his bedchamber at the vicarage that held some of his more interesting fossils and other stones. "Yes, of course I did. I suppose I could give her one of those."

"Most of all," his brother said, "you must convince her that you're marrying her not because you want to stop her from succeeding, but because you can't succeed without her. That you're better together than either one of you is apart."

"That's damned eloquent, vicar," said Maitland raising his glass.

All four men laughed, and Cam, the tightness in his chest dissipated for the moment, drank the rest of his ale before requesting another round.

Chapter 19

Gemma didn't venture up to the attics until after breakfast the next morning. She felt more at ease about the situation with Cam thanks to her discussion with her friends and her sister, and she was able to concentrate more fully on the search for the missing skull bone.

One thing had marred her evening, however, and that was finding some of her own notebooks in the workroom next to the collection had been disarranged. She was all but certain she'd reshelved them after looking through them that morning. But there they were, scattered over the worktable.

It was possible she had been so distracted by other things that she was mistaken, but she didn't think so. When considered in context with the feeling of being watched and the threat left on Sir Everard's body, the thought that someone had been in her workshop made her shiver.

By breakfast she'd convinced herself that she'd been imagining things, however, and putting it out of her mind, she headed upstairs.

It had been some time since Gemma had explored the attics, and she was surprised all over again by their tidiness.

She'd only just lit the lamps nearest the door when she heard the sound of footsteps in the stairwell.

"I hope you didn't think we'd let you search up here without help," said Sophia as she stepped into the cluttered, but tidy space.

To Gemma's surprise, she saw not Daphne and Ivy behind her but Cam.

She tried to keep her expression neutral, but she felt a familiar jolt of awareness and relief at seeing Cam there. She might not be completely sure that marrying him would be the best thing for her, but she knew that more than just a small part of her wanted him to be.

"Where do you want us?" he asked with a lopsided smile that softened his blunt features and made her stomach flip.

She wished for a moment that he hadn't been accompanied by Sophia, but then decided it was probably better that he had. It was far too early in the day for the activity that smile inspired her to want. And they did have work to do.

"I begin to doubt we'll find anything of use," she said aloud as she turned to survey the room at large. "If there were something that seemed likely to be associated with Lady Celeste's collecting, I think we'd have discovered it by now."

"Since your letter was cut short by her illness," Sophia said, stepping up beside her, "perhaps Lady Celeste wasn't able to extract the information she needed for it from up here. And we haven't searched the attics thoroughly, you must admit. We looked at her personal diaries but that was all."

"She was so orderly about everything else, though," Gemma said, moving toward the far wall where she remembered she'd discovered a few items that might have gone into the collection room. "I don't know that I believe she'd have left anything to chance."

"She was quite ill, though, dearest," Sophia said, placing a comforting hand on her sister's arm. "She may not have trusted the task to anyone else."

Before they could continue, Benedick appeared in the doorway.

"I'm afraid I just got word that Mrs. Wallace has fallen ill," he said, his usual good humor replaced with concern. "I'll need to go see to her at once, but you may remain here, my dear—"

But Sophia shook her head. "Of course not," she said. "Her little ones must be frantic. And they do not care for her sister at all."

In just a few short months, Sophia had adapted to her role as a vicar's wife with an ease that made Gemma respect her even more than she had already. Far from dampening her enthusiasm for her art, her marriage had transformed her into a fuller, happier version of herself.

Still, she did wish her sister could remain here now.

Perhaps sensing Gemma's disappointment, Sophia kissed her cheek and said, "It can't be helped. I'll see you tomorrow if I'm not needed there."

"Of course." Gemma hugged her, then made a shooing motion. "Go, go. I'm sure poor Mrs. Wallace's children are worried sick."

When they were gone, she and Cam stood silently assessing one another until Cam said with a touch of amusement, "Do not look so frightened. I won't ravish you amidst the discarded furniture and disturbing dress forms of your attic."

She bit her lip. Of course he knew precisely what she'd been thinking. "I thought perhaps you were frustrated at my change of heart yesterday."

He stepped further into the low-ceilinged room and stopped just a foot away from her. "I won't ravish you at all, Gemma," he said softly. "If you're not willing, then I don't want you. Just say the word and we can end this betrothal now."

His words sent a stab of fear through her—whether it was

the thought of dissolving their betrothal or his frankness, she wasn't sure.

"I meant what I said." She lifted her chin and met his gaze with a boldness she didn't feel. "I do wish to explore with you. It's just that yesterday was . . ."

"You needn't explain," he said softly, running a finger over her cheek. "I can wait. Until you're ready."

She lowered her eyes at the intensity of his gaze.

When she looked up again, though, he was smiling. "I will tell you, however," he said, his half smile revealing a dimple in his left cheek, "that exploration is my specialty."

She couldn't help her answering grin and she felt as if her heart would beat right out of her chest. Surely he could see it.

"Then perhaps we should—"

But he cut her off with a quick kiss. "We'll wait until tonight, in your bed."

"What if I don't want to wait?" she asked, growing impatient. "What if I want to get it over with?"

At that his eyes darkened. He slipped his arms around her and pulled her close. To her surprise, she felt him—one part of him in particular—pressing against her. "This is what you do to me," he said huskily. "And when I take you, I mean to take my time. You might not know it, but it makes a difference for a woman. The first time, especially, shouldn't be done in haste."

It was one area in which she was painfully ignorant. Despite having read as many of the books in the library on the subject, Gemma had no real experience, and even less understanding of the subtleties he described. And Sophia had been frustratingly vague, though Gemma was quite certain she and Benedick had anticipated their vows—in Sophia's studio, no less!

"I suppose in this," she said loftily, "I will have to trust you."

He smiled. "You'll trust me in more than this before it's all over," he said. "But for now, it'll do."

She shifted a little and he gave a hiss as she brushed against his arousal. Alarmed, she pulled away. "Did I hurt you?"

Huffing a laugh, Cam shook his head. "Not as such. I'll just need a minute."

He turned around and stared at the ceiling for a moment.

"How on earth do you manage to walk about like that?" she asked, curious now. She'd known of course about penises. Or was it penii? She'd have to ask Ivy when next she saw her. It wasn't the sort of thing one could write in a letter after all.

"I was exaggerating when I said I'd been like this ever since we kissed," he said. "But not by much."

"That still doesn't explain how—"

"Gemma?"

"Yes?"

"Perhaps you can begin searching now and we can save this discussion for later?"

She stared at his back for a moment. Well, if he didn't want questions, he ought not have brought it up.

Then she remembered distinctly his laughter when she'd said that precise phrase before.

"Brought it up," she said under her breath, understanding the double entendre now.

Stifling her laughter at the jest she moved to the trunk where she'd found some of Lady Celeste's papers before and began her search.

Once he'd managed to lose his erection—thanks to a memory of a neighbor in the vicinity of his father's estate who used copious amounts of scent in lieu of bathing—Cam wordlessly moved to Gemma's side and began to sort through a trunk next to one she was looking in.

She'd said this area was where the items related to Lady

Celeste's interest in fossils and collecting were to be found, and a cursory examination of the first few pages on top affirmed that assessment.

They worked in silence for some time, both of them removing the contents of the trunks they searched and placing item after item, document after document onto the floor beside where they knelt.

He was almost to the bottom of his trunk when a brisk knock sounded on the door of the attic.

"I thought you might be ready for a break," Serena said brightly, ushering the footman, William, into the room carrying a tray laden with sandwiches and the like. It had been a long time since luncheon.

"How did you know I wouldn't want to stop?" Gemma asked, standing and brushing her hands off on her gown.

"I have shared a house with you for almost a full year, Gemma," her chaperone said. "I think I should know your work habits by now."

Cam had risen as soon as he saw Serena, and moved over to where William, the footman, was setting up a small table and two chairs just inside the door.

"A picnic in the attic," he said dryly as he watched the servant place a small vase with what looked like one of Paley's hothouse roses on the table. "What a perfect setting for a newly betrothed couple."

He turned to eye Serena and she turned pink, confirming his suspicion. For whatever reason, she'd changed her assessment of him as a potential husband for her charge. He wasn't sure whether to be pleased or concerned.

It wouldn't make any difference in his own intentions, of course, but he did wonder what had changed her mind.

There would be no clues coming from Gemma, he thought wryly as she took her seat and impatiently gestured for him to be seated as well.

"I'm starving," she said, and her stomach gave a rumble then, as if to confirm it.

Seeing that they were not going to ignore the repast she'd arranged, Lady Serena gave a brisk nod.

"I'll be off and let you two eat, then," she said. "Enjoy your meal."

And before either of them could protest, she was gone, followed by the butler and footman.

Cam stared after her for a moment, then took his seat.

Gemma was indeed hungry, for she bit into a sandwich just then and sighed in a way that had him thinking of the scented neighbor again.

"Why aren't you eating?" she asked when minutes had passed without him selecting from the assorted food on offer.

"I am," he said, reaching for a bit of beef and cheese. "There, see?" he bit into it. And realized he was far more hungry than he'd realized.

Relaxing a bit, she continued to forage from the collation of cheese, fruits, meat and fruit tarts.

"You aren't one of those silly creatures who pretends no interest in food, I've noticed," he said with approval. He'd once thought—when he was fresh from university and full of himself—that a true lady would never deign to show interest in food or drink. No more.

"You know me too well now to have ever imagined that," she said with a shake of her head. "I shall never see the sense in pretending to be happy when I'm sad. Or pretending to be full when I'm still hungry."

"In some instances, pretending happiness might be necessary to prevent someone else from learning something painful," he said, thinking back to his father's behavior when the duchess had been ill.

"I suppose that's true," she said thoughtfully, "but I cannot imagine what—other than a need for gentlemen to feel superior—should make it necessary for a lady to pretend never to have human needs."

"It does become rather absurd when you see all the men at table stuffing their maws with every sort of delicacy while the ladies nibble small bites and never finish any of the dishes."

"Precisely," Gemma said with an approving nod.

Cam basked in the feeling for a moment.

"You've changed somehow," she said, tilting her head to really look at him. "It's as if you're—lighter. Less angry."

Had learning about the reasons behind his father's actions really wrought such a change in him in such a short time? Surely not.

She must have seen his skepticism, because she continued, "I don't know if it's something everyone would notice. But I see it."

That made him feel somewhat better. He'd never thought of himself as an easy read, but it made sense that Gemma, whom he'd spent the most time with, and been the most intimate with, would be the one to see it.

But was it something he was ready to share with her?

For once, the man who always knew exactly what his next move would be was uncertain.

As the silence between them lengthened, Gemma turned her attention back to the trunk she was examining. It was filled with the sorts of bits and bobs every collector of fossils and geological oddities gathered over a career of hunting for important finds. Too interesting to dispose of without a pang of guilt and too unimportant to place on display with the truly great pieces acquired on a hunt.

A glance at Cam revealed he too was poring over the contents of the trunk he'd opened.

They had worked quietly for nearly a quarter of an hour, however, when she realized that the floor of this particular trunk was not painted brown as she'd originally thought, but was lined with large, leather-bound books.

Her heart thumped as she recognized them as the same sort of notebooks Lady Celeste had used for her personal journals she and the others had looked through earlier in the year.

Hurriedly, but careful not to damage any of the fossils, she removed everything from the trunk.

Cam must have noticed her haste because he looked over, his eyes alert. "What did you find?"

"I don't know yet," she said, taking out the last large stone. "But I have a hope it's what we've been looking for."

She didn't name it aloud for fear of jinxing herself. She desperately wanted to find out if the fossil she'd discovered on the shore was actually the famed Beauchamp Lizard. She would accept the truth no matter what the outcome, but she could admit to herself, at least, that she'd be highly disappointed if it wasn't. Not only because it would mean she might have been wrong about the value of the stone she found, but also because it would mean that Lady Celeste hadn't, in fact, planted it there for her to find. The lack of her benefactress having made some kind of quest or plan for her enlightenment during the first year at Beauchamp House stung. And this seemed to be her last chance.

"Here," said Cam, as if sensing her fear, "I'll bring them out while you scan them."

Grateful for his lack of questions, she moved out of the way, and let him kneel down in front of the trunk.

While he worked, she moved closer to the lamp they'd hung on the wall just over where they'd been searching. There was an abandoned armchair there and she perched on the edge, scanning the pages.

The hand was one she also recognized from Lady Celeste's journals and the pages were lined with neatly inscribed dates, locales and descriptions of what she'd found there. In some cases, there were purchase dates and the name of the collector from whom she'd acquired the particular item or items, followed by a brief notation of where the items had been found.

The journal in her hands was dated some twenty years previous and contained five years' worth of discoveries and purchases as well as pencil sketches of the items. But nowhere in this particular volume, however, did she find a mention of any fossil that matched the skull fossil she'd discovered on the shore.

Cam finished removing all eleven remaining journals and offered them to her just as she set the first one she'd drawn out down on the table.

"You take these and I'll look in these," he said, not bothering to note that she'd obviously not found anything about the lizard in the first one.

Once more the attic was silent, though this time there was an air of excitement as they scanned the diaries for some mention of the stone Sir Everard had been convinced was the Beauchamp Lizard.

At last Gemma found it. The sketch was the only one in this volume Lady Celeste had rendered in any great degree of detail. The unimportant finds, Gemma had concluded, were only given cursory drawings. This one, however, was as finely rendered as any pen-and-ink drawing on display in the great museums. And there was no question it was the fossil they were looking for.

"Here, Cam," she said, her voice ringing with excitement. "A particularly fine fossilized skull of a marine lizard, found Beauchamp House cliffs, Little Seaford, Sussex, Ldy C. Beauchamp and Lrd Crutchley. 4 Sept. 1813."

"Crutchley?" Cam frowned. "Doesn't he have an estate near Lyme?"

Lord Richard Crutchley was not a particularly renowned

collector, but he was known to have a small collection of finds he'd purchased from Mary Anning. He'd also written a few notes and letters to the various geological magazines.

"Yes," Gemma said thoughtfully. "I do recall Lady Celeste mentioning him in her personal diaries, at social gatherings and the like, but this seems more friendly than those entries did."

"She clearly had a large circle of acquaintances," he said wryly. "I suppose working for the Home Office can expand one's reach like that."

While Sophia and Benedick had been investigating a local art forgery ring, they'd discovered, among other things, that Lady Celeste had been an agent for the Home Office for a time. It had not come as a shock to the heiresses, who had come to understand that their benefactress was not only intelligent and kind, but also had her finger in far more pies than they could ever have imagined.

"How did you know about that?" Gemma asked with a frown. She'd thought the heiresses had agreed not to spread word of Lady Celeste's work for the crown.

"I overheard Sophia telling Ben," he said ruefully. "But I promise not to say anything to anyone. I'm quite good at keeping secrets."

Turning her attention back to the notebook, Gemma considered what they'd discovered. "It would appear that we've found evidence that here was a Beauchamp Lizard, at the very least."

"Whether the specimen you found was the same fossil, however . . ." Cam said, trailing off at her glare. "I admit the signs are all there," he said, holding up his hands in a gesture of surrender. "It's just a matter of corroborating that information with someone who's seen the one Lady Celeste unearthed."

Rising from her chair, Gemma began marching toward the attic doors.

"Where are you going?" he asked, climbing to his feet.

"To change into something warmer," she told him over her shoulder. "You should call for your curricle. We've got a long journey ahead of us."

She felt the reverberation in the floor as he jogged to catch up with her.

"You might ask me if I wish to drive nearly to Lyme first," Cam complained as he reached her side. "Perhaps I'm tired."

"My dear Lord Cameron," she said with a raised brow. "If you are too tired to drive to Crutchley's estate then I fear you are too fatigued for any other activity."

He paused, then shook his head a little. "Point taken. I'll meet you in the entrance hall in thirty minutes."

"Fifteen," she said, "and don't be late."

Chapter 20

Normally, Cam would wish to spend some time planning a journey like this. Not because Lyme was particularly far, but because the weather at this time of year was unpredictable and one look at the skies as he lifted Gemma into the curricle was enough to have him seriously considering an attempt to put her off.

They'd secured hot bricks and his curricle was already equipped with blankets and furs, but he had a pang of conscience about taking her out on the road in the cold with the possibility of rain on the horizon.

"I've sworn George to secrecy," she said as she arranged a blanket around her and rubbed her hands together. "Serena was, fortunately, with Jem in the nursery, so there's little danger of her discovering we've gone until we're at least into the village."

They drove in silence for a long while, Cam lost in his thoughts, while Gemma all but vibrated with excitement about the coming interview with Crutchley.

"You do realize that as soon as Lady Serena notices we're gone, she'll assume we've eloped," Cam told her just as they reached the far side of Little Seaford.

If he'd expected Gemma to be cowed by the notion of Serena's assumptions, however, he was grossly mistaken.

"Of course she won't," Gemma explained. "I told George we were going to speak with Lord Crutchley and that we would be back not long after supper."

"Gemma, do you have any notion how far it is to Lyme?" he asked, bemused at her blithe disregard for the limits of time and space.

"Of course I do," she said with a shake of her head as the curricle hit a stone and she had to cling to his arm. "Why are you so cross about this?"

He had to admit, he thought as her violet scent teased him, being this close to her in a confined space would be no hardship.

"I'm not cross," he said with a huff of disbelief. "But why do you assume our trip to Crutchley's estate will only take a couple of hours. At this time of year, Lyme is at least three. And that's in excellent weather, which this is not."

She stiffened beside him. "What do you mean?" she asked. "I distinctly recall the day you came to rip up at me over the article for your benighted journal that you said you'd come from Lyme. It was early afternoon, so I assumed it was a trip to be made in a few hours."

"It is," he said patiently. "In late summer. But in late autumn, when the roads are in poor conditions thanks to rainstorms like the one that made it possible for you to find your skull fossil, it takes longer. Not to mention that the horses must rest."

Gemma was silent as she pondered this information. "She'll think we've eloped. So will Sophia and Benedick."

"Yes," he said. "Do you wish me to turn around? We can just as easily set out tomorrow. It was foolish of me to let you talk me into traveling today."

She snorted. "Yes, it's all my doing. Good heavens, Cam, do you not have sense enough to tell me when a plan is ill conceived? You seem to have opinions enough on every other matter."

"You were very obviously excited about finding Lord Crutchley's connection to the Lizard," he said defensively. "I got caught up in it. And I've been thinking about other things."

"What other things?"

"You know what other things," he said with a glare. She had him so tied up in knots he didn't know which way was up.

"Oh, you mean the—" she gestured with one hand.

"Yes," he said glancing at her, then turning back to watch the road. "That."

"Well, it's hardly my fault that you cannot concentrate on anything else," she said with a shrug. "I wonder that men are allowed to conduct business at all if they're so incapable of prying their thoughts away from carnal matters."

He ignored the slight, and turned back to the subject at hand. "Do you wish to go back?"

They were already well over a third of the way to Crutchley's estate, but if they were to return without Serena any the wiser, they'd need to go now.

When she didn't respond, he directed the horses to a roadside clearing.

"Why are you stopping?" she asked, frowning.

"Because I wish to know what you've decided," he said, feeling more than a little frustrated with her. Gemma wasn't normally given to behaving like a flibbertigibbet, but today was a marked exception.

"We have to continue," she said with a slight shake of her head. "I hadn't thought to alarm Serena, but knowing how long it will take us to reach Crutchley's home doesn't change my mind about the necessity for the trip. We need to know who stole the fossil. And who killed Sir Everard. He may not have been a particularly good person, but he didn't deserve to be murdered."

Cam leaned back against the padded seat of his curricle. The wind had begun to pick up and the horses were impatient to be on the road again if their huffs of white breath were any indication.

"You are the most maddening lady, Gemma," he said, his own breath a visible vapor in the shelter of the curricle roof. "I thought you were intent on exploring whatever this is between us without the risk of being forced into marriage."

At his words, understanding dawned in her eyes. "Oh, I see now. You're worried this will mean we have to wed."

"Not worried," he said hastily. "Or, perhaps on your behalf. You're the one who wishes to make a life for yourself alone."

He'd told his brother he would try to convince her to change her mind about her plan for a solitary life, but he didn't wish to win her over by default. He wouldn't marry her unless it was of her own free will. He'd seen too many arranged and forced marriages end in unhappiness for both parties.

"I'm embarking on this journey of my own volition, Cam," she told him, putting a gloved hand on his arm. "If it turns out that this hasty trip ends up causing me to abandon my plans, then I'm willing to live with the consequences."

He wanted to protest that he didn't want her that way, but it would be a lie. He wanted her any way he could get her. And the rapidity of his change of heart on that matter was something that frightened him. Only last week, he'd considered her to be one of the most difficult and uncomfortable ladies of his acquaintance. Now he was becoming certain that a life without her would be dreadfully dull.

"If you're sure," he said, placing his hand over hers. And

when he caught her gaze going to his mouth, he gave in and leaned forward to kiss her.

It was just a brief meeting of warm mouths, but the contrast with the cold air around them made it that much harder to pull away. But he did so, despite wishing he could wrap her in his arms and keep out the cold. This was a public thoroughfare, however, and he wouldn't expose her to that sort of damage to her reputation, at least.

Still, when he pulled away, she smiled at him and he was almost lost.

"We have to go," she said firmly, before slipping her arm into his. "It looks as if it might rain."

Now she noticed, he thought wryly, "Yes, it does," he said aloud. "If we're lucky it will hold off until we reach Lyme."

But they weren't lucky.

Not long after they had gone another mile, a fat raindrop plopped onto the rump of the left leader. Then more followed that and soon they were experiencing that most uncomfortable of circumstances, driving against the wind into a rainstorm.

Cam's coat and hat were enough to protect him from the worst of it, but Gemma's clothing was made for fashion and not practicality. Thus, her jaunty hat, while pretty, did little to protect her from the shower. Nor did her coat.

Fortunately, they reached a village not far from Lyme a short while later. The inn there, which Cam had had occasion to stay in before, was not particularly luxurious, but clean and comfortable. But its proximity to Lyme meant it was a favorite with tourists visiting the seaside, and even at this time of year it did brisk business.

As he drew the horses to a stop, Cam leapt from the vehicle and when he crossed the wet inn yard to Gemma's side she was already being assisted to the ground by a familiar figure.

"Lord Cameron," said Lord Paley briskly as he slipped his arm through Gemma's and led her into the taproom. "You'd best get out of the rain."

Cam felt the man's presence like a punch to the gut. Of all the people to encounter on this benighted journey, it had to be Paley.

He didn't mistake the way the blackguard's hand rested on Gemma's as they walked, either.

Paley might have agreed to leave her be but it was obvious he found her attractive. What's more, why was he here at all? Wasn't he meant to remain at Pearson Close until Northman gave him permission to leave the area?

He'd just stepped into the interior of the inn when he heard Paley say, "What a surprise to find the two of you here so close to Lyme, Miss Hastings."

Gemma glanced at Cam before responding. "It was an impulse on my part, Lord Paley. I simply had to come to see Mary Anning's collection. Especially after learning that Lady Celeste purchased some things from her."

"So you were able to learn more about Lady Celeste's collection, then?" Paley asked, looking far too avid for Cam's comfort.

"Indeed," she replied, her mouth a little pursed at his obvious curiosity. "And Lord Cameron was kind enough to drive me here."

"What a dreadful bit of luck to encounter such bad weather, then," Paley said, his eyes narrowed at Cam. "I would have thought Lord Cameron would take better care of his betrothed."

And something about the fellow's air of disapproval, coupled with the knowledge that Gemma's reputation was in real jeopardy thanks to this happenstance meeting, Cam pinned Paley with a glare. "Indeed, she is no longer my betrothed, Lord Paley."

At a gasp from Gemma and a frown from Paley, he continued. "She is now my bride. You may wish us happy."

The sight of Lord Paley at the entrance to The Fish & Fowl had caught Gemma by surprise. Especially since she hadn't considered the notion they'd see anyone of their acquaintance on their journey. It was foolish, she realized now, but she had genuinely been so focused on meeting with Lord Crutchley and questioning him about the lizard skull, and then on arguing with Cam, that it hadn't occurred to her.

For someone who prided herself on her intellect, she was behaving remarkably foolishly these days.

But she noted that Cam seemed far more put out by Lord Paley's presence than she was. If ever there were a man staring daggers, it was Cam and his eyes were, metaphorically at least, stabbing Lord Paley to bits.

"What a dreadful bit of luck to encounter such bad weather, then," Lord Paley was saying. "I would have thought Lord Cameron would take better care of his betrothed."

This ruffled Gemma's feathers on Cam's behalf. Especially given that she'd been the one to insist on making the drive today.

She was about to say so when Cam, looking like a man who was about to lay down a trump card on the table, said with a smile that didn't reach his eyes, "Indeed, she is no longer my betrothed, Lord Paley."

His words surprised her, but they also gave her a sense of foreboding.

Because rather than moving away from her, as would a man who was ending an engagement would do, Cam pulled her to his side, and away from Lord Paley's grasp.

"She is now my bride," he said, his voice ringing with triumph. "You may wish us happy."

Gemma stood as still as a stone for a moment while she

watched Lord Paley's eyes narrow on them both. Recognizing that whatever game Cam was playing at there must be a reason for it, she filed away her sense of outrage to be examined later, and turned what she hoped would be interpreted as a smitten gaze on Cam. He, meanwhile, looked genuinely pleased with himself.

"I . . . that is a surprise," Lord Paley said with a puzzled frown.

"Nothing was planned. I hoped, but I was biding my time, you see," Cam told him, squeezing Gemma's hand in warning. "I came to Little Seaford with a special license in my pocket. I just had to convince Miss Hastings—that is, Gemma—to go through with it. My brother performed the ceremony."

To Gemma's relief, Lord Paley seemed to believe the story. And to Gemma's surprise he pumped Cam's hand in an enthusiastic handshake before asking if he could kiss her hand.

Bemused, she extended her hand to him and he bent over it. "I wish you both every happiness," he said with a mix of wistfulness and congratulations. "I do wish I'd met you earlier, Miss Hastings." Then correcting himself, he said, "Lady Cameron, I mean. You're a lucky man, Lord Cameron."

"I well know it, Paley," her false bridegroom responded with a loving glance in her direction. Really, if she hadn't known it was all a hum, she'd have been fooled completely. Cam was a far better actor than she'd first supposed.

Just then, someone opened the door of the taproom and a breeze came in and Gemma realized she was cold and wet and desperately uncomfortable.

"I'll leave you to it, then," said Lord Paley, with a sudden expression of discomfort.

He thinks he's interrupted our wedding night, Gemma thought with a start.

And Cam, who had likely read the other man's expression in the same way, gave him a brisk nod and, keeping her close by his side, moved to where the proprietor had been standing aside waiting until their business with Paley was concluded rather than interrupting.

"Milord," said the man with a deep bow. "I couldn't help but overhear. I'd be happy to offer you our best room. But I'm afraid there's only the one. The rest are full up thanks to the mail coach, which came in just an hour ago."

Gemma bit back an exclamation of frustration. She might have been planning to welcome Cam into her bedchamber at Beauchamp House, but that was before he put himself into her black books by declaring them wed before Lord Paley. He would be lucky if he allowed him to kiss her hand tonight, much less sleep with her in the large bed looming before them. And besides, she had no intention of remaining here tonight. The weather would no doubt turn and they could get to Lord Crutchley's home in time for an evening call.

She said none of this, however, just waited for Cam to reply to the proprietor.

"My—ah, wife," her "husband" said with the air of a man who is not used to the notion of having a bride yet, "will need a hot bath and we'd also like supper in our room."

"Of course," he said with a nod, leading them up a wide staircase to a corridor of doors.

The room he ushered them into was, as Cam had told her, comfortable, but not particularly lush. But the floors were swept and the counterpane and windows looked newly cleaned.

Once the innkeeper left them, and shut the door behind him, Gemma turned to face Cam.

To his credit, he didn't shy away from her scowl.

"You may rip up at me once you're out of your wet clothes," he said firmly. "I may be a liar and a rogue, but at least I won't countenance you catching your death."

She lifted her brows, but untied the ribbons on her hat

and removed it. "It seems as if catching my death has been a real possibility in your company of late," she said as she placed the straw confection, now sadly drooping with moisture, on the mantelpiece.

Meanwhile, Cam had shrugged out of his many caped greatcoat and blue superfine. His neckcloth was as limp as Gemma's hat, and though it must be uncomfortable, he didn't remove it.

"Do not give up your comfort for my sensibilities' sake," Gemma said as she began unbuttoning her pelisse. "After all, we're as good as married now."

Cam looked up from an examination of his boots—he was clearly trying to figure out if he should remove them or not—and was arrested by the sight of the bare skin above her bodice. It had been covered by the pelisse, which was long-sleeved and high-necked. As Gemma watched, his eyes darkened and she felt an answering flush run through her.

"I meant your cravat," she said moving her gaze to rest on the knotted linen at his neck.

Wordlessly, he began to loosen the knot that someone—his valet?—had spent a great deal of time perfecting.

It was dreadfully intimate, Gemma realized, just this simple act of watching him unknot his neckcloth. She felt a flutter in her belly and her breath quickened at the realization. This was far more intense than she'd imagined it would be.

When he was finished removing his tie, he stepped closer to her.

She'd never seen a gentleman in shirtsleeves before. Never even seen one with his neck bare. His fine lawn shirt opened into a vee at the hollow beneath his throat, dark curling hair drawing her eye there like a bit of shale in a bed of lime.

"Are you very angry?" he asked softly, reaching out to touch her cheek. His hands were rough. Rougher than those of most gentlemen she guessed. Very likely because he spent much of his time digging in the soil and cleaning fossils and stones. The thought reminded her that she had far more in common with this man who had the ability to bring her to all sorts of strong emotions within the space of a moment.

And yes, anger was one of them.

"A bit," she admitted, but she didn't object as he pulled her against that broad chest she couldn't take her eyes off of. With a sigh, she leaned into his warmth and allowed him to hold her. "You must admit it was a scurvy trick."

To his credit, he didn't laugh at her turn of phrase—an epithet she'd picked up from the footman, William, who had a brother in the Royal Navy.

"It was, indeed," he said, kissing her on the top of the head as he pulled her closer against him, so that her softness was flush against his solid strength. "I couldn't let Paley leave with the kind of gossip seeing us here together alone would have started, though," he said, his breath warm against her ear. "I'd have had to call him out in truth, this time."

"I know," she said, her own voice sounding breathy to her own ears. "But, without warning. I wasn't ready. I mean, I'd come to the realization that this trip was taking a risk. But . . ."

"There's no way I'd have let you go after you let me into your bed, though, Gemma." His voice sounded apologetic, but there was a hint of steel there that she recognized for what it was. Determination.

She pulled away a little so that she could look him in the eyes. "But you said you would let me go," she said, frowning. "Did you lie?"

He sighed. "I didn't lie. Let us instead call it a temporary agreement about which I hoped to change your mind."

His mouth curved into a sensual smile.

Despite her annoyance with him, she laughed. "Do you really think you're so skilled at this lovemaking business that you'd be able to sway me from my life goals?"

When he only grinned, she laughed again. "You are incorrigible," she said breathlessly. He pulled her close again and took her mouth in a kiss that told her just how confident in his skills he was.

When a knock signaled the servants bringing up the bath, they pulled apart, but Gemma couldn't help but touch her swollen lips.

She watched the play of muscles beneath his shirt and waistcoat as he directed them with the hip bath.

If he was as good as he thought he was, she mused, perhaps it was a good thing they were away from Beauchamp House for this.

Chapter 21

Before she left, the maid, who'd come up with toweling and borrowed nightclothes from the proprietor's wife, asked tentatively, "Would you like me to assist you, milady?"

Cam had been preparing to put his coat back on, as well as his soggy neckcloth, so that he could go down to the taproom while Gemma bathed, and was startled to hear her tell the girl no and send her on her way.

When they were alone again, he turned from looking at the door to find her watching him.

He hadn't been this overwhelmed by the prospect of bedding a woman since he was a lad. And just having her gaze on him was almost enough to send him over the edge.

"I'll need your help with my gown," she said, her nerves betrayed only by a hint of color in her cheekbones. It had taken some degree of bravery for her to say it so calmly, and he realized he was behaving like a halfling.

She turned her back to him as she stood beside the steaming tub, and wordlessly he crossed to where she waited. When he brushed his fingers over the nape of her neck, he heard her intake of breath, and watched as goose pimples rose on the soft skin there.

The pearl buttons that ran down to the dip just above her

heart-shaped bottom were tiny, and not particularly easy to slip through the wool of her gown. So he took his time, unfastening them one by one, allowing himself the luxury of a touch here, a brush of his fingers there, as button by button, the soft creamy skin of her back just visible through the think chemise she wore beneath, revealed itself to him like a flower opening to the sun.

It was impulse that made him kiss her as he went. He let his fingers follow the line of buttons as he concentrated his mouth on the gentle slope of her shoulder, the gossamer place below her ear.

He could feel her shiver at his touch, and it wasn't from cold.

But he wanted her to know that he did nothing that she didn't want too.

"Is this agreeable?" he asked, as his fingers stole their way down her back, unfastening as they went.

She giggled a little, and he paused. "What's funny?"

Turning to face him, she held up the bodice of her gown, which was now gaping in the back.

"I hadn't expected you to be the sort of man who asked permission," she said with a raised brow.

He blinked. That was rather a lowering thought. "You think I take without asking?" he asked, tilting his head to look at her. He supposed he hadn't always been the picture of kindness in her presence, but nor had he expected her to assume he was the kind of fellow who would ravish a lady without gaining any kind of agreement from her.

His dismay must have shown on his face because her brows knit. "I didn't mean it as a criticism," she said, her expression troubled now. "Only that you surprised me. I thought asking you to share my bed at Beauchamp House was a sort of blanket permission."

"That was before I set the cat amongst the pigeons by

telling Paley we were wed," he said with a shake of his head. "I should have thought you might at the very least need to revisit the issue, given that not very long ago you seemed as if you wanted to toss me bodily from the window."

She glanced at the window, which was rather small, but would have done the job if she had the strength of anger on her side.

"I do not understand you, Cam," she said finally. "One moment you seem to want nothing more than to hold me in your arms, and the next you're almost diffident."

"Because I'm trying not to ride roughshod over you," he said, pulling away and thrusting a hand through his hair. "I know you think I'm a . . . a bully, but I am trying not to be for your sake."

He heard her gasp and then felt her hand on his back. "Cam, I don't think you're a bully," she said firmly. "No more than I am. And I know quite well that I can be as stubborn as they come."

"I . . . regret that first meeting between us, Gemma," he said on a sigh. "More than you can ever know."

"Well, I don't," she said, and he had to turn to see her face because her words were so jarring.

"You despised me that day," he said frowning. "I despised me that day."

"But we've got past that, haven't we?" she asked, still grasping her gown to her chest. "There's more to a person's personality than one moment."

"Of course there is," he agreed. "But I want to be better for you. I was so angry then. At everything. I misunderstood some things about . . . life. And I'm not that bitter man anymore."

"I know you're not," she said softly. "I wouldn't be here with you otherwise. No matter how much I wanted to learn the truth about this business with Sir Everard."

He had no time to respond because she let go of her gown then and she was standing before him in nothing more than her shift and stockings. With the fire behind her, he could see her sweet curves outlined in the light. Unable to stop himself, he reached out to touch her where her waist dipped in.

But she danced away from him. And moving to the side of the tub, she looked him in the eye then reached down and unfastened her garters, then rolled down her stockings. She took her time, just as he'd done with her buttons and by the time she was finished he was in danger of losing his control entirely.

When he reached down to lift her chemise, he knew he should turn away but a team of oxen couldn't have pulled his gaze away from his first sight of her gloriously naked.

Without a backward glance, she stepped into the hip bath and sighed as she sank into the warm water.

He was in danger of pulling her out of the bath and onto the bed when a knock sounded on the door. He made sure the screen was blocking the view of her, and opened the door to reveal the innkeeper and a couple of footmen with a table and trays of food.

The man seemed to wish to chat about everything from the weather to the state of the roads, but Cam finally had to cut him off in mid-sentence and send him on his way.

Gemma had left the bath and was rosy cheeked and dressed in a very practical flannel nightdress and dressing gown by the time he turned back to her. He felt a pang of disappointment before remembering he'd be taking off those prim garments before much time had passed.

"That smells divine," she said, padding over to the table in her bare feet. "I hadn't realized I was so hungry."

His senses once more in control, Cam took the seat opposite her. He had to admit that the food—fish stew, crusty bread and small beer—was delicious, and like Gemma he was hungrier than he'd thought.

As if by agreement, they talked about inconsequential matters while they ate. She told him about a recent encounter she and Sophia had with Squire Northman's wife, who still hadn't forgiven the ladies of Beauchamp House for an ill-fated dinner party when they first arrived. Cam related an amusing story about his brother Freddie and his angst about the prospect of his infant daughter ever being of an age to have gentleman callers.

"But why should that bother him," Gemma asked, tearing off a bit of bread. "I should think it was something that fathers took for granted."

"Freddie is the one of us who—before he was wed, mind you—had the most rakish reputation," Cam explained. He'd always found Freddie's ability to charm the wings off a ladybug a bit annoying if truth be told. It all seemed so easy for Freddie. Cam didn't hurt for female company, but he certainly didn't have the gift for easy conversation that his brothers did. Aloud, he continued, "I suppose he's afraid that his baby daughter will one day meet the latter day equivalent of . . . himself?"

Gemma laughed at that. "Poor Freddie. But at least he'll know what to look out for. It takes one to know one, after all."

It was a good point. "I'll tell him you said so," Cam said with a nod. "Though in fairness, he's been as straight as an arrow since he married Leonora. He's desperately in love with her."

Even as he said it, he wished he'd kept his mouth shut. He might be hellbent on marrying Gemma at this point, but love hadn't really entered into their conversation thus far. And he didn't wish to force it there just now either.

But, Gemma had no such reservations. "Will you be disappointed to be the brother who didn't marry for love?" she asked softly. There was something tentative in her tone, as if she knew it would be a sore subject. But his Gemma wasn't one to shirk difficult conversations.

He reached across the table to take her hand. "There might be love between us," he said seriously. "I hope there will be. There is certainly passion. And affection."

"I see how it is between my sister and Benedick," she said with a smile. "I hope it will be like that with us."

"For now, let's see how it is with us there," he nodded to the bed, which had been looming in the background throughout the meal.

With a nod, she rose. He did too, and crossed to where she stood.

Before things could become awkward between them, he pulled her against him and kissed her with all the passion he'd been holding in check.

"Yes," she said against his mouth. "The answer to your question is yes."

Without replying, he took her in his arms again and carried her the short distance to the bed.

Chapter 22

Gemma felt her heartbeat jump as he carried her to the bed, but rather than laying her down on it, he set her on her feet beside it.

"What are you doing?" she asked, puzzled.

"Removing this chastity belt of a nightdress," he said with a wry look.

But when he began to remove the dressing gown, she shooed his hands away and said primly, "You remove your clothes, sir. I will manage my own."

And without argument, his hands went to the buttons on his waistcoat and she shrugged out of the dressing gown and then began unbuttoning what really was the most unenticing flannel nightdress she'd ever seen. She paused, however, when he pulled his lawn shirt over his head.

The hint of hair she'd seen earlier when he uncoiled his neckcloth proved to trail down the center of his chest, and she took in the sight of his broad, muscled chest—the skin slightly tanned from some time spent out of doors in the sun. She'd felt its firmness with her own hands, but the sight of it, and the trail of curly dark hair that disappeared into his breeches was enough to make her mouth dry with wanting. This was what it meant to be intimate, she realized. Knowing what a man looked like out of his clothes as well as in them.

He tossed his shirt to the floor, and turned back to find her watching him.

"You seem very well made," she said, trying to maintain some dignity even as she felt her cheeks heat. Then, realizing what she'd said, she felt her ears turn red as well.

But to her relief, he didn't laugh, only said gravely, "Thank you. As are you."

And gently, as if he were trying not to spook a nervous horse, he moved his hands to where hers clutched the buttons of her nightdress and finished unbuttoning it for her. The enormity of what was to come sent a wave of emotion through her then, and she was grateful for the care he took with her. She looked down when the idea of meeting his eyes became too much, but she saw the bulge in his breeches there and looked up and focused on a freckle on his bare shoulder instead.

But then she was looking into his eyes again because he'd pushed the flannel gown off her shoulders and it fell with a shushing sound to the floor.

"My bosom is far too small," she said as she felt his eyes roam over her. "And I'm too fleshy around the middle."

She was about to continue with a critique of her legs, but he stopped her with his mouth. His voice husky he said to her, "You are the most beautiful thing I've ever seen."

He pulled away, and cupped her breast. "See how it fits perfectly in my hand."

She glanced down and the sight of his dark hand on her pale skin sent a wave of heat through her.

"And in my mouth," he said lifting her onto the bed, then following her up.

Just his words were enough to send a stab of sensation to her core.

And then he suited his words to deed and took her rosy nipple into his hot mouth and she thought she would combust. "Oh." She clutched at his shoulders as if she could pull him closer. Then he stroked a thumb over her other breast and she felt another jolt of fire run between her breast and her center.

"Perfection," he said, his deep voice vibrating through her as he kissed his way down her breast and over her ribs. "As soft as silk and so responsive."

A restlessness was taking over her, however, and she wanted him back with his mouth on her.

"You're as well formed as one of Elgin's marbles come to life," he said opening his mouth over the dip of her waist and then kissing his way further down.

Gemma was awash in desire at the sensations he roused, but when she felt his hand grip her hip, she realized what lay at the destination his mouth seemed intent on visiting. "Wait, Cam, where are you . . . ?"

She felt his laugh softly against her lower belly. Pushing himself up a little, he looked up at her and she was taken aback by the view of him looking up her naked body at her.

"Do you trust me, sweet?" he asked, his eyes dark with passion. "Because I very much want to kiss you here. And I think it will make your pleasure when I take you better."

"You think?" she asked, suddenly very aware of the fact that this was the strangest conversation she'd ever engaged in.

He had the decency to look abashed. "I'm afraid I don't have any experience bedding virgins," he said with a slight shrug. "But the last thing I want is to give you pain and I know there can be pain the first time . . ."

His expression betrayed his concern about causing her discomfort and Gemma felt her chest constrict at the knowledge. He was so much kinder than he revealed to the world.

"Very well," she said with a small nod. "If you think this will help with . . ."

And without waiting for her to finish her statement, he shifted so that her knees were over his shoulders. Her complaint, however, lodged in her throat as she felt his hot tongue slide up the center of her, right where she hadn't even known she needed him.

It was as if her body came alive at his touch, each new stroke of his tongue stoking the fire within her to higher flames. When he added his fingers, stroking then gently pressing inside of her, she cried out. That was what she needed. There, his fingers filling her. Of their own volition, her hips bucked against his staying hands, and she felt an overwhelming rush of excitement as she spiraled over some imaginary precipice into darkness.

When she came back to herself, she was slightly embarrassed, but her limbs were far too limp to do anything about it.

She felt Cam kiss her thigh before he moved up her body. Somewhere along the line he must have shed his breeches because she felt his strong legs slide against hers as he shifted to kneel between them.

His kiss was remarkably tender as he slid her knee over his hip, placing his arousal at the heart of her, and the press of him, when it came, was uncomfortable but not painful. She waited for him to be fully seated, and when he stopped, she exhaled slowly.

"All right?" She could feel the tension in his body, and knew his patience was not without cost to him. But he made no complaint.

She reached up a hand to stroke her thumb over his furrowed brow. "Yes," she said softly, memorizing his expression in this moment so that she'd remember it always. And before she finished the syllable he began to withdraw.

This was different from the anxiety of that first stroke, and Gemma felt bereft as he left her.

"Can't go slow," Cam said, in a voice both strained and apologetic, as he began to move faster and Gemma thought she would weep with relief. With each thrust, she struggled to hold on to him, and of their own volition her knees clasped him to her. His movements sent her into another frenzy of sensation, and she began to spiral up, up, up into the ether once more, even as she heard the sound of their breaths, and felt every touch of skin and sweat between them.

"Come for me, sweet," he said as his movements became more desperate and unable to hold back, she let herself fly.

As she let the feeling of bliss overtake her, she heard him cry out her name.

Not wanting to crush her, Cam flipped them so that she was lying on his chest, though it took every ounce of strength he had left to do it.

Never in his life had he felt more inclined to sleep than at this moment.

"Just a few minutes," he promised her, kissing the top of head as he struggled to get his breath back.

As it happened, however, a few minutes turned into a few hours and when he awoke again it was to find she'd moved to settle at his side, her gloriously naked leg entwined in his and her hair a tangle of curls.

He let his gaze drift lazily over her as he considered the consequences of what had been, all things considered, the most important act of his adult life.

He knew she'd been intent on ending their betrothal once the year was over. He'd been intent upon it too. But once he'd made the decision to wed her, it had become a goal he had no intention of giving up. And now that she'd lain with him, there would be no ending their betrothal. Especially not with the possibility of a child.

"You're thinking quite hard, I believe," she said, and he saw that she'd been watching him.

Her lips curved into a mischievous smile as she stretched her arms over her head.

"Thinking about you," he said, pulling her up onto his chest. Gemma gave a slight shriek at the manhandling then she sat with her knees on either side of him.

"You're going to rouse the inn with cries like that," he chided, brow raised. "Though I suppose they've already decided we're shameless newlyweds."

To his amusement, the unfazeable Miss Gemma Hastings looked abashed. "Do you think they heard us?" she asked, looking worried.

"You were quite loud at times," he said with shrug. "But," he added, "so was I, if it comes to that. I feel sure this inn has heard worse than the pair of us."

That must have relieved her concerns because she nodded, then leaned forward to kiss him. "I had no idea you had such a gift for tender talk," she said as she stroked her thumb over the stubble of his jaw. "In fact, you were much more considerate than I'd have imagined."

He let her control the kiss for a moment, letting her tongue stroke his until it was impossible to tell who was leading. When she pulled her mouth away, he stayed her torso with a hand. "Why should it surprise you I'm a considerate lover?" he asked softly.

He wasn't sure why it mattered, but he didn't want to think Gemma had thought he'd be an inconsiderate lout either.

"Well, I have no one to compare you to," she admitted with a shrug. "But, given our tendency to rip up at one another, I had thought perhaps you'd be—I don't know—more demanding, I suppose."

"And what did you find?"

She grinned. "That you were gentle and sweet," she said, laying her head on his chest, and stretching her legs out over the top of his. "But also, forceful when I needed you to be."

"Forceful, eh?" he stroked a hand down her spine to the soft roundness of her bottom. "You liked that?"

"Very much," she said, toying with his chest hair.

"Gentle and sweet and forceful," he said. "Quite a combination."

"But you can change them up when the mood suits," she said with equanimity.

"Thank you so much, my dear," he said wryly. "And what of my wishes?"

"Of course you must tell me what you like too," she said, and she sat up again and looked down at him. A long lock of dark blonde hair fell down to cover her breast and he couldn't help but reach out and wrap it around his finger.

"Cam," she said, calling his attention back to her face. "I mean it, you mustn't feel as if you can't tell me what you want. I can assure you that I won't hold back from telling you."

He heard the note of concern in her voice and let go of her hair and took her hand. Kissing her palm, he assured her, "I will. Though I'm sorry to say that my wants are quite uncomplicated. I want you, however I can get you. The ways and iterations aren't all that important."

Her brow furrowed and he watched in amusement as she considered that there were likely more iterations than she'd previously imagined.

"Do you mean to say you do not wish to take me bent over a chair?" she asked, with a frown. And suddenly he could think of nothing in the world he wanted more. He glanced at the wooden chairs they'd sat in for supper and considered if it were feasible.

She must have read his expression right because she

laughed. "So, perhaps your wants aren't quite as uncomplicated as you'd thought," she said wryly.

He shrugged. "Perhaps not," he agreed. "I will amend my statement and say that I very much want you in every way possible. You are the part of the equation that cannot vary."

"I feel sure Daphne would have something to say about your arithmetic," Gemma said.

And having decided they'd talked enough—especially given that his prick had very much liked the chair idea and wanted to be appeased, he flipped her onto her back again.

"You cannot keep doing that," she scolded, though it was evident from her wide smile that she wasn't as unhappy as she seemed. "What if I wished to control things?"

"Later," he told her, "you told me you liked it when I'm forceful."

He pressed her hands above her head and held them there with one hand while his other stroked over her straining breast, and down her belly.

"Yes," she said in a husky tone. "I do like it."

"Good," he said against her neck.

And when his hand reached the wetness at her center, he stroked over her once before guiding himself into her. With one swift thrust he filled her and they both cried out with relief at the joining.

"Let me touch you," she said, pulling her hands. "Oh please, Cam."

But he lifted her knee over his hip and thrust again. "Not yet. Trust me, sweet." He leaned down to kiss her.

And as he built up the fire between them, using the friction of her nipples against his chest to stoke them both, she began to twist beneath him.

"Cam," she exhaled as she followed his strokes with her hips and they began to move in tandem. He felt her inner muscles clutch him and he quickened his pace bringing

her toward an edge that both of them longed to go over.
When he felt the telltale tingle in his spine, he let go of her
hands and she cried out again, the sudden freedom spurring
her climax. And then they were both soaring over the edge
into pleasure's abyss.

Chapter 23

When Gemma awoke the next morning, feeling sated and a little sore, she was disappointed to find herself in the bed alone. But, much as she would like to remain here forever, there were still important things to be done outside of their cocoon of bliss. So when the maid scratched on the bed-chamber door and entered with hot water for washing, she welcomed the girl in and set about putting herself to rights.

By some miracle they'd managed to brush out her gown and pelisse and she'd be able to wear it to Lord Crutchley's without fear of disgracing herself.

She was putting the final pins into the simple chignon she'd managed with her hair—thanks to pins borrowed from the maid since she couldn't find where hers had gone the night before—when Cam returned. He too had had his waterlogged coats from the day before brushed and dried out and his cravat was even snowy white again.

"I thought we'd set out after breakfast," he said, clearly mindful of the maid's presence.

When the girl was gone, and Gemma had turned to face him, he stepped forward and kissed her properly.

"Good morning," he said, pulling away, though he did take her hands in his.

"I missed you," she said simply. It was the truth, and if she were going to be in this with him she wouldn't suppress her feelings.

"I wanted to let you sleep for as long as you could," he said with a smile. Then, ruefully, he added, "And I wasn't sure I could keep myself from reaching for you again."

"But I wouldn't have minded," she told him, her heart beating faster at the thought.

"That's precisely why I had to leave," he told her firmly. "You might not care about your poor, ill-used body, but I do."

"Your being the sensible one is very tedious," she complained. "Though I will admit to some soreness, so perhaps you were right."

He pulled her arm through his, but not before kissing her hand. "If we are to find your lizard then you need to be in fighting shape."

At the mention of the Beauchamp Lizard, Gemma sighed. "Right again. So let's be off."

It took nearly an hour for them to breakfast in a private dining room, and by the time Cam lifted her into his curricle, it was almost mid-morning.

They made good time, however, and since yesterday's rain had all but passed, leaving in its wake the same cloudy skies and brisk winds that had come before it, they remained dry if chilled.

The innkeeper had given Cam the direction of the Crutchley estate, and when the curricle turned into the evergreen-lined drive, Gemma sent up a tiny prayer that he'd have the information they needed.

Grooms were at the ready to take the reins from Cam and when he helped Gemma down, they were greeted by a dour-looking butler flanked by bewigged, liveried footmen.

"You're expected, Lord Cameron, Lady Cameron," said the butler as he gestured them into the imposing wide doors of the sandstone manor house.

Gemma's eyes widened at the words, and a glance at Cam revealed him to be as surprised as she was.

How did anyone at Lord Crutchley's estate know about their ruse at the inn? Besides the innkeeper and his staff, only Lord Paley had . . .

As if conjured by her thought, that gentleman himself stepped forward and took her hand. "Lady Cameron," he said with a silky smile, "How good to see you again."

"Paley," said Cam from beside her. She hadn't noticed the way he held her against his side, as if to protect her from the urbane gentleman before them. "What a surprise."

"Only if you think it a surprise to find me at my godfather's estate," said Lord Paley with a charming smile that didn't meet his eyes.

"Godfather?" Gemma shook her head. The possibility of a connection between the men hadn't even occurred to her.

"But let's not discuss it in the hallway," said Paley with a welcoming gesture. "Come into the drawing room. Lord Crutchley is quite eager to meet you both."

Not as eager, Gemma guessed, as she was to meet him. There were many things she wished to question the man about, not least of which was more about what Lord Paley might have told him about the goings-on at Pearson Close and Beauchamp House.

Feeling Cam's strong hand at her lower back, she followed the viscount up the double-sided staircase and into a lushly carpeted hallway.

The drawing room was a lavish chamber with brightly colored wall hangings and floor to ceiling windows that looked out over what was, at this time of year, a rather dour landscape.

Before the fire sat an elderly gentleman, who rose upon their entrance.

"Miss Hastings," he said as they neared him. "What a delight to finally make your acquaintance."

She curtseyed before him, then offered him her hand, which he kissed.

Behind her, she heard Cam clear his throat before saying, "I'm afraid she is no longer Miss Hastings, Crutchley, but Lady Cameron Lisle."

And as Cam stepped forward to exchange bows with the older gentleman, Crutchley laughed. "Too right, my boy. If this were my lady I'd be quick to claim her as my own as well. Especially if, as Paley has told me, she's the gift of knowing wheat from chaff."

Before Gemma could respond to that, Paley gestured for them to all be seated and once he was also in a chair, he said, "I wish you'd confided in me when we met yesterday that you intended to visit my godfather. But I suppose you had other things on your mind."

The insinuation hung in the air between them for a moment before Lord Crutchley spoke up, apparently oblivious to his nephew's gaffe. "I must admit, I have wished to make your acquaintance, Lady Cameron, ever since I learned Lady Celeste had chosen you to be one of her heiresses. That lady had as good an eye for fossils as anyone I've ever known and it wounded me dreadfully to know she was taken from this world so prematurely."

"But I don't understand," Gemma said with a frown. "How did you even know who I was?"

"Oh I didn't, I didn't," he assured her with a wave of a gnarled hand. "But I did know Celeste, and if she chose you to be the keeper of her collection, well, then that was endorsement enough for me. I may not move about in local society much anymore but I do have my ways of learning about the goings-on in the area. Paley, for instance, has been most informative about the goings-on at Beauchamp House and of course the gathering of fossil hunters at Pearson Close."

"Imagine my surprise," Lord Paley said before Gemma could respond, "when I learned that the collection at Beauchamp House I'd so recently toured was one which he'd played a role in shaping with Lady Celeste."

"You're overstating it, boy," said the older man with a frown. "I merely accompanied Celeste on a few of her fossil-hunting expeditions. That collection was all Celeste's doing. Especially once we had our falling-out."

This was the first Gemma had heard of a rift, and she risked a glance at Cam to see if he too was surprised. His answering nod told her he was.

"I had seen some mention of you in her collection notebooks," Gemma said, trying not to appear too eager for information lest Lord Crutchley should regret his confidences. "But nothing about an argument."

"Oh it wasn't really an argument, my dear," said the old man. "It was really more wounded pride on my part."

He shook his head at the memory, then continued, "You see, she found a fossil skull that she was convinced held the key to some major understanding of the way that animal life developed on the Sussex coast. Found it right there on the bit of shore beneath Beauchamp House. And despite her trying to keep quiet about it until she was able to do some investigation into it, word spread among the collecting circles. Well, since I was there with her when she found the blasted thing, she thought I'd been the one to spread the news. It wasn't me, of course, and she even went so far as to take measures to hide the thing away because she became convinced someone would try to steal it from her."

"And did you know where she hid it?" Gemma asked, her breath catching.

"No," Lord Crutchley said with a mournful shake of his head. "And what's more, I didn't ever talk to her again after that dustup between us. I was stubborn in those days, and that bit of doubt on her part was enough to make me storm off in a huff and never go back. But I always regretted it. Always."

To Gemma's surprise, he wiped away a tear. "I'm a sentimental old fool, you see, and I thought we'd make it up again some way. But she was gone before someday ever came."

"I feel sure she would have liked to see you again," Gemma said quietly. Having read her benefactress's journals and other writings, she knew that while proud, Lady Celeste had been a loving person and she didn't doubt that if Lord Crutchley had initiated contact with her, Lady Celeste would have welcomed him with open arms.

"So you have no idea where she might have hidden the fossilized skull?" Cam asked, changing the subject back to the fossil.

"I don't," said Lord Crutchley. "Though we did have a mad conversation once about the best place to hide one's valuables. I thought of it because Paley, here, mentioned that you'd found a particularly impressive skull on that same stretch of shore, Miss H—er, Lady Cameron."

"And what was that?" Gemma held her breath, not quite daring to hope what he was about to say. They'd come here to ask the man about his dealings with Lady Celeste, but if he could give them some way to secure the provenance of the skull, they'd be that much closer to finding the person who stole it.

"Well," Crutchley said with a laugh, "we decided the best place to hide a thing was in plain sight, and for a thing dug up from the earth, that would be back in the same place where you'd found it."

At Lord Crutchley's confirmation that Gemma's fossil and the Beauchamp Lizard were one and the same, Cam saw Gemma's eyes light with triumph for a split second before she shuttered her gaze.

"Of course," Crutchley continued, "I would have no way of knowing if Celeste followed through on the scheme. For all I know, she locked the Beauchamp Lizard away in a safe place. But I must admit when Paley told me about the fossil you'd found, Lady Cameron, I did wonder."

"The business with Sir Everard does make it seem even more likely that the fossil is one and the same," Lord Paley added with a shrewd look. "Though I do wonder how he could possibly have known where to search for it. I only found out about my godfather's involvement with Lady Celeste last evening, so it wasn't me."

"And you've never met Sir Everard yourself, Lord Crutchley?" Gemma asked, frowning. Cam could all but hear the theories spinning through her head.

Then, another possibility occurred to him.

"Was there anyone else who might have heard your discussion with Lady Celeste about possible hiding places, Crutchley?" Cam asked. While he thought it was more likely Sir Everard had merely stumbled upon Gemma's work, there was something a bit too coincidental about the blackguard's boasts that it might be the famed Beauchamp Lizard.

"Or," Gemma added, "someone she might have confided in?"

Crutchley's lined face twisted into an expression of distaste. "There was one person who spent a great deal of time around her that year, but I never thought she trusted him enough to confide something like that in him. And if she had told him, he'd have stolen it long ago."

"Who was it, Lord Crutchley?" Gemma's impatience was beginning to show, Cam thought, noting her white knuckles on the arms of her chair.

"I suppose there's no harm in telling you," the old man said with a frown. "Though I know she was dreadfully embarrassed about the whole matter at the time."

Cam was beginning to understand Gemma's impatience.

Finally, though, Crutchley continued.

"I always understood that Celeste had decided at a certain point that she would never marry," he explained. "Especially as by that time she'd built up the estate at Beauchamp House on her own and was known as a scholar in her own right on many subjects including fossils. But there was a man who wanted desperately to marry her. I always suspected it was more because he wanted to own her, like a specimen in his collection."

Cam saw Gemma shiver at the description. He'd certainly known men like that—who saw women not as their own persons but instead as objects to possess. He was glad, suddenly, that Lady Celeste, who by all accounts was an independent and strong woman, had managed to evade this scoundrel.

"You may be wondering why I am so slow to reveal who this man was," Crutchley said with a rueful shake of his head. "But it's because in the years since Lady Celeste discovered the Beauchamp Lizard, he's come to be well known in the world of fossil collecting, though he himself has never once been the one to dig up his own specimens."

Something about the description made the hair on the back of Cam's neck stand on end.

It couldn't be.

But Crutchley's next words confirmed it.

"I believe you both are well acquainted with him," he said, with a nod to both Cam and Paley. "I'm speaking, of course, of Maximillian Pearson."

"Pearson?" Gemma asked, her shock evident. "But how is that possible? He cannot be old enough to have courted Lady Celeste twenty years ago, for one thing."

"Oh he was a stripling at the time," Crutchley assured her. "Barely twenty years old and yet he thought himself cock of the walk. He didn't care if Celeste wanted him or not. He wanted her and that was what mattered."

"But surely his parents," Gemma protested. "I cannot imagine any young heir's father being sanguine about his son marrying a lady so many years his senior."

"His father died when young Max was barely fifteen," Crutchley explained. "And his mother was no match for his strong will. Though Celeste did try to speak to her about the way he wouldn't take no for an answer. It was no help, obviously."

"Since she didn't marry Pearson," Cam said, "then I can only assume something managed to convince him to let her be."

"I'm afraid, Lady Cameron, that it might be a tale too delicate for your ears."

Cam almost laughed when Gemma tried to control her impulse to scoff at the notion.

Instead, however, she said simply, "I am a married lady, Lord Crutchley. I'm sure it will not scandalize me overmuch."

When the elderly gentleman turned his beseeching gaze to Cam, he shrugged. "I will not make up my wife's mind for her," he said. Though it did amuse him to note how quickly he'd come to think of her as his wife in the twelve hours or so since their pretend marriage.

"If you insist, Lady Cameron," said the elderly lord. "One

afternoon, not long after Celeste found the lizard skull, we were . . . ah . . . behaving amorously on the shore below Beauchamp House when Pearson came looking for her. He had become suspicious of the amount of time we spent together, and made it his practice to simply show up without invitation at odd hours, in an effort to ensure that he had no serious rivals."

Gemma's cheeks turned a bit pink, but other than that, she remained unfazed by the confession. "And what did he do?" she asked, frowning. "I cannot imagine how dreadful it must have been for Lady Celeste to be spied on in such a manner."

"Oh, she was furious," Crutchley confirmed. "As was I. I wanted to call him out but she wouldn't let me. Pearson himself was more shocked than angry. He was, after all, little more than a lad. He'd put her on a pedestal and hadn't considered that she might be, as a woman some two decades older, someone with desires that he knew nothing about."

"And that ended things for him?" Cam asked. It was a bit difficult to believe that a man who was so covetous would simply give up at the first sign of difficulty.

"It was the beginning of the end," Crutchley said. "He called on her the next day and informed her that he was disappointed, but would forgive her if she promised she would agree never to see me again. Of course she refused."

"Of course she did," Gemma said with a scowl. "The nerve of the man."

"He took that badly, but he spent a few more weeks trying to bully her into accepting him. But gradually, he became more and more withdrawn. By the time she and I parted ways, he no longer left his estate. And, I'm quite sure it was the beginning of his hatred of all women. It wasn't until his mother's death some ten years later that he was able to eradicate all women from his life—even the servants. From what Paley has told me, he's become a total recluse now."

"You mentioned, Lord Crutchley," Gemma said, bringing the conversation back to their reasons for being here, "that you thought Pearson might have known Lady Celeste had hidden the lizard skull where she found it. Why is that?"

"That day he spied on us," Crutchley explained, "was the same day we discussed her fears that someone would steal the fossil. It was also not long afterward that Pearson became a fossil collector himself."

That was a bit of news Cam hadn't expected. "You mean to say Pearson had no interest in stones and fossils until Lady Celeste rejected him?"

"I think at first," Crutchley said, "the boy considered it was a way to take something from her. She wanted to add to her collection, so he wanted to ensure that the fossils she most coveted she didn't get."

"That's certainly mean-spirited," said Lord Paley with a frown. "I must admit, I had no notion that Pearson knew Lady Celeste at all, much less that he'd once been fixated on her. He must be livid that Lady Celeste left her collection to you."

It was news to Cam as well, and he couldn't help but wonder if Pearson's vendetta against Lady Celeste went beyond the lady's death.

"But if he knew that she planned to rebury it," Gemma asked, brows furrowed, "then why did he not go dig it up himself ages ago?"

"Perhaps he didn't put two and two together," Cam offered. "He was likely far more focused on the—happenings—on the beach. Remember it was Celeste he wanted then, not her fossils. It was only later that he decided to compete with her in that arena. And by then, the lizard had become an unseen legend. No one knew where it was. And after a time, it was forgotten."

"For all that he began to fancy himself an expert," Lord Crutchley offered, "it was always quite clear to me that Pearson wasn't particularly gifted in the brain box. He was far more about spending his coin to acquire things than in learning about why they mattered."

The visit had been even more illuminating than Cam could have imagined. He was about to rise and usher Gemma back out to his curricle when they all heard a disturbance downstairs.

"So many visitors," said Lord Crutchley with ill-disguised excitement. It made Cam feel a pang of pity for the old gentleman, who clearly craved company.

But when the butler appeared at the door to the drawing room, his words made him switch his pity from Crutchley to himself.

"The Reverend Lord Benedick Lisle and Lady Benedick Lisle," the servant said as Ben and Sophia entered looking travel-worn and somewhat harassed.

Well, perhaps only Ben. Sophia looked happy enough.

"What a relief it is to find you are both safe," Sophia said with a smile. "You must forgive us, gentlemen. We were expecting them back—"

"Dear Sophia," Gemma interrupted her, and Cam noticed that she was trying to communicate something to her sister with her eyes, "we did tell you that we would be paying a call at Lord Crutchley's estate after our wedding night in Lyme."

At the words "wedding night" Cam noticed a muscle in his brother's jaw jump.

Still, to his relief, Benedick smiled indulgently and said, "You know how your sister worries about you, Gemma. I fear she is having a difficult time—and I admit, I am as well—believing that you and my brother have married. It seems only yesterday we were discussing the surprise of your betrothal."

Cam was grateful for his brother's going along with their ruse, but he knew with the surety of a lifetime as Ben's younger brother that he would pay dearly for it later.

Chapter 24

Gemma watched the interplay between the Lisle brothers as Viscount Paley introduced Sophia and Ben to his godfather.

Benedick, it turned out, was a far better actor than she'd supposed because it was obvious to her, at least, that he wanted nothing more than to drag his brother out of the drawing room by the ear.

For his part, Lord Crutchley just seemed delighted to have more visitors.

"It's delightful to see you both again so soon," said Lord Paley as he rang for refreshments. It was clear to Gemma, at least, that he spent a great deal of time in Crutchley's house, which made her feel somewhat better for the elderly man's situation. It had bothered her once she learned of his connection with Lady Celeste that he seemed to be lonely for company.

"It's certainly a surprise," Benedick agreed as he moved to stand with his back to the fire. "Though you mustn't allow us to burden you with unexpected visitors. We merely wished to assuage my wife's worry for her sister's welfare. Now that we've done that, we will all leave you to your peace and quiet, of course."

"But that's absurd," Lord Crutchley protested. "You cannot mean to make the drive back to Little Seaford without a meal at the very least."

And that was how the party from Beauchamp House ended up partaking of the midday meal at the home of Lord Crutchley.

It felt somewhat absurd, Gemma thought, considering that she and Cam were pretending to be married, while her sister and brother-in-law pretended to believe it. And Lord Crutchley and Lord Paley believed the pretense to be the truth.

Sheridan couldn't have written a more absurd farce.

The delay of their departure, however, allowed her and Cam to explain what they'd learned from Lord Crutchley about his time spent with Lady Celeste and just how much they'd not known about Maximillian Pearson's history with her.

"What a dreadful time Lady Celeste must have had with him watching her all the time," Sophia said with a frown. "I am no longer surprised that she chose not to marry. I wonder that she ever entertained the prospect at all."

"Oh, she was made of stern stuff," Lord Crutchley assured her. "Your benefactress was one of the most intelligent and strong-minded ladies I ever had the pleasure to meet."

He gave a wink in Gemma's direction. "Though I believe your sister may be the first I've met in years to hold a candle to Celeste. If I were twenty years younger, and I'd met her first, I'd have given Lord Cameron a run for his money."

Gemma blushed at the elderly gentleman's blandishments. "I'm quite sure I don't deserve such praise, my lord."

But Cam surprised her by agreeing with their host. "Gemma is the cleverest lady of my acquaintance, Crutchley. But I must admit to a bit a relief at having won her before she made your acquaintance, for I feel quite sure I'd have had a time convincing her I was worthy."

"If you would believe it, Crutchley," said Ben drolly, "these two were at loggerheads with one another only a week ago. I still can't quite believe they're wed."

Gemma suppressed her desire to kick her brother-in-law in the shin. But Sophia must have done it for her if his sudden yelp were anything to go by.

The meal passed without further incident, and soon enough, the sisters and brothers were taking their leave of Crutchley and his godson.

"Thank you all for giving an old man a chance to relive happy memories," their host said as he took Gemma's hands in his. "I know without a doubt that Celeste would have been pleased as punch to know she'd left her collection in the hands of such a special lady."

"Thank you for sharing your stories," she told him, then kissing him on the cheek. "I feel as if I know Lady Celeste even better now. And I hope we'll be able to find her Beauchamp Lizard and put it back in her collection where it belongs."

When Lord Paley took his leave of them, Gemma noticed that he pulled Cam to the side and they talked quietly for a few minutes while the carriages were brought around. She filed that bit of information away to query him about later.

It was decided that since Benedick and Sophia had brought the brougham from Beauchamp House, Gemma and Cam would ride in the more comfortable closed carriage with them while one of the grooms drove Cam's curricle back to Little Seaford. She couldn't have imagined a less congenial prospect than a four-hour drive with her angry sister and brother-in-law—because she was under no illusion that their sunny conversation at Lord Crutchley's had been anything but a polite fiction for the sake of their host—seated across from them.

And once the carriage pulled away from Crutchley's house, the fireworks began.

"Of all the mutton-headed, arrogant, reckless things you have ever done, Cameron," Ben said, his voice eerily calm despite the tenor of his words, "this is by far the worst."

Something about the way he immediately blamed their situation on Cam made Gemma's hackles rise. "I am not a young innocent being led into misbehavior, Benedick," she argued. "It was my idea for us to travel to meet Crutchley in the first place. And we couldn't have accounted for what would happen with the weather. So, you may keep your sharp words to yourself."

"Do you know what could happen to you if word gets out that the two of you spent the night together in an inn, Gemma?" Benedick asked, not backing down from his position one bit. "If you thought the risk from what happened in Pearson Close was great, then this escapade is far worse. You were even seen by Paley, for heaven's sake."

"But Paley thinks we're wed," Cam said, squeezing Gemma's hand as she slipped it into his. "And we will be as soon as I can procure a special license."

She felt a pang of conscience over the rift she'd caused between the brothers. She'd never considered that Benedick would take his role as her pseudo-guardian so seriously. A glance at Sophia revealed her sister was concerned about his anger over the situation as well.

"That's not the point," Ben was saying in response to Cam. "And lying about your marital status is hardly the way to begin your life together."

"Dearest," Sophia said, placing a hand on her husband's arm. "You must remember that none of us at Beauchamp House has precisely followed the usual order of things when it comes to marriage. Even you and I didn't wait until we—"

"But that was different," Benedick said with a frown. "We didn't go about telling people we were wed when we were not. And I dashed well knew I intended to make good on my promise to marry you."

As soon as he spoke the words, Gemma felt Cam stiffen beside her. A glance in her sister's direction told her that she'd also realized just how far over the line Benedick's words had been.

"What. Did. You. Say?" Cam asked, his tone as deadly quiet as his brother's had been.

"I'm sure he didn't mean it like it came out, did you, Benedick?" Gemma clung to Cam's arm as if she feared he would launch himself across the carriage at the vicar.

To his credit, Ben sighed and rubbed a hand over his face. "I don't know, damn it. I don't know anything anymore."

"You just suggested that I seduced and intend to abandon your sister-in-law," Cam said coldly, "so I think if you didn't believe it, you were being just as reckless as you accused me of being."

"It was badly worded," Ben said with a shrug, "but you must admit that you've never shown any inclination to marriage. And you certainly had no particular fondness for Gemma before this business with the Beauchamp Lizard."

"Nor did you show any particular desire to marry before you met Sophia," Cam protested. "And relationships change. Gemma and I may have argued a great deal, but that doesn't mean I didn't want her."

At that confession, Gemma wanted to tell him she'd wanted him too, but decided that might be too intimate a conversation for the present moment.

"I didn't say you didn't want her," Benedick said. "Just that you didn't want to marry her."

"Perhaps we can save this conversation for later," Sophia said before Cam could speak up. "After all, you may both wish to speak more freely and that doesn't seem possible while Gemma and I are here, does it?"

Ben had the grace to look abashed. "I hadn't considered your feelings, Gemma," he said with a look of apology. "Perhaps we had better save this until later, as Sophia suggested."

But Cam shook his head. "I have no secrets from Gemma. She knows that we've both undergone a change of heart over the last week or so. And I freely admit that I had no intention of marrying last week. This week is different, however."

"Is that what you want, Gemma?" Ben asked her, his sympathy now making her want to throw it back in his face for the way he'd hurt his brother. "For us to speak freely, I mean."

"Yes," she said. "Don't hold back on my account."

Sophia made a sound of dismay, but didn't speak up.

"Very well," Benedick said with the air of a man who was doing his duty but not with any kind of relish, "didn't you tell me just a few days ago that you preferred to marry someone entirely different from Gemma?"

Since this confession on Cam's part had been one that Gemma herself overheard, she should be inured to its power to hurt her. And yet, it still stung.

"That was a stupid thing said in the heat of the moment," Cam said, and he brought Gemma's hand up to kiss her palm. "Gemma and I discussed it and she knows I regretted saying it."

She had forgiven him the slight days ago, but she could feel from the tension in his body that Cam still carried the guilt of it.

"I think perhaps rather than calling your brother to account," she said to Benedick with a scowl, "you should consider that I am the one who was more against the notion of marriage. If anyone is likely to run away before we are married, it will most certainly be me."

She felt three sets of eyes on her.

"What?" Cam demanded, turning to face her. "Why would you do that?"

She patted him on the hand. "I didn't say I would do it, just that of the two of us, I would be the one more likely to scarper off. You know it's true. If you are stubborn, I am positively a brick wall of will."

Sophia laughed. "My money would be on Gemma as the one to run as well."

Ben looked at his wife in disbelief.

"What?" she asked with a shrug. "I know my sister. She's quite correct about her stubbornness."

Her husband pinched the bridge of his nose. Gemma had no doubt that he was regretting his decision to bring up the matter at all.

Cam, meanwhile, was still concerned about the possibility that Gemma would follow through on her hypothetical plan to run away. "You won't leave before we marry, though, right?"

She was touched to hear the tinge of worry in his voice. "Of course I won't," she said, hugging his arm. "It was just a silly comparison. I have no intention of leaving before you marry me."

He relaxed a little. And mindless of the presence of the other couple in the carriage, he kissed her.

Then, realizing exactly what she'd just said, she pulled away and added, "Nor *after* you marry me either."

They all laughed, and the mood inside the carriage lightened considerably.

"Good," he said, lifting her hand to his lips, "because I love you."

The rest of the drive was far less eventful, though Cam felt as if he'd run naked through the streets of Little Seaford after confessing his love to Gemma in front of his brother and sister-in-law.

It was not lost on him that she didn't say she loved him too, but of course that wasn't something he required. After all, it had only been a few days—as had been pointed out to him multiple times today—since they'd even come to like one another. He could hardly expect her to tumble head over ears into love at the same rate he had.

Still, the ease with which she took his decision that he would return to stay at the vicarage when the brougham drew up before Beauchamp House was troubling.

"I'll see you in the morning," she told him as he handed her down from the carriage. "We need to pay a call on Pearson to question him about the fossil but I am far too fatigued to do so now."

Her knowing smile reminded him of the reasons why she was so tired, and he felt a bit better at her sending him away.

But only a bit.

Her next words, however, made some degree of sense.

"I wish you could stay here," she said as she leaned into him, "but I don't wish to add more reason for strife between you and your brother. I'm quite cross with him already."

At her defense of him, Cam smiled. "Do not be too angry with him," he told her. "Ben has had to endure years of my selfishness and I think he genuinely doesn't want to see you hurt."

"But what about you?" she asked, still not convinced. "I could just as easily hurt you."

He kissed her quickly. "You could, at that. But I hope you can find it in yourself to forgive him. For my sake as well as Sophia's. Because I think it would be very uncomfortable for her if you loathed her beloved husband."

She lifted her chin. "I don't loathe him."

"Good." He grinned at her. "Now, you'd better get inside and show yourself to Serena. I have a feeling she will have a few words for you."

At the mention of her chaperone, she sighed. "I cannot wait until we are wed in truth so that I need only answer to myself."

Cam considered telling her that she would have to answer to him, but he'd had enough arguments for one day.

He escorted her up the steps of Beauchamp House then jogged back down them and climbed into the carriage with his brother and his wife.

Soon, he thought as he watched the house fade from view. Soon he would be entitled to go inside with Gemma and shut the door behind them.

Chapter 25

Gemma had no sooner stepped through the door of Beauchamp House when she was waylaid by Serena, who, rather than scolding, simply enveloped her in a fierce hug.

"I thought you'd be furious," Gemma said with a startled laugh once her chaperone had let her go.

To her further surprise, Serena was wiping tears from her eyes.

"I guessed you were with Cam, of course." The lady, who was most often as calm as her name implied, shook her head a little. "But after the dangers that the others faced when they began digging into my aunt's past, I feared that you both might have been kidnapped or worse."

That possibility hadn't even occurred to Gemma and she suddenly understood why both Ben and Sophia had been angry as well as relieved upon finding them.

"I am so sorry," she said, grasping her chaperone's hand. "It didn't occur to me that you'd worry on that score. I did tell George that we'd be back last night but we were delayed because of weather and—"

"—and now will be married by special license as soon as Cam can obtain one, I'll wager," said Serena with a twist of her lips. "I will go down in the annals of chaperonage as the most incompetent ever. That will make four of you who managed to slip past my ruthless attempts to preserve your reputations."

Though she said it with a bit of a laugh, Gemma knew she genuinely felt the sting of her failure. "And four who have married happily," she reminded her. "That is no small thing, I believe."

"Come, let's go upstairs and you can tell me what you've discovered in your search for your fossil," Serena said.

Once they were in Gemma's bedchamber, Serena called for tea and a bath for her charge and while they waited, Gemma filled her in on the details of the journey—minus the pretend marriage and night in the inn—and when she began to tell of the relationship between Lady Celeste and Lord Crutchley, Serena looked thoughtful.

"I think I remember that," she said with a faraway look. "Kerr, Maitland and I were children, but I do remember one summer in particular when my aunt had one gentleman friend who brought along his . . . godson, I think it was? My cousins will perhaps remember more of the time than I do. I was only Jeremy's age, but I do remember the godson because he was a bit of a terror. He broke my favorite dolly, you see and that was the most—"

Gemma interrupted her. "Godson? Are you sure of it? Do you remember his name?"

She was furious with herself for not realizing it sooner. Had Paley been following their every move with them none the wiser?

"Toby?"

"Topher?" Gemma asked, with a rising sense of excitement remembering that Topher was sometimes used as a diminutive form of Christopher—as in Christopher, Lord Paley.

"Yes," Serena said with a nod. "I knew it was something

I'd never heard before because I remarked upon it. I think that's why he retaliated with my doll, if I recall correctly."

Serena's maid arrived then with the tea tray, and despite her earlier fatigue, Gemma moved to the wardrobe and removed her cloak.

"Where are you going?" Serena asked. "You just returned. What about your bath?"

"I need to speak to Cam," Gemma explained as she pulled the hood of her cloak over her head. "And it can't wait until morning."

"Gemma, you just apologized for running off with him yesterday."

She paused in the doorway. "I know, but please trust me. I think I know who killed Sir Everard. And we have to alert Mr. Northman."

Not waiting to hear Serena's reply, she hurried down the hall toward the cellar entrance to the tunnel.

Cam felt at loose ends almost as soon as he entered the vicarage with Sophia and his brother.

It felt wrong to have left Gemma at Beauchamp House.

They'd spent the past two days in one another's pockets and her absence was a physical ache. An ache that had nothing to do with the intimacies they'd shared and everything to do with the love he'd professed for her.

He closed the door to his bedchamber in the vicarage, having decided to allow his brother and his wife some time alone without his interference. He had little doubt that Sophia would have some choice words for Benedick after his accusations in the carriage.

The knowledge that his brother thought him capable of seducing and abandoning Gemma had stung. How could it not have? But not as much as it would have if he hadn't known, deep down in his bones, that the accusation was dead wrong.

He knew better than anyone what his intentions had been when he entered that inn with her, and there was nothing for him to be ashamed of.

And Gemma knew that too, if her leave-taking kiss had been anything to judge by. It did bother him that she'd not returned his sentiment, but he knew better than to rush his fences. Especially in such a delicate situation as this.

Tomorrow he would travel to London and get a special license, and when he returned they'd be married. Gemma's feelings would catch up to his. He was confident of it.

He began to unravel his cravat, and realizing the curtains were still open, he moved to close them against the already dark night. But as he did so, a flash of light caught his eye.

This side of the house faced west, toward the shore below Beauchamp House. Another flicker shone then and he swore under his breath.

Had the killer returned to the scene of the murder? Or was someone searching for more fossils where the famous Beauchamp Lizard had been recovered?

He made haste down the stairs, not caring if he disturbed his brother and sister-in-law. If someone was there, it could be the key to finding Sir Everard's murder. And getting the Beauchamp Lizard back for Gemma would be the perfect wedding gift.

Retrieving his greatcoat from the butler, he told the man not to lock the cellar door to the secret passageway, and with a lit lantern in hand, he stepped into the darkness.

Because the secret passageways to the beach weren't linked, Gemma had to step out onto the shore before she could locate the door leading into the vicarage tunnel.

Thus, when she stepped out onto the shore, she was hit by a brisk, cold wind that made her pull her cloak closer.

Then, almost as suddenly, a dark figure moved closer and she was suddenly in the grip of very strong arms.

"Convenient of you to bring a lantern, my dear," said Lord Paley as he pulled her out onto the rocky beach, one gloved hand covering her mouth so that she couldn't cry out. "It will make my search that much easier."

Why was he here? she wondered. He already had the Beauchamp Lizard, she was sure of it now.

"If you'll promise not to scream," he said coldly, "then I'll remove my hand. But if you renege, I'll kill Lord Cameron."

The threat against Cam sent a jolt of fear through her, and despite her wish to thwart the man holding her, she nodded.

He removed his hand, but then began to tie her hands behind her back with rope he must have had on his person.

"What are you doing here?" she asked, thinking to distract him with talk as he shoved her along toward the chalk cliff where she'd found the skull fossil. "No one would be foolish enough to hide the same fossil here a third time."

He laughed softly and she heard a note of disgust there. "I have the Beauchamp Lizard, you dolt. I want the rest of it. There can't be just a skull with no body. There has to be a full skeleton there beneath the chalk. And I intend to find it."

"But, it was a fossil," she said, puzzled. "If it were an actual bone, perhaps, but there's no guarantee that the entire lizard . . ."

"I'm not a simpleton," he snapped. "I know the chances are slim, but I need something to set me apart. And I won't be able to declare I've found the Beauchamp Lizard for decades thanks to Sir Everard and his blasted boasting. It will mark me as his murderer as surely as if declared it on the front page of the *Times*."

"Then why kill him for it?" she asked, genuinely curious. It made little sense if he'd only wanted the fossil.

"Because the blackguard intended to cut me out of our arrangement," Paley said with a scowl. "I'm the one who told him about the Lizard in the first place. And where I thought it was hidden."

"Because you were there," she said softly. "When Lady Celeste and your godfather found it."

"Lady Serena remembered, then," he said with a sour smile. "I knew it was a risk, but I assumed that enough time had passed and I'd grown enough that she would have forgotten."

"You broke her doll," Gemma said simply. "Of course she remembered."

"She was too young to play with us lads, anyway," Paley said with the pique of a remembered childhood anger. "I thought it would make her leave, but it just made her cousins angry. I went out to the shore because they shunned me."

"And saw your godfather with Lady Celeste," Gemma guessed. Not particularly appropriate viewing for a child, no matter how nasty he grew up to be.

"Actually," he said with a shrug, "I was surprised to learn that from Crutchley this morning. I'd guessed, of course, but I'm grateful I missed that bit. But I did come upon Pearson. He was furious, and brushed past me as if the hounds of hell were on his heels. I don't even know that he saw me, he was so incensed."

"What did you see, then?" Gemma asked.

"The Lizard, of course," he said as if she were stupid. "They were obviously excited about it. Lady Celeste held it up in the light and it was glorious. And then I heard my godfather tell her that she'd be famous for it. *She* would be famous."

He shook his head in disgust. "It was just as much his find as hers. He was there too. But he was giving her the credit."

"Because she unearthed it," Gemma said before she could stop herself.

Paley glowered. "Of course you would think like that. Women have no business putting their names on artifacts. If it were up to me, they wouldn't be involved in the collecting world at all. In that, at least, Pearson and I are in perfect agreement."

"So Pearson had nothing to do with Sir Everard's death, then?" Gemma asked.

"Of course not," he said with a smile that didn't reach his eyes. "But he made the perfect scapegoat once I heard the story of his unrequited youthful passion for Lady Celeste. What better person to blame for the murder of the man who stole her most famous find?"

The wind was picking up, and Gemma couldn't stop the shiver that ran through her. She was beginning to lose feeling in her fingers.

"What will you do with me?" she asked, realizing that Serena thought she was at the vicarage and would very likely not search for her if she didn't come back tonight, thinking she'd just chosen to remain at her sister's house.

"You'll keep me company while I dig," said Lord Paley. "And if I don't find anything I will find . . . other ways to amuse myself with you."

Gemma swallowed. "But it's so cold," she said in a plaintive tone. "Won't you at least let me use my cloak?" He'd removed it before tying her hands.

"If you think yourself a man's equal, Miss Hastings," he said with a cruel smile, "then you can manage a few hours in the cold. I have endured far worse in the quest for evidence of our natural history."

"That's Lady Cameron Lisle to you," she said with equal coldness. Perhaps reminding him that she was not without a champion would give him pause.

But Paley laughed. "You don't really think I believed that charade at the inn?" he asked with a shake of his head. "My dear Miss Hastings, you were both as transparent as a pane of glass. It comes from being truthful most of the time, I would imagine. Though I did enjoy it when your sister and brother-in-law arrived at my godfather's house looking just like what they were—angry relations searching for a couple on the run."

"If you knew, why didn't you say anything?" Gemma asked, genuinely wondering. "You might have sent us on our way."

"Because I needed to hear the whole blasted story from my godfather's perspective," he said with a shrug. "He never would tell it to me. I think because he suspected I would resent him for his weakness in the matter. Which he was perfectly correct about. But being faced with Lady Celeste's chosen collector, he couldn't resist."

"You really hold him in no affection at all?" Gemma asked.

"Why should I?" he asked sullenly. "He might have taken me under his wing when I showed an interest in geology, but instead he claimed it was too painful for him because it reminded him of her. Simpering fool."

She'd been standing the whole while they spoke and suddenly, she felt a tremor run through her as the cold wind hit her.

"Oh sit down, you foolish child," Paley said as he saw her wobble. Before she could brace herself, he placed a hand on her shoulder and shoved her into a sitting position. The rocks were hard on her bottom and back, but Gemma didn't make a sound.

He was shuffling back up to where he'd been digging when Gemma saw movement at the other side of the little crescent of shoreline.

As she watched, Cam crept soundlessly across the rocks.

He held a finger to his lips, indicating that she should keep quiet and she clenched her teeth so that she wouldn't cry out her relief at seeing him.

Some sixth sense, or perhaps some sound of boots on stone, alerted Lord Paley to his presence, however, because he turned suddenly.

On seeing who was creeping up on them, he stood up and opened his arms wide.

"Oh look, it's the debaucher of innocents come to rescue his false bride," he said with a sneer. "Do come closer so that I may greet you properly, Lord Cameron."

And to Gemma's horror, she saw that in one of those outstretched hands Lord Paley held a pistol.

Chapter 26

As soon as Cam stepped through the door leading to the beachhead, he saw that the light he'd glimpsed from his window was a lamp. The next thing he noted, and what made his heart leap into his throat, was Lord Paley, shoving Gemma, her hands tied behind her back toward the sloping chalk cliff where she'd found the fossil they knew now was the Beauchamp Lizard.

Not wanting to alert the other man to his presence, he waited while Gemma questioned him about his role in Sir Everard's murder. He wasn't sure if she was stalling until someone came to save her, or if she simply sought to understand the man's motive.

Either way, he used the time to his advantage, searching for and finding a large enough stone to cause the other man damage if Cam were to strike him with it. He clutched it in his hand while Paley continued to talk, until he saw him shove Gemma to the ground. And he knew he had to act.

As quietly as he could, he walked across the rocks toward the far side of the shore, and when Gemma saw him, he indicated that she should remain silent. She gave a slight nod, and he continued.

But something must have warned Paley because he turned around, and to Cam's horror, when he rose to his feet he was holding a pistol in one hand. A pistol he aimed at Gemma.

"Oh look, it's the debaucher of innocents come to rescue his false bride," Paley said with a sneer. "Do come closer so that I may greet you properly, Lord Cameron."

"Don't hurt her, Paley," Cam said, suddenly wishing he'd gone back for Benedick's help when he saw Paley had Gemma. "If you hurt someone, make it me. Don't hurt her. You haven't harmed a lady yet. Don't start now."

"How would you know?" Paley scoffed. "Just because I murdered Sir Everard, that doesn't mean he was the extent of my criminal career. Not all of us are bound to some outdated code of honor where women are concerned. I had hoped you were one of us, but then you fell prey to this hussy's charms. It will never cease to amaze me that otherwise intelligent men so often find themselves tied up in knots over something that can be had for a few bob on the nearest street corner."

"Either I'm an innocent or a hussy, Lord Paley," Gemma said boldly. "Make up your mind. I cannot be both."

Cam bit back a curse at her taunt. She was going to get herself killed.

"She's not worth it, Paley," he shouted, desperate to take the man's attention off Gemma and onto himself. "Don't waste your shot."

But Paley had already turned to face his prisoner. "You are bold for someone on the other end of a pistol, Miss Hastings," he said coldly.

"Because I have more courage in my little finger than you ever will, you murderer," Gemma shouted. "If you were any sort of collector you wouldn't have to steal to get what you wanted. In fact, you would have—"

To Cam's horror, Paley made a growling sound and raised his hand to fire.

Even as he watched, Cam ran as fast as he could toward the other man and a shot rang out in the night, followed closely by another.

By the time he reached where Gemma and Paley struggled on the ground, he found them both covered in blood.

Furious, he pulled Paley off her and raised his fist to punch the man, but somehow Gemma's voice penetrated the red fog of his anger.

"Cam! Cam! He's hit already."

And to his shock he realized that Paley was indeed the one who was bleeding.

He turned to Gemma. "Are you hit as well?" he asked as he shoved the other man to the side. "I heard two shots."

"No, I'm not hit," she said with a shake of her head. "But I don't know who fired the other shot."

"That was me, I'm afraid," said a voice from the stairs leading from the top of the cliffs to the beach.

They looked up to see Maximillian Pearson coming toward them, followed close behind by Serena.

Not waiting to greet the man, Cam turned Gemma so that he could remove the ropes binding her hands.

Mindless of the blood on her gown, he pulled her to him.

"I thought you'd be killed, you stubborn girl," he said as he held her against him with trembling arms. "What were you thinking to taunt him like that?"

"I was thinking that I very much wanted him not to shoot you," she said against his shoulder. "What were *you* thinking?"

"Perhaps you can carry on this conversation indoors?" Serena asked from where she stood beside Pearson. "We'll need to make room for the footmen to remove Lord Paley into the house."

"Of course," Cam said, then much to Gemma's chagrin

if her squeal was to be believed, he swung her into his arms and carried her toward the door leading to the tunnel into Beauchamp House.

Though her bath from earlier was cold by now, Gemma washed quickly in the water and changed into a clean gown before she made her way to the drawing room, where she found Serena, Mr. Pearson, and Cam.

The latter two were sipping brandy, and when Serena offered her a cup of tea, Gemma declined it and turned to the sideboard to pour herself a bit of brandy too.

Not caring about the propriety of it—on a night like this she would do what she pleased—Gemma took a seat beside Cam and curled up against his side, welcoming his arm around her shoulders.

"Lord Paley is being seen to by Dr. Holmes upstairs," Serena said without commenting on her charge's boldness. "I've sent for Mr. Northman as well so that he may hear the full story of Lord Paley's misdeeds."

"I must confess, Lady Serena," said Pearson with a frown, "I blame some of this on myself. If I hadn't been so unwilling to speak about what I knew about the Beauchamp Lizard, I feel sure that Paley wouldn't have felt it necessary to kill Sir Everard over it."

"What did you know, sir?" Gemma asked, curious now whether, as Lord Crutchley had told them, Pearson had been there the day Lady Celeste found the fossilized skull.

"I was here the day Lady Celeste found it," he said with a pained expression. "I was . . . infatuated, I suppose is the word . . . and I was watching her. I saw her unearth it, with Lord Crutchley by her side. I saw more as well—"

He broke off and Gemma knew he was speaking of the intimacy he'd also seen that day.

"I decided, and I'm not proud of it, but I decided to steal the fossil from her." Pearson shook his head. "If I couldn't have her, I would have that damned fossil she was so proud of."

"So it was your theft attempt that made her decide to hide it?" Gemma asked.

"Yes," he said with a look of shame. "I did many things I'm not proud of. Then, as well as now."

"How did you come to be here tonight?" Cam asked. He was grateful for the man's shot that saved Gemma, but wondered why he'd been here at all.

"I received a note from Lord Crutchley," he said with a bemused look. "I hadn't thought of the man in decades. Not since those days when I was so taken with your aunt, Lady Serena. But he was concerned that his godson might be about to do something foolish. He spoke specifically of danger to you, Lady Cameron."

He turned to Gemma and Cam. "Felicitations on your marriage, by the way."

Gemma didn't have the heart to tell him that she and Cam weren't married just yet, so she simply said, "Thank you," and Cam echoed her.

There was an awkward silence before Serena leapt into the breach with her usual social aplomb. "Why don't you tell them what happened when you received Lord Crutchley's note," she said kindly.

As if surprised to find her still there, Pearson nodded. "I set out for Beauchamp House at once. I had found Paley to be interested to the point of obsession about the Beauchamp Lizard over the course of the gathering at Pearson Close. And when Sir Everard turned up dead, after boasting about having found it, I had a suspicion that Paley might have been involved."

He took a deep breath. "I should have said or done something, but you must understand. Tonight is the first time I've left my estate in decades."

Recognizing true contrition when she saw it, Gemma placed her hand over his. "And I am so grateful for it. I have no doubt you saved my life tonight, sir."

His cheeks colored and he looked at the floor. "Thank you, Lady Cameron."

The drawing room door opened then to admit Sophia and Benedick.

Unmindful of the others, Sophia hurried to her sister's side and knelt beside her. "Are you trying to give me an apoplexy?" she asked, taking Gemma's hands in hers.

Ben, meanwhile introduced himself to Pearson and said, "We had word from Serena that my services might be needed here tonight. Little did I realize that when we ate luncheon with Paley and his godfather he'd attempt to murder Cam and Gemma later in the evening."

"If you ask me," Gemma said with a scowl, "Lord Paley doesn't deserve last rites. He's already murdered one person and intended to murder me and Cam as well."

"But that's the thing about the lord's forgiveness, Gemma," her brother-in-law told her gently. "It's there for everyone. Even the murderers among us."

He came forward and kissed her on the cheek, though to take the sting out of his words. "I'm glad you're unharmed."

As she watched, he placed a hand on Cam's shoulder. "And you, as well. I would have spent the rest of my days regretting it if our quarrel in the carriage were my last words to you."

Cam moved to clasp his brother's hand in his. "But it wasn't. So you'd better go say some holy things over Paley before he dies of his wounds."

The brothers exchanged grins and Gemma knew that whatever animosity had been between them was healed now.

When Benedick was gone, Pearson stood. "I will be off

then," he said, clearly a little uncomfortable with the family scene before him.

He was interrupted, however, by the appearance of Squire Northman in the doorway. "I think not, Pearson, if you were here when Lord Paley was shot."

Realizing that they had a long night ahead of them, Gemma turned to Serena. "I think I will have that cup of tea after all."

Chapter 27

When Cam finally slipped into Gemma's bedchamber some two hours later, he was bone tired. But he'd been almost constitutionally incapable of returning to the vicarage with his brother and sister-in-law. After almost losing Gemma to a madman's shot, he had to hold her in his arms or he'd never get a moment's rest.

She'd gone up a half hour before and when he shut the door behind him, he saw that she had left a lamp burning on the bedside table.

Despite that, she was fast asleep, her hair glinting around her like a halo as she lay curled beneath the blankets.

As quickly and quietly as he could, Cam shucked off his boots and coats and stripped down to his smallclothes before slipping beneath the covers with her.

She murmured something as he pulled her warm body against him, but didn't wake up. And for the first time since they'd left the inn that morning, he relaxed and breathed in the violet scent of her, then fell fast asleep.

When he came awake again the first rays of light were peeking through the narrow gap between the curtains, and a warm mouth was working its way down his neck.

"Who is this intoxicating creature?" he asked, his voice still thick with sleep.

"You're dreaming," she said, crawling up his body to kiss him on the mouth. "I'm a mere figment of your imagination, Lord Cameron."

"If that's the case then I don't know what I will tell my intended," he said, sliding his hands down to cup her bottom. "Because I fear she's a very jealous lady. She won't like your being here with me at all. In fact, I think you'd better go, imaginary lady."

"And what if I told you she wouldn't mind?" Gemma took his lower lip in her teeth, and Cam felt himself harden against her.

"Would she not?" he asked, moving his hands to grasp the fabric of her nightdress and slide it up her body. "I don't think you know her as well as I do."

She shifted to let him remove the gown completely, and sighed against him as her bare breasts brushed against his chest. "I think I do," she said, moving her hips to tease herself against his hardness. "She likes this very much, I think."

"Does she now?" Cam asked, grasping her hips and moving her so that he was right where she wanted him.

Gemma breathed out a sigh of pure pleasure before shifting to brace her hands on his chest. Then in one fluid motion, she sat up, seating him fully inside of her.

Cam looked up at her, naked and glorious as she sat impaled on him. He moved one hand to cup her breast, while the other guided her hip as she began to move. There were no more words, then, only sensation as she experimented, finally finding a rhythm that they both found pleasing. And he watched her for as long as he could, her eyes closed and her mouth wide with ecstasy as she rode him to completion.

When he felt her quiver around him, Cam held her tight, and flipped them so that he was on top and let himself go, taking her, claiming her, loving her with his body as he whispered words of love against her neck until he felt himself fly over the edge into bliss.

He came to himself again with the soft stroking of her fingers in his hair. He'd collapsed on top of her, he realized with a start, before he began to roll to the side.

"Don't you dare move, Cameron Lisle," she said, clasping him to her with her ankles locked around him. "You're perfect just where you are."

"I don't want to crush you," he protested, moving a little so that he could see her face.

She moved her hand to brush an errant lock of hair from his face. "I like it. You may be sure that if I ever find you are doing something I dislike, I will tell you."

He laughed. "I suppose that's right."

"Now," she said firmly, "lay your head back down so that I can stroke you."

"Your hair," she said in response to his raised brow.

Laughing again, he laid his head on her breast while she continued to toy with his hair.

"We'll have to marry soon," she said conversationally. "If only so that we don't have to sneak around in order to do what we just did."

"There's also the small detail that we've already passed ourselves off as a married couple," he said wryly. Though he too would like to marry so that they could enjoy one another without fear of being caught.

"But there is one thing we haven't talked about," she said thoughtfully. "The matter of where we will live."

"We haven't discussed it, of course," Cam said, moving so that he was lying beside her where he might see her face. "But I do have a tidy little manor house just down the coast on the other side of Brighton."

She frowned. "Do you, indeed?"

"You didn't think I'd wed you without having something to offer you besides a collection of fossils, did you?"

Her expression was sheepish. "Well, I had thought since it was so sudden—" she began.

"Gemma," he said with a shake of his head. "Did you really believe I had nothing more to my name than fossils? That I wished to marry you so that I might lay claim to Beauchamp House?"

He wasn't sure whether to be annoyed or amused.

"Not to get Beauchamp House, no," she corrected him, sitting up with her back against the ornately carved headboard. "But if it were necessary, I would not have objected to our living here. I am the last of the heiresses after all, so . . ."

"But we've a full month before the year ends," he reminded her, kissing the end of her nose. "So, last or not, you too will be wed before the first year is up. You'll all have to share joint ownership."

"About that," she said with a look of embarrassment. "What if we waited until after the first of the year to marry?"

He stared at her. "Are you serious?"

She stared back. For so long that his heart began to beat with alarm.

Gemma watched as his eyes shone with real alarm, and she couldn't punish him any longer.

"Of course not, you madman," she said as she threw her arms around his neck. "I am in love with you. I don't want to wait, and I wouldn't wait even if it meant full ownership of Beauchamp House."

He breathed out a sigh and she realized she'd held out a little too long for his comfort.

"Just for that," he said pettishly, "I won't give you the present I brought you."

She pulled back to see his face, to determine whether he was jesting.

His response was raised brows. "Yes, I have a present for you, but I'm not sure I wish to give it to someone who would toy with my feelings like that," he said in mock-pique.

Deciding she'd have to win him back no matter the cost, Gemma began peppering his face with kisses, until, that is, he caught her face between his large hands and stilled her so that he could kiss her properly.

When they were both breathless, he pulled away and lifted her off him.

She watched with great appreciation as he strode naked across the room to where his greatcoat lay draped over a chair.

"I wondered why you brought that up with you," she said, sitting up and fluffing the pillow behind her.

He kept his back to her as he removed something from the inner pocket of the coat. To her great disappointment, he hid whatever it was behind his back as he came back and slid beneath the bedclothes and sat beside her against the headboard.

She turned to look at him, and to her wonderment, he actually looked a bit nervous.

"Before I give this to you," he said solemnly, "if you think it's foolish you need only tell me and we'll forget it ever happened."

Gemma blinked. She never thought she'd see Lord Cameron Lisle so shy. It was a side of him she'd never thought to see. And her heart seemed to flip over at the knowledge he'd trusted her enough to show it to her.

As she watched, he proffered his closed fist and, in one fluid motion, opened it.

There, nestled atop his palm was one of the brightest blue banded agate stones she'd ever seen. With a shaking hand she took it from him and traced the bands of different hues of blue that surrounded the asymmetrical triangle of lighter blue in the center.

"It's beautiful," she breathed, too moved to say more. She knew without him telling her that this was important to him.

"I found it on the shore near Lisle Hall when I was a small boy," he said softly. "It was my first find. My father helped me polish it, and he found a man to shave off the side so that the striations would be revealed. It was the beginning of a lifelong love."

"It's lovely," she said, leaning forward to kiss him. "But I can't take it from you."

But Cam shook his head. "I need to give it to you. To show you how much you mean to me, Gemma."

He cupped her face in his hands.

"You mean more to me," he said fiercely. "More than this stone. More than geology. If it takes me giving it up to make you happy, I will do it. I love you that much."

Gemma felt tears fill her eyes. All this time, she'd been afraid that somehow marrying Cam would mean she'd have to give up some part of herself. The scholar, the fossil-hunter, the bluestocking.

Aunt Dahlia was wrong. Marrying this generous, loving, wonderful man wouldn't diminish her. It would make her stronger.

They would make a formidable team.

"Thank you," she said, kissing him again. "But I could no more ask you to give up fossils than you'd ask me. I love you, you see. I'm not quite sure how we will manage it, but I do know that I can imagine no one else I'd rather comb beaches and quarries for specimens with."

As she spoke, she watched as his smile transformed his entire face. There was joy there, and relief, but also love.

"Are you sure?" he asked, though it was clear from his expression that he believed her.

Still, she couldn't help but say, "I think I've loved you since that day that we fought over your silly geology magazine. I simply didn't know it yet."

He pulled her against him. "But why didn't you say? I poured my heart out in the carriage yesterday and you never said a thing. I could have kept my prize agate."

She gave him a playful punch in the shoulder.

"I wasn't sure of it," she told him honestly. "I've never felt this way before and I didn't want to tell you I loved you when I might discover later it was . . . I don't know, indigestion."

"So now you know it's not indigestion?" he asked, his mouth curved into a smile.

Her heart clenched. "I knew it when I saw Lord Paley holding that pistol."

She clasped him to her and held on tight.

"I love you so much, Cam. More than I can ever show you."

He whispered a suggestion of how she might do so in her ear.

"You, sir, are a tease," she said before kissing him.

"But you love me anyway?" he asked, pulling back a little.

"Of course I do," she said with a serene smile. "How could I possibly resist such a rogue?"

Epilogue

ONE MONTH LATER

"I can hardly believe almost a full year has passed since we arrived here," said Ivy staring out at darkened parkland beyond the window. "I didn't know any of you, and now I can't remember life without you."

"I feel the same way," said Sophia, slipping an arm round her friend's waist.

Gemma, who had married Cam only a few days after the incident with Lord Paley on the cliffs, sat with Daphne at the library table where they'd spent many happy hours in quiet study punctuated by the occasional laughter and sometimes tears.

"I can," Daphne said dryly, "and it was much less pleasant."

"And we hadn't met Serena either," Gemma said. "I hope she'll be amenable to our scheme. Without her, it will be difficult. Not impossible, of course, but I'm not sure I could trust anyone as I do her."

It was hard for Gemma to believe that it was nearly time for them to go their separate ways.

They could come and go as they pleased, of course. The

house belonged to all of them equally. But marriage meant that their comings and goings couldn't always be dictated by their wishes. And once children came, even with the best intentions, they would not be able to live in one another's pockets. Not as they had here at Beauchamp.

In the month since Gemma and Cam had discovered that it had been Lord Paley who murdered Sir Everard and stole the Beauchamp Lizard, the four Beauchamp House heiresses had been hard at work on a scheme that would see to it that even once they were all departed to live with their husbands, the house itself would remain a haven for lady scholars.

"You did ask Serena to meet us here, didn't you?" asked Sophia with a frown. "I haven't seen her since luncheon."

The four heiresses and their husbands had spent the holidays in the house together, along with their chaperone, Lady Serena, and her son, Jeremy.

"Of course," Gemma said. "I think she's tucking Jeremy in. She said she'd come up to see us as soon as she was finished."

"I still can't believe you managed to find the Beauchamp Lizard," said Ivy with a shake of her head as she stepped over to one of the other chairs at the table. "With only an unfinished letter from Lady Celeste and those odious men trying to steal it from you."

Gemma had been sad, at first, that she alone of the four heiresses hadn't had a full letter and quest from their late mentor. But the truth of the matter was that she felt as connected to the bluestocking leader as she would have if she'd left her a whole trunkful of personal letters. Because she alone knew the same excitement Lady Celeste had when she saw the fossilized skull emerge from the chalk cliffs only a few hundreds of yards from where she sat now. And she'd been able to restore it to its rightful place in Lady Celeste's collection.

"It wasn't easy," she said aloud. "But I had help from Cam, and I feel a certain degree of satisfaction knowing that Lord Paley wasn't able to enjoy the fruits of his evil deeds."

Once he'd recovered from his gunshot wound, Lord Paley had been taken to London to await his trial by the House of Lords, which wouldn't happen for another month or so. But Gemma had little doubt that even if they didn't sentence the man to hang, he would, at the very least, spend the rest of his life in gaol.

"I was a little surprised we were able to tear you away from polishing the Lizard," said Sophia wryly. "I don't believe any of the other pieces in the collection is afforded that kind of treatment."

"It's a very important find," Gemma protested. "Once I hear from Cuvier in Paris I'll know more, of course. But I am fairly certain this fossil will shed some light on how life developed in this part of England. In fact—"

She broke off when she realized her sister had been teasing her. "Well, it's important," she ended lamely. Then spoiled her vehemence by sticking out her tongue at Sophia.

"Ladies," said Serena as she came into the room. "Must I remind you what constitutes good behavior? One does not stick out one's tongue, no matter what the provocation."

Her wide smile took any sting from her words, and the four heiresses welcomed their chaperone for the past year into the room by offering her a chair at the mahogany table and putting a glass of brandy in her hand.

"You were all so secretive about this little gathering," she said after she'd taken a sip. "I couldn't even persuade Maitland to tell me, and you all know my poor brother is hopeless at keeping secrets."

"It's one of his most admirable qualities," said Daphne

with a grin. "I was able to winkle every last one of my Christmas gifts from him."

"But in this case, he held firm," Serena said with a shake of her head.

"You don't have the same sorts of persuasive tactics at your disposal," Gemma said dryly.

"There is that," Serena said with raised brows.

"Now," she continued her blue eyes sparkling, "you'd better tell me what you're plotting before I die of curiosity."

Ivy looked round at the other three and with their nods of agreement, she said, "First of all, we would like to know if you've decided where you'll go once you've decided to leave Beauchamp House. Or, rather, if you truly wish to go at all."

Serena looked from one to the other of them. "I had thought to return to the Maitland estate," she said carefully. "Though if that is no longer agreeable to you, Daphne—"

"If you wish it," Daphne said carefully, "then I am agreeable. But we have another offer."

"We, the Beauchamp heiresses," said Gemma with a smile.

"For you, and Jeremy if you wish it," Sophia added.

"We-would-like-to-turn-Beauchamp-House-into-a-school-for-bluestockings-and-we-would-like-for-you-to-run-it," said Ivy in one long breath.

When the other three heiresses stared at her, the classical linguist shrugged. "I made up my own compound word."

Serena blinked. "What did you say?"

"In a slower fashion," said Gemma wryly, "we would like to turn Beauchamp House into a sort of haven for lady scholars like ourselves, and we would like you to serve as chaperone to them. And perhaps oversee a few scholars we employ to live here and instruct them. Like a school, but without all of the strictures and silliness that are emphasized at ladies' schools. More like university learning for ladies."

"You wouldn't need to interact with them on a daily basis if you didn't wish it," said Sophia hastily. "Since I'll be only a few miles away at the vicarage, I can come and manage things for you from time to time if you become overwhelmed."

"Or we could hire someone to be the headmistress," said Ivy quickly. "You needn't do it at all if you don't wish it. I know being forced to stay here for the past year must have been tiresome at times, when you wished to visit friends, or see family. We simply thought that since you'd done such a good job of it with us. And there's no one we'd trust to protect Beauchamp Hall than you."

At that Serena began to laugh. And laugh. Until tears were streaming down her face.

"You needn't make fun of us," said Daphne stiffly. "If you don't want to do it, you need only say so."

"Oh my dears," said Serena, wiping her eyes, and reaching across the table to take Daphne's hand with her free one. "I'm not making fun. Truly, I'm not. It's just that, I think I can say unequivocally that I have been the most inept chaperone ever to hold the title."

"Of course you haven't," Ivy protested. "You were quite cross when I had to marry Quill after only a few days' acquaintance."

"And you were most firm when you overheard Maitland and me in the wine cellar," Daphne added with a nod.

"You looked properly upset when you caught Benedick coming into the breakfast parlor that time," said Sophia solemnly.

Gemma shrugged. "I think by the time I disappeared overnight with Cam you were used to misbehavior. But you did call the magistrate when Lord Paley tried to shoot me, which cannot be overlooked."

"My dear girls," said Serena beaming at all of them. "You

cannot think I am the right person to head up this endeavor. I cannot believe it."

"But you're the perfect person," Ivy protested. "You are kind, you are a paragon of good behavior yourself and therefore a good role model."

"And you never fail to say and do the right thing," said Daphne. "I know, because I've watched hoping you would fail, but you never do. It's most frustrating."

"But I know nothing about running a school," Lady Serena protested.

"That's the perfect part," Gemma said with a smile, "it wouldn't be a school as we all understand schools to be. It would be more of a house of learning where the female scholars we choose—we've decided they needn't come from the gentry or the aristocracy, because why should education be only for those with money—would be afforded the tutelage they need to become proficient in their fields of study. They could go on to become teachers or governesses themselves, or time in Beauchamp House would give them the propriety and manners they need to rise in society."

"But that sounds like a finishing school," Serena argued.

"A finishing school with scholarly learning too," Sophia said. "And the arts, of course. I would be happy to come once a week and teach painting, for instance."

"And what is the mission of this endeavor to be?" Serena asked. "To turn out intelligent wives?"

"To turn out educated women," Gemma corrected her. "Who can mix in whatever society they like, and pursue their scholarly endeavors with the confidence needed to hold their own in a world of men."

"I'm not a scholar, though," Serena insisted. "I've only ever been a wife and mother. I haven't one ounce of the scholarly learning the four of you have."

"You're a scholar of society," said Daphne. "You know more than I ever will about the rules of precedence. Or how to properly address the wife of a baronet's younger son."

"You know what month it's best to air out the linen closet, and what dishes might be made from a goose," said Ivy.

"Your needlework puts all of ours to shame," Gemma said wryly.

Serena couldn't argue with any of that. Because she'd found almost as soon as the four heiresses arrived at Beauchamp House that what they knew about household management paled in comparison with what they knew about their fields of study.

"Even if one knows all there is to know about maths," Daphne said, "it is still necessary to speak to the housekeeper about the dashed menus."

Menus were a particular trial to Daphne now that she'd spent some time at the ducal estate.

"I have been wondering if it might be possible to remain here," Serena said slowly, and knowing they'd won, the heiresses cheered.

"You won't be sorry!" cried Ivy as she clapped her hands.

"I knew you would agree," said Gemma as she pulled Serena into a hug. "You've enjoyed this year, admit it."

Tears shone in Lady Serena's eyes as she welcomed the hugs of her former charges. "It's been the happiest year of my life, you scapegraces, and well you know it."

"I say this calls for a toast," said Gemma, suddenly needing to pay tribute to the woman whose brilliance and generosity had brought them all together.

Raising her brandy glass, she waited until the others had done the same.

"To Lady Celeste Beauchamp," Gemma cried with a glance toward the portrait of their benefactress, which hung above the fireplace. "May we never forget her generosity of spirit."

And almost at the exact moment they touched glasses the candles in the chandelier flickered.

The quintet were silent for a moment, exchanging wide-eyed glances.

"You saw that too, did you not?" Daphne asked, her blue eyes wide.

"I believe my aunt approves of your toast," Lady Serena said with a nod toward the portrait.

Gemma lifted her glass again. "Thank you, Lady Celeste. Thank you for everything."

The candles didn't flicker that time, but Gemma was quite sure she saw the portrait wink.

Acknowledgments

No project of mine makes it to completion without an army of folks working behind the scenes to make sure every last detail is taken care of. Thanks to my fantastic and magical agent, Holly Root, who soothes my ruffled feathers and takes care of business (not necessarily in that order); to my friend, catcher of mistakes, and partner in mischief, Lindsay Faber; to my plotting buddies, Angela Quarles, Katie Reus, and Cynthia Eden; the amazing art department who never fail to outdo themselves with covers for my books; my marketing and promo whizzes, Titi Oluwo and Meghan Harrington; and last but not least, my editorial team of Jennie Conway and Holly Ingraham. You are all wonderful and I don't deserve you.